Praise for
Diane Chamberlain

"Diane Chamberlain is a marvellously gifted author.
Every book she writes is a gem."
—*Literary Times*

The Bay at Midnight
"So full of unexpected twists you'll find yourself wanting
to finish it in one sitting. Fans of Jodi Picoult's style
will love how Diane Chamberlain writes."
—*Candis*

"This complex tale will stick with you forever."
—*Now Magazine.*

"Emotional, complex and laced with suspense, this
fascinating story is a brilliant read"
—*Closer*

"A moving story"
—*Bella*

"A fabulous thriller with plenty of surprises"
—*Star*

"A brilliantly told thriller"
— *Woman*

"This compelling mystery will have you
on the edge of your seat"
—*Inside Soap*

The Lost Daughter
"A strong tale that deserves a comparison with
Jodi Picoult"
—*www.lovereading.co.uk*

Before
the Storm

Diane
Chamberlain

MIRA

All the characters in this book have no existence outside the imagination of the author, and have no relation whatsoever to anyone bearing the same name or names. They are not even distantly inspired by any individual known or unknown to the author, and all the incidents are pure invention.

Published in Great Britain 2010
MIRA Books, an imprint of Harlequin (UK) Limited,
Eton House, 18-24 Paradise Road,
Richmond, Surrey, TW9 1SR

© Diane Chamberlain 2008

ISBN 978 0 7783 0338 1

58-0610

MIRA's policy is to use papers that are natural, renewable and recyclable products and made from wood grown in sustainable forests. The logging and manufacturing processes conform to the legal environmental regulations of the country of origin.

Printed and bound by CPI Group
(UK) Ltd, Croydon, CR0 4YY

ACKNOWLEDGEMENTS

On my first research trip to Topsail Island, I stumbled into a realty office to ask directions. When realtor Lottie Koenig heard my name, she told me she loved my books and gave me a hug. That was my introduction to the friendly people who call Topsail Island home. Lottie gave me a tour of the island and hooked me up with another valuable resource, fellow realtor and longtime Topsail Island resident Patsy Jordan. In turn, Patsy introduced me to Anna Scott, one of the few teens on the island. Anna gave me a wealth of information about what life would be like for the teenagers in *Before the Storm*. I'm grateful to these three women for their help and enthusiasm.

Thank you to special friends Elizabeth and Dave Samuels and Susan Rouse for generously allowing me to use their Topsail Island homes as I did my research.

I could not have written this story without the help of Ken Bogan, Fire Marshal of the Town of Surf City's fire department. Ken went out of his way to give me an understanding of my firefighting characters, instruct me in arson investigation and much, much more. Ken and his wife, Angie, also introduced me to Sears Landing Grill, where I arrived armed with a list of forty-five questions for them to answer over dinner. They answered them all and would have answered another forty-five had I asked. Thank you, Ken and Angie! Thanks also to these other Surf City firefighters: Tim Fisher, Kevin "Butterbean" Head and Bill Lindsey.

I found several excellent resources on Foetal Alcohol Spectrum Disorder, but none better than Jodee Kulp, an FASD activist, author and mother of a daughter with FASD. *The Best That I Can Be*, a book Jodee wrote with her daughter, Liz, was a huge help to me in understanding Andy. Jodee not only answered my questions, but read Andy's first chapter to make sure I was on target with his character.

For helping me understand the legal and juvenile justice system, I'm indebted to attorneys Barrett Temple and Evonne Hopkins, as well as to Gerry McCoy.

I kept Ray McAllister's book, *Topsail Island: Mayberry by the Sea*, close at hand as I wrote. It's an excellent, lovingly written treat for anyone wanting to read further about the Island.

In a raffle sponsored by the North Carolina Writers' Network, Jabeen Akhtar won the right to have her name mentioned in *Before the Storm*. I hope she's happy I named a coffee shop after her! Although some of the places mentioned in *Before the Storm* do exist, Jabeen's Java, Drury Memorial Church and The Sea Tender are, like the characters themselves, figments of my imagination.

I'm also grateful to the following people for their various contributions: Sheree Alderman, Trina Allen, Brenda Burke-Cremeans, BJ Cothran, Valerie Harris, Christa Hogan, Pam "bless your heart" Lloyd, Margaret Maron, Lynn Mercer, Marge Petesch, Glenn Pierce, Emilie Richards, Sarah Shaber, Meg Skaggs, David Stallman, MJ Vieweg, Brittany Walls, Brenda Witchger, Ann Woodman and my friends at ASA.

Thanks to the readers of my blog, especially Margo Petrus, for inspiring this book's title.

Finally, I often hear that agents and editors are so busy that they can't take the time to help their authors create the best books possible. That certainly is not true in my case. Thank you to my agent, Susan Ginsburg, and my editor, Miranda Stecyk, for their skill, wisdom, commitment and passion. You two are the best!

For John, both helpmate and muse

Laurel

They took my baby from me when he was only ten hours old.

Jamie named him Andrew after his father, because it seemed fitting. We tried the name out once or twice to see how it felt in our mouths. Andrew. Andy. Then, suddenly, he was gone. I'd forgotten to count his fingers or note the color of his hair. What sort of mother forgets those things?

I fought to get him back, the way a drowning person fights for air.

A full year passed before I held him in my arms again. Finally, I could breathe, and I knew I would never, ever, let him go.

Chapter One

Andy

WHEN I WALKED BACK INTO MY FRIEND Emily's church, I saw the pretty girl right away. She'd smiled and said "hey" to me earlier when we were in the youth building, and I'd been looking for her ever since. Somebody'd pushed all the long church seats out of the way so kids could dance, and the girl was in the middle of the floor dancing fast with my friend Keith, who could dance cooler than anybody. I stared at the girl like nobody else was in the church, even when Emily came up to me and said, "Where were you? This is a lock-in. That means you stay right here all night." I saw that her eyebrows were shaped like pale check marks. That meant she was mad.

I pointed to the pretty girl. "Who's that?"

"How should I know?" Emily poked her glasses higher up her nose. "I don't know every single solitary person here."

The girl had on a floaty short skirt and she had long legs that flew over the floor when she danced. Her blond hair was in those cool things America-African people wear that I could never remember the name of. Lots of them all over her head in stripes.

I walked past some kids playing cards on the floor and straight over to the girl. I stopped four shoe lengths away, which Mom always said was close enough. I used to get too close to people and made them squirmy. They need their personal space, Mom said. But even standing that far away, I could see her long eyelashes. They made me think of baby bird feathers. I saw a baby bird close once. It fell out of the nest in our yard and Maggie climbed the ladder to put it back. I wanted to reach over and touch the girl's feather lashes, but knew that was not an appropriate thing.

Keith suddenly stopped dancing with her. He looked right at me. "What d'you want, little rich boy?" he asked.

I looked at the girl. Her eyes were blue beneath the feathers. I felt words come into my mind and then into my throat, and once they got that far, I could never stop them.

"I love you," I said.

Her eyes opened wide and her lips made a pink O. She laughed. I laughed, too. Sometimes people laugh *at* me and sometimes they laugh *with* me, and I hoped this was one of the laughing-with-me times.

The girl didn't say anything, but Keith put his hands on his hips. "You go find somebody else to love, little rich boy." I wondered how come he kept calling me little rich boy instead of Andy.

I shook my head. "I love *her*."

Keith walked between me and the girl. He was so close to me, I felt the squirmies Mom told me about. I had to look up at him which made my neck hurt. "Don't you know about personal space?" I asked.

"Look," he said. "She's sixteen. You're a puny fourteen."

"Fifteen," I said. "I'm just small for my age."

"Why're you acting like you're fourteen then?" He laughed and his teeth reminded me of the big white gum pieces Maggie liked. I hated them because they burned my tongue when I bit them.

"Leave him alone," the pretty girl said. "Just ignore him and he'll go away."

"Don't it creep you out?" Keith asked her. "The way he's staring at you?"

The girl put out an arm and used it like a stick to move Keith away. Then she talked right to me.

"You better go away, honey," she said. "You don't want to get hurt."

How could I get hurt? I wasn't in a dangerous place or doing a dangerous thing, like rock climbing, which I wanted to do but Mom said no.

"What's your name?" I asked her.

"Go home to your fancy-ass house on the water," Keith said.

"If I tell you my name, will you go away?" the girl asked.

"Okay," I said, because I liked that we were making a deal.

"My name's Layla," she said.

Layla. That was a new name. I liked it. "It's pretty," I said. "My name's Andy."

"Nice to meet you, Andy," she said. "So, now you know my name and you can go."

I nodded, because I had to hold up my end of the deal. "Goodbye," I said as I started to turn around.

"*Retard*." Keith almost whispered it, but I had very good hearing and that word pushed my start button.

I turned back to him, my fists already flying. I punched his stomach and I punched his chin, and he must have punched me too because of all the bruises I found later, but I didn't feel a thing. I kept at him, my head bent low like a bull, forgetting I'm only five feet tall and he was way taller. When I was mad, I got strong like nobody's business. People yelled and clapped and things, but the noise was a buzz in my head. I couldn't tell you the words they said. Just bzzzzzzzzz, getting louder the more I punched.

I punched until somebody grabbed my arms from behind, and a man with glasses grabbed Keith and pulled us apart. I kicked my feet trying to get at him. I wasn't finished.

"What an asshole!" Keith twisted his body away from the man with the glasses, but he didn't come any closer. His face was red like he had sunburn.

"He doesn't know any better," said the man holding me. "You should. Now you get out of here."

"Why me?" Keith jerked his chin toward me. "He started it! Everybody always cuts him slack."

The man spoke quietly in my ear. "If I let go of you, are you going to behave?"

I nodded and then realized I was crying and everybody was watching me except for Keith and Layla and the man with glasses, who were walking toward the back of the church. The man let go of my arms and handed me a white piece of cloth from his pocket. I wiped my eyes. I hoped Layla hadn't seen me crying. The man was in front of me now and I saw that he was old with gray hair in a ponytail. He held my shoulders and looked me over like I was something to buy in a store. "You okay, Andy?"

I didn't know how he knew my name, but I nodded.

"You go back over there with Emily and let the adults handle Keith." He turned me in Emily's direction and made me walk a few steps with his arm around me. "We'll deal with him, okay?" He let go of my shoulders.

I said "okay" and kept walking toward Emily, who was standing by the baptism pool thing.

"I thought you was gonna kill him!" she said.

Me and Emily were in the same special reading and math classes two days a week. I'd known her almost my whole life, and she was my best friend. People said she was funny looking because she had white hair and one of her eyes didn't look at you and she had a scar on her lip from an operation when she was a baby, but I thought she was pretty. Mom said I saw the whole world through the eyes of love. Next to Mom and Maggie, I loved Emily best. But she wasn't my girlfriend. Definitely not.

"What did the girl say?" Emily asked me.

I wiped my eyes again. I didn't care if Emily knew I was crying. She'd seen me cry plenty of times. When I put the cloth in my pocket, I noticed her red T-shirt was on inside out. She used to always wear her clothes inside out because she couldn't stand the way the seam part felt on her skin, but she'd gotten better. She also couldn't stand when people touched her. Our teacher never touched her but once we had a substitute and she put a hand on Emily's shoulder and Emily went ballistic. She cried so much she barfed on her desk.

"Your shirt's inside out," I said.

"I know. What did the girl say?"

"That her name's Layla." I looked over at where Layla was still talking to the man with the glasses. Keith was gone, and I stared at Layla. Just looking at her made my body feel funny. It was like the time I had to take medicine for a cold and couldn't sleep all night long. I felt like bugs were crawling inside my muscles. Mom promised me that was impossible, but it still felt that way.

"Did she say anything else?" Emily asked.

Before I could answer, a really loud, deep, rumbling noise, like thunder, filled my ears. Everyone stopped and looked around like someone had said Freeze! I thought maybe it was a tsunami because we were so close to the beach. I was really afraid of tsunamis. I saw one on TV. They swallowed up people. Sometimes I'd stare out my bedroom window and watch the water in the sound, looking for the big wave that would swallow me up. I wanted to get out of the church and run, but nobody moved.

Like magic, the stained-glass windows lit up. I saw Mary and baby Jesus and angels and a half-bald man in a long dress holding a bird on his hand. The window colors were on everybody's face and Emily's hair looked like a rainbow.

"Fire!" someone yelled from the other end of the church, and then a bunch of people started yelling, "Fire! Fire!" Everyone screamed, running past me and Emily, pushing us all over the place.

I didn't see any fire, so me and Emily just stood there getting pushed around, waiting for an adult to tell us what to do. I was pretty sure then that there wasn't a tsunami. That made me feel better, even though somebody's elbow knocked into my side and somebody else stepped on my toes. Emily backed up against the wall so nobody could touch her as they rushed past. I looked where Layla had been talking with the man, but she was gone.

"The doors are blocked by fire!" someone shouted.

I looked at Emily. "Where's your mom?" I had to yell because it was so noisy. Emily's mother was one of the adults at the lock-in, which was the only reason Mom let me go.

"I don't know." Emily bit the side of her finger the way she did when she was nervous.

"Don't bite yourself." I pulled her hand away from her face and she glared at me with her good eye.

All of a sudden I smelled the fire. It crackled like a bonfire on the beach. Emily pointed to the ceiling where curlicues of smoke swirled around the beams.

"We got to hide!" she said.

I shook my head. Mom told me you can't hide from a fire. You had to escape. I had a special ladder under my bed I could put out the window to climb down, but there were no special ladders in the church that I could see.

Everything was moving very fast. Some boys lifted up one of the long church seats. They counted one two three and ran toward the big window that had the half-bald man on it. The long seat hit the man, breaking the window into a zillion pieces, and then I saw the fire outside. It was a bigger fire than I'd ever seen in my life. Like a monster, it rushed through the window and swallowed the boys and the long seat in one big gulp. The boys screamed, and they ran around with fire coming off them.

I shouted as loud as I could, "Stop! Drop! Roll!"

Emily looked amazed to hear me tell the boys what to do. I didn't think the boys heard me, but then some of them *did* stop, drop and roll, so maybe they did. They were still burning, and the air in the church had filled up with so much smoke, I couldn't see the altar anymore.

Emily started coughing. "Mama!" she croaked.

I was coughing, too, and I knew me and Emily were in trouble. I couldn't see her mother anywhere, and the other adults were screaming their heads off just like the kids. I was thinking, thinking, thinking. Mom always told me, in an emergency, use your head. This was my first real emergency ever.

Emily suddenly grabbed my arm. "We got to hide!" she said again. She had to be really scared because she'd never touched me before on purpose.

I knew she was wrong about hiding, but now the floor was on fire, the flames coming toward us.

"Think!" I said out loud, though I was only talking to myself. I hit the side of my head with my hand. "Brain, you gotta kick in!"

Emily pressed her face against my shoulder, whimpering like a puppy, and the fire rose around us like a forest of golden trees.

Chapter Two

Maggie

MY FATHER WAS KILLED BY A WHALE.

I hardly ever told people how he died because they'd think I was making it up. Then I'd have to go into the whole story and watch their eyes pop and their skin break out in goose bumps. They'd talk about Ahab and Jonah, and I would know that Daddy's death had morphed into their entertainment. When I was a little girl, he was my whole world—my best friend and protector. He was awesome. He was a minister who built a chapel for his tiny congregation with his own hands. When people turned him into a character in a story, one they'd tell their friends and family over pizza or ice cream, I had to walk away. So, it was easier not to talk about it in the first place. If someone asked me how my father died, I'd just say "heart." That was the truth, anyway.

The night Andy went to the lock-in, I knew I had to visit my father—or at least try to visit him. It didn't always work. Out of my thirty or forty tries, I only made contact with him three times. That made the visits even more meaningful to me. I'd never stop trying.

I called Mom to let her know the lock-in had been moved from Drury Memorial's youth building to the church itself, so she'd know where to pick Andy up in the morning. Then I said I was going over to Amber Donnelly's, which was a total crock. I hadn't hung out with Amber in months, though we sometimes still studied together. Hanging out with Amber required listening to her talk nonstop about her boyfriend, Travis Hardy. "Me and Travis this," and "me and Travis that," until I wanted to scream. Amber was in AP classes like me, but you wouldn't know it from her grammar. Plus, she was such a poser, totally caught up in her looks and who she hung out with. I never realized it until this year.

So instead of going to Amber's, I drove to the northern end of the island, which, on a midweek night in late March, felt like the end of the universe. In fourteen miles, I saw only two other cars on the road, both heading south, and few of the houses had lights on inside. The moon was so full and bright that weird shadows of shrubs and mailboxes were on the road in front of me. I thought I was seeing dogs or deer in the road and I kept braking for nothing. I was relieved when I spotted the row of cottages on the beach.

That end of the island was always getting chewed up by storms, and the six oceanfront cottages along New River Inlet Road were, every single one of them, condemned. Between the cottages and the street was another row of houses, all waiting for their turn to become oceanfront. I thought that would happen long ago; we had to abandon our house after Hurricane Fran, when I was five. But the condemned houses still stood empty, and I hoped they'd remain that way for the rest of my life.

Our tiny cottage was round, and it leaned ever so slightly to the left on long exposed pilings. The outdoor shower and storage closet that used to make up the ground floor had slipped into the sea along with the septic tank. The wood siding had been bleached so pale by decades under the sun that it looked like frosted glass in the moonlight. The cottage had a name—The Sea Tender—given to it by my Grandpa Lockwood. Long before I was born, Grandpa burned that name into a board and hung it above the front door, but the sign blew away a couple of years ago and even though I searched for it in the sand, I never found it.

The wind blew my hair across my face as I got out of the car, and the waves sounded like nonstop thunder. Topsail Island was so narrow that we could hear the ocean from our house on Stump Sound, but this was different. My feet vibrated from the pounding of the waves on the beach, and I knew the sea was wild tonight.

I had a flashlight, but I didn't need it as I walked along the skinny boardwalk between two of the front-row houses to reach our old cottage. The bottom step used to sit on the sand, but now it was up to my waist. I moved the cinder block from behind one of the pilings into place below the steps, stood on top of it, then boosted myself onto the bottom step and climbed up to the deck. A long board nailed across the front door read *Condemned,* and I could just manage to squeeze my key beneath it into the lock. Mom was a pack rat, and I found the key in her desk drawer two years earlier, when I first decided to go to the cottage. I ducked below the sign and walked into the living room, my sandals grinding on the gritty floor.

I knew the inside of the cottage as well as I knew our house on Stump Sound. I walked through the dark living room to the kitchen, dodging some of our old furniture, which had been too ratty and disgusting to save even ten years ago. I turned on my flashlight and put it on the counter so the light hit the cabinet above the stove. I opened the cabinet, which was empty except for a plastic bag of marijuana, a few rolled joints and some boxes of matches. My hands shook as I lit one of the joints, breathing the smoke deep into my lungs. I held my breath until the top of my head tingled. I craved that out-of-body feeling tonight.

Opening the back door, I was slammed by the roar of the waves. My hair was long and way too wavy and it sucked moisture from the air like a sponge. It blew all over the place and I tucked it beneath the collar of my jacket as I stepped onto the narrow deck. I used to take a shower when I got home from the cottage, the way some kids showered to wash away the scent of cigarettes. I thought Mom would take one sniff and know where I'd been. I deserved to feel guilty, because it wasn't just the hope of being with Daddy that drew me to the cottage. I wasn't all that innocent.

I sat on the edge of the deck, my legs dangling in the air, and stared out at the long sliver of moonlight on the water. I rested my elbows on the lower rung of the railing. Saltwater mist wet my cheeks, and when I licked my lips, I tasted my childhood.

I took another hit from the joint and tried to still my mind.

When I was fifteen, I got my level-one driver's license and was allowed to drive with an adult in the car. One night I had this crazy urge to go to the cottage. I couldn't say why, but one minute, I was studying for a history exam, and the next I was sneaking out the front door while Mom and Andy slept. There was no moon at all that night and I was scared shitless. It was December and dark and I barely knew how to steer, much less use the gas and the brake, but I made it the seven miles to the cottage. I sat on the deck, shivering with the cold. That was the first time I felt Daddy. He was right next to me, rising up from the sea in a cloud of mist, wrapping his arms around me so tightly that I felt warm enough to take off my sweater. I cried from the joy of having him close. I wasn't crazy. I didn't believe in ghosts or premonitions or even in heaven and hell. But I believed Daddy was there in a way I can't explain. I just knew it was true.

I felt like Daddy was with me a couple more times since then, but tonight I had trouble stilling my mind enough to let him in. I read on the Internet about making contact with people who'd died. Every Web site had different advice, but they all said that stilling your mind was the first thing you needed to do. My mind was racing, though, the weed not mellowing me the way it usually did.

"Daddy," I whispered into the wind, "I really need you tonight." Squeezing my eyes more tightly closed, I tried to picture his wavy dark hair. The smile he always wore when he looked at me.

Then I started thinking about telling Mom I wouldn't be valedictorian when I graduated in a couple of months, like she expected. What would she say? I was an honors student all through school until this semester. I hoped she'd say it was no big thing, since I was already accepted at UNC in Wilmington. Which started me thinking about leaving home. How was Mom going to handle Andy without me?

As a mother, Mom was borderline okay. She was smart and she could be cool sometimes, but she loved Andy so much that she suffocated him, and she didn't have a clue. My brother was my biggest worry. Probably ninety-five percent of my time, I thought about him. Even when I thought about other things, he was still in a little corner of my mind, the same way I knew that it was spring or that we lived in North Carolina or that I was female.

I talked Mom into letting Andy go to the lock-in tonight. He was fifteen; she had to let go a little and besides, Emily's mother was one of the chaperones. I hoped he was having a good time and acting normal. His grip on social etiquette was pretty lame. Would they have dancing at the lock-in? It cracked me up to imagine Andy and Emily dancing together.

My cell phone vibrated in my jeans pocket and I pulled it out to look at the display. Mom. I slipped it back in my jeans, hoping she didn't try to reach me at Amber's and discover I wasn't there.

The phone rang again. That was our signal—the call-twice-in-a-row signal that meant *This is serious. Answer now.* So I jumped up and walked into the house. I pulled the door closed to block out the sound of the ocean before hitting the talk button.

"Hi, Mom," I said.

"Oh my God, Maggie!" Mom sounded breathless, as though she'd run up the stairs. "The church is on fire!"

"*What* church?" I froze.

"Drury Memorial. They just cut into the TV to announce it. They showed a picture." She choked on a sob. "It's completely engulfed in flames. People are still inside!"

"No way!" The weed suddenly hit me. I was dizzy, and I leaned over the sink in case I got sick. *Andy.* He wouldn't know what to do.

"I'm going over there now," Mom said. Her car door squeaked open, then slammed shut. "Are you at Amber's?"

"I'm…" I glanced out the door at the dark ocean. "Yes." She was so easy to lie to. Her focus was always on Andy, hardly ever on me. I stubbed out the joint in the sink. "I'll meet you there," I added. "At the church."

"Hurry!" she said. I pictured her pinching the phone between her chin and shoulder as she started the car.

"Stay calm," I said. "Drive carefully."

"You, too. But *hurry!*"

I was already heading toward the front door. Forgetting about the Condemned sign, I ran right into it, yelping as it knocked the air from my lungs. I ducked beneath it, jumped to the sand and ran down the boardwalk to my Jetta. I was miles from the church in Surf City. Miles from my baby brother. I felt so sick. I began crying as I turned the key in the ignition. It was my fault if something happened to him. I started to pray, something I only did when I was desperate. *Dear God,* I thought, as I sped down New River Inlet Road, *don't let anything happen to Andy. Please. Let it happen to me instead. I'm the liar. I'm the bad kid.*

I drove all the way to Surf City, saying that prayer over and over in my mind until I saw the smoke in the sky. Then I started saying it out loud.

Chapter Three

Laurel

THERE IS ONLY ONE STOPLIGHT ON THE twenty-six miles of Topsail Island. It sits two short blocks from the beach in the heart of Surf City, and it glowed red when my car approached it and was still red when I left it behind. If there'd been a dozen red lights, they wouldn't have stopped me. People always told me I was a determined woman and I was never more so than the night of the fire.

Miles before the stoplight, I'd seen the yellow glow in the sky, and now I could smell the fire itself. I pictured the old church. I'd only been inside it a few times for weddings and funerals, but I knew it had pine floors, probably soaked with years of oily cleaner, just tempting someone to toss a match on them. I knew more than I wanted to know about fires. I'd lost my parents to one, plus Jamie had been a volunteer firefighter before he died. He told me about clapboard buildings that were nothing but tinder. Probably one of the kids lit a cigarette, tossed the match on the floor. Why oh why did I listen to Maggie? I never should have let Andy go. Maggie was around him so much, she thought of him as a normal kid. You got that way when you were around him a lot. You got used to his oddities, took his limitations for granted. Then you'd see him out in the world and realize he still didn't fit in, no matter how much you'd tried to make that happen. It was easy to get seduced into thinking he was okay when the environment around him was so carefully controlled and familiar. Tonight, though, I threw him to the wolves.

The street near Drury Memorial was clotted with fire trucks and police cars and ambulances and I had to park a block away in front of Jabeen's Java and The Pony Express. I'd barely come to a stop before I flew out of my car and started running toward the fire.

A few people stood along the road watching clouds of smoke and steam gush from the church into the bright night sky. There were shouts and sirens and a sickening acrid smell in the air as I ran toward the front doors of the church. Huge floodlights illuminated the building and gave me tunnel vision. All I saw were those gaping doors, smoke belching from them, and they were my target.

"Grab her!" someone shouted.

Long, wiry arms locked around me from behind.

"Let go of me!" I clawed at the arms with my fingernails, but whoever was holding me had a grip like a steel trap.

"We have a staging area set up, ma'am," he shouted into my ear. "Most of the children are out and safe."

"What do you mean *most?*" I twisted against the vise of his arms. "Where's my *son?*"

He dragged me across the sandy lot before loosening his hold on me. "They've got names of the children on a list," he said as he let go.

"*Where?*" I spun around to see the face of Reverend Bill, pastor of Drury Memorial. If there was a person on Topsail Island I didn't like, it was Reverend Bill. He looked no happier to realize it was me he'd been holding in his arms.

"One of *your* children was here?" He sounded stunned that I'd let a child of mine set foot in his church. I never should have.

"Andy," I said. Then I called his name. "Andy!" I shaded my eyes from the floodlights as I surveyed the scene. He'd worn his tan pants, olive green-striped shirt, and new sneakers tonight. I searched for the striped shirt, but the chaos of the scene suddenly overwhelmed my vision. Kids were everywhere, some sprawled on the sand, others sitting up or bent over, coughing. Generators roared as they fueled the lights, and static from police radios crackled in the air. Parents called out the names of their children. "*Tracy!*" "Josh!" "*Amanda!*" An EMT leaned over a girl, giving her CPR. The nurse in me wanted to help, but the mother in me was stronger.

Above my head, a helicopter thrummed as it rose from the beach.

"*Andy!*" I shouted to the helicopter, only vaguely aware of how irrational I must have seemed.

Reverend Bill was clutching my arm, tugging me across the street through a maze of fire trucks and police cars to an area lit by another floodlight and cordoned off with yellow police tape. Inside the tape, people stood shoulder to shoulder, shouting and pushing.

"See that girl over there?" Reverend Bill pointed into the crowd of people.

"Who? *Where?*" I stood on my toes trying to see better.

"The one in uniform," he shouted. "She's taking names, hooking parents up with their kids. You go see—"

I pulled away from him before he could finish the sentence. I didn't bother looking for an entrance into the cordoned-off area. Instead, I climbed over the tape and plowed into the clot of people.

Parents crowded around the officer, who I recognized as Patty Shales. Her kids went to the elementary school in Sneads Ferry where I was a part-time nurse.

"Patty!" I shouted from the sea of parents. "Do you know where Andy is?"

She glanced over at me just as a man grabbed the clipboard from her hands. I couldn't see what was happening, but Patty's head disappeared from my view amid flailing arms and angry shouting.

From somewhere behind me, I heard the words "killed" and "dead." I swung around to see two women, red eyed, hands to their mouths.

"*Who's* killed?" I asked. "*Who's* dead?"

One of the women wiped tears from her eyes. "I heard they found a body," she said. "Some kids was trapped inside. My daughter's here somewhere. I just pray to the Lord—" She shook her head, unable to finish her sentence.

I felt suddenly nauseated by the smell of the fire, a tarry chemical smell that burned my nostrils and throat.

"My son's here, too," I said, though I doubted the woman even heard me.

"Laurel!" Sara Weston lifted the yellow tape and ducked under it, running up to me. "Why are you here?" she asked.

"Andy's here. Is Keith?"

She nodded, pressing a trembling hand to her cheek. "I can't find him," she said. "Someone said he got burned, but I—"

She stopped speaking as an ominous creaking sound came from the far side of the church—the sort of sound a massive tree makes as it starts to fall. Everyone froze, staring at the church as the rear of the roof collapsed in one long wave, sending smoke and embers into the air.

"Oh my God, Laurel!" Sara pressed her face against my shoulder and I wrapped my arm around her as we were jostled by people trying to get closer to Patty. Parents stepped on our feet, pushing us one way, then another, and Sara and I pushed back as a unit, bullish and driven. I probably knew many of the people I fought out of my way, but in the heat of the moment, we were all simply desperate parents. *This is what it was like inside,* I thought, panic rising in my throat. *All the kids pushing at once to get out of the church.*

"Patty!" I shouted again, but I was only one voice of many. She heard me, though.

"Laurel!" she yelled. "They took Andy to New Hanover."

"Oh God."

"Not life threatening," Patty called. "Asthma. Some burns."

I let out my breath in a silent prayer. *Thank you, thank you, thank you.*

"You go." Sara tried to push me away, but I held fast to her. "Go, honey," she repeated. "Go see him."

I longed to run back to my car and drive to the hospital in Wilmington, but I couldn't leave Sara. "Not until you've heard about Keith," I said.

"Tracy Kelly's parents here?" Patty called.

"Here!" a man barked from behind me.

"She's at Cape Fear."

"Is Keith Weston on the list?" Sara shouted into the din.

I was afraid Patty hadn't heard her. She was speaking to a man who held a pair of broken glasses up to his eyes.

"Keith Weston was just airlifted to New Hanover," Patty called.

"Oh, no." Sara grabbed my arm so hard I winced. I thought of the helicopter rising into the sky above me.

"Let's go," I said, pulling Sara with me through the sea of people. Tears I'd been holding in spilled down my cheeks as we backed away, letting other parents take our places. "We can drive together."

"We'll go separately," Sara said, already at a run away from me. "In case one of us has to stay longer or—"

"Mom!" Maggie suddenly appeared at my side, winded and shivering. "They told me Uncle Marcus is here somewhere, but I couldn't find out anything about Andy."

"He's at New Hanover." I grabbed her hand. "I'm parked over by Jabeen's. Let's go."

I took one glance back at the smoking church. The ragged siding that still remained standing glowed red against the eerie gray sky. I hadn't thought about my former brother-in-law being there, but of course he was. I pictured Marcus inside the church, moving slowly through the smoke with his air pack on, feeling his way, searching for children who never stood a chance. Could he have been hurt when the roof collapsed? *Please, no.* And for the briefest of moments, I shifted my worry from Andy to him.

Maggie and I barely spoke on the way to Wilmington. She cried nearly the whole time, sniffling softly, shredding a tissue in her lap. My eyes were on the road, my foot pressing the gas pedal nearly to the floor. I imagined Andy trying to make sense out of the chaos of a fire and its aftermath. Simply moving the lock-in from the youth building to the church had probably been more than he could handle.

"Why did you say they moved the lock-in to the church?" I asked when we were halfway there.

"The electricity went out in the youth building." Her voice broke. "I heard some kids *died*," she said.

"Maybe just rumors."

"I'm so sorry I talked you into letting Andy—"

"Shh." I reached for her hand. "It's not your fault, all right? Don't even think that." But inside I was angry at her, at how cavalierly she'd told me, *Oh, Mother, he'll be fine!*

I tried to pull my hand from hers to make a turn, but she held it tightly, with a need that was rare for Maggie, and I let our hands stay locked together for the rest of the trip.

The crammed waiting area of the emergency room smelled of soot and antiseptic and was nearly as chaotic as the scene at the church. The throng of people in front of the glass reception window was four deep. I tried to push through, carving a space for Maggie and myself with my arms.

"Y'all have to wait your turn," said a large, wide woman as she blocked my progress.

"I need to find out how my son is." I kept pushing.

"We all need to know how our children are," said the woman.

A man in the waiting area let out sudden gut-wrenching sobs. I didn't turn to look. I wanted to plug my ears with my fingers. Maggie leaned against me a little.

"Maybe it was the electrical," she said.

"What?"

"You know, how the electricity was out in the youth building? Maybe that's connected to the fire somehow."

The woman ahead of us left the window and it was finally our turn. "They told me my son was brought here," I said. "Andrew Lockwood."

"All right, ma'am. Have a seat."

"No!" I wailed, the sound escaping my mouth like a surprise. "Please!" I started to cry, as though I'd been holding the tears in by force until that moment. "Tell me how he is! Let me go to him. He's...he has special needs."

"Mom..." Maggie tried to pull me away from the window.

The receptionist softened. "I know, honey," she said. "Your boy's okay. You take a seat and someone will come get you right quick."

I nodded, trying to pull myself together, but I felt like fabric frayed too much to be mended. Maggie led me to one of the seats in the waiting area and when I looked at her I realized that she, too, had dissolved in tears once more. I hugged her, unable to tell whether it was her shoulders quaking or my own.

"Laurel?"

I saw a woman heading toward us from the other side of the room. Her face and T-shirt were smeared with soot, her hair coated with so much ash I couldn't have said what color it was. Beneath her eyes, two long, clean trails ran down her cheeks. She'd had a good cry herself. She smiled now, though, as she took both my hands in hers. I recognized the slightly lopsided curve of the lips before I did the woman. Robin Carmichael. Emily's mother.

"Robin!" I said. "Are you all right?"

"Fine," she said. "And Andy's fine, too," she added quickly, knowing those were the words I needed to hear before anything else.

"They won't let me see—"

"What about Emily?" Maggie interrupted.

Robin nodded toward the other side of the waiting area, where I spotted Emily curled up on a chair, hugging her knees and holding a bloodstained cloth to her forehead.

"She's gonna be okay," Robin said, "but we're waiting to get her seen. She cracked her glasses right in two and got a little cut over her eyebrow." Robin still held my hands and now she looked hard into my eyes. "Andy saved Emily's life." Her voice broke and I felt her grip tighten on my fingers. "He saved a load of people tonight, Laurel."

"*Andy?*" Maggie and I said at the same time.

"Yeah, I know." Robin clearly shared our amazement. "But I swear, it's the truth."

"Mrs. Lockwood?" A woman in blue scrubs stood at the entrance to the waiting area.

"Yes!" I stood up quickly.

"Come with me."

We were ushered into one of the treatment areas I remembered from three years earlier when Andy broke his arm at the skating rink. The room had several beds separated by curtains. Someone was screaming behind one of the curtains; someone else cried. But the curtain was not drawn around Andy's bed. He was bare chested and barefooted, but wearing his now-filthy pants. A woman in blue scrubs was bandaging his left forearm, and he wore an oxygen cannula below his nose. Andy spotted us and leaped off the bed, the gauzy dressing dangling from his arm, the cannula snapping off his face.

"Mom!" he shouted. "There was a big fire and I'm a hero!"

"Andy!" the nurse called sharply. "I need to finish your arm."

Maggie and I pulled Andy into a three-way hug, and I breathed in that horrible acrid scent from the fire in great gulps. "Are you okay, sweetie?" I asked, still holding him tight. He fidgeted beneath my arms, and I knew they'd given him something for the asthma. I could tell by the spring-loaded tension in the muscles of his back, that's how well I knew my son. Still, I wouldn't let go of him.

Maggie came to her senses first, pulling away from us. "The nurse still needs you, Panda Bear," she said. She lifted his arm and I saw the angry red swath that ran from his wrist to the bend of his elbow. First degree, I thought with relief. I led him back into the cubicle and looked at the nurse as Andy climbed onto the bed.

"Is that the worst of it?" I asked, pointing to his arm.

She nodded as she fit the cannula to his nostrils again. "Check it tomorrow for blisters. We'll give you a prescription for pain. He'll be okay, though. He's a lucky fella."

"I made a new friend," Andy said. "Layla. I saved her."

"I'm glad, sweetie." I dusted ashes from his hair until its nutmeg color showed through.

The nurse carefully taped the gauze to his arm again. "He doesn't seem to feel pain," she said, looking at me.

"Not when he's wired like this." Maggie boosted herself onto the end of the bed.

"He'll feel it later." I remembered the swim meet last year when he hit his head on the side of the pool. He swam lap after lap, blood trailing behind him, not even aware he was hurt until the adrenaline had worn off.

"Did you *hear* me, Mom?" Andy said. "I saved Layla."

"Emily's mother told us you saved several people." I smoothed the elastic strap of the cannula flat behind his ear. My need to touch him, to feel the life in him, was overpowering. "What happened?"

"Not several," he corrected me. "*Everybody.*"

"You need to talk to him?" The nurse was looking over our heads, and I turned to see a man in a police uniform standing a few feet behind us. He looked at Andy.

"You Andy Lockwood?" he asked.

"Yes," I answered for him.

The man took a few steps closer. "You're his mother?"

I nodded. "Laurel Lockwood. And this is my daughter, Maggie."

The nurse patted Andy's bare shoulder. "Give a holler, you need anything," she said, pulling the curtain closed around us as she left.

"I'm ATF Agent Frank Foley," the man said. "How about you tell me what happened tonight, Andy?"

"I was the hero." Andy grinned.

The agent looked uncertain for a moment, then smiled. "Glad to hear it," he said. "We can always use more heroes.

Where were you when the fire began?" He flipped open a small notebook.

"With Emily."

"That's his friend," I said. "Emily Carmichael."

"Inside the church?" Agent Foley asked, writing.

"Yes, but she's my friend everywhere."

Maggie laughed. I knew she couldn't help herself.

"He's asking if you and Emily were inside the church when the fire broke out," I translated.

"Yes."

"Where in the church were you? Were you standing or sitting or…"

"One question at a time." I held up a hand to stop him. "Trust me," I said. "It'll be easier that way." I looked at Andy. "Where were you in the church when the fire broke out?"

"I don't remember."

"Try to think," I prodded. "Were you by the front door or closer to the altar?"

"By the baptism pool thing."

"Ah, good." The agent wrote something on his notepad. "Sitting or standing?"

"I stood next to Emily. Her shirt was inside out." He looked at me. "She used to do that all the time, remember?"

I nodded. "So you were standing with Emily near the baptism pool thing," I said, trying to keep him focused. "And then what happened?"

"People yelled fire fire fire!" Andy's dark eyes grew big, his face animated with the memory. "Then they started running past us. Then some boys grabbed a…the long thing and said one two three and broke the window with the bald man."

It was my turn to laugh as the words tumbled out of his mouth. An hour ago, I'd been afraid I'd never hear my precious son speak again.

Agent Foley, though, eyed him with suspicion. "Were there drugs there, Andy?" he asked. "Did you drink or take any substances tonight?"

"No, sir," Andy said. "I'm not allowed."

The agent stopped writing and gnawed his lip. "Do you get it?" he asked me. "The long thing? The bald man?"

I shook my head.

"Are you still talking about being inside the church, Panda?" Maggie asked.

"Yes and the boys caught on fire, but there were no ladders, so I told them to Stop! Drop! Roll! and some of them did. Keith was there." He looked at me. "He was mean to me."

"I'm sorry," I said. Sara was my best friend and I was worried sick about her son, but Keith could be a little shit sometimes. "You mean there were no ladders to escape the fire, like the ladder we have in your room at home?"

"Right. There weren't any," Andy said.

"Okay," Agent Foley said. "So while this was happening, where were you?"

"I *told* you, at the baptism thing." Andy furrowed his forehead at the man's denseness.

The agent flipped a few pages of his notepad. "People told me you got out of the church and—"

"Right," Andy said. "Me and Emily went out the boys' room window, and there was a big metal box on the ground, and we climbed onto it."

"And then what happened?"

"We were outside."

"And what did you see outside? Did you see any person out—"

"One question at a time," I reminded him.

"What did you see outside, Andy?" Agent Foley asked.

"Fire. Everywhere except by the metal box. And Emily was screaming that nobody could get out the front door because fire was there. I saw somebody *did* get out the door and they were on fire. I don't know who it was, though."

"Oh God." Maggie buried her face in her hands, her long dark hair spilling in waves over her arms. I knew she was picturing the scene as I was. Sitting there with Andy, it was easy to forget how devastating the fire had been for so many people. I thought again of Keith. Where was he?

"Did you see anyone else outside beside the person on fire?" the agent asked.

"Emily."

"Okay. So you went back in."

"You went back *in,* Andy?" I repeated, wondering whatever possessed him to reenter the burning church.

Andy nodded. "I climbed on the metal box and got into the boys' room and then called for everyone to follow me."

"And they did?" the agent asked.

"Did they what?"

"Follow you?"

"Not exactly. I let some of them, like my friend Layla, go first." He pulled the cannula from his nostrils and looked at me. "Do I still have to wear this?"

"A little longer," I said. "Until the nurse comes back and says you can take it off."

"So you let Layla go out the window first?" Agent Foley nudged.

"And some other kids. Then *I* followed *them*. But some were still following me, too." He wrinkled his nose. "It's hard to explain."

"You're doing fine, sweetie," I said.

"How did you know the…metal box was there?" the agent asked.

"I don't remember."

"Try to remember," I said.

"I saw it when I went to the bathroom."

"When was that?" the agent asked.

"When I had to pee."

Agent Foley gave up, closing his notepad with the flick of a wrist.

"Sounds like you *are* a hero, Andy," he said.

"I know."

The agent motioned me to follow him. We walked outside the curtained cubicle. He looked at me curiously.

"What's his, uh, disability?" he asked. "Brain injury?"

"Fetal Alcohol Spectrum Disorder," I said, the words as familiar to me as my own name.

"Really?" He looked surprised, glancing over my shoulder as though he could see through the curtain. "Don't those kids usually…you know, have a look to them?"

"Not always," I said. "Depends on what part of them was developing when the alcohol affected them."

"You're his adoptive mother then?"

The police on Topsail Island know me and they know Andy

and they know our story. An ATF agent in Wilmington, though, was a world away.

"No, I'm his biological mother," I said. "Sober fifteen years."

His smile was small. Tentative. Finally he spoke. "You've got a year on me," he said. "Congratulations."

"You, too." I smiled back.

"So——" he looked down at his closed notepad "——how much of what he says can I believe?"

"All of it," I said with certainty. "Andy's honest to a fault."

"He's an unusual kid." He looked over my shoulder again.

"You don't need to tell *me* that."

"No, I mean, in a fire, seventy-five percent of the people try to get out the front door. That's their first reaction. They're like a flock of sheep. One starts in that direction and they all follow. The other twenty-five percent look for an alternate exit. A back door. Bash open a window. Who's the bald-headed guy he was talking about?"

"I have no idea."

"Anyway, so Andy here goes for the window in the men's room. Strange choice, but turns out to be the right one."

"Well," I said, "kids like Andy don't think like that first seventy-five percent, or even the twenty-five percent. It was sheer luck. He could just as easily have gone for...I don't know, the ladies' room window, let's say, and still be stuck there." I hugged my arms across my chest at the thought. "Do you know if everyone got out okay? I heard rumors that some didn't."

He shook his head. "This was a bad one," he said. "Last report, three dead."

I sucked in my breath, hand to my mouth. "Oh, no." Some parents wouldn't have the luxury of hearing their children tell what happened tonight. "Do you know who?" I thought of Keith. Of Marcus.

"No names yet," he said. "Two of the kids and one adult is all I know. A lot of serious burns and smoke inhalation. This E.R.'s packed tight as a can of sardines."

"What's the metal box?" I asked.

"The AC unit. Whoever laid the fire skipped around it."

"Whoever... You're saying this was *arson?*"

He held up a hand as if to erase his words. "Not for me to say."

"I know there was an electrical problem at the youth building. Could that have affected the church?"

"There'll be a full investigation," he said.

"Is that why you asked Andy if he saw anyone else outside the church?"

"Like I said, there'll be a full investigation," he repeated, and I knew that would now be his answer, no matter what question I asked.

I opened the curtain around Andy's bed once I returned to his cubicle, and noticed a man sitting on the edge of a bed on the other side of the room. His head was bandaged and his T-shirt-clad broad shoulders drooped. When he looked up to say something to his nurse, the movement made him wince. I recognized the dark hair, the thick-lashed brown eyes. He passed a tremulous hand over his face and I saw the sheen of tears on his cheek.

Andy's nurse was listening to his lungs. She asked him to breathe deeply. To cough. I took that moment to whisper to Maggie.

"Ben Trippett's over there," I said. Ben was a volunteer firefighter, twenty-seven or twenty-eight. He was also Andy's swim-team coach and I wasn't sure how Andy would react to seeing him there, injured and upset.

Maggie started as if I'd awakened her from a dream, then followed my gaze to the other side of the room. She knew Ben fairly well, since she coached the younger kids' swim team.

Maggie got up, and before I could stop her, walked across the room toward Ben. He'd be embarrassed that we'd seen him crying, but Maggie was seventeen and I had to let her make her own errors in judgment. Her back was to me as she greeted Ben and I couldn't see his reaction. But then she pulled a rolling stool close to the bed and sat down and they talked, both of them with their heads bowed as though they were sharing a prayer. Ben's shoulders shook, and Maggie reached out and rested her hand on his wrist. She amazed me at times. Had she learned that compassion from me, watching me with Andy? I doubted it. All good things about Maggie had been Jamie's doing. A seventeen-year-old girl finding it in herself to comfort a grown man. I was, for just a moment, in awe of her.

Andy's nurse straightened up. "Let me take your vitals and then I'll see about getting you discharged," she said.

Andy stuck out his left arm for the blood pressure cuff.

"Your other arm, Andy," the nurse said. "Remember? You need to be careful with the burned arm for a few days."

She took his blood pressure and temperature and then left us alone.

"I'm going to write a book about being a hero," Andy said, as I reached beneath the bed for the plastic bag containing his shirt and shoes.

"Maybe someday you will." I considered bringing him down

to earth a little, but how often did he get to crow about an accomplishment? Other people would not be so kind, though.

Opening the bag, I recoiled from the pungent scent of his clothes. "Andy, what you did tonight was very brave and smart," I said.

He nodded. "Right."

I thought about letting him leave the hospital without his odorous shirt or shoes, but it was chilly outside. I handed him the striped shirt.

"But the fire was a very serious thing and a lot of people were hurt." I hesitated. It was best that he heard it from me. "Some died."

He shook his head violently. "I saved them."

"You couldn't save everyone, though. That's not your fault. I know you tried. But don't talk to people about how you're a hero. It's bragging. Remember, we don't brag."

"Is it bragging if it's in a book?"

"That would be okay," I said.

Behind me, the glass door plowed open and I turned to see Dawn Reynolds fly through the room toward Ben.

"Oh my God! *Ben!*" She nearly knocked Maggie off the stool as she rushed to pull Ben into her arms. "I was so scared," she said, crying. Tears welled in my own eyes as I watched the love and relief pour from her. She and Ben lived together in a little beach cottage in Surf City, and Dawn worked with Sara at Jabeen's Java.

"I'm okay." Ben rubbed her arms in reassurance. "I'm all right."

Maggie quietly stood up, offering the stool to Dawn, then walked back to us.

"Is he okay?" I nodded toward Ben.

"Not exactly." She bit her lip. "He has a seven-year-old daughter who lives with his ex-wife in Charlotte. He keeps thinking about her being trapped like that. He's upset that people…" She looked at Andy, then me. "You know."

"I explained to Andy that some people died in the fire," I said.

Maggie started to cry again. She reached in her jeans pocket for her shredded tissue. "I just don't understand how this could happen."

"I'm going to write a book about it so it won't be bragging," Andy said as he pulled on one of his shoes.

Maggie stuffed her tissue in her pocket again. She lifted Andy's leg so his foot rested on her hip as she tied his shoelaces. "Ben said a beam landed on his head," she said. "Uncle Marcus was with him."

Marcus. I remembered what the ATF agent had said: *Two kids and one adult.* And for the second time that night, my fear and worry shifted from my son to my brother-in-law.

Chapter Four

Marcus

I DIALED LAUREL'S NUMBER FOR THE THIRD TIME as I swerved onto Market Street. Voice mail. Again. *Cute, Laurel. Now's not the time to pretend you don't know me.*

"Call me, for Christ's sake!" I shouted into the phone.

I still couldn't picture Laurel letting Andy go to a lock-in, especially one at Drury Memorial.

I'd just come out of that fire pit when Pete ran up to me.

"Lockwood!" He'd only been a few feet away, but he had to shout above the racket of generators and sizzling water and sirens. "Your nephew's at New Hanover. Get out of here!"

It took a second for his words to register. "Andy was *here?*" I shrugged out of the air pack and peeled off my helmet. My hands had been rock steady inside the church. Suddenly, they were shaking.

"Right," Pete called over his shoulder as he raced back to the truck. "Drop your gear and get going. We'll take care of it."

"Does Laurel know?" I shouted as I stripped off my turnout jacket, but he didn't hear me.

I ran the few blocks to the fire station, yanking off my gear along the way until I was down to my uniform. Jumped into my pickup and peeled out of the parking lot. They'd closed the bridge to all traffic other than emergency vehicles, but when the officer guarding the entrance recognized me, she waved me through. I'd tried Laurel at home as well as her cell. Now I called the emergency room at New Hanover. I had to dial the number twice; my hands were shaking that hard. I set the phone to speaker and dropped it in the cup holder.

"E.R.," a woman answered.

"This is Surf City Fire Marshal Marcus Lockwood," I shouted in the direction of the phone. "You have a patient, Andy Lockwood, from Drury Memorial. Can you give me a status on him?"

"Just a moment."

The chaos at the hospital—sirens and shouting—filled the cab of my pickup. Someone screamed words I couldn't make out. Someone else wailed. It was like the frenzied scene at the fire had moved to the hospital.

"Come on, come on." My fists clenched the steering wheel.

"Mr. Lockwood?"

"Yes."

"He's being treated for smoke inhalation and burns."

Shit.

"Hold on a sec..."

I heard her talking to someone. Then she was back on the phone. "First-degree burn, his nurse says. Just his arm. He's stable. His nurse says he's a hero."

She had the wrong boy. The words "Andy" and "hero" didn't go together in the same sentence.

"You sure you're talking about Andy Lockwood?"

"He's your nephew, right?"

"Right."

"His nurse says he led some kids out of the church through the men's room window."

"What?"

"And she says he's going to be fine."

I couldn't speak. I managed to turn off the phone, then struggled to keep control of the pickup as the road blurred in front of me. As nerve-racking as the fire had been, it hadn't scared me half as much as those last couple of minutes on the phone.

Now that I knew Andy was going to be okay, I was royally pissed off. The fire was arson. I had been on the first truck out and done a quick walk around. The fire ring was even on all four sides of the building. That didn't happen by accident.

I understood arson. I'd been the kind of kid who played with matches and I once set our shed on fire. I tried to blame it on Jamie, but my parents knew their saintly older son would never be that stupid. I don't remember my punishment—just the initial thrill of watching Daddy's oily rags explode into flame on his workbench, followed by terror as the fire shot up the wall. So I got it—the thrill, the excitement. But damn it, if some asshole had to start a fire, why a church filled with kids? Why not one of the hundreds of empty summer homes on the island? The building itself was no great loss. Drury Memorial had been on a fund-raising kick for years, trying to get the money to build a bigger church. So, was that just a coincidence? And was it a coincidence that the lock-in was moved from the youth building to the church? Whatever, it felt good to be thinking about the investigation instead of Andy.

Ben Trippett and Dawn Reynolds were coming out of the E.R. as I ran toward the entrance. Now *there* was a guy who could call himself a hero. As much as I wanted to see Andy, I had to stop.

"There's the man!" I said, clapping him on the shoulder.

"Dude," Ben said, with a failed effort at a smile. He leaned against Dawn and in the light from the entrance I saw her eyes were red.

"How's the head?" He'd been crawling in front of me in the church when something—a joist or a statue or who knew what—crashed on top of him, knocking off his helmet. In the beam from my flashlight, I'd seen blood pouring down his cheek.

"Seventeen stitches." Dawn pressed closer to him. "Maybe a concussion."

"You saved at least one life tonight, Trippett," I said. "You can have my back anytime."

Truth was, I hadn't liked going in with him. Ben had been a volunteer for less than a year, and I was sure he wouldn't last. He had the desire, the ambition and the smarts, but he was claustrophobic. He'd put on the SCBA gear, take that first breath through the face piece and freak out. Full-blown panic attack. The guys razzed him about it. Good-natured teasing at first, but when the severity of the problem became clear, the taunting turned ugly, and I couldn't blame them. No one wanted to go into a fire with a guy they couldn't trust. Ben had been ready to quit. Ready to leave the island altogether. But he finally made it through the controlled burn during a training session, and a month or so ago, he told me he was ready to go live.

"You sure?" I'd asked him. "There's a huge difference between a controlled fire and a live burn."

"I'm sure," he'd said. He hadn't been kidding. He was ahead of me tonight, inching on his hands and knees through the burning church, when his low-air alarm sounded. We'd both started out with full tanks, but nerves made you chew up the air faster and he was running on empty.

"Let's go!" I'd shouted to him, the words muddy from behind my mask. He heard me, though. I knew he did, but he didn't turn around. Instead, he kept moving forward and I thought he was losing it. I heard the dull thud of whatever hit his helmet. Heard his grunt of pain. Saw the streak of red on his cheek. "Ben!" I'd shouted. "Turn around!" But he kept right on going.

I called into my radio. "I've got an injured man with low air," I said, but through the murk, I suddenly saw the screen of his thermal image camera. There was someone in front of us. He was going after one of the kids.

The girl had crawled into her sleeping bag and somehow found an air pocket. Ben grabbed her, and together we dragged her from the church. She was unconscious but alive.

"Your boyfriend's a stubborn SOB," I said now to Dawn. "But there's a girl who's lucky he is."

"I know," Dawn said.

"I heard some kids didn't make it," Ben said. "I should've stayed. Maybe we could have—"

"You couldn't stay, man." I gripped his shoulder. "Your head was split open."

Ben pressed his sooty fingers to his eyes. He was gonna come unglued any second.

"It's okay, buddy," I said. "You did good tonight." The hospital lights fell on his dark hair and all of a sudden, he reminded me of Jamie. That brawny bulk of him that made me feel scrawny by comparison. Big man with a soft heart.

"Do you hear him, Ben?" Dawn turned to Ben, one hand on his chest. "You did all you could, sugar." She looked at me. "Do you know how it started?"

"Arson, most likely."

"Who would do something like that?" Dawn asked.

I shook my head. "Y'all happen to see my nephew inside?" I looked past them through the glass doors of the E.R. "Andy?"

"He's there." Dawn touched my arm. "He's okay."

Andy sat cross-legged on a bed in the E.R., looking like a skinny little Buddha with a bandaged forearm, and my throat closed up. Laurel sat next to the bed, her back to me, black hair falling out of a barrette. Maggie was curled up at the end of the bed, hugging her knees.

Andy spotted me as I opened the glass door.

"Uncle Marcus!" he called.

I reached the bed in a few strides and leaned past Laurel to hug him. His back felt boyish and narrow—a little kid's back, though his muscles were tight from swimming. I inhaled the smoke from his hair, unable to speak. Finally, I got a grip on myself and stood up.

"Good to see you, Andy." My voice felt like sandpaper in my throat.

"I'm a hero," Andy said, then glanced quickly at Laurel. "Can I tell Uncle Marcus that?"

Laurel chuckled. "Yes," she said. "Uncle Marcus is family." She looked at me. "I told Andy that he shouldn't brag."

I put an arm around Maggie and hugged her to me. "How're *you* doin', Mags?"

"Okay," she said. She didn't look okay. Her face was waxy. Beneath her eyes, the skin was purplish and translucent.

"Don't worry," I said, squeezing her shoulders. "He's okay."

"*Who's* okay?" She was definitely out of it.

"Andy, babe," I said.

"Oh, I know." She leaned forward, rubbed her hand over Andy's knee.

"How about you, Marcus?" Laurel asked. "You're a mess. Are you okay?"

"Fine," I said. "But I'd like Andy to tell me why he's a hero."

There was no place to sit, so I leaned against the side of Laurel's chair, hands in my pockets. Andy jumped into the story with a zeal that made me forget my anger at Laurel for not calling me. He was suddenly a storyteller.

Laurel glanced up at me as Andy spun his tale. Our eyes locked for about half a second. She was quick to look away.

Andy was on a roll. "So, I clumb out the—"

"Climbed, sweetie." Laurel stroked her thumb over his hand.

"I climbed out the boy's room window and onto the metal box with Emily and then went back in and got everyone else to follow me out."

"Unreal," I said. "Like the Pied Piper of Hamelin."

"Who's that?" Andy asked.

"The Pied Piper is a man from a fairy tale, Andy," Laurel said. "Children followed him. That's what Uncle Marcus meant. You were like the Pied Piper because the children followed you."

"I thought it was rats that followed him," Maggie said.

I groaned. "Never mind. It was a bad analogy to begin with."

Laurel looked at her watch, then stood up. "Can I talk with you a minute?" she asked.

I leaned toward Andy, my hands on the sides of his head as I planted a kiss on his forehead. Breathed in that stench of fire I never wanted to smell on him again. "See you later, Andy," I said.

I had to run to catch up with Laurel outside the room. She was a jogger—a vitamin-chomping health nut—and she didn't walk as much as dart. Now she turned toward me, arms folded—her customary posture when talking with me. That was the way I usually pictured her in my mind—arms across her chest like a shield.

"Why the hell didn't you call me?" I asked.

"Everything happened so fast," she said. "And look. Keith Weston's here somewhere."

Whoa. "Keith was at the lock-in, too?"

She nodded. "He was airlifted. Sara left the fire about the same time I did, but I haven't seen her."

"Come on." I started walking toward the reception desk.

"An ATF agent was here talking to Andy," Laurel said.

"Good." They were moving fast. That's how I liked it.

"He said three people were killed. Do you know who?"

"No clue." I knew she was scared Keith was one of them. So was I. I touched her back with the flat of my palm. "There were plenty of injuries, I know that much."

We'd reached the desk, but the clerk was too overwhelmed to be bothered. I stopped a guy in blue scrubs heading toward the treatment area.

"Can we find out the condition of one of the fire victims?" I asked after identifying myself. "Keith Weston?"

"Sure," he said, like he had nothing better to do. He disappeared down a hallway.

I looked at Laurel. "Is this for real?" I nodded toward the treatment room. "He led other kids out?"

"Unbelievable, isn't it? But the agent said it was true. I think it was because he didn't think like everyone else—you know, heading for the front doors."

"And he has no fear," I added.

Laurel was slow to nod. Andy had plenty of fears, but she knew what I meant. He had no sense of danger. No real understanding of it. He was impulsive. I thought of the time he dove from the fishing pier to grab a hat that had blown off his head.

The guy in scrubs came back. "He's not here," he said. "They took him straight up to UNC in Chapel Hill."

Laurel covered her mouth with her hand. "The burn center?"

He nodded. "I talked to one of the medics. They induced a medical coma on the beach."

"Is he going to make it?" Laurel's hand shook. I wanted to hang on to my anger at her, but that trembling hand did me in.

"That I don't know," the guy said. "Sorry." His beeper sounded from his waistband, and he spun away from us, taking off at a run.

"Is his mother with—" Laurel called after him, but he was already halfway down the hall.

Laurel pressed those shaky hands to her eyes. "Poor Sara."

"Yeah," I said. "I'm just thankful Andy's okay."

"Oh, Marcus." She looked at me. Right at me. More than a half second this time. "I was so scared," she said.

"Me, too."

I wanted to wrap my arms around her. I needed the comfort as much as I needed to comfort her. I knew better, though. She'd stiffen. Pull away. So I settled for resting my hand on her back again as we headed toward the treatment area and Andy's bed.

Chapter Five

Laurel
1984

JAMIE LOCKWOOD CHANGED ME. For one thing, I could never again look at a man on a motorcycle without wondering what lay deep inside him. The tougher the exterior, the greater the number of tattoos, the thicker the leather, the more I'd speculate about his soul. But Jamie also taught me about love and passion and, without ever meaning to, about guilt and grief. They were lessons I'd never be able to forget.

I was eighteen and starting my freshman year at the University of North Carolina when I met him. I was pulling out of a parking space on a Wilmington street in my three-month-old Honda Civic. The red Civic was a graduation present from my aunt and uncle—technically my adoptive parents—who made up for their emotional parsimony through their generosity in tangible goods. I checked my side mirror—all clear—turned my steering wheel to the left, and gave the car some gas. I felt a sudden *thwack* against my door and a meteor of black leather and blue denim streaked through the air next to my window.

I screamed and screamed, startled by the volume of my own voice but unable to stop. I struggled to open my door without success, because the motorcycle was propped against it. By the time I escaped through the passenger door, the biker was getting to his feet. He was huge pillar of a man, and if I'd been thinking straight, I might have been afraid to approach him. What if he was a Hells Angel? But all I could think about was that I'd hurt someone. I could have killed him.

"Oh my God!" I ran toward him, moving on sheer adrenaline. The man stood with his side to me, rolling his shoulders and flexing his arms as if checking to see that everything still worked. I stopped a few feet short of him. "I'm so sorry. I didn't see you. Are you all right?"

A few people circled around us, hanging back as if waiting to see what would happen.

"I think I'll live." The Hells Angel unstrapped his white helmet and took it off, and a tumble of dark hair fell to his shoulders. He studied a wide black scrape that ran along the side of the helmet. "Man," he said. "I've got to send a testimonial to this manufacturer. D'you believe this? It's not even dented." He held the helmet in front of me, but all I saw was that the leather on his right sleeve was torn to shreds.

"I checked my mirror, but I was looking for a car," I said. "I'm so sorry. I somehow missed seeing you."

"You need to watch for cyclists!" A woman shouted from the sidewalk. "That could have been my son on his bike!"

"I know! I know!" I hugged my arms. "It was my fault."

The Hells Angel looked at the woman. "You don't need to rag on her," he said. "She won't make the same mistake twice." Then, more quietly, he spoke to me. "Will you?"

I shook my head. I thought I might throw up.

"Let's, uh—" he surveyed the scene "—let me check out my bike, and you back your car up to the curb and we can get each other's insurance info, all right?" His accent was pure Wilmington, unlike mine.

I nodded. "Okay."

He lifted his motorcycle from in front of my door, which was dented and scraped but opened with only a little difficulty, and I got in. I had to concentrate on turning the key in the ignition, shifting to Reverse, giving the car some gas, as if I'd suddenly forgotten how to drive. I felt about fourteen years old by the time I managed to move the car three feet back into its parking space. I fumbled in the glove compartment for my crumpled insurance card and got out.

The Hells Angel parked his motorcycle a couple of spaces up the street from my car.

"Does it run okay?" I asked, hugging my arms again as I approached. It wasn't cold, but my body was trembling all over.

"It's fine," he said. "Your car took the brunt of it."

"No, *you* did." I looked again at the shredded leather on his arm. "I wish you'd... *yell* at me or something. You're way too calm."

He laughed. "Did you cut me off on purpose?"

"No."

"I can tell you already feel like crap about it," he said. "Why should I make you feel worse?" He looked past me to the shops along the street. "Let's get a cup of coffee while we do the insurance bit," he said, pointing to the café down the block. "You're in no shape to drive right now, anyway."

He was right. I was still shivering as I stood next to him in line at the coffee shop. My knees buckled, and I leaned heavily against the counter as we ordered.

"Decaf for you." He grinned. He was a good ten inches taller than me. At least six-three. "Find us a table, why don't you?"

I sat down at a table near the window. My heart still pounded against my rib cage, but I was filled with relief. My car was basically okay, I hadn't killed anyone, and the Hells Angel was the forgiving type. I'd really lucked out. I put my insurance card on the table and smoothed it with my fingers.

I studied the width of the Angel's shoulders beneath the expanse of leather as he picked up our mugs of coffee. His body reminded me of a well-padded football player, but when he took off his jacket, draping it over the spare chair at our table, I saw that his size had nothing to do with padding. He wore a navy-blue T-shirt that read Topsail Island across the front in white, and while he was not fat, he was not particularly toned either. *Burly. Robust.* The words floated through my mind and, although I was a virgin, having miserably plodded my way through high school as a social loser, I wondered what it would be like to have sex with him. Could he hold his weight off me?

"Are you doin' all right?" Curiosity filled his brown eyes, and I wondered if the fantasy was written on my face. I felt my cheeks burn.

"I'm better," I said. "Still a little shaky."

"Your first accident?"

"My last, too, I hope. You've had others?"

"Just a couple. But I've got a few years on you."

"How old are you?" I asked, hoping it wasn't a rude question.

"Twenty-three. And you're about eighteen, I figure."

I nodded.

"Freshman at UNC?"

"Yes." I wrinkled my nose, thinking I must have *frosh* written on my forehead.

He sipped his coffee, then nudged my untouched mug an inch closer to me. "Have a major yet?" he asked.

"Nursing." My mother had been a nurse. I wanted to follow in her footsteps, even though she would never know it. "What about you?" I opened a packet of sugar and stirred it into my coffee. "Are you a Hells Angel?"

"Hell, no!" He laughed. "I'm a carpenter, although I *did* graduate from UNC a few years ago with a completely worthless degree in Religious Studies."

"Why is it worthless?" I asked, though I probably should have changed the subject. I hoped he wasn't going to try to save me, preaching the way some religious people did. I was beholden to him and would have had to listen, at least for a while.

"Well, I thought I'd go to seminary," he said. "Become a minister. But the more I studied theology, the less I liked the idea of being tied to one religion like it's the only way. So I'm still playing with what I want to be when I grow up." He reached toward the seat next to him, his hand diving into the pocket of his leather jacket and coming out with a pen and his insurance card. On his biceps, I saw a tattooed banner, the word *empathy* written inside it. As sexually excited as I'd felt five minutes ago, now I felt his fingertips touch my heart, hold it gently in his hand.

"Listen," he said, his eyes on the card. "Your car runs okay, right? It's mostly cosmetic?"

I nodded.

"Don't go through your insurance company, then. It'll just cost you in the long run. Get an estimate and I'll take care of it for you."

"You can't do that!" I said. "It was my fault."

"It was an easy mistake to make."

"I was careless." I stared at him. "And I don't understand why you're not angry about it. I almost killed you."

"Oh, I was angry at first. I said lots of cuss words while I was flying through the air." He smiled. "Anger's poison, though. I don't want it in me. When I changed the focus from how I was feeling to how *you* were feeling, it went away."

"The tattoo…" I pointed to his arm.

"I put it there to remind me," he said. "It's not always that easy to remember."

He turned the insurance card over and clicked the pen.

"I don't even know your name," he said.

"Laurel Patrick."

"Nice name." He wrote it down, then reached across the table to shake my hand. "I'm Jamie Lockwood."

We started going out together, to events on campus or the movies and once, on a picnic. I felt young with him, but never patronized. I was drawn to his kindness and the warmth of his eyes. He told me that he was initially attracted to my looks, proving that he was not a completely atypical guy after all.

"You were so pretty when you got out of your car that day," he said. "Your cheeks were red and your little pointed chin trembled and your long black hair was kind of messy and sexy." He coiled a lock of my stick-straight hair around his finger. "I thought the accident must have been fate."

Later, he said, it was my sweetness that attracted him. My innocence.

We kissed often during the first couple of weeks we saw one another, but nothing more than that. I experienced my first ever orgasm with him, even though he was not touching me at the time. We were on his bike and he shifted into a gear that suddenly lit a fire between my legs. I barely knew what was happening. It was startling, quick and stunning. I tightened my arms around him as the spasms coursed through my body, and he patted my hands with one of his, as though he thought I might be afraid of how fast we were going. It would be a while before I told him that I would always think of his bike as my first lover.

We talked about our families. I'd lived in North Carolina until I was twelve, when my parents died. Then I went to Ohio to live with my social-climbing aunt and uncle who were ill-prepared to take on a child of any sort, much less a grief-stricken preadolescent. There'd been a "Southerners are dumb" sort of prejudice among my classmates and a couple of my teachers. I fed right into that prejudice in the beginning, unable to focus on my studies and backsliding in every subject. I missed my parents and cried in bed every night until I figured out how to keep from thinking about them as I struggled to fall asleep: I'd count backward from one thousand, picturing the numbers on a hillside, like the *Hollywood* sign. It worked. I started sleeping better, which led to studying better. My teachers had to revise their "dumb Southerner" assessment of me as my grades picked up. Even my aunt and uncle seemed surprised. When it came time to apply to colleges, though, I picked all Southern schools, hungry to return to my roots.

Jamie was struck by the loss of my parents.

"Both your parents died when you were twelve?" he asked, incredulous. "At the same time?"

"Yes, but I don't think about it much."

"Maybe you *should* think about it," he said.

"It's all in the past." I'd healed from that loss and saw no point in revisiting it.

"Things like that can come back to bite you later," he said. "Were they in an accident?"

"You're awfully pushy." I laughed, but he didn't crack a smile.

"Seriously," he said.

I sighed then and told him about the fire on the cruise ship that killed fifty-two people, my parents included.

"Fire on a cruise ship." He shook his head. "Rock and a hard place."

"Some people jumped."

"Your parents?"

"No. I wish they had." Before I'd perfected my counting-backward-from-one-thousand technique, vivid fiery images of my parents had filled my head whenever I tried to go to sleep.

Jamie read my mind. "The smoke got them first, you can

bet on it," he said. "They were probably unconscious before the fire reached them."

Although I hadn't wanted to talk about it, I still took comfort from that thought. Jamie knew about fire, since he was a volunteer firefighter in Wilmington. For days after he'd fight a fire, I could smell smoke on him. He'd shower and scrub his long hair and still the smell would linger, seeping out of his pores. It was a smell I began to equate with him, a smell I began to like.

He took me to meet his family after we'd been seeing each other for three weeks. Even though they lived in Wilmington, I was to meet them at their beach cottage on Topsail Island where they spent most weekends. I'd probably been to Topsail as a child, but had no memory of it. Jamie teased me that my mispronunciation of the island—I said *Topsale* instead of *Topsul*—was a dead giveaway.

By that time, he'd bought me my own black leather jacket and white helmet, and I was accustomed to riding with him. My arms were wrapped around him as we started across the high-rise bridge. Far below us, I saw a huge maze of tiny rectangular islands.

"What *is* that down there?" I shouted.

Jamie steered the bike to the side of the bridge, even though ours was the only vehicle on the road. I climbed off and peered over the railing. The grid of little islands ran along the shoreline of the Intracoastal Waterway for as far as I could see. Miniature fir trees and other vegetation grew on the irregular rectangles of land, the afternoon sun lighting the water between them with a golden glow. "It looks like a little village for elves," I said.

Jamie stood next to me, our arms touching through layers of leather. "It's marshland," he said, "but it does have a mystical quality to it, especially this time of day."

We studied the marshland a while longer, then got back on the bike.

I knew Jamie's parents owned a lot of land on the island, especially in the northernmost area called West Onslow Beach. After World War II, his father had worked in a secret missile testing program on Topsail Island called Operation Bumblebee. He'd fallen in love with the area and used what money he had to buy land that mushroomed in value over the decades. As we rode along the beach road, Jamie pointed out property after property belonging to his family. Many parcels had mobile homes parked on them, some of the trailers old and rusting, though the parcels themselves were worth plenty. There were several well-kept houses with rental signs in front of them and even a couple of the old flat-roofed, three-story concrete viewing towers that had been used during Operation Bumblebee. I was staggered to realize the wealth Jamie had grown up with.

"We don't live rich, though," Jamie had said when he told me about his father's smart investments. "Daddy says that the whole point of having a lot of money is to give you the freedom to live like you don't need it."

I admired that. My aunt and uncle were exactly the opposite.

All the Lockwood houses had names burned into signs hanging above their front doors. The Loggerhead and Osprey Oasis and Hurricane Haven. We came to the last row of houses on the Island and I began to perspire inside the leather jacket.

I knew one of them belonged to his family and that I'd meet them in a few minutes. Jamie drove slowly past the cottages.

"Daddy actually owns these last five houses," he said, turning his head so I could hear him.

"Terrier?" I read the name above one of the doors.

"Right, that's where we're headed, but I'm taking us on a little detour first. The next house is Talos. Terrier and Talos were the names of the first supersonic missiles tested here."

Those two houses were mirror images of each other: tall, narrow two-story cottages sitting high on stilts to protect them from the sea.

"I love *that* one!" I pointed to the last house in the row, next to Talos. The one-story cottage was round. Like all the other houses, it was built on stilts. The sign above its front door read *The Sea Tender*.

"An incredible panoramic view from that one." Jamie turned onto a narrow road away from the houses. "I want to show you my favorite spot," he said over his shoulder. We followed the road a short distance until it turned to sand; then we got off the bike and began walking. I tugged my jacket tighter. The October air wasn't cold, but the wind had a definite nip to it and Jamie put his arm around me.

We walked a short distance onto a spit of white sand nearly surrounded by water. The ocean was on our right, the New River Inlet ahead of us and somewhere to our left, although we couldn't see it from our vantage point, was the Intracoastal Waterway. The falling sun had turned the sky pink. I felt as though we were standing on the edge of an isolated continent.

"My favorite place," Jamie said.

"I can see why."

"It's always changing." He pointed toward the ocean. "The sea eats the sand there, then spits it back over there," he moved his arm to the left of us, "and what's my favorite place today may be completely different next week."

"Does that bother you?" I asked.

"Not at all. Whatever nature does here, it stays beautiful." Neither of us spoke for a moment. Then Jamie broke the silence. "Can I tell you something?" For the first time since we met, he sounded unsure of himself. A little shy.

His arm was still around me and I raised mine until it circled his waist. "Of course," I said.

"I've never told anyone this and you might think I'm crazy."

"Tell me."

"What I'd really like to do one day is create my own church," he said. "A place where people can believe whatever they want but still belong to a community, you know?"

I wasn't sure I understood exactly what he meant, but one thing I'd learned about Jamie was that there was a light inside him most people didn't have. Sometimes I saw it flash in his eyes when he spoke.

"Can you picture it?" he asked. "A little chapel right here, full of windows so you can see the water all around you. People could come and worship however they chose." He looked toward the ocean and let out a sigh. "Pie in the sky, right?"

I did think he was a little crazy, but I opened my mind to the idea and imagined a little white church with a tall steeple standing right where we stood. "Would you be allowed to build something here?" I asked.

"Daddy owns the land. He owns every grain of sand north

of those houses. Would *nature* let me build it? That's the thing. Nature's got her own mind when it comes to this spot. She's got her own mind when it comes to the whole island."

The aroma of baking greeted us when we walked into Terrier. Jamie introduced his parents Southern style as Miss Emma and Mr. Andrew, but his father immediately insisted I call him Daddy L. Miss Emma had contributed the gene for Jamie's full head of wavy dark hair, although hers was cut in a short, uncomplicated style. Daddy L was responsible for Jamie's huge, round brown eyes. They each greeted their son with bear hugs as if they hadn't seen him in months instead of a day or so. Miss Emma even gave *me* a hug and a kiss on the cheek, then held my hands and studied me.

"She's just precious!" she said, letting go of my hands. I caught a whiff of alcohol on her breath

"Thank you, ma'am," I said.

"Didn't I tell you?" Jamie said to his mother as he helped me out of my leather jacket.

"I hope you're hungry." Daddy L leaned against the doorjamb. "Mama's cooked up a storm this afternoon."

"It smells wonderful," I said.

"That's the meringue on my banana pudding you're smelling," Miss Emma said.

"Where's Marcus?" Jamie asked.

I hadn't met him yet, but I knew Jamie's fifteen-year-old brother was something of a bad boy. Eight years younger than Jamie, he'd been a surprise to parents who'd adjusted to the idea of an only child.

"Lord only knows." Miss Emma stirred a big bowl of potato

salad. "He *was* surfing. Who knows what he's doing now. I told him dinner is at six-thirty, but the day he's on time is the day I'll keel over from the shock."

Jamie gave his mama's shoulders a squeeze. "Well, let's hope he's not on time, then," he said.

An hour later, we settled around a table laden with fried chicken, potato salad and corn bread. Marcus was not with us. We were near one of the broad oceanside windows and I imagined the view was spectacular in the daylight.

"So, tell me about your people, darlin'," Miss Emma said as she handed me the bowl of potato salad for a second helping.

I explained that my mother grew up in Raleigh and my father in Greensboro, but that I lost them on the cruise ship and was raised by my aunt and uncle in Ohio.

"Lord have mercy!" Miss Emma's hand flew to her chest. She looked at Jamie. "No wonder you two found each other."

I wasn't sure what she meant by that. Jamie smiled at me and I figured I could ask him later.

"That explains your accent." Daddy L looked at his wife and she nodded. "We were trying to peg it."

Daddy L helped himself to a crisp chicken thigh. He glanced at his watch, then at the empty chair next to Jamie. "Maybe you could talk to Marcus about his grades, Jamie," he said.

"What about them?"

"We just got his interim report, and he's fixin' to flunk out if he doesn't buckle down," Miss Emma said quietly, as if Marcus could overhear us. "Mostly D's. And it's his junior year. I don't think he knows how important this year is for getting into college." She looked at me. "Jamie's Daddy and I never made it to college, and I want my boys to get an education."

"I love going to UNC," I said, although I was really thinking that she and Daddy L had done quite well for themselves without a college degree.

"I'll talk to him," Jamie said.

"He spends all the time he's not in school on that surfboard," Miss Emma said, "and then is off with his friends on the weekends, no matter what we say."

"Boy's out of control," Daddy L added.

I'd been in the house only an hour, but already the primary Lockwood family dynamic was apparent: Jamie, despite the long hair and the tattoo and the motorcycle, was the favored son. Marcus was the black sheep. I hadn't even met him and I already felt sympathy for him.

We were nearly finished when we heard the downstairs door open and close. "I'm home!" a male voice called.

"And your dinner's cold as ice!" Miss Emma called back.

I heard him on the stairs. He came into the dining room barefooted, wearing a full-length wet suit, the top unzipped nearly to his navel. He had a lanky, slender build that would never fill out to Jamie's bulk, even though Jamie had eight years on him. A gold cross hanging from his neck glittered against the tan that must have been left over from summer, and his hair was a short, curly cap of sun-streaked brown. He had Miss Emma's eyes—blue, shot through with summer sky.

"Hey." He grinned at me, pulling out the chair next to Jamie.

"Go put some clothes on," Daddy L said.

"This is Laurel," Jamie said. "And this is Marcus."

"Hi, Marcus," I said.

"You're a sandy mess," Miss Emma said. "Get dressed and I'll heat you a plate in the microwave."

"Not hungry," Marcus said.

"You still need to change your clothes if you're going to sit here with us," said his father.

"I'm going, I'm going." Marcus got up with a dramatic sigh and padded toward the bedrooms.

In a few minutes, I heard the music of an electric piano. The tune was halting and unfamiliar.

Jamie laughed. "He brought the piano with him?"

"If you can call it that," Miss Emma said.

Daddy L looked at me. "He wants to play in a rock-and-roll band," he explained. "For years, we offered to buy him a piano so he could take proper lessons, but he said you can't play a piano in a band."

"So he bought a used electric piano and is trying to teach himself how to play it," Miss Emma said. "It makes me ill, listening to that thing."

"Ah, Mama," Jamie said. "It keeps him off the streets."

After we'd eaten the most fabulous banana pudding I'd ever tasted, I wandered down the hall to use the bathroom. I could hear Marcus playing a song by The Police. When I left the bathroom, I knocked on his open bedroom door.

"Your mother said you're teaching yourself how to play."

He looked up, his fingers still on the keys. He'd changed into shorts and a navy-blue T-shirt. "By ear," he said. "I can't read music."

"You could learn how to read music." I leaned against the doorjamb.

"I'm dyslexic," he said. "I'd rather have all my teeth pulled."

"Play some more," I said. "It sounded good."

"Could you recognize it?"

"That song by The Police," I said. "'Every Breath You Take'?"

"Awesome!" His grin was cocky and he had the prettiest blue eyes. I bet he was considered a catch by girls his age. "I'm better than I thought," he said. "How about this one?"

He bent over the keys with supreme concentration, the cocky kid gone and in his place a boy unsure of himself. The back of his neck looked slender and vulnerable. He grimaced with every wrong note. I struggled to recognize the song, to let him have that success. It took a few minutes, but then it came to me.

"That Queen song!" I said.

"Right!" He grinned. "'We are the Champions.'"

"I'm impressed," I said sincerely. "I could never play by ear."

"You play?"

"I took lessons for a few years."

He stood up. "Go for it," he said.

I sat down and played a couple of scales to get the feel of the keyboard. Then I launched into one of the few pieces I could remember by heart: *Fur Elise.*

When I finished, I looked up to see Jamie standing in the doorway of the bedroom, a smile on his face I could only describe as *tender.* I knew in that moment that I loved him.

"That was beautiful," he said.

"Yeah, you're good," Marcus agreed. He tipped his head to one side, appraising me. "Are you, like, a sorority chick?"

I laughed. "No. What made you ask that?"

"You're just different from Jamie's other girlfriends."

"Is that good or bad?" I asked.

"Good." Marcus looked up at his brother. "She's cool," he said. "You should keep this one."

I heard the sound of dishes clinking together in the kitchen and left the brothers to help clean up. I found Miss Emma up to her elbows in dishwater.

"Let me dry." I picked up the dish towel hanging from the handle of the refrigerator.

"Why, thank you, darlin'." She handed me a plate. "I heard you playing in there. That was lovely. I didn't know a sound like that could come out of that electric thing."

"Thanks," I said, adding, "Marcus plays really well by ear."

"It's his *choice* of music that makes me ill." I had the feeling nothing Marcus did would be good enough for her.

"It's what everybody listens to, though," I said carefully.

She laughed a little. "I can see why Jamie likes you so much."

I felt my cheeks redden. Had he talked about me to his parents?

"You care about people like he does."

"Oh, no," I said. "I mean, I care about people, but not like Jamie does. He's amazing. Three weeks ago, I almost killed him. I did. Now I feel like…" I shook my head, unable to put into words how I felt. Taken in. By Jamie. By his family. More at home with them than I'd felt in six years with my icy aunt and silent uncle.

"Jamie does have a gift with people, all right," she said. "The way some people are born with musical talent or math skills or what have you. It's genetic."

I must have looked dubious, because she continued.

"I don't have the gift, Lord knows," she said, "but I had a

brother who did. He died in his thirties, rest his soul, but he was…it's more than kindness. It's a way of seeing inside a person. To really feel what they're feeling. It's like they can't *help* but feel it."

"Empathy," I said.

"Oh, that stupid tattoo." She squirted more dish soap into the water in the sink. "I about had a conniption when I saw that thing. But he's a grown man, not much his mama can do about it now. He doesn't *need* that tattoo." She scrubbed the pan the corn bread had been baked in. "My aunt had the gift, too, though she said it was more of a curse, because you had to take on somebody else's pain. We were at the movies this one time? A woman and boy sat down in front of us before the lights were shut out. They didn't say one single word, but Aunt Ginny said there was something wrong with the woman. That she felt a whole lot of anguish coming from her. That was the word she used—*anguish*."

"Uh-huh," I said, keeping my expression neutral. Miss Emma was going off the deep end, but I wasn't about to let her see my skepticism.

"I know it sounds crazy," she said. "I thought so too at the time. When the movie was over, Aunt Ginny couldn't stop herself from asking the woman if she was all right. Ginny had a way of talking to people that made them open right up to her. But the woman said everything was fine. As we were walking out of the theater, though, and the little boy was out of earshot, she told us that her mother'd had a stroke just that morning and she was worried sick about her. Ginny'd picked right up on that worry and took it inside herself. She ended up with a bleeding ulcer from taking on too many other people's worries. That's how Jamie is, too."

I remembered Jamie after the accident, when I wondered why he'd expressed no anger toward me. *You already feel like crap about it,* he'd said. *Why should I make you feel any worse?*

I shivered.

Miss Emma handed me the corn-bread pan to dry. "Here's what happens with people like Jamie or my brother or my aunt," she said. "They feel what the other person feels so strong that it's less painful for them to just...give in. I knew when Jamie was small that he had the gift. He knew when his friends were upset about something and he'd get upset himself, even if he didn't know what had them upset in the first place." She reached into the dirty dishwater and pulled the stopper from the drain. "One time, a boy he barely knew got his dog run over by a car. I found Jamie crying in bed that night—he couldn't have been more than eight or nine. He told me about it. I said, you didn't even know that dog and you barely know that boy. He just kept crying. I thought, oh Lord have mercy on me, please. Here's my brother and Aunt Ginny all over again. It's a scary thing, raising a child like that. Most kids, like Marcus, bless his heart, you have to teach them how other children feel and how you need to be sensitive to them and all." She pulled another dish towel from a drawer and dried her hands on it. "With Jamie, it was the opposite. I had to teach him to take care of himself."

I bit my lip as I set the dry pan on the counter. "Are you trying to...are you warning me about something?" I asked.

She looked surprised. "Hmm," she said. "Maybe I am. He likes you. I can tell. You're a nice girl. Down-to-earth. You got a good head on your shoulders. He's had a few girlfriends who took advantage of his kindness. I guess I'm asking you not to do that. Not to hurt him."

I shook my head. "Never," I said, thinking of how good it felt to have Jamie's arms around me. "I couldn't."

I thought I knew myself so well.

Chapter Six

Laurel

"I GUESS WE'RE SUPPOSED TO SIT UP THERE." Maggie pointed to the front row of seats in the crowded Assembly Building. Trish Delphy's secretary had called us the day before to say the mayor wanted us up front at the memorial service. I was sure our special status had to do with Andy, who was scratching his neck beneath the collar of his blue shirt. I'd had to buy him a new suit for the occasion. He so rarely had need of one that his old suit no longer fit. I let him pick out his own tie—a loud Jerry Garcia with red and blue swirls—but I'd forgotten a shirt and the one he was wearing was too small.

"We'll follow you, sweetie," I said to Maggie, and she led the way down the narrow center aisle. The air hummed with chatter, and the seats were nearly all taken even though there were still fifteen minutes before the start of the service. There'd been school buses in the parking lot across the street, and I noticed that teenagers occupied many of the seats. The lock-in had attracted children from all three towns on the island as well as from a few places on the mainland, cutting across both geographic and economic boundaries, tying us all together. If I'd known how many kids would show up at the lock-in, I never would have let Andy go. Then again, if Andy hadn't been there, more would have died. Incredible to imagine.

I sat between my children. Next to us were Joe and Robin Carmichael, Emily's parents, and in front of us was a podium flanked by two dozen containers of daffodils. Propped up on easels to the left of the podium were three poster-size photographs that I was not ready to look at. To the right of the podium were about twenty-five empty chairs set at a ninety-degree angle to us. A paper banner taped between the chairs read *Reserved for Town of Surf City Fire Department*.

Andy was next to Robin, and she embraced him.

"You beautiful boy," she said, holding on to him three seconds too long for Andy's comfort level. He squirmed and she let go with a laugh, then looked at me. "Good to see you, Laurel." She leaned forward a little to wave to Maggie.

"How's Emily doing?" I asked quietly.

Joe shifted forward in his seat so he could see me. "Not great," he said.

"She's gone backward some," Robin said. "Nightmares. Won't let us touch her. I can hardly get her to let me comb her hair. She's scared to go to school again."

"She had her shirt on inside out," Andy piped in, too loudly.

"Shh," I hushed him.

"You're right, Andy," Robin said. "She was already sliding back a ways before the fire, but now it's got real bad." She raised her gaze to mine. "We're going to have to take her to see that psychologist again."

"I'm so sorry," I said. Emily had suffered brain damage at birth, and I knew how far they'd come with her over the years. How hard it had to be to have a child who hated to be touched! Many FASD kids hated being touched, too, but I'd gotten lucky with Andy; he was a hugger. I needed to rein that hugging in with people outside the family, though, especially now that he was a teenager.

Robin looked behind us. "So many people affected by this...mess," she said.

I didn't turn around. My attention was drawn to the Surf City firefighters who were now filing into the seats reserved for them. In their dress blues and white gloves, a more sober looking bunch of men—and three women—would be hard to find, and as they sat down, a hush washed over the crowd. I saw Marcus glance at us, and I quickly turned my attention to the pink beribboned program I'd been handed when I entered the building.

Some people had wanted to put the memorial service off for another couple of weeks so the new Surf City Community Center would be open and the event could be held in the gymnasium. But the somber mood of the island couldn't wait that long. In the week since the fire, that's all anyone talked about. The part-time counselor at the elementary school where I worked was so inundated with kids suffering from nightmares about being burned or trapped that she'd had to refer the overflow, those whose fears showed up as stomachaches or headaches, to me. People were not only sad, they were angry. Everyone knew the fire was arson, although those words had not been uttered by anyone in an official capacity, at least not publicly.

Maggie hadn't said a word since we walked into the building. I glanced at her now. Her gaze was on the firefighters and I wondered what she was thinking. I was never sure how much she remembered of her father. She had a framed picture of Jamie in his dress blues on her bureau beside a picture of Andy taken on his twelfth birthday. There was another picture, taken a couple of years ago at a party, of herself with Amber Donnelly and a couple of other girls.

She had no picture of me on the bureau. I realized that just the other day.

Andy started jiggling his leg, making my chair vibrate. I used to rest a hand on his knee to try to stop his jiggling, but I rarely did that anymore. I'd learned that if I stopped the energy from coming out of Andy in one place, it would come out someplace else. Jiggling his legs was preferable to slapping his hands on his thighs or cracking his knuckles. Sometimes I pictured a tightly coiled spring inside my son, ready to burst out of him with the slightest provocation. That's most likely what happened when Keith called him names at the lock-in. It was rare for Andy to react with violence, but calling him names could do it.

"Hey, I know him!" Andy said suddenly.

"Shh," I whispered in his ear. I thought he meant Marcus or Ben Trippett, but he was pointing to the third poster-size photograph at the front of the room. It was Charlie Eggles, a long-time real estate agent in Topsail Beach. Charlie'd had no kids of his own but often volunteered to help with community events. I'd been saddened to learn he was one of the fire victims. I looked at his engaging smile, his gray hair pulled back in his customary ponytail.

"It's Mr. Eggles," I whispered to Andy.

"He held on to me so I couldn't hit Keith again." I watched a crease form between Andy's eyebrows as reality dawned on him. "Is he one of the dead people?"

"I'm afraid he is," I said.

I waited for him to speak again, but he fell silent.

"What are you thinking, love?" I asked quietly.

"Why didn't he follow me when I said to?"

I put my arm around him. "Maybe he didn't hear you, or he was trying to help some of the other children. We'll never know. You did the very best you—"

Somber piano music suddenly filled the room, swallowing my words, and Trish Delphy and Reverend Bill walked up the center aisle together. Reverend Bill stood behind the podium, while the mayor took the last empty seat in our row. Reverend Bill was so tall, skinny and long necked that he reminded me of an egret. Sara told me that he came into Jabeen's Java every afternoon for a large double-fudge-and-caramel-iced coffee with extra whipped cream, yet there was not an ounce of fat on the man. He was all sticks and angles.

Now he craned his long neck forward to speak into the microphone. "Let us pray," he said.

I bowed my head and tried to listen to his words, but I felt Maggie's warm body against my left arm and Andy's against my right. I felt them breathing, and my eyes once more filled with tears. I was so lucky.

When I lifted my head again, Reverend Bill began talking about the two teenagers and one adult killed in the fire. I forced myself to look at the blown-up images to the left of the podium. I didn't know either of the teenagers, both of whom were from Sneads Ferry. The girl, Jordy Matthews, was a smiling, freckle-faced blonde with eyes the powder-blue of the firefighters' shirts. The boy, Henderson Wright, looked about thirteen, sullen and a little scared. A tiny gold hoop hung from one end of his right eyebrow and his hair was in a buzz cut so short it was difficult to tell what color it was.

"...and Henderson Wright lived in his family's old green van for the past three years," Reverend Bill was saying. "We have people in our very own community who are forced to live that way, through no fault of their own." Somewhere to my right, I heard quiet weeping, and it suddenly occurred to me that the families of the victims most likely shared this front row with us. I wondered if it had been necessary for Reverend Bill to mention the Wright boy's poverty. Shrimping had once sustained Sneads Ferry's families, but imported seafood was changing all that. There were many poor people living amidst the wealth in our area.

I thought of Sara. Ever since I'd heard that Keith had referred to Andy as *rich,* apparently with much disdain, I'd been stewing about it. Andy and Keith had known each other since they were babies and the disparity between our financial situations had never been an issue, at least as far as I knew. I wondered now if there was some underlying resentment on Sara's part. God, I hoped not. I loved her like a sister. We were so open with each other—we had one of those friendships where nothing was off-limits. We'd both been single mothers for a decade, but Jamie had left my children and me more than comfortable. We had a handsome, ten-year-old four-bedroom house on the sound, while Sara and Keith lived in an aging double-wide sandwiched in a sea of other mobile homes.

My cheeks burned. How could I have thought that didn't matter to her? Did she say things to Keith behind my back? Had Keith's resentment built up until it spilled out on Andy at the lock-in?

Sara had been at the UNC burn center with Keith since the fire, so we'd had no good chance to talk. Our phone conversations were about Keith's condition; he was still battling for his life. Although the most serious burns were on his arms and one side of his face, his lungs had suffered severe damage, and he was being kept in a medicated coma because the pain would otherwise be unbearable.

Neither of us brought up the fight between our sons. Maybe she didn't even know about it. She had one thing on her mind, and that was getting Keith well. I'd offered to help her pay for any care he needed that wouldn't be covered by his father's military health insurance, but she said she'd be fine. Was it my imagination that she'd sounded chilly in her response? Had I insulted her? Maybe she simply resented the fact that Andy was safe and whole while her son could die.

Everyone around me suddenly stood up. Even Andy. I'd been so caught up in my thoughts that I didn't realize we were supposed to be singing a hymn, the words printed on the back of the program. I stood up as well, but didn't bother singing. Neither did Andy or Maggie, and I wondered where *their* thoughts were.

Long ago, Sara helped me turn my life around. When I got Andy out of foster care, he was a year old and I had no idea how to be a mother to the little stranger. After all, Jamie'd been both mother and father to Maggie when she was that age. It was Sara who helped me. Keith was nearly a year older than Andy, and Sara was a goddess in my eyes, the mother I wanted to emulate. Keith was adorable, and our boys were friends. They stayed friends until Andy was about nine. That's when Keith started caring what other kids thought, and my strange little son became an embarrassment to him. Andy never really understood the sudden ostracism. In Andy's eyes, everyone was his friend, from the janitor at school to the stranger who smiled at him on the beach. Over the past few years, though, I was glad Keith and Andy had drifted apart. Keith got picked up for drinking once, for truancy a couple of times, and last summer, for possession of an ounce of marijuana. That was the last sort of influence I needed over Andy. Andy longed to fit in and, given his impulsiveness, I worried how far he'd go to reach that goal.

We were sitting again and I felt ashamed that I'd paid so little attention to the service. Reverend Bill swept his eyes over the crowd as he vowed that "a new Drury Memorial will rise from the ashes of the old," embracing everyone with a look of tenderness, skipping over my children and me. Literally. I saw his eyes light on the man sitting next to Maggie, then instantly slip to the Carmichaels on the other side of Andy. We were the heathens in the crowd, and Reverend Bill carried a grudge for a good long time. I was willing to bet his eyes never lit on Marcus either when he looked in the direction of the firefighters. Still, I felt for the man. Even though his congregation was planning to build a new church, he'd lost this one. I knew some families were talking about suing him for negligence.

Others wondered if Reverend Bill himself might have set the fire for the insurance money. I was no fan of the man, but that was ridiculous.

My gaze drifted to Marcus. His face was slack and I could suddenly see the first sign of age in his features. He was young. Thirty-eight. Three years younger than me. For the first time, I could begin to see how he'd look as he got older, something I'd never have the joy of seeing in Jamie, who'd only been thirty-six when he died.

Reverend Bill and Trish Delphy were changing places at the podium. Trish licked her lips as she prepared to speak to the crowd.

"Our community will be forever changed by this terrible tragedy," she said. "We mourn the loss of life and we pray for those still recovering from their injuries. But I'd ask you to look around you and see the strength in this room. We're strong and resilient, and while we'll never forget what happened in Surf City on Saturday, we'll move forward together.

"And now," she continued, "Dawn Reynolds has an announcement she'd like to make."

Ben Trippett's girlfriend looked uncomfortable as she took her place behind the podium.

"Um," she began, "I just wanted to let y'all know that I'm coordinating the fund-raising to help the fire victims." The paper she held in her hand shivered and I admired her for getting up in front of so many people when it obviously made her nervous. "The Shriners have come through like always to help out with medical expenses, but there's still more we need to do. A lot of the families have no insurance. I'm working with Barry Gebhart, who y'all know is an accountant in Hampstead, and we set up a special fund called the Drury Memorial Family Fund. I hope you'll help out with a check you can give me or Barry today, or you can drop by Jabeen's Java anytime I'm working. Barry and I are thinking of some fund-raising activities and we'd like your suggestions in that…um…about that." She looked down at the paper. "We'll make sure the money gets to the families who need it the most."

She sat down again at the end of our row. I saw Ben, his head still bandaged, smile at her.

Trish stood up once more at the podium.

"Thank you, Dawn," she said. "We have a generous community with a generous spirit and I know we'll do all in our power to ease the suffering of the families hurt by the fire.

"Now I'd like to recognize the firefighters and EMS workers who did such an amazing job under grueling circumstances. Not only our Town of Surf City Fire Department, but those firefighters from Topsail Beach, North Topsail Beach and the Surf City Volunteer Fire Department as well."

Applause filled the building, and as it ebbed, I saw Trish drop her gaze to us.

"And I'd like to ask Andy Lockwood to stand, please."

Beside me, I felt Andy start.

"Go ahead, sweetie," I whispered. "Stand up."

He stood up awkwardly.

Before the mayor could say another word, applause broke out again, and people rose to their feet.

"Are they clapping for me?" Andy asked.

"Yes." I bit my lip to hold back my tears.

"Why did they stand up?"

"To honor you and thank you."

"Because I'm a hero?"

I nodded.

He grinned, turning around to wave at the crowd behind us. I heard some subdued laughter.

"Can I sit down now?" Andy asked finally.

"Yes."

He lowered himself to his seat again, his cheeks pink. It took another minute for the applause to die down.

"As most of you know," Trish said, "Andy not only found a safe way out of the church, but he risked his own life to go back in and lead many of the other children to safety. Our loss is devastating, but it would have been much worse without Andy's quick thinking and calm in the face of chaos."

Andy sat up straighter than usual, his chest puffed out a bit, and I knew he was surprised to find himself suddenly the darling of Topsail Island.

Chapter Seven

Andy

MOM PUT HER VITAMINS IN A LINE by her plate. She ate breakfast vitamins and dinner vitamins. Maggie and I only ate breakfast ones. Maggie passed me the spinach bowl. Dumb. She knows I don't eat spinach. I tried to give it to Mom.

"Take some, Andy," Mom said. "While your arm is healing, you need good nutrition."

"I have lots of nutrition." I lifted my plate to show her my chicken part and the cut-up sweet potato.

"Okay. Don't spill." She put her fingers on my plate to make it go on the table again.

I ate a piece of sweet potato. They were my favorite. Mom made sweet potato pie sometimes, but she never ate any. She didn't eat dessert because she didn't want to ever be sick. She said too many sweet things could make you sick. Maggie and I were allowed to eat dessert because we weren't adults yet.

"Andy," Mom said after she swallowed all her vitamins, "your arm looks very good, but maybe you should skip the swim meet tomorrow."

"Why?" I *had* to swim. "It doesn't hurt!"

"We need to make sure it's completely healed."

"It *is* completely healed!"

"You've been through a lot, though. It might be good just to take a rest."

"I don't *need* a rest!" My voice was too loud for indoors. I couldn't help it. She was pressing my start button.

"If your arm is all better, then you can."

"It's better enough!" I wanted to show her my arm, but I punched it out too hard and hit my glass of milk. The glass flew across the table and crashed to the floor. It broke in a million pieces and milk was all over. Even in the spinach.

Mom and Maggie stared at me with their mouths open. I saw a piece of chewed chicken in Maggie's mouth. I knew I did an inappropriate thing. My arm did.

"I'm sorry!" I stood up real fast. "I'll clean it up!"

Maggie catched me with her hand.

"Sit down, Panda," she said. "I'll do it. You might cut yourself."

"I'll get it." Mom was already at the counter pulling off paper towels.

"I'm sorry," I said again. "My arm went faster than I thought."

"It was an accident," Mom said.

Maggie helped her pick up the pieces of glass. Mom put paper towels all over the milk on the floor.

"My arm did it because it's so strong and healed," I said.

Mom was scrunched on the floor cleaning milk. Sometimes when I talk, she looks like she's going to laugh but doesn't. This was one of those times.

I put my napkin on top of the spinach to clean off the milk.

"Andy," Maggie said, while she got five or maybe six more paper towels. "I know you're upset that you might not be able to swim, but you've *got* to think before you react." She sounded exactly like Mom.

"I *do*," I said. That was sort of a lie. I *try* to think before I act, but sometimes I forget.

Mom stood up. "We'll check your arm again in the morning." She threw away the milky paper towels. "If it still looks good and you feel up to it, you can swim."

"I'll feel up to it, Mom," I said. I *had* to be there. I was the secret weapon, Ben told me. I was the magic bullet.

The pool was the only place where my start button was a very good thing.

Chapter Eight

Maggie

I WAS SPACED-OUT AS I LINED UP MY TEAM of ten little Pirates at the end of the indoor pool. Aidan Barber pranced around like he had to pee and I hoped that wasn't the case.

"Stop dancing, Aidan," I called to him, "and find your mark."

He obeyed, but then Lucy Posner actually sat down on the edge of the pool and started picking at her toenails.

"Lucy! Stand up! The whistle's going to blow any minute."

Lucy looked surprised and jumped to her feet. I usually loved these kids. I was good with them. Incredibly patient. That's what the parents always told me. *You're so much more patient with them than I am, Maggie,* they'd say. Now that I was floating through this meet like I was in a weird dream, I had no patience at all. I wanted it to be over.

People talked about canceling the meet, since it was only a week since the fire. It was like Mom had called me to say the church was on fire minutes ago instead of days; I was still that shaken up. I couldn't sleep. I kept seeing flames and smoke pouring out of the church and was afraid of what I'd dream if I shut my eyes.

Since I coached the little kids' team, I had some say about if we should hold today's meet between our team, the Pirates, and the Jacksonville team, the Sounders. I voted for canceling. I told Ben, who coached Andy's team, that it was totally insensitive to hold it, but mostly I didn't think I could concentrate. Ben wasn't much in the mood for a meet either. He still had a bandage over the gash on his forehead, and he was on pain meds for his headache.

One of the girls who was in the burn center at UNC was on Ben's team, though, and her parents wanted us to have the meet. *The kids need it,* her mother said. *They need the normalcy.* They persuaded Ben, and I didn't have much choice but to go along.

The whistle blew and my kids were off, paddling furiously through the water in a way that usually made the people in the bleachers laugh, but either there was less laughter today or I couldn't hear it through the fog in my head. I shouted encouragement to my kids without really thinking about what I was saying.

I got through their event—they lost every match and that was probably my fault—but they didn't care. I hugged every one of their cold, wet little bodies as they came out of the pool and told them they did great. I was so glad it was over. I pulled my shorts on over my bathing suit and headed for the bleachers. Ben passed me as his team came together at the end of the pool.

"They're getting better," he said.

I almost laughed. "Yeah, sure."

I climbed the bleachers to sit next to my mother. "You're so good with those kids," she said, as usual. "I love watching you."

"Thanks."

I looked for Andy at the end of the pool and found him right away. Even though he was on a team with kids his age, he was a little shrimp and easy to pick out. He was jabbering to a couple of kids who were, most likely, tuning him out. Ben put his hand on Andy's shoulder and steered him to the edge of the pool in front of lane five.

Andy's burn was so much better. I looked at him lined up with the other high schoolers. I would have felt sorry for him if I didn't know his skill. His tininess always faked out the other teams. He was ninety pounds of muscle. He had asthma, but as long as he used his inhaler before a meet, no one would ever guess. I watched him at the edge of the pool, coiled up as tight as a jack-in-the-box. Ben called him his team's secret weapon. I smiled, watching him lean forward, waiting for the whistle. Next to me, my mother tensed. I thought we were both holding our breath.

A whistle lasts maybe a second and a half, but Andy always seemed to hear the very first nanosecond of the sound and he was off. This time was no different. He leaped through the air like he'd been shot from a gun. In the water, he worked his arms and legs like a machine. I used to think his hearing was more sensitive than the other kids', that he could hear the sound of the whistle before they could. Then Mom told me about the startle reflex, how babies have it and outgrow it, but how kids with fetal alcohol syndrome sometimes keep it until their teens. Andy still had it. At home, if I walked around the corner from the living room to the kitchen and surprised him, he'd jump a foot in the air. But in the pool, his startle reflex was a good thing. Ben's secret weapon.

Mom laughed as she watched the race, her hands in fists beneath her chin. I didn't know how she could laugh at anything so soon after the fire. I wasn't sure I'd ever be able to laugh again.

"Hey, Mags." Uncle Marcus suddenly showed up on the bleachers. He squeezed onto the bench between me and the father of one of the kids on Ben's team.

"Hey." I moved closer to Mom to give him room. "I didn't know you were here."

"Just got here," he said. "Sorry I missed your team. How'd they do?"

"The usual," I said.

"Looks like Andy's doing the usual, too." Uncle Marcus looked toward the water, where my brother was a couple of lengths ahead of everyone else. "Hey, Laurel." He leaned past me to look at my mother.

"Hi, Marcus," Mom said, not taking her eyes off Andy, which could just be a mother-not-wanting-to-look-away-from-her-son kind of thing, but I knew it was more than that. My mother was always weird about Uncle Marcus. Cold. Always giving him short answers, the way you'd act with someone you were tired of talking to, hoping they'd get the hint. I asked her about it once and she said it was my imagination, that she didn't treat him differently than anyone else, but that was a total crock. I thought it had to do with the fact that Uncle Marcus survived the whale while Daddy didn't.

Uncle Marcus was always nice to her, pretending he didn't notice how bitchy she acted. A few years ago, I started thinking of how cool it would be if Mom and Uncle Marcus got together, but Mom didn't seem interested in dating anyone, much less her brother-in-law. Sometimes she and Sara went to a movie or to dinner, but that was it for my mother's social life. I thought her memory of my father was so perfect she couldn't picture being with another man.

The older I got, the more I thought she should have something more in her life than her part-time school nurse job, her every single day jogs, and her full-time job—Andy. I said that to her once and she turned the tables on me. "You're a fine one to talk," she said. "Why don't *you* date?" I told her I wanted to focus on studying and coaching, that I had plenty of time to date in college. I shut up then. Less said on that topic, the better. If Mom knew how my grades had tanked this year, she'd realize I wasn't studying at all. That was the good thing about having a mother who only paid attention to one of her kids.

The race was down to the last lap and I stood up along with everyone else on the bleachers. I spotted Dawn Reynolds in the first row near the end of the pool. She had no kids on the swim team; she was there to watch Ben. I followed her gaze to him. Ben had on his yellow jams with the orange palm tree print. His chest was bare, with some dark hair across it. He was tall and a little overweight, but you could see muscles moving beneath the tanned skin of his arms and legs.

"Go, Pirates!" Dawn yelled, her hands a megaphone around her mouth, but she wasn't even looking at the swimmers. She was so obvious that I felt embarrassed watching her. It was like watching someone do something very personal, like inserting a tampon. I imagined climbing down the bleachers when the race was over to sit next to her. I could ask her how the fund was doing. I could ask if there was a way I could help. I wanted to in the worst way. I knew Mom put in three thousand, and I gave five hundred from the money I was saving for extra college expenses, although I told Mom I only gave a hundred. Andy gave thirty from his bank account. Money was not enough. I needed to do more. I watched Dawn cheer on Ben's team, imagining the conversation I'd never have with her.

The race was almost over. Andy was in the lead. Surprise, surprise. "Come on, Andy!" I yelled. Mom raised her fists in the air, waiting for the moment of victory, and Uncle Marcus let out one of his ear-piercing whistles.

Andy slapped the end of the pool, and the applause exploded for him, like it had two days before in the Assembly Building, but he just turned and kept swimming at the same insane pace. Mom laughed and I groaned. He'd never understood about ending a race. At the end of Andy's next lap, Ben leaned over, grabbed him by his arms and lifted him out of the pool. I saw him mouth the words *You won!* to Andy, and something else that looked like *You can stop swimming now.*

We all sat down again. Andy looked at us, grinning and waving as he walked to the bench.

Uncle Marcus leaned forward again. "I've got something for you, Laurel," he said.

My mother had to break down and look at him then. "What?"

Uncle Marcus pulled a small folded newspaper article from his shirt pocket and reached across me to hand it to her.

"One of the guys was up in Maryland and saw this in the *Washington Post*."

I looked over my mother's shoulder to read the headline: Disabled N.C. Boy Saves Friends.

Mom shook her head with a laugh. "Don't they have enough of their own news up there?" She looked at Uncle Marcus. "I can keep this?"

"It's yours."

"Thanks."

Uncle Marcus took in a long breath, stretching his arms above his head as he let it out. Then he sniffed my shoulder. "You wear chlorine the way other women wear perfume, Mags," he teased.

He was not the first guy to tell me that. I liked that he said "women" and not "girls."

The pool had been my home away from home since it was built when I was eleven. Before that, I could only swim during the summer in the sound or the ocean.

Daddy taught Andy and me how to swim. "Kids who live on the water better be good swimmers," he'd said. He taught me first of course, before Andy even lived with us. One of my earliest memories was of a calm day in the ocean. It was nothing major. Nothing special. We just paddled around. He held me on his knees, tossed me in the air, swung me around until I practically choked on my laughter. Total bliss.

When I was a little older, Andy joined us in the water and he took to it the same as I did. Daddy'd told me that Andy probably wouldn't be able to swim as well as I could, but Andy surprised him.

I couldn't remember ever playing in the water with my

mother. In my early memories, Mom was like a shadow. When I pictured anything from when I was a little girl, she was on the edge of the memory, so wispy I couldn't be sure she was there or not. I didn't think she ever held me. It was always Daddy's arms around me that I remembered.

"How's Ben's head?" Uncle Marcus asked.

"Better," I said, "though he's still taking pain meds."

"You know who he reminds me of?"

"Who?"

"Your father." He said this quietly, like he didn't want Mom to hear.

"Really?" I tried to picture Ben and Daddy standing next to each other.

"Not sure why, exactly." Uncle Marcus put his elbows on his knees as he stared at Ben. "His build. His size, maybe. Jamie was about the same height. Brown eyes. Same dark, wavy hair. Face is different, of course. But it's that…brawniness or something. All Ben needs is an empathy tattoo on his arm and…" He shrugged.

I liked when he talked about my father. I liked when anyone, except Reverend Bill, talked about Daddy.

I was probably five or six when I asked Daddy what the word "empathy" meant. We were sitting on the deck of The Sea Tender, our legs dangling over the edge, looking for dolphins. I ran my fingers over the letters in the tattoo.

"It means feeling what other people are feeling," he said. "You know how you kissed the boo-boo on my finger yesterday when I hit it with a hammer?"

"Uh-huh." He'd been repairing the stairs down to the beach and said, "Goddamn it!" I'd never heard him say that before.

"You felt sad for me that I hurt my finger, right?"

I nodded.

"That's empathy. And I had it tattooed on my arm to remind me to think about other people's feelings." He looked at the ocean for a long minute or two and I figured that was the end of the conversation. But then he added, "If you're a person with a lot of empathy, it can hurt more to watch a person you care about suffer than to suffer yourself."

Even at five or six, I knew what he meant. That was how I felt when something happened to Andy. When he fell because his little legs weren't steady enough yet, or the time he pinched his fingers in the screen door. I cried so hard that Mom couldn't figure out which of us was hurt at first.

When I heard that Andy might be trapped by the fire—that *any* of those children might be trapped—the panic I felt might as well have been theirs.

"I was worried about him," Uncle Marcus said.

I dragged my foggy brain back to our conversation. "About who?" I asked. "Daddy or Ben?"

"Ben," Uncle Marcus said. "He had some problems in the department at first and I didn't think he'd last. Claustrophobia. Big guy like that, you wouldn't think he'd be afraid of anything. But after the fire at Drury—"he shook his head "—I realized I'd been wrong about him. He really proved himself. All he needed was the fire."

And right then I knew it wasn't fog messing up my brain. It was smoke.

Chapter Nine

Marcus

EXCELLENT DAY FOR THE WATER, AND the boaters knew it. From the front steps of Laurel's house, I stopped to look at Stump Sound. Sailboats, kayaks, pontoon boats. I was jealous. I had a kayak and a small motorboat. I used the kayak for exercise and fished from the runabout. Or on those rare occasions I had a date, I'd take the boat for a sunset spin on the Intracoastal. I had this fantasy of taking Andy out with me someday. *Never happen,* I told myself. *Give it up.*

I rang Laurel's doorbell.

Nearly every Sunday that I wasn't scheduled to work, I did something with Andy. Ball game. Skating rink. Fishing from the pier. Maggie used to come, too, but by the time she reached Andy's age, she had better things to do. I got it. I was fifteen once myself. I liked the time alone with Andy, anyway. He needed a man in his life. Father figure.

My beautiful niece opened the door and gave me a kiss on the cheek. I'd dated a woman a while back who turned out to be too artsy-fartsy for my taste, but I did learn a few things from her. We were standing in the National Gallery in Washington one time, in a room full of paintings of women. Most of the women had thick wavy hair and big, heavy-lidded eyes. They looked like they were made of air. You could lift any one of them up with a finger.

"These paintings remind me of my niece," I told my date.

"Really?" she asked. "She has a Pre-Raphaelite look to her?"

Whatever, I thought.

"I'd like to meet her," my date said.

We broke up before she could meet Maggie, but since then, whenever I saw my niece, the term Pre-Raphaelite popped into my mind even though I didn't know what it meant. I would have given my right arm—*both* my arms—for Jamie to have the chance to see the long-haired, heavy-lidded beauty his daughter had become.

"What are you up to today, Mags?" I asked.

"Studying at Amber's," she said. "I have some exams this week."

I sat down on the stairs that led to the second story. "You can see that ol' light at the end of the tunnel now, huh?"

She nodded. "You better have my graduation on your calendar."

"Can't imagine you gone next year," I said.

"I'll only be in Wilmington."

"It's more than geography, kiddo," I said.

She looked up the stairs, then lowered her voice. "How's Mom gonna manage Andy without me?" she asked.

"Hey," I said, "I'm not going anywhere. All your mom has to do is say the word and I'm here."

"I know."

"You decide on a major yet?"

She shook her head. "Still between psych and business."

I couldn't see a Pre-Raphaelite woman in one of those stiff, pin-striped business suits. Her choice, though. I'd keep my trap shut.

"You've got plenty of time to decide," I said.

Maggie swung her backpack over her shoulder. "Do they know what caused the fire yet?" she asked.

I shrugged. "We're still waiting on results from the lab."

"You're in charge, aren't you?" she asked.

"On the local side, yeah. But once there are fatals..." I shook my head. "The State Bureau of Investigation and ATF are involved now."

"Oh, right. That guy who talked to Andy at the hospital."

"Right." I got to my feet. "Your brother upstairs?"

"Yeah." She smiled. "Wait till you see his room. It looks like a Hallmark store. Oh, and Mom said don't mention anything about him writing a book. She hopes he'll forget about it."

"He's still talking about that?"

"Every once in a while." She clipped her iPod to her low-rise jeans.

"Your mom home?"

"Went for a run." She popped in the earbuds. "Later," she said, pulling open the door.

Maggie wasn't kidding about the Hallmark store, I thought as I walked into Andy's room. Greeting cards were propped up on his desk and dresser and the windowsills. Tacked to the cork wall he used as his bulletin board, clustered around the charts Laurel had made to keep him organized. *What I Do Before Going to Bed on a School Night: 1. Brush teeth 2.Wash face 3. Put completed homework in backpack. 4. Pick out clothes to wear to school.* And on and on and on. Laurel was a very patient woman.

Andy was at his computer and he swiveled his chair around to face me.

"What's with the cards?" I asked.

"They're thank-yous." He stood up and handed me one. The front was a picture of an artificially elongated dachshund. Inside it read, *I want to extend my thanks.* Then a handwritten note: *Andy, you don't know me, but I live in Rocky Mount and heard about what you did at the fire and just want you to know I'd want you around any time I needed help!*

He handed me a few others.

"Some are from people I know," he said as I glanced through them. "And some are from people I don't know. And some girls sent me their pictures." He grinned, handing me a photograph he had propped up next to his computer. "Look at this one."

I did. *Yowks.* She had to be at least twenty. Long blond hair and wispy bangs that hung to her eyelashes. She wore a sultry look and little else. Well, all right, she had on some kind of skimpy top, but it didn't cover much. I looked up at Andy and caught the gleam in his eye. He scared me these days. He used to see girls as friends, like his little skew-eyed pal, Emily. Now, he was getting into *fights* over girls. When did that happen? His voice was starting to change, too, jarring me every once in a while with a sudden drop in pitch. Sometimes standing next to him, I smelled the faint aroma of a man. I bought him a stick of deodorant, but he told me Laurel'd already gotten him one. That was part of the problem. If Laurel would just *talk* to me about Andy, we wouldn't be buying him two sticks of deodorant. It had to scare her, too, the changes in him. The temptations he could fall victim to because he wanted to be one of the guys. By the time I was Andy's age, I'd been having sex for two years and drank booze nearly every day. I didn't have a disability and I still managed to screw myself up. What chance did Andy have of surviving his teens?

"How about we fly your kite on the beach today?" I suggested.

"Cool!" Andy never turned me down.

Laurel suddenly appeared in the doorway. She had on her running shorts and a *Save the Loggerheads* T-shirt. Her cheeks were a bright pink. She leaned against the jamb, arms folded, a white sheet of paper dangling from her hand. "What are y'all going to do today?" she asked.

"We're going to fly my kite," Andy said.

"That'll be fun," she said. "Why don't you go get it? It's in the garage on the workbench."

"I can get it when we leave," Andy said.

"Get it now, sweetie," Laurel said. "We should check it and make sure it's all in one piece. It's been a while since you flew it."

"Okay." Andy walked past her and down the stairs.

So Laurel wanted to talk to me without Andy there. A rarity. I tried to look behind the half smile on her face.

"You won't believe the e-mail I got this morning," she said.

"Try me." I was stoked she wanted to share something with me. Who cared what it was? She looked down at the paper instead of at me. With her head tipped low like that, I could see that the line of her jaw was starting to lose its sharpness. To me, she'd always be that pretty eighteen-year-old girl Jamie brought home so long ago. The girl who played *Fur Elise* on my electric piano and who took me seriously when I said I wanted to play in a band. Who never made me feel second-best.

"It's from a woman at the *Today* show," she said, handing me the paper. "They want Andy and me to fly to New York to be on the show."

"You're kidding." I took the paper from her and read the short e-mail. She was supposed to call the show Monday to make arrangements. Would appearing on TV be good for Andy or not? "Do you want to do it?" I asked.

"I think I'd like to," she said. "It's a chance to educate people. Make them aware they can't drink while they're pregnant. And that kids with FASD aren't all bad and out of control and violent and...you know."

Once you got Laurel started on FASD, it was hard to reel her in.

"Those bits they do are short." I didn't want her to get her hopes up. "They might just want to hear about Andy and the fire and not give you a chance to—"

"I'll get my two cents in," she said. "You know I will."

"Yeah." I smiled. "You will." I looked around the room at the cards. Swept my arm through the air. "It's bound to generate more of this stuff." I picked up the photograph of the blond from Andy's desk. "Did you see this one?"

Her eyes widened. "Lord, no!" she said. "Ugh. I'll keep a better eye on his mail."

"His e-mail, too."

"Marcus." She gave me one of her disdainful looks. "I check *everything*. His e-mail, where he surfs, his MySpace page. You know me."

I heard Andy on the stairs and quickly plucked the picture from her hand and set it back on his desk.

"It's perfect!" Andy blew into the room, the box kite just missing the doorjamb.

"Okay, you two," Laurel said. "Don't forget the sunscreen. It's in the drawer by the refrigerator. You'll grab it, Marcus?"

"I'll do that." I put my hand on the back of Andy's neck. "Let's go, And."

I trotted down the stairs with him, feeling pretty good. It was a step forward, Laurel telling me about the *Today* show, although she was so psyched, she probably would have told the plumber if he'd been the only person available. Still, it was progress.

For a year or so after Jamie died, Laurel didn't let me see the kids at all. My parents were dead. My brother as well. Laurel, Maggie and Andy were all the family I had left, and she cut me out. I'd had some shitty periods in my life but that year was my worst. I'm sure it was Sara who got her to let me back in. It was slow going at first. I could only see the kids with Laurel skulking someplace nearby. Then she finally gave me freer rein. "Just not on the water," she'd said.

I didn't blame her for her caution. How could I? She had good reason not to trust me.

After all, she believed I killed her husband.

Chapter Ten

Laurel
1984-1987

JAMIE COULD INDEED KEEP HIS WEIGHT off me when we made love. I discovered, though, that I didn't want him to. Blanketed beneath him, I took comfort in the protective mass of him. Being with him, whether we were making love or riding his bike or talking on the phone, made me feel loved again, the way I'd felt as a young child. Loved and whole and safe.

We dated my entire freshman year at UNC. When I went home to Ohio for the summer, we kept in touch by phone and mail and made plans for him to come visit for a week in July. I told Aunt Pat and Uncle Guy about him as carefully as I could. They didn't like the fact that he was four years older than me. I could only imagine what they would say if I told them that there were really five years between our ages. They liked his religious studies degree, jumping to the conclusion that he was a Presbyterian like they were—and like they thought I still was. I'd been swayed by Jamie's negativity about organized religion and was gradually coming to understand his own deep, personal and passionate tie to God. They didn't understand why he was a carpenter when he should be using his degree in a "more productive manner." I wanted to tell them he was a carpenter because he liked being a carpenter and that his family had more money than they could ever dream of having. But I didn't want them to like Jamie for his family's wealth. I wanted them to like him for himself.

On the evening Jamie was due to arrive, Aunt Pat and Uncle Guy waited with me on the front porch of their Toledo home. They sat in the big white rocking chairs sipping lemonade, while I squirmed on the porch swing, my nerves as taut as the chains holding the swing to the ceiling. I tried to see my aunt and uncle through Jamie's eyes. They were a handsome couple in their late forties, and they looked as though they'd spent the day playing golf at a country club, although neither was a golfer and they couldn't afford the country club.

Although it was July, Uncle Guy had on a light blue sweater over a blue-and-white-striped shirt, and he didn't appear to be the least bit uncomfortable. He had chiseled good looks accentuated by the fact that he combed his graying hair straight back.

Aunt Pat wore a yellow skirt that fell just below her knees as she rocked. She had on sturdy brown shoes and panty hose. Her yellow floral blouse was neatly tailored, and her light brown hair was chin length, curled under, and held in place with plenty of spray. I tried to see my gentle mother in her face many times over the years, but I never could find her in my aunt's hard-edged features.

As dusk crept in from the west, I suddenly heard Jamie's motorcycle, still at least two blocks away. My heart pounded with both trepidation and desire. It had been a month since I'd seen him and I couldn't wait to wrap my arms around him.

"What's that ungodly sound!" Aunt Pat said.

"What sound?" I asked, hoping she was hearing something I could not hear.

"Sounds like a motorcycle," Uncle Guy said.

"In *this* neighborhood?" Aunt Pat countered. "I don't think so."

I saw him rounding the corner onto our street, and I stood up. "It's Jamie," I said, and I knew the meeting between my relatives and the man I loved was doomed before it even began.

He pulled into the driveway. His bike sounded louder than it ever had before, the noise bouncing off the houses on either side of the street. I walked down the porch steps and across the lawn. I wanted to run, to fling myself into his arms, but I kept my pace slow and even and composed.

I saw him anew as he pulled off his helmet. His hair fell nearly to the middle of his back. He took off his jacket to reveal what I'm sure he considered his best clothes—khaki pants and a plain black T-shirt. I saw how out of place he looked in this starched and tidy Toledo neighborhood.

He opened his arms and I stepped into them, only long enough to whisper, "Oh God, Jamie, they're going to be insufferable. I'm so sorry."

They were worse than insufferable. They were downright rude to him, shunning his attempts at conversation, offering him nothing to eat or drink. After a half hour of the coldest possible welcome, I told Jamie I'd show him to the guest room and we walked inside the house.

Upstairs, I led him into the spare room that I'd dusted and vacuumed that morning and closed the door behind us.

"Jamie, I'm sorry! I knew they'd be difficult but I really had no idea they'd be this…mean. They're not mean people. Just cold. They—"

"Shh." He put his finger to my lips. "They love you," he said.

"I…what do you mean?"

"I mean, they love you. They want the best for you. And here comes this big, hairy, scary-looking guy who probably doesn't smell so good right now and who has a blue-collar job and no car. And all they can see is that the little girl they love might be traveling down a path that can get her hurt."

I pressed my forehead to his shoulder, breathed in the scent of a man who'd been riding for two days to see the woman he loved. I loved him so much at that moment. I envied him, too, for his ability to step outside himself and into my aunt and uncle's shoes. But I wasn't sure he was right.

"I think they just care what the neighbors will think," I said into his shoulder.

He laughed. "Maybe there's some of that, too," he said. "But even if that's true, it's their fear coming out. They're scared, Laurie."

"Laurel?" my aunt called from the bottom of the stairs.

I pulled away from him, kissing him quickly on the lips. "The bathroom's at the end of the hall," I said. "And I'll be back as soon as I can."

I walked downstairs, where Aunt Pat waited for me. Her

face was drawn and lined and tired. "Come out on the porch for a minute," she said.

On the porch, I took my seat on the swing again while Aunt Pat returned to the rocker. "He can't stay here," she said.

"*What?*" That was worse than I'd expected.

"We don't know him. We don't trust him. We can't—"

"*I* know him," I said, keeping my voice low only to prevent Jamie from hearing me. I wanted to scream at them. "I wouldn't be in love with someone who wasn't trustworthy."

Uncle Guy leaned forward in the rocking chair, his elbows on his knees. "What in God's name do you see in him?" he asked. "You were raised so much better than that."

"Than *what?*" I asked. "He's the best person I know. He cares about people. He's honest. He…he's very spiritual." I was desperately trying to find a quality in Jamie that would appeal to them.

"What does that mean?" Aunt Pat asked.

"He plans to start his own church some day."

"Ah, jeez." My uncle looked away from me with disgust. "He's one of those cult leaders," he said, as if talking to himself.

"I think your uncle's right," Aunt Pat said. "He has some kind of power over you, or you wouldn't be with someone like him."

She was right that he had power over me, but it was a benevolent sort of power.

"He's a good person," I said. "Please. How am I supposed to tell him he can't stay here when he just rode all the way from North Carolina to see me?"

"I'll pay for him to stay in a hotel for one night," Uncle Guy said.

I stood up. "He doesn't need your money, Uncle Guy," I said.

"He has more money than you would know what to do with. What he needed from you was some tolerance and—" I stumbled, hunting for the right word "—some *warmth*. I should have known he wouldn't find it here." I opened the screen door. "He'll go to a hotel, and I'll be going with him."

"Don't...you...dare!" My aunt bit off each word.

I turned my back on them and marched into the house, amazed—and thrilled—by my own audacity.

In the end, Jamie wouldn't let me go with him. He told my aunt and uncle that I was a special girl and he could understand why they'd want to protect me so carefully.

"You talk like a sociopath, Mr. Lockwood," my uncle said, any remaining trace of cordiality gone.

Even Jamie was at a loss for words then. He left, and I sat on the porch steps the entire night, alternating between tears and fury as I imagined Jamie alone in a hotel room, tired and disappointed.

My aunt and uncle tried to coerce me into changing colleges in the fall, but my parents had been very wise. Even though they died in their early forties, they'd left money for my college expenses as well as a legal document stating the money was to be used at "the college, university or other institute of higher learning of Laurel's choice."

When I left Toledo for UNC that fall, I took everything with me. I knew I'd never be coming back.

Jamie proposed to me during the summer of my junior year and we set a wedding date for the following June. I exchanged an occasional letter with my aunt and uncle, but the wedding invitation I sent them went unanswered and, as far as I was concerned, that was it. I was finished with them. I didn't miss them—I was already so much a part of the Lockwood family and knew Miss Emma and Daddy L better than I'd ever known Aunt Pat and Uncle Guy. Daddy L was mostly a benign presence, a quiet man with an uncanny business sense when it came to real estate. Miss Emma couldn't survive without her three or four whiskey sours every afternoon-into-the-evening, but no one ever said a word about her drinking, as far as I knew. She was the sort of drinker who grew more mellow with each swallow. Marcus was cute and sweet but self-destructive, and he knew how to push his parents' buttons—as well as Jamie's. He'd long ago been labeled the difficult child and did his best to live up to expectations. He landed in the hospital with a dislocated shoulder after wiping out on his surf-board because he was so drunk. He got beaten up by a girl's father for bringing her home late—by twelve hours. And twice before Jamie and I were married, he was arrested for driving under the influence. Daddy L bailed him out once. The second time, Jamie took care of it quietly so their parents wouldn't know. Marcus was a real challenge to Jamie's yearning to be empathic.

But I loved each of the Lockwoods, warts and all. I was so happy and full of excitement in those days that I no longer needed to count backward from a thousand to fall asleep. We were married the week after I received my nursing degree. Daddy L surprised us with the gift of The Sea Tender, the round cottage on the beach, my favorite of his properties. I took a job in a pediatrician's office in Sneads Ferry, where I fell in love with every infant, toddler and child that came through the door. With every baby I held, I longed for one of my own. I felt the pull of motherhood in every way—biological, emotional, psychological. I wanted to carry Jamie's baby. I wanted to nurse it and love it and raise it with the love my parents had showered on me before their deaths. I had no family of my own any longer. I wanted to create a new one with Jamie.

While I worked in the doctor's office, Jamie left carpentry to get his real estate license, manage his father's properties, and join the Surf City Volunteer Fire Department on the mainland. He even cut his hair—a radical change in his looks it took me a while to get used to—and bought a car, although he never did get rid of his motorcycle.

Living on the island in the eighties was extraordinary. I'd commute the easy distance to my job, then drive to the docks in Sneads Ferry to buy fresh shrimp or fish, then drive home to paradise. In the warm weather, I'd open all the windows in the cottage and let the sound of the waves fill the rooms as Jamie and I made dinner together. It was a time that would live in my heart always, even after things changed. I would never forget the peaceful rhythm of those days.

I knew Jamie had never lost his yearning for a church, so I wasn't surprised when he asked his father if he could build a little chapel on the land next to the inlet.

Daddy L laughed.

"It'll wash away in the first storm," he said, but he told Jamie to go ahead. He couldn't deny his favorite son anything.

We'd made friends with a few other year-round people on the island and across the bridge in Sneads Ferry, and three or four of them bought into Jamie's idea of a new kind of church and volunteered to help him build it. Daddy L suggested he build the foundation and walls out of concrete like the Operation Bumblebee towers that seemed able to withstand anything Mother Nature handed out. Jamie built his chapel in the shape of a pentagon with a steeple on top, so that no one would mistake it for anything other than a house of worship. Panoramic windows graced four sides of the building. He made heavy wooden shutters that could be hung over the windows when the weather threatened the island. Over the years, the wind stole the steeple four times, but no window was ever broken until Hurricane Fran in '96. Even then, the concrete shell of the chapel remained, rising out of the earth like a giant sand castle.

There was no altar in the chapel, no place for a minister to stand and preach. That's the way Jamie wanted it. He would be one of the congregation. Marcus, who was still living at home in Wilmington while attending community college, came down to help Jamie build pews out of pine, even though he never really bought into the whole idea of Jamie starting his own church. The pews formed concentric pentagons inside the building. Daddy L burned the words *Free Seekers Chapel* into a huge piece of driftwood, and Jamie hung the sign from a post buried deep in the sand near the front door.

Despite Jamie's desire to be one of the congregation, he did become an ordained minister of sorts. He saw an ad in the back of a magazine, and for thirty dollars, purchased a certificate showing him to be an ordained minister in the Progressive Church of the Spirit. He didn't take it seriously. He thought it was pretty funny, actually, but it enabled the people who loved his vision to call him *Reverend,* and that meant something to them.

Jamie and I agreed to wait to start a family until after the chapel was built, and as soon as the last pew was in place, I stopped my pills. The pediatrician I worked for warned me it would take a while to get pregnant after being on the pill for several years, but I must have conceived almost immediately, because within a couple of weeks, I knew something about my body was different. Sure enough, the pregnancy test I took in the obstetrician's office was positive.

I managed to keep the secret until that night, when Jamie and I indulged in one of our favorite pastimes: bundling up—it was October—and lying on the beach behind the cottage. Each of us wrapped in a blanket, we lay close together like two cocoons, wool hats pulled over our heads, staring in contented wonderment at the autumn sky.

"There's one," Jamie said, pointing north. We were trying to distinguish satellites from the stars.

"Where?" I followed his finger to the only constellation I recognized—Pegasus.

"Look southeast of Pegasus," he said. "And watch it closely."

"You're right." I followed the slow drift of the light toward the north.

The sky behind our house was always full of stars, especially in the fall and winter when we had the dark northern end of the island nearly to ourselves. The sound of the waves was music in our ears. Suddenly, I felt nearly overcome with the miracle my life had become. I lived in one of the most beautiful places on earth, in a round house like something out of a fairy tale, with a man whose love for me was matched only by mine for him. I thought of the tiny collection of cells inside me that would become our baby, how soon the globe of sky above us would be mirrored by the globe of my belly. I thought of how our child—our *children*—and our children's children would someday lie on this beach and watch the same stars and hear the same waves. And suddenly the thoughts were too enormous for me to contain any longer. Overwhelmed, I started to cry.

"Hey." Jamie lifted his head. "What's the matter?"

"I'm happy."

He laughed. "Me, too."

I leaned even closer to my husband. "And I'm pregnant."

I could barely see him in the darkness, but I heard his sharp intake of breath. "Oh, Laurie." He opened his blanket and pulled my cocoon inside his, planting kisses all over my face until I giggled. "How do you feel?"

"Fantastic," I said. And I did.

He looked down at me, touching my cheek with the tenderness that I'd come to love in him. "Our whole world is going to change," he said.

He had no idea how right he was.

The next morning at ten o'clock, thirteen people including Jamie and myself, arrived at the Free Seekers Chapel for its first service. Four were friends who had helped Jamie build it. Four others were acquaintances, and the last three were strangers, curious to see what was going on inside the five walls of the diminutive building. I was a bit curious myself. Jamie had said little about his plans for a service. I'd wanted to sew him a stole. I'd make it different than any other I'd seen, bright with blues pulled from the sea and sky.

"Thanks, Laurie," he'd said when I suggested it. "But I don't want a stole. I don't want anything that sets me apart that much, okay?"

I understood.

The small chapel smelled of new wood, a delicious smell I would always associate with the promise of my young marriage and the life I carried inside me, and I breathed in deeply as we moved into one of the pews.

We waited a few minutes, then Jamie stood up in his jeans and leather jacket. He cleared his throat, the only giveaway that he was nervous. When he spoke, his voice echoed off the walls and the pews.

"Let's talk about where we experienced God this week," he said.

No one spoke as he took his seat again. The sound of the sea was muted by the double glass of the windows. In the silence, I heard one of the strangers, a man wearing a thick red flannel jacket who was chewing tobacco, spit into the blue plastic cup he carried. We sat there quietly for what seemed like minutes.

The first time I'd heard Jamie describe God as an *experience* instead of as a *being,* it scared me. It felt somehow blasphemous. Yet, slowly I started to understand what he meant. Something awakened in me, pushed the big man in robes out of my consciousness and replaced it with a powerful feeling hard to put into words.

I remembered the night before, lying on the beach with Jamie. I stood up suddenly, surprising myself as much as him.

"Last night I was lying out on the beach watching the stars," I said. "The sky was beautiful and suddenly a...a happiness came over me." I looked down at where my hands clutched the back of the pew in front of me. "That's not the right word. Not a strong enough word." I chewed my lower lip, thinking. "I felt *overwhelmed* by the beauty of the world and I felt…a joy that wasn't just on the surface but deep inside me, and I knew I was feeling…*experiencing* something that was outside of me." I didn't think I was explaining myself well. Words were so inadequate at expressing what I'd felt the night before on the beach. "I felt something bigger than myself last night," I said. "Something sacred."

I sat down slowly. Jamie took my hand and pressed it between his palms. I glanced at him and saw the smile I loved seeing on his face. It was a small smile, one that said *everything is right in our world*.

Another moment passed and then the man chewing tobacco stood up. "So, we supposed to say when we felt God's hand in something?" he asked.

Jamie hesitated. "It's an open-ended question," he said. "You're free to interpret it however you like."

"Well, then, I'd say I experienced God when I laid eyes on this here church for the first time this morning," he said. "I hear about it over to the Ferry, hear how a crazy young fella thinks he's a preacher made a five-sided church outta concrete and clapboard. And when I got outta my car and started walking 'cross the sand and saw this—" he waved the hand holding the blue cup through the air, taking in the five walls and expanse of windows "—when I saw this out here…well I felt it. What you talkin' about, missy." He looked at me. "Something good and big come over me. It's a feelin' I wouldn't mind havin' again."

The man sat down. I heard Jamie swallow. I could always

tell when Jamie was moved because he would swallow that way, as if he was swallowing tears.

Silence filled the little room. I wanted someone else to say something, but Jamie seemed unconcerned. Finally a woman got up. She was about my age—twenty-two—with very short blond hair.

"My name's Sara Weston," she said, "and I think I'm the only person who lives in North Carolina who doesn't go to church."

A few people chuckled at that.

"I moved down here because my husband's stationed at Camp Lejeune," she said, which explained her accent. I wasn't sure where she was from, but it wasn't North Carolina or anyplace else south of the Mason-Dixon Line. "Everyone's always asking, what church do you go to?" Sara continued. "And they look at me like I've got two heads when I say I don't go. To be honest, I don't like church. I don't like all the rituals and...I don't even know if I believe in God."

I heard Jamie whisper, "That's all right," though I was certain no one could hear him but me.

"Sorry." Sara let out a breath, giving away a touch of anxiety. "I'll try to keep this positive. Usually when people ask me what church I go to, I just say I haven't decided yet, but then they always want to take me to *their* church. Now, I'm going to tell them I go to the Free Seekers church."

She sat down, blushing, and the man in the flannel jacket set his cup down and gave her a short but hearty round of applause.

The next Sunday, there were seventeen people inside Free Seekers...but there were also seventeen people outside, and one of them was Reverend Bill from Drury Memorial. He was preaching through a bullhorn, saying that Free Seekers wasn't really a church and that Jamie Lockwood was a heretic and blasphemer and his tiny congregation was full of atheists and agnostics.

Inside, Jamie said, calm as ever, "Let's share where we experienced our own personal God this week," and people began to stand and speak and it was as though no one could hear what was going on outside.

Finally Floyd, the man with the red flannel jacket and blue plastic cup, stood up. "I have a mind to go tell that man to shut his trap."

Jamie didn't budge from his seat. "Imagine how threatened he must feel that he'd come here and try to disturb our service," he said. "Let's treat him kindly."

Reverend Bill became Jamie's nemesis. He tried to shut Free Seekers down by attacking it on all fronts. It was in an area not zoned for a church, he argued. Jamie was a fraudulent minister. The building itself was a blight on the unspoiled landscape near the inlet. I stayed out of it, worried that Reverend Bill had several legal legs to stand on. I don't know how, but Jamie wriggled out of every possible attack. Perhaps the Lockwood name was enough to offset any wrongdoing. Where Reverend Bill *did* succeed was in turning his own small congregation against us. Jamie Lockwood and his followers were heathens. That bothered Jamie, whose intention was never to cause friction, never to force people to take sides. His vision was one of peace and tolerance. As he'd once said himself: pie in the sky.

I was four months' pregnant when Miss Emma and Daddy L kicked Marcus out of the house. He'd dropped out of college before he could flunk out, but he was working in construction and Jamie was upset by his parents' decision.

"I don't understand Mama and Daddy," he said to me one morning at breakfast. "Marcus already feels like the second-class son. Getting kicked out of the house is only going to make him feel worse."

I poured milk onto my granola. "Let's take him in," I said simply. "There's plenty of work for him on the island and we've got room. We can help him get on his feet."

Jamie stared at me, his spoon midway to his mouth. "You're utterly amazing, do you know that?"

I shrugged with a smile. "You're just rubbing off on me," I said.

"I thought of having him live with us for a while, but I was afraid to ask you." Jamie rested the spoon in his bowl. "I know he can be a pain. You already have to put up with a lunatic husband, and with the baby coming and everything…" His voice trailed off then, and he shook his head. "I've always been the golden child," he said. "I love my parents, but they've never treated Marcus the same way they treated me."

"He could never measure up to you."

"I'll feel better if he's with us and we can keep an eye on him." Jamie leaned across the table to kiss me. "Maybe we can straighten him out."

"Maybe we can," I agreed.

But that was not what happened.

Chapter Eleven

Laurel

THE SECURITY LINE AT THE WILMINGTON airport was longer than I'd anticipated for six in the morning, and I was afraid I hadn't allowed enough time to make our plane. Andy slumped against me as we waited, and I could hardly blame him. We'd gotten up at 4:00 a.m. to make the six-thirty flight to New York, but everything had taken longer than it should have. Getting Andy out of bed took fifteen minutes alone. Changing his routine was always dicey. I nearly had to brush his teeth for him and when I turned my back, he'd crawled into bed again. The cab had to wait for us in the driveway. I told myself we'd be fine. We were only going to be in New York a couple of nights so we had no bags to check. Still, it was nearly six by the time we reached the security line.

We were due at Rockefeller Plaza early the following morning for our appearance on the *Today* show. I knew what I wanted to say about FASD, and I'd done enough speaking on the subject over the years that I knew I could get the information across quickly without seeming didactic or preachy. That was my goal. I also needed to mention the Drury Memorial Family Fund. Dawn had asked if I could get them to air the Internet address for the fund so viewers could make contributions. I promised I would try.

We were nearly to the security checkpoint. Finally. I nudged Andy, who was still leaning against me, his eyes closed.

"Come on, sweetie. Let's start taking our shoes off."

He bent over and untied his tennis shoes. "When did I go on a plane before, Mom?" he asked.

"When you were little." I kicked off my pumps and bent over to pick them up. "You were two or three. We flew to Florida to visit your grandmother who was spending the winter there."

"Grandma Emma, right?"

"That's right."

"I don't remember her."

"You were little when she passed away." We'd reached the conveyor belt and I slid him a plastic bin. "Put your shoes and your jacket in here."

He dumped his shoes in the bin. "Why do we have to take our shoes off?"

That was the sort of question I had to answer carefully. If I said anything about a bomb or terrorists, he'd fixate on the threat and the flight would be sheer misery.

I hoisted our carry-on bag onto the belt.

"They have to make sure we're only carrying safe things onboard," I said.

"I saw the sign."

"What sign?"

"That said don't carry guns, liquids and all those things."

"Right."

The conveyor belt swept the bins into the X-ray machine.

"Bye-bye shoes." Andy waved after them.

I smiled at the bored-looking security guard standing next to the metal detector as I handed him my driver's license and boarding pass.

"Hold your boarding pass so the security guard can see it," I told Andy.

I walked through the metal detector first, relieved I didn't set off the alarm.

"My turn?" Andy asked me.

"Hurry up, sweetie," I glanced at my watch. "We're running late."

Andy stretched his arms out to his sides as if for balance and walked toward the metal detector, a look of concentration on his face. I was afraid he was going to crash into the metal detector with his arms, but he dropped them to his sides just before stepping through.

The alarm pinged.

"Oh, great," I said, blowing out my breath and walking toward Andy. "It's his belt buckle," I said to the guard. "I should have thought of it."

"Step back, ma'am," the guard said to me. "You have a belt on?" he asked Andy.

Andy lifted his jersey to display his metal belt buckle. "It's not liquid or anything," he said.

"Are you trying to joke with me, boy?" the guard asked. "Take off your belt."

"He's not trying to joke," I said as Andy pulled off his belt. "He really thinks you're—"

"Ma'am, just let me do my job." The guard coiled the belt into a plastic bowl. "Walk through again," he said to Andy.

Andy stepped through the metal detector again.

Ping!

I was lost. What could he possibly be wearing that would set it off?

"I don't understand," I said. "He's not wearing a watch or—"

"Step over here." The guard motioned Andy to walk over to the other side of the conveyor belt, where a stocky, uniformed woman stood. She wielded a baton-shaped metal detector like a billy club.

"Hold your hands out to your sides," she instructed.

Andy looked at me as if for permission.

"Go ahead, Andy," I said. "It's all right. The guard just needs to figure out why you set the alarm off." I pulled our carry-on bag from the conveyor belt, then gathered our shoes, jackets and my pocketbook from the bins. My arms were shaking.

"We're very late for our flight," I said to the guard as she ran the wand over Andy's chest.

"Is that a microphone?" Andy asked. "We're going to be on TV and talk into microphones."

"We are." I hoped I could soften the woman up a little. "We're actually heading to New York to be on the—"

Dih-dih-dih-dih. The wand let out a staticky sound as it passed over Andy's left sock.

"Take off your sock," the woman commanded.

"His sock?" I was completely perplexed.

The guard ignored me.

"Go ahead, Andy," I said.

Andy pulled off his sock and something small and silver *plinked* to the floor.

"What's that?" I asked.

"My lighter," Andy said.

I leaned closer. "Your *lighter?*"

"Stand back, ma'am." The guard carefully picked up the object with her gloved fingers.

"Andy!" I was astonished. "Why do you have a cigarette lighter?"

Andy shrugged, splotches of red on his cheeks. He was in trouble with me and he knew it.

"Put your shoes on," the woman said, "and then I'll have to ask the two of you to come with me."

"Come with you?" I dropped one of the shoes from my overladen arms, and dropped two more when I bent over to pick it up. "Where?" I scrabbled around on the floor trying to fit everything into my arms again.

"You can sit here to put your shoes on." The guard motioned to a row of chairs.

Giving in, I sat down and motioned to Andy to do the same. We put on our shoes, the guard watching our every move.

"Where do you want us to go?" I asked, getting to my feet. Our jackets and my pocketbook were over my arm and my free hand wheeled the carry-on.

"To the Public Safety Department for questioning," she said, turning on her heel. "Follow me."

Andy started to follow her. "Wait!" I said. "Our plane leaves in fifteen minutes. Can't you just confiscate the lighter and let us go?"

"No, ma'am." She rambled on in a monotone about federal regulations, all the while leading us down a corridor from which I feared we'd never escape.

She led us into a small office where a uniformed officer, his bald head gleaming in the overhead light, sat behind a desk. He looked up at our entry.

"Sir," the guard said, "this boy tried to get through security with a lighter concealed in his sock."

"I'm his mother, Officer," I said. The man had kind eyes beneath high, expressive eyebrows. "I'm so sorry this happened, but we're going to miss our plane if—"

"Sit down." He motioned to the two chairs in front of his desk.

"We have to go to New York to be on the *Today* show," Andy said as he sat down.

I remained standing. "Is there a chance you can have them hold the plane for us?" I asked.

He looked at me. "If you don't take this seriously, ma'am, how do you expect your son to respect the law?" So much for the kind eyes.

I sank into the chair next to Andy, wondering how long it was until the next plane to New York.

The man folded his arms on his desk and leaned forward. "How old are you, son?" he asked Andy.

"Fifteen."

"You're fifteen?" He looked like he didn't believe him.

"He is," I said.

"I'm small for my age," Andy said.

"Why did you have a lighter in your sock?" the officer asked.

"Because of the sign."

"And what sign is that?"

"The one that said don't carry guns and knives onboard. It said don't carry lighters, too."

"Oh, no," I said under my breath. "He took it literally," I said to the officer.

"Ma'am, I have to ask you to be quiet." Then to Andy, "If you knew the sign said not to bring lighters onboard, why did you have a lighter in your sock?"

I saw tears in Andy's eyes. "I put it in my sock so I wouldn't be carrying it," he said.

I reached over and rested my hand on his knee. "I can explain—"

"Ma'am." The officer gave me a warning look. Then he sat back in his chair, tapping a pen on his desk. "We have these regulations in place for your protection, son," he said, looking at Andy. "We don't take joking about them lightly."

"Please, Officer," I said. "He has a disability."

The man ignored me. "What were you planning to use the lighter for?" he asked.

Andy darted his gleaming eyes at me. "In case I wanted a cigarette."

"Do you know you can't smoke on the plane?"

"I wouldn't smoke on the plane."

"And where are your cigarettes?"

"I don't have any."

"But you had a lighter that was so important to you that you carried it on your person."

Andy had had it. "Mom?" He looked at me for help, one tear slipping over his lower lashes.

"Sir, Andy has Fetal Alcohol Spectrum Disorder," I spoke quickly. I wouldn't let the man stop me again. "He doesn't understand the fine point of what you're saying. If he sees a sign that says 'don't carry something,' he takes that literally to mean he shouldn't *carry* something. You carry things in your hands. I didn't know he had a lighter. I didn't even know he smoked." I darted my eyes at Andy with a look that said we would talk about *that* later. "But I can assure you, he had no idea he was doing anything wrong. We're flying to New York to be on the *Today* show tomorrow morning, because Andy saved some lives in a fire in Surf City."

The man's eyebrows shot halfway up his forehead. "You're *that* boy?" he asked.

"Yes, sir," Andy said in a small voice. "People followed me out the window."

The man pursed his lips. He picked up the lighter from the desk in front of him, flipped open the top and thumbed the wheel to produce a long slender flame. "Well," he said, snapping the lid closed. "Needless to say, we're confiscating this lighter. We have some paperwork to attend to. And—" he looked at the computer monitor on his desk, clicked a few keys on his keyboard "—there's another flight to LaGuardia at ten-ten."

"Three *hours* from now?" I was nearly whining. "That's the next one?"

"Yes, ma'am. There's room on it, though, so you're lucky."

* * *

It was nearly seven-thirty by the time we returned to the main part of the terminal. "Let's get something to eat," I said. "That'll kill some time."

We each got a muffin and a bottle of water, then found seats at the gate.

"Okay, Andy," I said, once we'd arranged our belongings on the seats around us. We were the only two people at the gate. "We need to have a talk. You promised me you'd never smoke."

Andy studied the toe of his well-examined sneaker as he chewed a mouthful of blueberry muffin.

"Andy?"

He swallowed. "I sometimes do," he said, "but I don't suck the smoke into my chest. Just my mouth."

"*Why?*"

"Because it's cool."

"Which of your friends smoke?" I asked.

He hesitated again. "Do I have to tell you?"

I thought about it. What difference did it make?

"No," I said, sighing. "You don't. But you *do* have to tell me where you got that lighter." It hadn't been a cheap little Zippo.

"I traded for it."

"What did you trade for it?"

"Mom, I don't want to talk about it!"

"You have to, Andy."

"I traded my pocketknife."

"*What* pocketknife?" I hadn't known he had one.

He rolled his eyes. "The one I've always had."

I sighed. "I know you want to fit in," I said. "I know you want to be...cool. But teenagers do some stupid things." As disturbed as I was about the lighter, I was more upset to realize there were parts of my son I didn't know. If he'd lied to me about not smoking, what else was he lying to me about?

"What about drugs? You also promised me you wouldn't do drugs. How do I know you're not doing them, too?"

"I would *never* do drugs," he said with such vehemence I believed him. At least, I believed that he meant it at that moment in time.

"I'm tired," he said, slumping low in the seat.

"Me, too." I thought we'd had enough heavy discussion for one morning. I reached into my pocketbook for the novel I'd brought with me. "Why don't you close your eyes and take a nap?"

He leaned his head against my shoulder, my angelic little boy again. I let the book rest in my lap and shut my eyes.

How were we going to survive the rest of his adolescence? I wondered. I didn't like to think about what next year would be like without Maggie at home. She was a second set of eyes watching over him. Her own commitment to education—to excellence in everything she did—influenced him. She would be as surprised as I was to learn about the lighter.

We were both bleary-eyed by the time we filed into the small jet.

"Do you want to sit next to the window?" I asked, pointing to the two seats reserved for us.

"Yeah!" he said, sliding into the seat.

"Buckle your seat belt," I said as I buckled my own. He popped the buckle together and then I pulled it tight.

The flight attendant, an Asian woman with sad eyes and a bright smile, stood up and began going through her motions.

"Who is that lady?" Andy asked loudly.

"She's the flight attendant. She's explaining some things about the plane. Let's listen."

The attendant showed how to undo the seat belt and Andy obediently undid his.

"She's showing how for later," I said. "So buckle it back up now."

She demonstrated the use of the oxygen mask and Andy leaned forward, tongue pursed between his lips as he concentrated on her instructions.

He turned to me when the attendant had finished.

"Why did she say adults traveling with children should put their mask on first?" he asked.

"Because the adult can't take good care of the child unless she takes care of herself first," I said.

For some reason, that made him laugh.

"What's so funny?"

"You'd put mine on before yours," he said with certainty. "You always take care of me before anybody else."

Chapter Twelve

Maggie

LIGHTS WERE ON IN SOME OF THE HOUSES as I drove to The Sea Tender. It was the first week in April, and people were starting to take vacations. In a couple of months, the island would be totally different. The everybody-knows-everybody-else feeling would morph into wall-to-wall strangers with new faces every week as they moved in and out of the rental houses and mobile homes. I dreaded it. There'd be people in the houses near The Sea Tender and they'd be snoopy and curious.

I didn't have to lie to Mom about where I was going tonight, since she and Andy were in New York. I hated lying, but that seemed like all I did anymore. It looked like my little brother had been doing some lying himself lately. Mom called from

New York to tell me about the lighter. I had a feeling Andy smoked. I caught a telltale whiff on him sometimes, but when I came right out and asked him if he smoked, he said, "Of *course* not, Maggie!" I fell for it.

Andy's screwups scared me. So far, they'd been little things. As he grew up, the chance for him to make bigger mistakes would grow along with him.

Like I had room to talk.

I parked down the street and kept my flashlight off as I walked along the road. I turned up the little boardwalk between two of the front-row houses to where our old cottage sat on the beach.

I lugged the cinder block beneath the steps and climbed up to the front door. Inside the cottage, I didn't head for the rear deck like I did when trying to make contact with Daddy. I was there for a different reason tonight—a *worldly* reason, one that made lying absolutely necessary.

The bedroom that had been my parents' was smaller than the other two, but it was the only one with a view of the ocean. It was also the only room in the entire house without a broken or boarded-up window. I could see a couple of lights far out on the water. I watched them long enough to see that one was sailing north, the other south. Then I lit all six of the jasmine-scented candles on the little plastic table in the corner of the room. The full-size bed—just a saggy old mattress, box spring and rusty frame—was one of the pieces of furniture Mom left behind when we deserted The Sea Tender. I pulled back the covers on the bed and took out the sheets of fabric softener I'd left on the pillows. I never knew how long it would be before I came back, and I hated the smell of stale linen.

I just finished plumping up the pillows when I heard footsteps on the front deck, then the creak of the sticky old door.

"Anyone home?" Ben asked quietly.

I tore through the living room to get to him. He pulled me into his arms and I buried my face against his chest, suddenly crying.

"It's okay, angel," he said, stroking my hair. "It was too long this time. I know."

I couldn't stop blubbering. Total meltdown, like I'd been saving it all up for him—for the moment I could finally let it out. I always had to be the strong one in my family. With Ben, I could just be me. He held me till I stopped crying. He always knew what I needed.

"It's been torture," I managed to say.

We hadn't been together—not *this* way—since before the fire. We coached the Pirates together, acting like we hardly knew each other so no one would wonder about us and start gossiping. We talked and text-messaged and exchanged a few e-mails, but no way could that substitute for being alone together.

He leaned back from me and ran his hand over my cheek. A little candlelight spilled out of the bedroom and I could see his chocolatey-brown eyes and the gory new scar on his forehead.

"How is it?" I touched the scar lightly.

He winced and I pulled my hand away.

"Sorry! Sorry!" I hated that I'd hurt him.

"Just tender," he said. "Got the stitches out this morning." He touched the scar himself. "I'll always have a reminder of that night."

"You're safe, though," I said.

"Others weren't so lucky."

"I was so scared."

"Shh." He kissed me, then suddenly lifted me up, the way an old-fashioned groom carries a bride over the threshold. He carried me into the bedroom. The jasmine smell was so strong, I felt drunk. Ben put me down on the bed and started undressing me. My throat still felt clogged with tears. I didn't want to start crying again, though. I wouldn't. Ben needed a woman tonight. Not a little girl.

I wasn't one of those wide-eyed girls who believed in love at first sight, but the first minute I saw Ben, something happened to me. It was my seventeenth birthday, nearly a year ago, and I was in the lounge at the rec center waiting to meet the new coach of the older kids. Their old coach, Susan Crane, was moving to Richmond, so a new guy was taking her place. Susan was thirty-five, so I don't know why I expected the new guy to be my age, but I did.

Ben stood at the check-in counter, filling out paperwork and laughing with David Arowitz, one of the managers. I thought he was opening a membership at the center, and I took him in in one big gulp. He wore blue-and-green-striped jams, like he was checking in to use the pool, and a short-sleeve blue shirt and sandals. He was big. He'd probably been one of those boys who had to wear those "husky-size" clothes. His hair was short, dark and wavy. He had a straight nose, dimples—at least on the side of his face I could see—and long, heavy-duty eyelashes. I swear, I took in all those details in one instant and literally felt something happen to my heart, like someone squeezed it hard enough to send tingles down my arms.

I knew what he was like just by looking at him. He was kind, he loved animals, he'd rather play volleyball than golf, he believed in God but wasn't religious, he loved scary movies, he could talk about emotional things, he smoked marijuana but never cigarettes. I knew all of this in the time it took the tingling to run from my heart to my fingertips. I also knew he was way too old for me, but I didn't care. I was in love.

Suddenly David pointed in my direction. Ben said something to him, then started walking toward me. The one thing I hadn't figured out about him was that he was the new coach.

"Maggie?" He held out his hand. The dimple was only on one side of his mouth. "I'm Ben Trippett."

I wasn't all that used to shaking hands with people. When I shook his, I felt heat coming off his palm, like he ran a few degrees warmer than everyone else on the planet. I would learn that about him——his hands were *always* hot. Maybe it was the heat that did it to me. All I knew was that I was completely, totally lost.

He was all I could think about. I suddenly understood why my girlfriends developed tunnel vision when they were hung up on a guy. I couldn't wait for our twice-weekly swim team practice. Sometimes he and I would stop at McDonald's afterward. I'd get a soda; he'd get a milk shake. We'd talk about our swimmers——who was strong, who needed more work on a certain stroke. We'd set goals for our team. The whole time, I'd be thinking *I love you, I love you, I love you.*

He lived with Dawn Reynolds, but I tried not to think about that. I didn't know Dawn well; she'd only been on the island for about a year. I didn't believe in breaking anybody up, but I couldn't help what I felt for him. I made up reasons to see him. He worked at the Lowes in Hampstead, and sometimes after school I'd think of an excuse to go there. I bought paint for my room that I never got around to putting on the walls and a lamp I knew I didn't like and would have to return.

We started talking about other things when we went to McDonald's. Movies—we both loved scary ones, as I predicted. His divorce, which was "messy," and his seven-year-old daughter, Serena, who lived with his ex-wife in Charlotte. He missed her a lot. I could tell he was a good father. I loved that about him.

Then one night, he said he wanted to talk about Dawn.

"When I first moved here, I rented one of the mobile homes in Surf City," he told me. "I was in Jabeen's Java one day and started talking to her. She was about to tack a flyer on the bulletin board looking for a housemate. She'd gotten divorced around the time I did and she was going to lose her house on the beach if she didn't find someone to share expenses. So it was a no-brainer."

"So...you and Dawn are just housemates?"

When he nodded, I felt like I was sitting on a cloud instead of a molded plastic bench at McDonald's.

"Except it's a little more complicated than that," he said. "She'd just gotten divorced and I'd just gotten divorced and..." He looked straight at me with those chocolatey eyes. "Have you ever broken up with anyone?"

"Not really." I'd only had three dates in my life.

"Well then, it might be hard for you to understand, but when a marriage ends, especially if you tried hard to save it and you still care about the person, it leaves you really raw…and very lonely. Dawn and I were both in that place when I moved in." He took a sip of his milk shake. Then another. He wasn't looking at me. "She's a pretty woman," he said finally, "and I was attracted to her physically."

I cringed. "Am I gonna get TMI here?"

"TMI?"

"Too much information."

"Oh." He smiled. "Probably."

"Oh, no." I sat up straight and got ready to hear the worst. "Okay," I said. "Go ahead."

His cheeks had turned pink. I loved that he wanted to talk to me about something personal enough to make him blush. "Well, you've figured it out," he said. "I screwed up. We slept together the first week I moved in. By the second week, I knew it had been a mistake. She's a nice woman, but we were never going to be right for each other. I told her I just wanted to be friends and offered to move out. She was upset. In her mind, she thought—she still thinks—we're a good match and she didn't want me to leave. Not only that, but she needs the financial help. So that's why I'm there." He blew out his breath and poked down one of the little raised bumps on his milk-shake lid. "And the reason I'm telling you this is because I have very strong feelings for you, Maggie."

Oh…my…God. "Me, too." I was amazed I got the words out. My mouth was so dry I thought they'd stick to my tongue.

"I know you do," he said. "There's such a connection between us. You might be seventeen chronologically, but you're no kid. No immature teenager. I don't really want to fight the feelings I have for you. But…you're seventeen."

"You already mentioned that."

"And I'm ten years older. I don't want to take advantage of you."

"Ben." I hated the table between us. "I love you. I've loved you for months. And you're right. I'm not an immature teenager. I hardly ever date because guys my age are such—" I shook my head "—total losers. The way I feel about you is different. It's like the way I love my brother and my—"

"*What?*" He laughed.

"I mean, it's really, really deep and…" I was afraid I was starting to *sound* like an immature teenager. It was hard to explain how I felt about him. "It's…pure," I said finally. "I don't know how else to describe it."

"Well—" his dimple was so cute when he smiled "—I like that description." He leaned back and sighed. "Whew," he said. "I've wanted to have this conversation with you for weeks. I wasn't afraid of what you'd say. I knew you felt the same way I did. But it changes things, and I don't know what to do next. You're just starting your senior year. Maybe we should try to keep it…you know, *platonic,* until you're out of high school."

I'd pictured lying in bed with him a thousand times. One of my arms would be across his chest, and one of his would circle my shoulders protectively. I didn't really care about having sex with him. I wanted something more than that. Something deeper that would last the rest of my life.

"I don't want to wait," I said. "The age of consent in North Carolina is sixteen. I'm seventeen and five months. You have my consent."

"We can't be out in the open," he said. "Your mother… God, your *uncle.* They'd kill me."

"I know." He was right about that. I was certain Mom had been a virgin on her wedding night, and Uncle Marcus was always giving me that "guys are out for one thing" lecture. Maybe guys *my* age were. Ben was totally different.

"And there's really no place we can be together," Ben said.

It was my turn to smile.

"Yes," I said, "there is."

Later, when I realized I could tell him anything at all—almost, anyway—I told him how I felt in the beginning. How I didn't think I wanted him sexually. He laughed and said, "Well, *that's* certainly changed." I guess it did, but my favorite part of being with Ben was still lying in his arms in the bedroom of The Sea Tender, telling him everything I thought and felt. I even told him two of my biggest secrets.

The first was that I threw the most important swim meet of the season when I was fourteen because I felt sorry for my competitor. That girl was so gangly, dorky and uncoordinated that her teammates groaned when it was her turn to swim. I couldn't make myself beat her. I pretended to get a cramp on my third lap.

Ben said I was sweet, but insane.

Second, I told him about feeling Daddy's spirit on the deck of The Sea Tender. That's when I found out I'd been wrong about one thing: Ben was religious after all. First, he just teased me about it, saying he hoped Daddy didn't show up when we were in bed together. When he realized I was serious, though, he got serious himself. He said the devil was playing tricks on me and I should be careful. I was disappointed that he believed in the devil. I wanted him to be my mirror image, with my

thoughts and beliefs. I wanted him to be everything I needed—
my confidant and best friend and lover. I realized then that no
one person could be all those things to another. I was a little
more careful about what I told him after that.

I would never even consider telling him my third secret.

After we made love, Ben got the marijuana from the kitchen
while I crawled naked under the covers, breathing in jasmine
and fabric softener. Ben got back in bed and I snuggled close
to him while he lit a joint.

He took a hit, then passed it to me.

"God, this feels good, being here with you," he said. "It's
been such a shitty week."

"I know."

"I have these...not nightmares, exactly. But when I go to
bed, I start picturing Serena at a lock-in when she's a few
years older. She gets scared a lot. Thunderstorms. Strangers.
Dogs. You name it. She might have panicked if she'd been
there. She could've been one of the kids who didn't make it."

"Don't think about that, Ben." *I* didn't want to think about
it. I slipped the joint between his lips. "Think about that girl
you saved. Uncle Marcus said she'd be dead if it hadn't been
for you."

"I do think about her, believe me," he said. "She's still at New
Hanover and I've visited her a couple times. She's going to be
okay. Then I think about how close I came to leaving her there
because my air was getting low and I was..." He shuddered.
"I'll tell you, Maggie, I was sweatin' bullets."

"It must have been awful." I knew all about his claustrophobia, how he'd start to panic the moment he'd put the face

piece on. I hated the rude things the other firefighters said about him right to his face, like he had no feelings. Once, I overheard one of them say to Uncle Marcus, "I don't know why you even bother to give him a pager. He's useless." It made me *furious.* He told me he was even thinking of leaving, going back to Charlotte, because he couldn't take it anymore. I freaked out when he said that. What would I do without him?

"How did you stand wearing the face piece?" I asked.

"I turned the emergency bypass valve on, just for a second," he said. "It gave me a little rush of air. A beautiful sound. It wasn't the air so much as just reminding myself that I had the bypass valve if I needed it."

"But when you got that low-air warning, you must've freaked."

"Yes, ma'am, I was as freaked as you can get. But I could also see that girl in the camera. I had to get her."

"I'm really proud of you. Have the other guys stopped giving you a hard time?"

He nodded. "I think they've finally accepted me," he said, letting the smoke pour from his lungs. "Even got a couple of apologies from some of the worst offenders. So that's my silver lining. The cost was too high, though."

Those big photographs from the memorial service popped into my mind, past the wall I'd built inside my head to try to keep them out. At the service, I felt sick to my stomach as Reverend Bill talked about each of them. I'd wanted to run out of the Assembly Building but was afraid of making a scene.

"Do you see why I have to believe there's an afterlife?" I asked Ben now. "Why I'm so sure Daddy visits me out here? I have to believe those three people—Jordy and Henderson and Mr. Eggles—that they're someplace better."

"I believe that," Ben said. "I just don't believe dead people can contact us."

He hadn't experienced what I had with Daddy, so he didn't understand.

We'd reached the end of the joint and Ben stubbed it out in a clamshell we kept on the floor next to the bed. I remembered that night in the E.R., how scared I was to see him there and how invisible I felt when Dawn practically knocked me over to get to him. People always thought he and Dawn were an item and although he never came right out and agreed with them, he also never bothered to set them straight. She was our cover, he said, which only bothered me when I saw her staring at him the way she did Saturday at the swim meet. I could see how much she loved him. It was all over her face. I felt sorry for her the way I'd felt sorry for the gangly fourteen-year-old girl I let beat me years ago. But I wasn't letting her have Ben.

"Dawn loves you so much," I said. "When she saw you at the E.R., she looked so relieved to see you were all right. It was like when I saw that Andy was okay. I feel like I'm hurting her by being with you."

"I haven't misled her. You know that."

"But she thinks you're unattached. That gives her hope."

"What can I do about it, Maggie?" He sounded a little pissed off. "I can't very well tell her about us."

"I know," I said quickly. I had never heard him sound annoyed with me before and it shook me up. "I feel sorry for her, that's all." What *did* I want him to do? I didn't know.

A breeze suddenly blew into the room from the living room, putting out all but two of the candles. I stood up and walked to the corner to relight them. When I turned to come back to bed, the candlelight must have landed on my hip.

Ben rose up on his elbows. "What's that on your hip?" he asked.

"A tattoo," I said.

"You're kidding." He sat up. "Is it new?"

"No. You just never noticed it before." I'd had it for over a year, placed low enough that my mother would never see it.

"I can't tell what it is from here," Ben said.

"Just a word." I stepped close enough for him to read it.

"Empathy." He ran his fingers over the small calligraphied print. "Why?"

"To remind me to walk in other people's shoes," I said.

Ben laughed, pulling me down on the bed so that I straddled him. "You don't need any reminders of that, angel," he said, his superheated hands on my hips. "You wrote the book."

Chapter Thirteen

Andy

THEY PUT US ON A LITTLE COUCH THING. There were big cameras on stands and lots of men and ladies all over. One lady sat in a chair looking at us. I looked at the camera and smiled like you're supposed to do when you get your picture taken.

The lady in the chair said, "Andy, when we start talking, just look at me. Don't look at the camera. We'll pretend we're having a normal conversation, okay?"

"Okay." She was nice to look at. Pretty, with shiny hair like Mom's only blacker, and Chinesey eyes. Her voice was soft and reminded me of how Maggie talked sometimes.

Mom smiled at me and squeezed my hand like she always did. Her hand was cold as a Popsicle.

A man attached a teeny black microphone to my shirt and

said not to worry about it. A lady wearing a headset held up three fingers, then two fingers, then one finger.

Then the lady started talking to us, and I looked right at her, like she said to do. I told myself, *don't look anywhere else except at the lady.* I didn't want to screw up.

"Tell us about the fire, Andy," she said to me. Her eyes had sparkles in them.

"I was at the lock-in with my friend Emily and all of a sudden there was fire everywhere," I said. "Some boys got on fire and I told them to stop, drop and roll!"

"You did?" the lady asked. "Where did you learn that?"

I couldn't remember exactly where. I wanted to look at Mom to ask her, but remembered I was only supposed to look at the lady. "I think school, but I'm not sure," I said.

"That's right," Mom said.

My knee was bouncing like it does sometimes and I thought Mom would put her hand on it to make it stop, but she didn't.

"And what happened then, Andy? People were trying to get out of the church, right? But they couldn't?"

"Because of the fire."

"I understand the front doors were blocked by the flames."

"And the back door, too."

"That must have been very scary."

"Emily was scared. She had her shirt on inside out."

The lady looked confused and turned to Mom.

"His friend Emily is a special-needs child who doesn't like to have the seam of her clothing touch her skin," Mom said.

"Ah, I see," the lady said. "So how *did* you get out of the fire, Andy?"

"I went to the boys' room and outside the window was the

metal…the air-conditioner box thing and I climbed out onto it and helped Emily out. Then I went back in and got people to follow me out."

"Amazing," the lady said. When she turned her head a little, the sparkles in her eyes moved. "You saved a lot of lives."

I nodded. "I was a…" I remembered I wasn't supposed to talk about being a hero.

"He was a hero," Mom said, "but I've told him not to brag about it."

I accidentally looked at Mom for a minute. She had the sparkles in her eyes, too! Freaky.

"How do you feel about what you did, Andy?" the lady asked.

"Good," I said. "But some people died. I guess they didn't all hear me call to them. Your eyes are really pretty. They have sparkles in them."

The lady and Mom both laughed. "It's from the lights," the lady said. "But thank you for that compliment, Andy." She turned to Mom again. "Laurel, can you tell us a little about Andy and Fetal Alcohol Spectrum Disorder?"

"I can tell you about it," I said.

Mom did put her hand on my knee then, which meant *shut up.*

"Let's give your mother a chance to talk, Andy."

"Okay," I said, even though I've heard Mom talk about FASD so many times I could say it all myself. She talked about how she had a drinking problem when she was pregnant with me and that made me different than other kids. She went into rehab and hasn't had a drink since then. I was in a foster home and she got me back when I was one year old. She threw herself into making sure I got the best care and education possible. See? I could say it all myself.

"I'm on a swim team," I said. "And I always win."

Mom and the lady laughed again. Mom said I'm an excellent competitioner because of my startling reflex. And that I have an average IQ, which I know means I'm intelligent and can do things a lot better than I actually do if I'd just try harder.

"I'm as smart as most people," I said. "But my brain works different."

Mom said about the lighter and how we missed the plane, which I still don't really understand 'cause if you have a lighter in your sock you're not actually carrying it.

"There's a fund that's been created for the medical expenses of the children injured in the fire," the lady said to the camera. "If you'd like to help, the Internet site is on your screen."

"Many of the children who were hurt at the lock-in are from families with limited funds," Mom said.

"She means they're poor," I said, proud that I understood.

"You have another child, too," the lady said to Mom. "Does she also have FASD?"

"Does she mean Maggie?" I asked Mom, though I kept my eyes on the lady.

"Yes, Maggie is my older daughter. I wasn't drinking when I was pregnant with her and she's fine."

"Maggie's the best sister," I said.

"She is?" the lady asked.

"She'd put my oxygen mask on first, too," I said.

Chapter Fourteen

Laurel
1989

"LOOK AT HER HAIR!" MISS EMMA SAID as Jamie settled the baby in her arms. "Your hair was exactly like this when you were born," she said to her son. "A thick head of beautiful black curls."

"Isn't she something?" Jamie sat down next to his mother on our sofa. He hadn't stopped grinning in the three days since we'd come home with the baby. "You have to see when she opens her eyes," he said. "She looks right at you."

"Are they brown like yours and Laurel's?" She ran a fingertip over the nearly translucent skin of the baby's forehead.

"They're kind of gray right now," Jamie said, "but the pediatrician said they'll most likely be brown."

Miss Emma looked at me where I sat in the rocker. "You must be in seventh heaven, darlin'," she said.

I was too tired to speak, so I smiled the same smile I'd been wearing for the past three days. I'd pasted it to my face shortly after the baby was born, and it was still in place. There was something wrong with me, and so far I'd managed to hide it from everyone else. I watched Jamie and Miss Emma sitting with the baby on the sofa and it was as if I was watching them in a dream. I felt apart from them, a strange sense of distance between us. If I tried to walk from the rocker to the sofa, it could take me days.

My pregnancy had been far easier than I'd anticipated. Except for some nausea early on and some puffy ankles toward the end, I'd felt very well. The baby was two weeks early, and although labor was harder than I'd anticipated, I made it through ten hours of agony without an epidural. I was nearly as concerned about Jamie as I was with myself. With his "gift," he looked as if he felt every single contraction. The baby was eight pounds, eight ounces and I was grateful she hadn't waited the two extra weeks to make her entrance.

I knew the moment when I changed from a woman in love with the baby she'd carried to a woman who no longer knew what love felt like. In the delivery room, I heard the baby cry for the first time, and I reached down toward my spread-apart legs, anxious to touch her. A nurse placed her on my chest. Jamie kissed my forehead as I lifted my head to look at her, but I felt like I was looking down a long, spiral rabbit hole. My world started to spin, faster, faster, and then it went black.

When I woke up, I was in the recovery room, Jamie at my side. I'd hemorrhaged, he'd said, but I was going to be fine. Maggie was perfect, and I'd be able to have more children.

I barely heard him. I was stuck on the word *Maggie*. Who was Maggie? I had a cramping pain low in my belly and thought I was still in labor. I was frightened by my confusion. It took Jamie several minutes to set me straight.

I didn't get to hold the baby until thirty-six hours after she was born. When she was placed in my arms, I felt absolutely nothing. No maternal tug of recognition that this was the familiar little presence I'd been carrying inside me for nine months. No longing to explore her body. Nothing.

"Isn't she beautiful?" Jamie stood next to the bed, beaming, and that's when I pasted the smile on my face. Now at home, everyone seemed to think I'd returned from that rabbit hole. I was the only person who knew I was still stuck somewhere between the black abyss and the real world.

"Is she eating well?" Miss Emma asked.

Jamie looked to me to answer, which meant I was going to have to somehow force words out of my mouth.

"I'm—" I cleared my throat "—I'm having some trouble," I admitted. "She doesn't latch on well."

How I'd longed to nurse an infant! Working in the pediatrician's office, I'd watch with envy and anticipation as mothers slipped their babies inside their shirts for that secret, sacred bond. But my nipples were too flat for the baby to latch on easily. In the hospital, nurse after nurse tried to help me. A counselor from the La Leche League showed up in my room in the hours before I was discharged. Sometimes I was able to get the baby to suck, but more often she wailed in frustration. The woman from the La Leche League swore the baby was getting enough nourishment, but I was worried.

"Oh, switch to formula," Miss Emma said now, as though it

was no big deal. "I bottle-fed both my boys and they turned out all right."

Jamie'd turned out great, I thought, but Marcus was questionable. He was *still* being bottle-fed. I felt tears fill my eyes, though, at receiving her permission. She was the first person who made it sound like no big deal to stop nursing.

"Well, it's important, Mama," Jamie said.

From where I sat, I could see the baby's face tighten into her pre-howling expression. A knot the size of a boulder filled my stomach.

"Oh-oh," Miss Emma said. "What's the matter, precious?" She raised the baby to her shoulder and rubbed her back, but the howling started anyway. "She wants her mama, bless her heart." Miss Emma handed the baby to Jamie—he already handled her with more assurance than I did—who walked with her toward my rocker.

"I'll try to feed her." It took all my strength to get to my feet. Jamie settled the baby in my arms and I walked toward the bedroom. I needed privacy, not out of a sense of modesty but because I didn't want witnesses to my failure.

In the bedroom, I sat on the bed with my back propped up against the pillows and started the battle to get the baby to latch on. She cried; I cried. Finally she started sucking, but not with the fervor I'd witnessed in other infants. Not with the contentment of being in her mother's arms. Her expression was one of resignation, as though she *had* to suck on my breast because it was her only option. She would rather be anywhere else but with me.

From the bedroom, I heard Marcus come home.

"Hey, Mama." I pictured him striding through the living

room, leaning over to kiss Miss Emma's cheek. "When did you get here? Have you seen my little niece yet?"

"Lord have mercy, Marcus!" I heard Miss Emma say. "You smell like a barroom."

I couldn't hear the rest of the conversation, just the muffled sound of their voices—including that of a young woman—and I knew Marcus had brought home another of his girlfriends. He seemed to have one for every day of the week.

Closing my eyes, I listened to my own voice inside my head. *Your baby doesn't like you.*

I know. I know.

You can't even give her enough milk.

I know.

The baby turned her head away from my breast, wrinkling her nose in what I could only interpret as distaste. I felt dizzy with tiredness.

"Jamie," I tried to call.

I heard laughter from the living room.

Gathering my strength, I called louder. "Jamie!"

In a moment, he opened the door to the bedroom and peered inside. "You doing okay in here?"

"Can you burp her, please?" I asked. "I need a nap."

"Sure, Laurie." He took the baby from me and, as I burrowed under the covers and gave in to the exhaustion, I felt the guilty freedom of not having to think about her for an hour or so.

Marcus had moved in with us during the sixth month of my pregnancy and he'd been a mixed blessing. Between Jamie's work at the real estate office, the fire department and the chapel, his hours were long and unpredictable and I liked having Marcus's company, even if I often had to share it with his girlfriend du jour and a few six-packs of beer. Jamie'd gotten him a construction job where he used to work. On the evenings Marcus wasn't working, though, he'd sometimes have dinner ready by the time I got home from my job at the pediatrician's office. He helped me turn the third bedroom into a nursery, painting it in greens and yellows and setting up the crib and dresser I'd bought. He'd long ago given up the electric piano, but he played the stereo in his room so loud that if I walked on the beach, as I did most mornings and evenings, I could hear it a quarter mile away. He'd turn it down if I asked him to. He did anything I asked, actually. The problem was not between Marcus and me but between Marcus and Jamie. They rubbed up against each other like sandpaper, and I soon realized it had been that way for most of their growing-up years. Jamie was a different person around Marcus. To say that Jamie tried to understand another person's feelings was putting it mildly. With Marcus though, he reacted before he thought. The music was too loud? He'd yell, "Marcus, turn that crap down!" If Marcus came home in the middle of the night, crashing into furniture and slamming doors after hours of partying, Jamie would get out of bed and I'd cover my head with the pillow to block out the fight.

I discovered it was impossible to intervene in the dance of anger between the brothers. It had been going on too long and my voice must have been a tiny, annoying buzz in their ears when I tried to make nice. Their parents had choreographed the rivalry many years ago with their deferential treatment of their older son. Marcus was no angel, to be sure, and he'd play dense when I tried to talk to him about the way he behaved with his brother. He drank way too much. Although he was only twenty, six-packs of beer appeared and disappeared and reappeared in the refrigerator with such rapidity that I lost track. We began to understand why his parents had planned to kick him out.

"You knew what he's like," I said to Jamie on one of our morning walks along the beach. It was a rare March day when the weather had turned so warm we were walking barefoot in the sand. My hands rested on my belly as we walked, cradling the baby I couldn't wait to meet. "You knew he drinks, he parties, he's rowdy."

"Lazy and irresponsible."

"He's not lazy at all," I countered, thinking of the help he'd given me with the nursery. I couldn't argue with "irrespon-sible," though. Several times, Marcus didn't show up for work, and the foreman called Jamie to complain. Having gotten Marcus the job, Jamie naturally felt responsible for his performance.

"Why did you want him to live with us?" I asked. "Did you think you could change him?"

Jamie ran his hands through his hair and looked out to sea. "I thought I could change *me*," he said.

"What do you mean?"

"I always had problems with him when we were younger," he said. "But I feel good about myself. Good about the person I am now, so I thought I could learn to be more tolerant of him. But I swear, Laurie, he's a whiz-bang expert at pissing me off."

"I know." For all the help Marcus gave me, he did put Jamie to the test, like a rebellious teenager trying to see how far he could push his parents.

"Maybe it was a mistake letting him move in," Jamie said.

"We told him we'd try it for six months," I reminded him. "Can you tough it out that long?"

Jamie nodded. "If we don't kill each other first."

Jamie took three weeks off from real estate and the fire department after Maggie was born. It took me that long to begin thinking of her by her name. At her two-week checkup, the pediatrician I'd worked for confirmed what I already knew: she had colic. He took a finger-prick's worth of blood from me while I was there and told me I was still anemic, which accounted for my exhaustion and pallor.

"And I think you have a touch of the baby blues, Miss Laurel," he said, still referring to me the way he did when I worked there. He studied my face and I realized I'd forgotten to paste on my smile that morning. "Don't worry," he said. "Your hormones will sort themselves out in good time."

I told him about my struggle to breast-feed. Every couple of hours, Maggie and I were locked in a battle that left both of us drained and at least one of us in tears. He was hesitant about suggesting I stop, but something in my demeanor tipped him over the edge.

"The first two weeks were the most important," he said. "And if it's having a negative impact on how you feel about her and about yourself, I suggest you begin weaning her now."

I nodded, relieved. Things would be better, I thought. I wouldn't dread feeding time. I would start to love her.

But that didn't happen. She took to the bottle more easily than she had my breast, but she still seemed uncomfortable in my arms, fussing no matter how I held her. I could quiet her by slipping my finger in her mouth, but as soon as she realized there was no food coming from my fingertip, the crying started again.

She was undeniably different with Jamie. She'd sleep on his shoulder or in the crook of his arm. I was both envious of her comfort with him and relieved that *something* could put an end to her crying.

The night before Jamie returned to work, I begged him to take another week off.

We were lying in bed together, keeping our voices low so we didn't wake her even though she was a room away from us.

"I can't, Laurie," he said. "It's nearly high season and I've already taken too much time off."

"Please don't leave me alone with her!" I sounded desperate, which was exactly how I felt.

"She's your *daughter*, Laurie, not a rabid dog."

"You're so much better with her than I am," I said.

"I know you haven't felt well." He raised himself up on an elbow and smoothed my hair back from my face. "Just walk with her a little. I don't think you hold her enough. She wants to be held."

"She cries when I hold her."

"She picks up your tension. You just need to relax more with her."

"I used to be so good with babies," I said. I'd read nearly every book on babies ever written and suddenly seemed to know nothing at all. "Dr. Pearson always relied on me to help when a mother brought in her infant."

Jamie smiled. "And you'll be good with them again. You got off to a rough start with the hemorrhaging and everything. Don't be so hard on yourself."

So Jamie went back to work, and I didn't get better. I got worse. Having a baby had been a huge mistake, and only I seemed to know it. Sometimes I would look at Maggie—she could be screaming or sleeping, it didn't matter—and I'd have to remind myself she was my child. I felt detached from her. She could have been a wedge of cheese or a frying pan for all the emotion I felt looking at her. I began to feel the same way about Jamie. I'd look at him and wonder how I'd ended up living on this sparsely populated island with a man for whom I felt nothing.

The uncrowded quietness I'd relished living on the island suddenly felt like isolation. I realized I had very few friends nearby, and of those I did have, none were young mothers. I still had a few friends from college, but they lived in the city. The only one with a baby called to congratulate me on Maggie's birth, but her enthusiastic gushing over her own little boy only served to let me know I wasn't normal.

I apologized to Maggie repeatedly. "You deserve a better mommy," I'd say. "I'm sorry I'm so bad at this." Marcus still offered to cook a few evenings a week, but as long as he was sober, I'd hand Maggie over to him instead and make dinner myself. Even Marcus was better with Maggie than I was.

When Jamie came home from work, it was Maggie he rushed to see, not me, and that was fine. It gave me the chance to crawl back in bed with the covers over my head—my escape in the guise of a nap.

One day during that first week alone with my daughter, I put her in the infant seat on the kitchen counter while I heated her bottle in a pan of water on the stove. Maggie was screaming, her face red as a beet. I was keeping an eye on the water when I suddenly pictured myself standing above Maggie with a knife in my hand, plunging it through her little pink-and-white onesie into her tiny body.

I yelped, backing away from the stove, pressing myself against the pantry door. I saw the knife block on the counter and quickly grabbed the entire block, carrying it down the hall into Marcus's room, where I stashed it under his bed. Surely if I had to go to that much trouble to get a knife, I'd have time to talk myself out of harming Maggie with it.

Back in the kitchen, I trembled as I picked her up, took the bottle from the hot water, and settled down in the rocker to feed her. With the nipple in her mouth, she quieted down.

I thought of mothers who hurt their children. People who shook their babies so hard they caused brain damage. I was scared. Was I capable of doing that?

"I love you," I told her as I rocked, but the words sounded like a line uttered in a play by someone pretending to be someone else.

"I need to sleep," I muttered from bed the next morning when Jamie was getting dressed. We'd both been up half the night, taking turns walking with our colicky daughter.

"I'll take her to the office," Jamie said, surprising me. I didn't even wonder how he would manage having her at the real estate office with him. I rolled over and went back to sleep, my relief at the thought of a day without Maggie outweighing my guilt. Soon, he was taking Maggie with him every day while I slept. I vaguely wondered what his coworkers thought about the situation, but I didn't really care. Jamie would find a way to explain it.

I felt drugged half the time, as though someone was slipping narcotics into my drinking water. In my sleepy state, I fantasized about running away. I could go someplace where no one knew me and start over. When my chest hurt one afternoon, I hoped I was having a heart attack. A fatal heart attack would put an end to the numbness I felt inside. I wouldn't have to hear Maggie screaming any longer or do laundry or worry about what to make for dinner. And Jamie and Maggie would be better off without me. I was completely convinced of that.

"Do you remember Sara Weston?" Jamie asked me one Sunday afternoon.

It took me a minute to place the name. "The woman who came to the chapel a few times in the beginning?" I hadn't been to the chapel since Maggie was born, and the pentagonal building down the beach from our house seemed miles away.

"Right. She came back today with her husband, Steve. He's stationed at Camp Lejeune. Anyhow, the reason she hasn't been coming is because Steve wasn't interested but she finally talked him into it today."

"Did he like it?"

Jamie laughed. "I don't think it was his cup of tea, though he was a good sport about it. But anyway, what I'm getting at is that Sara asked about you and I said you could use some help with Maggie and she volunteered."

Oh no, I thought. "I don't want a stranger in the house, Jamie," I said.

"No, I know you're not up for that. But she can take Maggie when I'm tied up during the day."

"We hardly know her." I thought about the knives, which I'd

had to bring back to the kitchen to avoid having to explain their whereabouts to Jamie and Marcus. Sara Weston could hardly be as dangerous as I was. "If you feel okay about her, then that's fine," I said.

I was still in bed the following Tuesday morning when Jamie knocked on the bedroom door.

"Laurel?" he said. "Sara Weston's here. Come out and say hi."

I shut my eyes, trying to draw energy from someplace inside me. "I'll be out in a minute," I said, too softly.

"What?" Jamie was right outside the bedroom door.

"In a minute." I spoke louder.

I got out of bed, pulling on the same clothes I'd worn the day before, and stumbled into the living room.

Sara looked as she had many months earlier, when I first saw her at the chapel. Only now, in summer shorts and peach-colored polo shirt, I could see that she was athletically built. She looked like a soccer mom. She sat on the sofa, holding Maggie on her lap.

"You have one gorgeous baby." She smiled at me.

"Thank you." I pasted on the smile as I sank into the rocker.

Jamie set a glass of sweet tea on the coffee table in front of her.

"And I love your house," she said. "So unique."

"Thanks."

"I wanted to meet you since I'll be helping out with Maggie," she said. "You know, to see if you have any special instructions or anything."

"Just—" I shrugged "—you know...don't kill her or anything."

She and Jamie stared at me, and I laughed.

"You know what I mean." I knew I sounded insane. I didn't care. I wanted to go back to bed in the worst way.

"Well, okay." She laughed, glancing at Jamie. "I think I can manage that."

I had my six-week postpartum checkup with my obstetrician in Hampstead. Once he was finished examining me, I sat up, crinkling the paper sheet around my thighs.

"I'm still so tired all the time," I said.

"The new mother's lament." He smiled, then scratched his balding head. "You're still slightly anemic. Are you taking your iron?"

I nodded.

"How are you sleeping?"

"Not great at night. I take care of the baby during the night because my husband takes her during the day."

"But you sleep in the daytime?"

I nodded again.

"How's your appetite?"

"I don't really have one."

"I think you've got some depression in addition to the anemia," he said.

I hated that catchall word "depression." I knew there was something wrong with me, but depression was too simplistic a term for it. "If I could just get caught up on my sleep, I think I'd be fine," I said.

"I'd like to start you on a trial of Prozac." He pulled a prescription pad from the pocket of his white coat. "Have you heard of it?"

The new miracle antidepressant. "I don't want an antide-pressant," I said. "I don't feel *that* bad."

He hesitated. "Well," he said, "I want you to know it's avail-able to you if you'd like to try it. And I can refer you to a thera-pist. It might be good to have someone to talk to about how you're feeling."

"I don't think so, thanks." How could I tell a stranger that I'd thought about killing my child or running away? He'd send me to the loony bin and throw away the key.

The doctor reached for the doorknob, then turned back to me. "Oh, and you and your husband can begin having sexual relations again," he said, and I masked my antipathy with a smile.

Over the phone that afternoon, I told Jamie the doctor had said I was still anemic.

"Did he say we could start making love again?"

"A couple more weeks." I winced inwardly at the lie. "He said I could have an antidepressant if I wanted one, but that I didn't really need it yet."

"You don't need drugs."

I could picture his scowl. "I know," I said.

"I think all you need is to be in better touch with God, Laurel," he said seriously. "You've lost that part of yourself. Where did you experience God this week?"

I wanted to punch him. If he'd been there with me instead of miles away in his office, I would have. "Nowhere," I said sharply. "I haven't experienced God in six long, miserable weeks."

Jamie was undaunted. "Well," he said, "I think we've iden-tified the problem."

* * *

Sara stopped by a few weeks later. I was lying on the sofa in front of the TV watching an ancient rerun of *I Dream of Jeannie* when she knocked on the screen door.

"Let yourself in," I said.

She was carrying a pan of something as she shouldered her way through the doorway.

"I'm going to put a casserole in the fridge for you," she said, walking into the kitchen.

"Where's the baby?" I asked.

"I left her with Jamie. He's doing some paperwork at the chapel," she said. "I wanted to talk to you."

Oh, no.

Sara pulled one of the dining room chairs over until it was next to the sofa. I looked at the TV screen instead of at her. It was the episode where Tony and Jeannie got married, not that I cared.

"How are you feeling?" Sara asked.

"Okay," I said.

She leaned forward. "Really, how are you feeling?"

I sighed, wishing she would leave.

"Tired," I said.

"What does your doctor say?"

"About what?"

"Your tiredness."

I didn't like her pushiness. "I'm anemic," I said, although I doubted I still was.

"Jamie told me your doctor offered you Prozac."

"That's really personal information."

"He told me because he's worried about you," she said.

"Jamie's kind of old-fashioned about taking antidepressants, but I wanted to tell you that I have a friend in Michigan who takes Prozac and it's really helped her."

"I'm not that depressed, Sara," I said. "I'm *tired*. You'd be tired too if you were up all night with a screaming baby."

"Laurel, you're a *nurse*," she said. "I didn't even finish college and I can tell you're depressed. You want to sleep all the time. Jamie says you don't get excited about anything. Especially not about Maggie." She nearly whispered the last sentence as though someone might overhear her. "It's not normal to be so...uninterested in your baby."

I lifted my gaze to hers. "I want you to leave," I said.

"I'm sorry." She leaned back in the chair but made no move to get up. "I didn't mean to upset you, but I think you need help. It's not fair to Jamie to make him..." She made a clicking sound with her tongue and let out a sigh. "It's like he's a *single parent*," she said. "He's great with her, but that baby isn't even going to know who you are. Who her mother is."

I heard the screen door creak open again and looked up to see Marcus, home for lunch.

Sara finally got to her feet. "You must be Marcus," she said, reaching out a hand. "I'm Sara Weston."

Marcus shook her hand. I could smell booze on him from where I sat.

"You're the babysitter," Marcus said.

"Right. I just stopped over to—"

"To tell me I'm a basket case and a shitty mother," I said.

"Laurel!" Sara said. "That's not what I meant."

"I asked her to go but she won't leave," I said to Marcus, barely able to believe my own rudeness.

"You should go," Marcus said to her.

Sara raised her hands in surrender, as if trying to keep us calm. "I'm going," she said, heading for the door. She turned one more time before leaving. "The casserole goes in a three-hundred-fifty-degree oven for half an hour."

That night, Maggie started getting a cold. Her nose ran and her throat must have hurt because she screamed from nine o'clock until two in the morning. By that time, Jamie and I were both completely exhausted. I fell into a sleep so deep that when the phone rang, I thought it was the smoke alarm and I leaped out of bed and ran into the nursery—one very rare, small sign that I did indeed care about my baby girl.

I came back to the bedroom as Jamie was picking up the phone from the nightstand. I listened to his end of the conversation and knew it was Marcus.

"No, damn it, you can wait there until morning!" Jamie shouted before slamming the receiver into the cradle.

I sat down on the bed. "Marcus?"

"I've *had* it with him!" Jamie got out of bed and opened the dresser drawer, pulling out a T-shirt. "He got another DUI," he said. "He's at the jail in Jacksonville. Wants me to come bail him out."

"Are you going now?"

"Yes." He sounded tired. "I can't leave him there. But this is it, Laurel. This is the end. He's out of this house."

I knew Jamie was right. Kicking him out had seemed inevitable from the start.

"I've been thinking about it," Jamie said as he sat down on the bed to put on his sandals. "He's a big part of the problem."

"What problem?" I asked.

"With you. With your tiredness and everything. You have to worry about him as well as Maggie and me. You have to clean up after him. You can never predict what he'll do next, what woman he'll drag home with him. He wakes the baby up with his music. He's never sober. When's the last time you've seen him sober?"

I tried to think, but then realized Jamie wasn't really after an answer.

"He's keeping us from becoming a family. You, me and Maggie. And this is it. It's over. The great save-Marcus-from-himself experiment comes to an end tonight."

Marcus left The Sea Tender the following day. He packed up his stereo, his CDs, his clothes and his beer and moved into another of his father's many properties—Talos, the house next door to ours.

Chapter Fifteen

Marcus

FOR THE FIRST TIME SINCE THE FIRE, I took my kayak out on the sound at sunrise. Not a ripple in the water. The air full of marshland and salt. I was able to put the fire out of my mind for forty minutes while I paddled hard. Sometimes out there, I felt a bit of what Jamie called "experiencing God." I thought he was so full of it back then. I wished I could tell him I was wrong.

I lived in one of the old Operation Bumblebee towers that I'd converted into a house, and I made it home in time to catch Andy and Laurel's interview on the *Today* show. I was taping it just in case, but I got a kick out of seeing them live. Andy's knee jumped the whole time. He handled Ann Curry's questions like a pro. Laurel got her bit in, of course. Maggie'd already e-mailed me about the lighter fiasco, but I still got queasy hearing Laurel describe what happened. I'd have to have a talk with Andy about smoking. They both *looked* fantastic. Laurel had her hair down and she smiled a lot, which made me realize she doesn't smile much around me. And Andy was a good-looking kid. So young, though. More like twelve than fifteen.

Then it was back to reality at the fire station. I poured my first mug of coffee and was heading across the hall to my office when I collided—literally—with good ol' Reverend William Jesperson. Ordinarily, Reverend Bill and I went out of our way to avoid each other, but my shoulder connecting with his chest made that impossible.

"'Scuse me." I was glad I didn't spill on him. Wouldn't put it past him to sue my sorry Lockwood ass.

He looked down the hall toward Pete's office. "The chief in?" he asked.

"Just stepped out," I said. "Is this about the fire? Because if it is, it's me you should be talking to anyway."

He scowled. "Now come on, Lockwood. You know I'm not going to talk with you, so just tell Pete to call me."

Pete picked that moment to walk in the door carrying coffee and a pastry bag from Jabeen's. He stopped in the hall and looked from me to Reverend Bill and back again.

"Can I help you, Reverend?" he asked.

"You have any leads yet?" Reverend Bill asked him.

"You know we'll tell you soon's we know anything," Pete said.

"Oh, come on," Reverend Bill said. "You fellas know more than you're saying, and I think I have a right to know what your investigation's turned up so far, don't you?"

"It's ongoing, Reverend," I said. "Nothing solid yet." That was putting it mildly.

"Did you see his nephew on TV this morning?" Reverend Bill jerked his head in my direction.

"I missed it." Pete took a sip from his coffee. I knew he was itching to get at whatever he had in the bag.

"Well, it was quite informative," Reverend Bill said. "For example, did you know that Andy Lockwood got kicked off his flight to New York for concealing a cigarette lighter in his sock?"

Pete raised his eyebrows at me. "Andy?"

Son of a bitch. "He didn't get kicked off, Pete. You know what Andy's like. He saw the sign saying you couldn't carry a lighter onboard, so he stuck it in his sock."

"And they didn't let him board," Reverend Bill said.

"Security needed to talk to him, so he and Laurel *missed* their plane. They got on the next one."

Pete's jaw had dropped sometime during the back and forth.

"The boy carries a *lighter* around with him," Reverend Bill said. "And he turned out to be the big hero at the lock-in. Doesn't that seem a bit suspicious?"

"Andy's experimenting like every other fifteen-year-old," I said. "Didn't you try smoking when you were a kid?"

"Frankly, no. I thought it was disgusting then and I still think so now."

Bullshit. He grew up in tobacco country and never lit up?

"Look," I said, "we haven't ruled anyone out at this point."

"I'm really talking to Pete here, Mr. Lockwood." Reverend Bill cut his eyes at me.

"And I appreciate you bringing this to our attention," Pete said. "Like Marcus told you, we haven't ruled anyone out." He ushered Reverend Bill toward the door, his hand in a death grip on the pastry bag. "If you think of anything else, please don't hesitate to let us know."

Reverend Bill held his ground. "You know, it's easy for y'all to take this lightly," he said. "It wasn't *your* church that burned to the ground."

Now I was pissed. "Three people died," I said. "We didn't take the fire lightly when we were fighting it and you can bet we're not taking it lightly now." I turned and walked into my office, steam coming out of my ears.

As far as I was concerned, Reverend Bill looked like a mighty good suspect himself. He'd been bitchin' and moanin' about his raggedy old church for years, and his congregation was still a good bit shy of their fund-raising goal to build a new one. Why not set fire to his church, collect the insurance money for a new one and pass the guilt along to some innocent kid? Andy was a perfect target. Theory didn't hold water, though. Even Reverend Bill wasn't callous enough to burn the church with kids in it. Or stupid enough. Lawyers were already sniffing around for negligence. And the ATF agent said the good Reverend was at a parishioner's house when the fire broke out, anyway. Airtight alibi, he said.

The forensic evidence was slight so far. We'd cut portions of the remaining clapboard and sent it to the lab. It looked like the accelerant was a mix of gasoline and diesel. That set off lightbulbs in all our heads: the same mixture had been used in a fire in Wilmington about six months ago. Old black church slated to be turned into a museum, so they'd figured that one for a hate crime. Plus, that building was abandoned. No one was hurt. This fire was definitely different.

From the burn pattern, it looked like the mixture had been poured all around the perimeter, as I'd figured out from my walk-around. The only place no accelerant had been spread was between the air-conditioning unit Andy'd climbed over and the building.

"Why's that fella hate your guts?" Pete walked into my office and sat down across from me. He pulled a blueberry muffin from the bag and took a bite. Pete'd come to the department a year ago from Atlanta. He didn't know much when it came to the island's history.

"He hated my brother, and I'm a relation." I didn't add that Reverend Bill, like a handful of the old-timers, also had me figured for a murderer.

"Your brother who had that Free Seekers Chapel?"

"Uh-huh. Ol' Bill didn't like the competition."

"Do you think there's anything to his concern?"

I looked at him over the rim of my mug. "About Andy?"

He nodded. "Does he smoke?"

"I didn't think so," I said. "He might just carry a lighter to be cool. To fit in. One thing for sure is that Andy'd never intentionally hurt anyone."

"Well, he did fight with that kid, Keith Weston." Pete wiped his fingers on a napkin. "Roughed *him* up a bit."

"Pete," I said with a laugh, "that dog don't hunt."

There were only two people from the lock-in we hadn't been able to interview: Keith Weston, still in a medicated coma, and Emily Carmichael. Emily'd been tight in the grip of post-traumatic stress and wouldn't even look at us, much less talk. But that afternoon, Robin Carmichael called, saying she thought her daughter was well enough to answer our questions now. We'd already spoken with Robin, who'd been a chaperone at the lock-in.

"Could you bring her in after school tomorrow?" I held the phone between my chin and shoulder as I poured a tube of peanuts into a bottle of Coke.

"She's not *in* school," Robin said. "She's got separation anxiety somethin' terrible. Won't leave my side. But you can talk to her here, if that suits you."

I changed into street clothes before picking up Flip Cates, the Surf City detective involved in the investigation. I figured it'd be easier on Emily if I wasn't wearing a uniform. Flip apparently had the same idea. So when we walked into the Carmichaels' Sneads Ferry living room, with its dark paneling and the cloudy mirror above the sofa, we looked like your average guys on the street.

"Emily, you remember Andy's Uncle Marcus," Robin said. "And this is Detective Cates."

"Hey, Emily," I said, as Flip and I sat down on the sofa.

Emily sat in an old threadbare wing chair, hands folded in her lap. She looked at me with her good eye. She had on a pink T-shirt, inside out, and white capris. No shoes or socks.

Every time I saw Emily, I felt for her and her parents. There was a prettiness behind the funny eyes and repaired cleft palate. Couldn't they operate on that eye? Give her a chance at a normal teenage life? Not much money in this house, though. And not much normal about Emily.

"Robin," I said, "can we try talking to Emily alone?"

"*No!*" Emily wailed.

Well, it had been worth a shot.

Robin shrugged her apology as she sat down on an ottoman near her daughter.

"Tell us everything you remember from the time you arrived at the lock-in, Emily," Flip asked.

Emily looked at her mother. "It got moved," she said.

"Right," Flip said. "Did you notice anything unusual when you got to the church?"

"We walked there."

"Right. From the youth building." Flip had a notepad open on his thigh, but so far, the page was blank. "Did you see anyone you didn't know hanging around the church?"

"I didn't know lots of kids. They came from all over."

"Did you see anyone pouring or spraying something around the outside of the church?"

She shook her head.

"When you got inside the church, what did you do?" Flip asked

"What do you mean?"

"Did you play games? Who did you hang around with?"

"Andy." She looked at me as if remembering my connection to Andy.

"Were you with Andy the whole time?" I asked.

"Right."

"Even when you left the youth building, was it Andy you walked with to the church?" Flip asked.

"Right—"

"No, honey…" Robin interrupted.

"Oh, no!" Emily corrected herself. "Actually—" she pronounced every syllable of the word "—I walked over with my mom."

Robin nodded. "That's right," she said to Flip and me.

I knew Robin thought she'd smelled gasoline as they walked toward the church. She'd told that to the police the night of the fire, but added that she couldn't be sure it wasn't from someone filling a car or boat nearby. "It was just in the air," she'd said.

"Andy liked a girl at the lock-in," Emily volunteered. "She was dancing with a boy, Keith. Do you know Keith?"

She looked at me, but Flip and I both nodded. We knew every detail of the fight between Andy and Keith. That was one thing most of the people we'd interviewed remembered.

"Andy got in a fight with him," Emily said. "I hate fights."

Flip looked at his notepad. "Emily, did you happen to notice anyone outside the church in the hour before the fire?"

"How could I?" she said. "I was inside the whole time."

"Right." Flip ran a hand over his brown buzz cut. "Did you notice anyone leave the church during the lock-in?"

"You mean besides Andy?"

Huh?

Flip and I both hesitated.

"Did Andy leave the church during the lock-in?" Flip asked after a moment.

Emily nodded. "I told him he wasn't supposed to, but sometimes Andy don't understand."

"Are you talking about when Andy left *during* the fire?" I asked. "You know, when he climbed out the bathroom window?"

Emily glanced at her mother.

"Is that what you mean, honey?" Robin asked. "Is that when Andy left the lock-in?"

"He left when people started dancing and I couldn't find him."

I looked at Flip. "That must be when he initially went to the men's room and noticed the air-conditioning unit outside," I said.

"No," Emily said. "That was a different time, because when he went to the boys' room, I went to the girls' room. But then he left again and I tried to find Mom to tell her but then he come back so I just said don't do that again."

Could I possibly not know Andy as well as I thought I did? Ridiculous. No way could Andy mix up a brew of gasoline and diesel, cart it to the church and spread it around. Any kid who would misinterpret a "do not carry lighters aboard the aircraft" sign could not possibly plan and carry out arson.

"Did you ask him where he was?" Flip asked.

"No, I just yelled at him."

"Emily," I said, "did Andy disappear before or after the fight with Keith?"

"I don't remember." She looked at her mother. "Do you remember, Mom?"

Robin shook her head. "This is the first I heard that Andy left the church at all," she said. "If he did." She nodded toward her daughter as if to say *take what she says with a grain of salt.*

"Don't even think what you're thinking," I said, when Flip and I got into my pickup after the interview.

"I don't like that bit about Andy disappearing during the lock-in," Flip said.

"Consider the source." I turned the key in the ignition. "No one else has said anything about Andy disappearing."

"It's possible no one else was paying attention to him," Flip said. "At least not until the fight."

"Look, Flip, Andy can't *plan* anything." I pictured Laurel's step-by-step charts on the corkboard wall of Andy's room. "He lives in the here and now."

"He figured out how to escape from the building when no one else could," Flip pointed out. "That took some planning, didn't it?"

Chapter Sixteen

Laurel

I WALKED INTO THE LOBBY OF SARA'S CHAPEL Hill hotel and was relieved to find it spacious and nicely decorated, huge vases of flowers on every surface. I'd been worried about how she'd afford to stay in a hotel for so long in such an expensive area, but I guessed Keith's hospital had an agreement with this hotel and she'd been able to get a good rate. At least, I hoped so.

I decided the day before that I *had* to see Sara face-to-face. It had been nearly two weeks since the fire. Nearly two weeks since I'd seen her. I needed to know she was all right, as well as to lay to rest my new concern about her resentment over our financial differences. When I called to tell her I was planning to visit, she was quiet at first. I was relieved when she said she'd really like to see me. She asked if I could pick up some clothes and a few other things from her house. I was thrilled to be able to help her in some small way. I missed her so much.

I was to meet her in the hotel's coffee shop. I stood at the entrance to the restaurant, trying to see inside in case she'd gotten there ahead of me.

"Hi, stranger."

I turned to see her behind me and had to mask my shock. Sara was the type of woman who put on her makeup to run out to the mailbox, but she didn't have a speck of it on now. She was pale, the color washed from her face, which looked nearly skeletal. She'd lost a lot of weight in two weeks. Dark roots formed a line along the part of her hair, which was in need of a cut and, I feared, a shampoo.

I pulled her into my arms and hugged her hard. "I love you," I said, my tears surprising me. "I've missed you, and I've been so worried about you."

"I love you, too," she said. "You're so sweet to drive nearly three hours just for lunch."

I let go of her reluctantly.

She smiled at me. "I'm okay, Laurie," she said, smoothing a tear from my cheek. "I'm hanging in there."

The hostess led us to a table in the back of the coffee shop, as if sensing we needed the privacy.

Sara looked around as we sat down. "It's such a relief to be out of the burn center for a while," she said. "It's eighty-five degrees in his room. I'm so glad you came."

"I should have come sooner," I said. "How's Keith?"

She let out a tired breath. "A little better, so they say. It's hard for me to tell because they still have him in a drug-induced coma, but his vital signs and everything are better. They're pretty sure now that he's going to make it."

I reached across the table to wrap my hand over her wrist. "I'm so relieved."

She nodded. "The right side of his face is perfect," she said. "The left side was pretty badly burned, though. He'll have a scar, but right now, I just want him to *live*."

"Of course, sweetie," I said.

The waitress brought us glasses of water and menus.

"I wish I could *talk* to him," Sara said once the waitress left our table. "I miss him, Laurie."

"You *should* talk to him, Sara. He may be able to hear you."

"Oh, I do! Constantly. I tell him I love him and miss him and…I apologize for not doing such a great job with him."

"Oh, Sara. You're a terrific mom."

"Then why does he get in so much trouble?"

"It hasn't been all that much." I longed to reassure her. The truth was, you could be the best parent in the world and still have your kids screw up.

"Well, you're a single mother, too, Laurel," she said. "And look at Maggie. She's just a year older than Keith and at least five years more mature."

"She's a girl. And you and I both know it's Jamie who made her the way she is."

She looked down at the menu. "Give yourself some credit," she said. "Jamie died when Maggie was eight."

"Well, thanks," I said. "I just don't want you to doubt yourself, that's all."

"I know."

"Have you been in touch with Steve?"

She looked surprised, then shook her head.

"Don't you think he should know about Keith?" I asked.

"No. He's…you know the kind of father he's been."

I did. Steve and Sara divorced when Keith was barely a year old and Steve had never once been in touch with his son. Sometimes it took a tragedy like this one to wake people up, though. But it was Sara's decision to make. I wasn't sure what I would have done in her position.

The waitress returned to our table. Sara ordered soup. I ordered a green salad and a broiled, skinless chicken breast that was not on the menu and that I had to talk the waitress into writing on her little pad. Sara smiled. She understood why I ate obsessively well, ran every day, kept up with mammograms and Pap smears and flu shots. I was an orphan. My children had already lost one parent. I wasn't going to let them lose another if I could do anything to prevent it.

"I have zero appetite," she said after the waitress left.

"You've lost weight."

She smiled ruefully. "Well, there's the silver lining, huh?"

I'd been practicing my next words for days.

"Are things okay with you and me?" I asked.

"Of course. What do you mean?"

"Just…I guess it's just that we usually talk nearly every day and everything's changed since the fire. I feel distant from you."

"I'm totally focused on Keith right now, Laurie," she said. "I'm sorry if I—"

"*No.*" I interrupted her. "It's me. I'm being paranoid. Maybe you don't even know this because you've been away, but

Keith...at the dance, he called Andy a 'little rich boy' a few times. It got me worried that you might resent that my kids and I are so much more comfor—"

"Laurel." Sara smiled. "That has never ever been an issue between us, silly," she said. "I can't believe you've been worrying about that."

Right after lunch, Sara left the hotel to go to the hospital, and I waited until she was gone to approach the check-in counter. I hoped Sara was being straight with me about her lack of resentment, because I intended to pay her hotel bill.

I handed the young man behind the counter my credit card.

"I'd like you to use this to cover all of Sara Weston's hotel charges," I said. "She's in room four thirty-two."

He tapped his keyboard, eyes on the screen in front of him. "They've already been taken care of," he said.

"Well, you probably have her card number there," I said, "but I don't want her to have to pay for her room. I'd like to."

"It's taken care of, ma'am," he said with a smile. "Somebody beat you to it."

Chapter Seventeen

Laurel
1990

THE FIRST YEAR OF MAGGIE'S LIFE PASSED BY me in a haze. We had a birthday party for her at The Sea Tender in May. I had forgotten the exact date of her birth, but Jamie had not. I planned the festivities, inviting Sara and Steve, Marcus, who now lived next door but who was around so much it was like he'd never left, and Miss Emma. A few friends of Jamie's from his real estate job came, along with their spouses, and they all seemed to know Maggie very well, since Jamie still carted her with him most places. Daddy L had died during the winter of a quick-moving pneumonia, and I recognized in Miss Emma the mechanical movements of a grieving woman. She reminded me of myself. We both wore smiles that didn't reach our eyes. The only difference was that she had a right to the grief, while I did not. Behind my back, I knew she called me lazy and I'm sure she thought I was doing exactly what she'd pleaded with me not to do: take advantage of her son's generous nature.

I went through the motions of mothering a toddler as if I were a robot, a spiritless machine that clunked along at half speed, threatening to break down for good any moment. Maggie was already walking, and I'd found the energy to baby-proof every cupboard and drawer in the house, afraid that I might turn my back and she would get into something that would kill her. I had no confidence in my ability to protect her. I'd shifted from occasionally wishing she would die to being terrified I would somehow cause her death. If she was home alone with me, which happened only when Jamie couldn't take her with him and Sara was tied up, I'd drag myself out of bed and try to attend to the little dark-eyed stranger who was my daughter. I followed her around the house like a shadow and checked on her repeatedly when she napped. It was hard for me to watch her for long, though; my own need for the escape of sleep was so great. The weariness I'd felt in the weeks after her birth had never abated, although I was no longer anemic. I began hiding my symptoms from my doctor. I didn't care if I got better; I was that far gone. I didn't care what happened to me. I sometimes still fantasized about leaving, though, about letting Jamie find a normal woman who could be a better mother to Maggie.

Sara had finally persuaded Jamie I needed "professional help," and for several months, they both badgered me about it. Jamie even made an appointment for me with a psychiatrist in

Jacksonville and drove me there to make sure I kept it. But the man sat and stared at me and I stared back. I didn't cry. I'd moved beyond tears. The psychiatrist told Jamie he could force me into a psych unit for a couple of days, but Jamie didn't have the heart for that.

Maggie didn't like me. My early fears about that had come true, and who could blame her? She cried when I'd take her from Jamie's arms, sometimes screaming as if my hands were made of cold steel instead of flesh and blood.

"Dada!" she'd scream, reaching for him. "Dada!"

By her first birthday, she knew five words, recognizable to those close to her. *Dada. Bih,* which referred to her pacifier. *Missu,* which seemed to mean Miss Sara. *Nana,* which meant banana. And *wah,* which was water. She had no word for me.

Sara had become the closest thing I had to a friend, in spite of how I'd tried to push her away when Maggie was a baby. She'd bring us meals, occasionally do our grocery shopping and suggest ways I could deal with Maggie's developing person- ality. She had no children of her own, yet she knew better than I did how to mother my daughter.

One morning when Jamie had been called to the fire station and I was alone with Maggie, I had a sudden spurt of energy and decided to take her outside to the beach. It was Septem- ber and the weather was warm and mild.

Maggie screamed the whole time I changed her into her ruffly pink bathing suit.

"We'll go out on the beach and make a sand castle!" I said. "We'll have such fun!" My hands shook as I slipped the straps over her shoulders. *What mother is nervous about dressing her sixteen-month-old child?* I chided myself.

She continued screaming while I doused her with sunscreen, but calmed down as we walked onto the deck. I picked up her pail and shovel, and she held my hand as we toddled down the steps to the beach. We sat in the damp sand close to the water and I built a little sand castle, trying to engage her, but she preferred running through the waves where they splashed against the shore.

I was adorning the sand castle with shell fragments when Maggie suddenly screamed. I looked up to see her crouched over, still as a statue.

"Dada!" she wailed.

I ran to her and saw blood trickling from her hand.

"What did you do, Maggie?" I grabbed her hand. "What happened?"

I spotted a narrow, splintery board stuck in the sand, water flowing over it. Picking it up with my free hand, I saw the rusty nail jutting from the surface.

"Dada!" Maggie screamed again, the blood running from her hand onto mine.

Scooping her into my arms, I ran with her to the cottage. She wailed in my ear as I opened the door and darted toward the kitchen sink.

I turned at the sound of footsteps on the deck and saw Marcus through the window. He'd been fired a few days earlier after showing up plastered at work and falling off a roof. At that moment, I was glad he'd lost his job and was home. I needed help.

He pushed open the door. "What happened?"

"She cut her hand on a rusty nail!" I said, turning on the water.

Marcus moved swiftly toward us. "Good thing her mom's a nurse," he said.

I was a nurse. I'd nearly forgotten. It seemed as though some other woman had gone through nursing school and worked in a pediatrician's office. Some happy, capable woman.

Maggie screamed, trying to squirm out of my arms, blood splattering everywhere.

"Hold her!" I said.

Marcus wrapped his arms around Maggie's little body, capturing her unharmed hand with his so she could no longer fight me off. "It's okay, Mags," he said.

I straightened Maggie's arm to hold it under the faucet as water flowed over the wound. It was deep and ragged across her palm. She'd need stitches. A tetanus shot.

Maggie's wails turned to earsplitting screams. I wanted to grab her hand *hard* and twist it clean off her wrist. I could imagine the cracking, grinding feeling of it. Letting go of her, I jumped back from the sink. "I can't do this!" I started to cry.

"Yes, you can." Marcus was so close I could feel his boozy breath against my ear. "You have a clean dish towel?"

I fumbled in the drawer near the stove, pulling out a dish towel. Still crying, I rinsed Maggie's hand again, then pressed the towel to her palm.

"She needs stitches, doesn't she?" Marcus asked.

"I can't do this, Marcus," I said again. My voice was a child's whine in my ears. I wasn't even sure what I was talking about. What couldn't I do? I hated myself.

"She'll be okay." Marcus misinterpreted my tears.

I nodded, sniffling. The dish towel, where I held it to Maggie's hand, was turning red.

"We've got to get her to urgent care," he said.

I nodded again.

"Come on," Marcus said. "I'll drive. You hold her and keep pressure on her hand."

He shoved Maggie into my arms, and I followed him outside to the driveway.

Together, we managed to buckle Maggie into her car seat. I sat next to her, trying to keep pressure on her hand while she screamed and screamed and called out for her daddy.

When we arrived at urgent care, I longed to hand Maggie over to the staff, but they wanted me to hold her as they cleaned and stitched her cut, erroneously thinking that, as her mother, I would be a comfort to her. I looked down at her dark curls as the doctor worked on her. Beautiful curls. Huge tears glistened on her jet-black eyelashes. Why didn't I feel anything for her? How could I be holding my own frightened, hurting child and feel nothing? I pictured my bed. How good it would feel to crawl under the covers! I could call Sara to come watch Maggie so I could sleep. I had it all planned out, my mind a million miles away as they worked on my baby, whose screams might have been made by a machine for all they touched me.

"It's okay, Mama." The young female doctor smiled at me as she finished bandaging Maggie's hand. "She's going to be fine. She'll just have an extra lifeline across her palm. Too bad we can't all be that lucky."

That night, Jamie sat on the edge of the bed as I burrowed beneath the covers.

"What would you have done if Marcus hadn't been here?" he asked.

I thought about the question. What *would* I have done? I remembered the image of twisting Maggie's hand from her arm and shook my head quickly to make it go away.

"Why are you shaking your head?" he asked.

"I don't know."

"You could have called me."

"Jamie." I wrapped my hand around his arm. "I want to leave."

He tilted his head to one side. "What do you mean, leave?"

"You and Maggie would be better off without me." It was not the first time I'd said those words in the past sixteen months, but it was the first time he didn't contradict me. Whatever Jamie and I'd once had together had disappeared. We rarely made love. We hardly spoke to each other. He'd stopped trying to understand me, to empathize with me, the way he'd stopped trying to empathize with Marcus. "I don't trust myself with her," I said. "With being able to take care of her."

Jamie looked down at my hand on his arm and covered it with his own. "Are you saying you want a separation?" he asked.

I nodded. The word itself brought me relief. "I'm not sure where I'd go, though." That uncertainty was the only thing that scared me.

"You'd stay here," he said, and I knew he'd already thought this through, that he'd been thinking of it for a while. Even planning it. "Sara and Steve have a spare room I can move into. I'll pay them a little rent. They can use the money."

I gasped. "Don't leave Maggie with me!"

Jamie shook his head. "She'd come with me," he said. "That's the whole point. You…I don't know what's wrong with you, Laurie, but whatever it is, it's interfered with you being able to be a good mother to Maggie. If I'm staying with the Westons, Sara would be right there to help with Maggie when I get called to the fire station or can't take her to work with me or whatever."

It seemed like a perfect solution and I was grateful he'd figured everything out and I didn't need to do a thing. I was a shitty mother. A shitty wife.

"Okay," I said, closing my eyes. "Thank you. That sounds good."

And I rolled onto my side to face the wall.

Chapter Eighteen

Maggie

MONDAY MORNING, I DROVE ANDY TO school and faked like I was going into the building with him, but once he was out of sight, I went back to my car and drove to Surf City. I hadn't slept all night. It had been more than two weeks since the fire, but those posters from the memorial service were still on the back of my eyelids every time I closed my eyes. Around two in the morning, I got up and drove to The Sea Tender. I sat on the deck and cried, because I couldn't quiet my mind enough to make contact with Daddy. It'd been so long since I felt him with me! Every time I tried to still my thoughts, those posters popped up again. I wanted to grab that blue-eyed Jordy and that scared-looking little boy, Henderson, and Mr. Eggles, who'd probably saved Andy from getting pulverized by

Keith—I wanted to grab them and breathe life back into them. I kept saying, *"Please Daddy, please Daddy, please Daddy,"* like he could somehow magically make things better. But he wasn't coming. I finally decided something, though, sitting out there in the dark. I'd cut school today and go to that accountant, Mr. Gebhart, to ask how I could help with the fund-raising. I had to do *something* besides give money. That was the easy way out.

Mr. Gebhart's office was on the mainland side of Surf City and it wasn't open yet. I sat in the parking lot, listening to music on my iPod and trying to read *The Good Earth*. I was so behind. It was one thing not to be valedictorian, totally something else to flunk out in my senior year. No way I'd let that happen. I *had* to graduate, because once I was in college, Ben and I could pretend to start dating. Publicly. Mom and Uncle Marcus would freak, but they'd just have to deal. Then maybe after a year, we could get married. I hoped Ben wouldn't want to wait until I got out of college. We'd never talked about it. I just knew I wouldn't be able to wait that long. I didn't care about a big wedding and all that, like Amber. She had it all planned out. The flowers and the music and the color of her brides-maids' dresses, and I just wanted to say *grow up*. Ben and I could elope, for all I cared.

I'd fallen asleep when I heard the *tap, tap, tap* of stiletto heels walking past my car. I jerked awake and saw a woman unlock-ing Mr. Gebhart's office door.

I pulled out my earbuds, drank from my water bottle and followed her inside.

"Hey, honey." She was making coffee. "What can I do for you?"

"My name's Maggie Lockwood," I said, "and I—"

"You related to Andy?"

"Yes, ma'am. His sister."

She scooped coffee into the filter. "I bet you're real proud of him."

"Yes, ma'am."

"Unbelievable what that boy did. And wasn't he somethin' on the *Today* show?"

I smiled. "He was." No one with half a heart could have seen that interview and not fallen in love with my brother. He'd been too cute, all big brown eyes and jiggly knee and his simple view of the world that—as long as you weren't his teacher—couldn't help but suck you in. "I wanted to talk to Mr. Gebhart about helping with the fund-raising," I said.

"Oh, honey." She pushed the coffeemaker's On button, then sat down at her desk. "Mr. Gebhart only handles the money part of it. The donations. You need to talk to Dawn Reynolds. You know who she is?"

Oh, yeah. Unfortunately. "Yes, ma'am," I said. "I was hoping Mr. Gebhart could tell me what I could do, since I'm here right now."

"Well, he won't be in for another thirty minutes, and he's really not the one who knows what's going on," she said. "You go talk to Dawn, honey. You can find her at Jabeen's Java. She'll give you more work than you'll know what to do with."

I sat in my car across the street from Jabeen's for twenty minutes, trying to figure out what to do. Maybe there was some other way I could help. There were still six kids in the hospital—four at New Hanover and two at the burn unit at UNC in Chapel Hill. The elementary schoolkids had made cards for them and Amber and I'd volunteered to take them to the hospital in the next day or so, which I knew was going to really upset me but I had to do it. Still, that just wasn't enough.

I saw something move inside Jabeen's. Just a flash of white by the window. Someone's shirt or something. Suddenly, though, I spotted Uncle Marcus on the corner walking toward the café. I held my breath until he reached Jabeen's door and pulled it open. *Yes!* Instant courage. I wouldn't have to face Dawn alone.

I got out of my car and crossed the street.

"Hey, Uncle Marcus." I stopped behind him at the counter where Dawn was pouring coffee into a cardboard cup.

"Mags!" He grinned and gave me his usual one-armed hug. "What are you doing here?"

"I took off school this morning so I could talk to Dawn about volunteering."

Dawn looked up when she heard her name.

"You know—" I forced myself to look her in the eye "—for the Drury Memorial Family Fund."

Dawn snapped a plastic lid on the cup. "Well, bless your heart, Maggie," she said, handing the coffee to Uncle Marcus. "I can use all the help I can get."

I'd seen Dawn plenty of times, but not this close up. She was pretty, with reddish hair and freckled skin, but there were crow's-feet at the corners of her eyes and I realized I didn't know how old she was. A whole lot older than seventeen, that was for sure. The thought of Ben having sex with her made me feel nauseous.

"You know," she said, "I was hoping your high school would get involved in some kind of organized way, but so far, nothing."

"Maggie's gonna be valedictorian," Uncle Marcus bragged. "Maybe she could organize something at Douglas."

"I'm not going to be valedictorian, Uncle Marcus," I said, trying to get him to shut up.

"No?" He raised his eyebrows.

I shook my head. "I haven't told Mom yet, though, so—"

"My lips are sealed."

A woman next to me asked for a latte, and Dawn rang up the sale.

"Doesn't matter, sugar," Dawn said to me as she handed the woman her change. "You're going to graduate, right? That's what counts. But what d'ya think? Could you get something going at Douglas High?" She started working on the latte.

I liked the idea. I'd be doing something useful without having to actually work with Dawn. Douglas was great at car washes and pancake breakfasts, but maybe I could come up with something more original.

"Yeah, maybe," I said. "I'll talk to some of my friends and a couple of teachers and see what I can figure out."

"You're a doll!" Dawn said. "Call me in a few days and tell me what you've come up with."

Uncle Marcus's hand was on my shoulder. "Have a few minutes to sit?" he asked.

"Sure." I knew he was curious about the valedictorian thing. It was going to have to come out sooner or later.

We walked toward the table by the window, but before we got there, Reverend Bill came through the door and we had to do one of those move-to-the-left, move-to-the-right maneuvers as we tried to pass him. He didn't say anything and neither did we, and it felt really bizarre.

Uncle Marcus rolled his eyes at me as we sat down. "Reverend Personality," he whispered.

"Sara told Mom he orders some kind of giant fattening drink here every day," I whispered back.

"That must be all he has." Uncle Marcus looked down at his pager, then back at me. "So, Mags." He drew out my name. "You upset about not being valedictorian?"

I started to answer, but Reverend Bill suddenly walked up to our table and just stood there, skinny as a flagpole, not saying a word. We looked up at him.

"Reverend." Uncle Marcus nodded his head toward the third seat at our table. "You wanna join us?"

Reverend Bill hates my family, so I was totally shocked when he pulled out the chair and sat down. "I'm actually on my way to talk to Pete," he said to Uncle Marcus. "But I think you need to hear what I have to tell him."

Uncle Marcus looked like he was trying not to yawn, but he said, "And what's that?"

"Well." Reverend Bill lifted his cup and swirled the drink around a couple of times. "I went up to the hospital at UNC yesterday," he said. "As you know, one of my parishioners, Gracie Parry, is in the burn unit there, along with Keith Weston."

"Right," Uncle Marcus said. "How're they doing?"

"Gracie's being transferred to New Hanover tomorrow and she'll make a full recovery," he said, then added, "except she'll have some scarring on her—" he motioned toward his chest "—her torso."

"What about Keith?" I asked. I was afraid of what he would say. I loved Sara and although Keith could be a total asshole, I wanted him to get well.

"Keith Weston's improving, thank the Lord," he said.

"Glad to hear it," Uncle Marcus said.

"Yes, he's better." He sipped his drink. "But he's in a boatload of pain. That poor child was burnt mighty bad."

Uncle Marcus frowned. "Isn't he still in a coma?"

"They brought him out of it yesterday morning." Reverend Bill's lips curled up a little, like a twitch, then flattened out again. "He's able to talk now."

"Good," Uncle Marcus said. "I bet it was a comfort having you to talk to." He actually sounded like he meant it.

Reverend Bill looked at Marcus from beneath his bushy gray eyebrows. "I think it's the police he should be talking to."

I didn't like the way he said it, like he was saying *Nyah, nyah. I know something you don't know.*

"Well, we'll be interviewing him," Uncle Marcus said. "Did he give you some information about the fire?"

"Yes, he did," Reverend Bill said. "That's what I need to talk to Pete about."

"Spit it out, Reverend," Uncle Marcus almost snarled. I felt hot and sweaty all of a sudden.

"He told me about that fight he had with your nephew." He looked at me. "Your brother." Up till that moment, I wasn't sure he even realized who I was. "And he said that shortly prior to the fight, he happened to look out the window and saw Andy Lockwood walking around outside the church."

"He wouldn't have been outside," I said. "It was a lock-in."

"You haven't heard all I have to say, Miss Lockwood."

God. What a snotty freak this guy was.

"So, go on," Uncle Marcus said.

"That's a right sick boy in the hospital there," Reverend

Bill said. "I don't see as he has much cause to be making things up."

"So what else did he say?" Uncle Marcus was getting impatient.

"Just that he didn't think anything of it at the time, since your nephew's known for doing strange things. But when the fire started, he couldn't help but wonder if Andy had something to do with it. Since it started outside and all."

"What's this about a window?" Uncle Marcus asked. "The windows in the church are stained glass. How'd he look out of them?"

"My job wasn't to interrogate the boy," Reverend Bill said. "It was to provide comfort. But since he volunteered that information, I thought it important the investigators have it. I'll leave a message for Pete and Flip Cates in case you choose not to tell them what I've told you."

Ouch. "Get off it, Rev," Uncle Marcus said. "I'll not only tell him, I'll make sure we talk to Keith ourselves today."

"Maybe you should stay out of it. You've got a bias, don't you think?"

"It'll be taken care of," Uncle Marcus said.

Reverend Bill scraped back his chair and stood up. "Good day." He nodded to me.

As soon as Reverend Bill was out the door, Uncle Marcus got to his feet.

"I've gotta run, babe." He bent over to kiss my cheek. "Don't worry about that whole Reverend Bill thing. I'm sure it's nothing." He headed for the door. "Love ya," he called over his shoulder.

"You, too." I stared after him, thinking about Keith. I knew his arms and half his face had been burned. What did that feel like? When I was a kid, I touched the handle of a hot frying pan. It was a small burn. Mom cut an aloe leaf from the plant she kept on the windowsill and rubbed the juice onto the burn, but it still hurt enough to make me cry. How could anyone tolerate pain like that on so much of his body? My eyes filled, thinking of Keith going through that. I didn't want to cry in public. Especially not in front of Dawn. I got up to leave, but even outside in the fresh air, Keith was still stuck in my mind.

Why would he lie about Andy being outside? And why would Andy be out there? I didn't believe it; he knew the whole point of a lock-in was to stay put. I was afraid, though, that Keith might screw things up by spreading lies about Andy…and even more afraid he could be telling the truth.

Chapter Nineteen

Marcus

DAMN, IT WAS HOT IN KEITH'S HOSPITAL ROOM.

I'd driven the three hours to Chapel Hill with my pickup windows down. Sucked in fresh air like I was storing it. I knew what it would be like at the burn center. Sure enough, the smell of bleach and ruined flesh nearly knocked me over when I walked into Keith's room. I'd forgotten, though, about the heat. Ninety degrees at least in there.

Keith was asleep. His arms and hands lay above the covers in massive bandages. Five surgical pins protruded from the bandage covering his left hand. Thick gauze padded the left side of his face, though the right side looked nearly untouched. Just like he'd sat out in the sun too long. An IV ran beneath the covers, probably to a port in his chest.

I pulled a chair close to his bed. Breathed through my mouth. Sat there without saying a word until I was sure I could speak without a catch in my voice.

I leaned forward. "Keith?"

Nothing. I was ready to say his name again when he made a humming sound and his right eyelid slowly opened. He turned his head toward me, flinching.

"*You,*" he said.

Me, what? What did I hear in that one word? Disgust? Disappointment? Or was I projecting my own feelings on him? How many times had I asked myself, *What if we'd gotten there one minute sooner? What if we'd had one more firefighter?* Would it have made a difference?

"How're you feeling?"

"Like shit." His words were slurred. "How's it look like I'm feeling?"

"I'm sorry," I said. "I know you're hurting bad, but I have to tell you, I'm glad to see you awake and talking."

He closed his eyes.

"Reverend Bill told me you remembered some things from the night of the fire. If you're up to it, I'd like to hear what you remember."

He groaned, shifting a little on the bed. "No, you wouldn't."

"Why do you say that?"

"Your nephew, is why," he said, his eye still shut. "He started the fire."

"What makes you think that?"

"He was...walk around church...just before it started."

"Keith?" I moved my chair until my knees were up against his bed. "Try to stay awake for a few more minutes, all right?"

No response. I kept going. "My understanding is that you and he were in a fight just before the fire started, so that would place Andy inside right before the fire."

His eye fluttered open. "Place him?" It came out like *playsh um?* "Is that investigator talk?"

"I get that you're angry," I said. "You have every right to be angry at what happened."

Tears pooled in his eye. "Why *me?*" he asked. "Why the fuck *me?*"

I took a tissue from the box on the nightstand and blotted his cheek. "I know," I said. "It doesn't seem fair." How much did he know about the other kids at the fire? I wasn't going to be the one to say he was lucky to be alive.

"I saw Andy outside," he growled, "just before the fight, which started because he came onto Layla." He sniffled and started to lift his arm like he wanted to wipe his nose, till he remembered. "Shit," he said. "I can't do nothin' for myself."

I reached toward him with the tissue again, but he turned his head.

"No," he said. "Don't."

"Where were *you* when you saw him outside?" I lowered the tissue to my thigh.

"Inside."

"What part of the church?"

"By the window."

"Which window, Keith?"

He hesitated. "In that office or whatever—" he winced, hunching his shoulders for a second "—back of the church. I looked out the window and there he was."

I remembered the small room at the back of the church. It

was for brides to primp in. That sort of thing. It did have a clear-paned window or two. Or at least, it used to.

Snot was running toward his lips now, and when I reached with the tissue again, he let me take care of it.

"Why were you back there?" I asked.

"What's it matter?" He answered quickly, like he'd expected the question. "I was just hanging out."

I'd let it slide for now. "Were you alone?"

"Yes."

"And it was dark out, right?"

"Must of been a moon or something, 'cause it was light enough for me to tell it was Andy."

"What was he doing?"

Keith licked his lips. They looked dry, the skin cracked and flaking.

"Do you want a sip of water?" I asked.

He shook his head and shut his eye. I wasn't ready to let him fall back to sleep.

"Keith?" I prodded.

"He was walking by the side of the church," he said. "Looking at, like, where the ground and wall meet."

"You could see that?"

He opened his eye to cut me a look. "I'm not fucking making it up."

"Did he have anything in his hands?"

"Don't remember."

"Could it have been another boy who looked like Andy?"

He tried to laugh, but coughed instead. I held the plastic cup of water for him and he took a sip through the straw. "Only one Andy Lockwood," he said, shutting his eye again. "One's enough."

I'd let him sleep. Didn't want to hear more, anyway. I shouldn't have been there in the first place.

I called Flip Cates as soon as I got to the hospital lobby.

"Cates," he answered.

"It's Marcus, Flip," I said. "I'm taking myself off the investigation."

"I'm glad to hear it," Flip said. "Because I was about to take you off myself."

"You talked to Reverend Bill?"

"Yes."

"I don't believe Andy could be responsible for that fire," I said, "but as long as his name's getting tossed around, I figure I'd better—"

"There's something else," Flip interrupted.

"What?"

"A woman called the hotline last night. She said she was driving by the church the night of the fire on her way to Topsail Beach and saw a kid—a boy—walking alone outside the building."

"What time? Did she give a description?"

"She was vague on time. Between eight and nine. It was dark out, but she thought the boy had dark or brown hair and looked around thirteen. A young teenager or preteen, is what she said."

"Did you get her name? Why's she just calling now?"

"We got her name. She was renting a cottage the weekend of the fire and left that Sunday morning to go back to Winston-Salem. She didn't make the connection between what she saw and the fire until the hotline number was broadcast on her local news yesterday."

I rubbed the back of my neck. It felt like a noose was tightening around it.

"We're going to ask Laurel if we can search Andy's room," Flip said.

I don't know why I was surprised. If we had this kind of information on another kid, I'd expect the same action. But Andy? It seemed like overkill.

"Okay," I said, after a minute. "Keep me in the loop, all right?"

Chapter Twenty

Andy

I WAS MR. POPULARITY AT SCHOOL TODAY. That's what Miss Betts called me. They showed the *Today* show on the TV in all the classrooms. Everybody saw me. My friend Darcy said I was awesome. A boy I don't really know said, "Next, your ugly mug'll be on the cover of *People* magazine." He was the only one who said a mean thing, and I didn't mind. Could I really be on the cover of *People?*

Miss Betts had me tell what it was like to be on TV in front of everybody. *Don't brag,* I kept saying inside my head. *Remember, we don't brag.*

After school, I sat on the bench at the bus place when my friend Max showed up.

"Hey, Andy," he said. He was in the ninth grade but was way

taller than me. "I heard about your lighter," he said. "That sucked."

"Yeah," I said. "If you go on a plane, don't put a lighter in your sock."

"I'll remember that," Max said. "You got any coffin nails on ya?"

"Sure." I took off my backpack and put it on the bench. I reached into the secret zipper place to find my cigarettes. I liked how Max called them "coffin nails." When you first had one, you coughed a lot. I didn't get the "nails" part, though.

I found my package of coffin nails and gave him one. I took one for me, too, and he lit them with a cool green lighter.

"You're in the market for a new lighter now, I guess, huh?" he asked.

I used to think "in the market" meant going to the store, but I now I got it. "Yeah," I said. "You wanna trade me for that one?"

Me and Max were good traders. I got my old lighter from him. And one time a pen with water in it that had a girl in a bathing suit. You turned the pen upside down to make her bathing suit come off and then she was naked. I only had the pen for one day, because Max wanted it back. He traded me a whole package of cigarettes for it.

"You can have this lighter for five bucks," he said.

"I don't have five bucks," I said. "I'll trade the rest of my coffin nails for it."

"You only got four left, dorko. What else you got in that book bag?"

I took out my three books, my inhaler, my iPod. Two sticks of gum. A matchbox car.

"Why you carryin' around a retarded matchbox car?" he asked.

"I don't know," I said. I didn't. Matchbox cars were for little kids.

I saw something at the bottom of my book bag. "Look!" I pulled out a picture a girl named Angie sent me. I was sure Max wouldn't call the picture retarded.

"Oh, mama!" Max licked his lips. He looked like he wanted to *eat* Angie's picture.

"It's my favorite," I said. "I have four pictures."

"Who is she?" Max asked.

"My friend Angie."

"Your friend Angie's got some bodacious hooters."

Angie sat on a motorcycle in her picture with shorts and a shirt that let you see a lot of her hooters. Hooters are breasts. One day I said, "Emily's got almost no hooters," and Mom started yelling how we *never* call breasts hooters. But around Max, I still did.

"I'll trade you the lighter for this picture," Max said.

I had to think hard. I'd miss Angie's picture a whole lot. It was bent though. Kind of crinkly from being in my book bag. Max's lighter wasn't bent at all.

"Okay," I said. We traded fair and square. I'd have to hide the cool green lighter good, like in the secret zipper part of my book bag where I kept the coffin nails. I didn't like hiding things from Mom, but sometimes I had to.

The bus came and I got on it but Max didn't. He took a different bus than me. I waved to him, but he was staring at Angie's picture and didn't see me. I missed Angie's picture all of a sudden. I'd probably have more in the mail when I got home, though. Then maybe Mom or Maggie could take me to the store.

I wanted to see if my face was on the cover of *People*.

Chapter Twenty-One

Laurel

FROM THE PORCH OF OUR HOUSE, I could see the lights on the mainland across the sound. It was the first night warm enough to be outside without a sweater, and I welcomed the salty balm of the air as I sat on the old glider, my feet propped up against the railing. Maggie was studying at Amber Donnelly's and I'd finally gotten Andy settled down enough to fall asleep and could take a minute for myself.

I'd really had to rein Andy in today, his first day at school since being on the *Today* show. I had to remind him not to brag about his heroism or newly found celebrity status. I was beginning to wonder if appearing on TV had been a good idea. Today's mail brought dozens more cards and letters from around the country, and I knew he was being inundated with e-mail. For a boy whom the world ordinarily treated with sympathy, curiosity or suspicion, such attention was heady stuff.

I heard a car door slam, the sound rippling across the water. Standing up, I peered around the corner of the house and saw the tail end of a pickup in my driveway. Marcus?

The doorbell rang as I walked back into the house. I pulled the door open to see him standing on the front porch.

"Is everything okay?" I asked. It was unusual for Marcus to show up like that, and I thought of Maggie, the only one of my small family not safe at home.

"Mostly okay." The porch light caught concern in his smile. "Just wanted to run a thing or two by you. Can I come in?"

"What does mostly okay mean?" I asked as he walked past me into the living room.

"Let's sit on the porch," he said. "It's a great night."

I led the way back through the family room to the porch. "Do you want some iced tea?" I asked.

"I don't need anything."

I sat on the glider once again, but without the sense of calm I'd had earlier. I couldn't recall the last time I'd been alone with Marcus. He visited Maggie and Andy frequently, because I decided long ago that whatever happened in the past, I wouldn't stand in the way of his relationship with them. I knew he loved them. My guidelines were simple: always let me know where you're taking them and when they'll be back, and no boats of any sort. So he visited them, but he didn't visit me. My arms automatically folded themselves across my chest, holding everything in. Holding me together.

"I wanted to let you know I'm not part of the fire investigation any longer," he said, sitting down on the old wicker rocker.

I wasn't sure why he'd make a special trip to tell me that. "Because Andy was there?" I asked.

"Because…there's some small…right now it's only hearsay and I'm sure it will stay only hearsay, but—"

I saw his discomfort, and it wasn't at being alone with me. It was something else.

"But what?" I prompted.

"We've had some reports that Andy was outside the church shortly before the fire."

I still wasn't getting it. "What do you mean?"

"Look, this is all confidential, okay?" he said. "I shouldn't even be telling you, but I don't want you to be blindsided by it."

"By *what?*"

"I went up to Chapel Hill today and talked to Keith Weston, and—"

"They've taken him out of the coma?" That sounded like good news.

"Yes. And Reverend Bill went to see him and Keith told him he saw Andy outside shortly before the fire. So I went to see him myself and he told me the same thing."

"Why would he be outside?" I asked.

"I don't know. But we also had a woman call the hotline to report seeing a boy with…a small stature outside the church that evening. And Emily Carmichael said that Andy disappeared for a while before the fire. Then there's that bit about him hiding a lighter in his sock."

"Oh, Marcus," I said. "You don't honestly think Andy had anything to do with the fire, do you?"

"No, I don't. But no one's reported seeing anyone *else* outside. So he has to be ruled out."

I was more annoyed than worried. "Okay, Marcus," I said. "So let's say it *was* Andy. Where did he get the gasoline or whatever was used? How did he get it to the church, huh?"

"I know it doesn't make sense," he said. "And I'm sorry he's being dragged into this. I just wanted you to hear it from me first, all right? We—they—have to explore every possibility."

Panic rose inside me, expanding in my chest. "I'm mad!" My fists curled around the edge of the seat cushion. "I'm mad you could…go along with this. That you could even *think* about it. You need to tell whoever's doing the investigation to leave Andy out of it."

Marcus didn't respond, and I continued. "Keith's a trouble-maker," I said. "He smokes dope and he's done things you don't know about."

"I know."

"You *know?* You know about the truancy? Possession of marijuana?"

He nodded. "Sara talks to me sometimes."

I felt a kernel of jealousy that surprised me. Sara was my best friend. Why didn't I know that she'd confided in Marcus? Why didn't I know that Marcus cared enough to talk to her about Keith?

"Well, maybe *Keith* set the fire," I said. "Why else would he be trying to blame it on someone else? Someone who can't really defend himself?"

"He'll be questioned, but let's face it, why would he set a fire and get trapped by it?"

"Why would *Andy* set a fire and get trapped by it?" I snapped.

"Well, he didn't get trapped, did he?"

I stared at him. "It was just lucky he found his way out."

"Or he wanted to be seen as a hero, and he's the only one who seemed to know the safe way out of the building."

"Marcus!"

He held up his hands as if to ward off a blow. "Devil's advocate, Laurel," he said. "I'm just trying to think the way the investigators will."

"Of which you're one."

"Hi, Uncle Marcus."

I looked up quickly at the sound of Andy's voice. He stood in the doorway between the family room and the porch in his pajamas, his eyes squinty with sleep. I changed my expression from angry to benign.

"Hey, Andy." Marcus got up and pulled Andy into a hug.

Judas, I thought.

"Are you fighting with Mom?" Andy asked.

"We're having a noisy talk," Marcus said. I was glad he could find his voice. Mine was trapped somewhere behind my breast-bone. "You ever have noisy talks with people?"

"Sometimes." Andy smiled.

"Go back to bed, sweetie," I managed to say.

"I'll take him." Marcus put his hand on Andy's shoulder. "Come on, Andy."

I thought of stopping him, concerned he would say something to Andy that would worry or confuse him, but I seemed to be frozen to the glider. And, anyway, Marcus wouldn't want Andy upset any more than I would.

I listened to their footsteps on the stairs inside the house.

I remembered the agent interviewing Andy at the hospital,

how he'd needed me as a translator of sorts. If they talked to him again, I had to make sure I was present. I imagined him being questioned by interrogators not so much *smarter* than him, but more adept at thinking and reasoning. People with an agenda. I couldn't let that happen.

When he returned to the porch, Marcus surprised me by sitting next to me on the glider. He gave me a hug and for a moment, I was too stunned to pull away. But only for a moment.

"Marcus, please don't."

He let go, then leaned forward with a sigh, elbows on his knees.

"I know Andy's innocent, and that'll come out," he said quietly. "But there are a lot of people who don't know him. Who don't see what you and I see when we look at him. They see an uncool kid who wants desperately to be cool. To be a hero."

"It's…it's ridiculous." I still felt unsettled by the sudden hug. I'd forgotten how he smelled. It was a scent I would always associate with longing. With the sea. With deceit.

"I'll go," he said, standing up. "Stay here—I'll let myself out." But he didn't make a move toward the door. Instead, he put his hands in his pockets and looked toward the dark water of the sound and the lights on the mainland. He wanted to say something more to me; I could see the war inside him.

"What?" I asked.

He looked down at me, letting out a sigh. "They want to search Andy's room," he said. "Look into getting a lawyer, Laurel."

Chapter Twenty-Two

Marcus

WHEN I GOT HOME FROM LAUREL'S, I made a Coke-and-peanuts cocktail, then climbed to the roof of my tower to think. There were a couple of old lounge chairs up there, but I liked sitting on the oceanside edge of the roof itself, my feet hanging over the side of the building. A couple of women I'd dated refused to sit on the edge with me. One was so afraid of heights that she wouldn't sit on the roof at all. *You're a fool if you don't install a railing up here,* she'd told me. Didn't bother calling *her* again.

Laurel and Jamie once sat up here with me. It was a hot summer night when I was still doing the renovations. I must have spoken to Jamie on the phone, telling him I was wiped. Next thing I knew, they'd gotten a babysitter and showed up with a bowl of gulf shrimp and a bottle of sparkling cider. We sat on the edge of the roof for an hour at least, talking and eating, dropping shrimp tails onto the patio below for me to clean up the next morning. Maybe Laurel had been uncomfortable sitting between Jamie and me, but she hadn't been at all afraid to sit on the edge of the roof.

I shook my head now, thinking of her. Man, I'd kicked a few holes in my ethical boundaries today. Taking it upon myself to talk to Keith before anyone else could. Telling Laurel about the search. But she had to know how serious this had become. I pictured her after I left, going into Andy's room, watching him sleep. He might have a little smile on his face. I'd seen him sleep like that a time or two.

In my mind's eye, Laurel reached out, pulling the covers over Andy's shoulders. I saw them both—two people who'd always have my heart—and I wished I could protect them from what I was afraid their future held.

Chapter Twenty-Three

Laurel
1990

I SLEPT NEARLY NONSTOP FOR DAYS AFTER JAMIE and Maggie left. I can't say I was happy they were gone, because nothing made me happy, but with Jamie gone, I could sleep all day if I wanted to without feeling guilty. With Maggie gone, I didn't have to feel her disdain or listen to her cry or worry about plunging a knife into her heart or throwing her into the sea. I didn't have to feel Jamie's helplessness. So, while there may not have been happiness, there was at least relief in my solitude.

But after three or four days, I awakened to find Marcus standing near the end of my bed, silhouetted against the evening sky. His arms were folded across his chest. I was so dopey with sleep that I wasn't even startled to see him there.

"I'm supposed to check on you," he said. "Make sure you eat and all. Have you been out of this bed since they left?"

I had to think. "To use the bathroom," I said.

"How 'bout to eat?"

I knew I'd had water and apple juice, but I couldn't remember eating anything. "Not really."

Marcus shook my foot beneath the blanket. "Get up and come next door. I picked up some shrimp, and I'll make grits. You'll feel better with some food in you."

"No, thanks." It was so much easier just to dig deeper under the covers.

"Do you know it stinks in this room?" he asked. "This whole house?"

I nearly laughed. "I bet you vacuum every day," I said. Marcus lived in Talos like the irresponsible, alcoholic, twenty-one-year-old bachelor he was.

"Yeah, well, my house doesn't stink."

I recalled the stench of stale beer and cigarettes from my last visit next door, but I was too tired to argue. "Go away, Marcus." I rolled on my side and put the pillow over my head.

The next thing I knew, he'd pulled the covers off me and was dragging me in my underpants and T-shirt toward the bathroom. "You've been sleeping in the same clothes for days, I bet," he said.

I didn't fight him as he pushed me, still dressed, into the shower and turned on the faucet. I screamed as the cold water spiked against my skin. He leaned against the shower door when I tried to push it open.

"I'm going to get pneumonia!" I shrieked.

"It'll warm up soon enough."

"Marcus, you bastard!" I backed into a corner of the shower to try to avoid the cold spray.

"You got shampoo in there? Soap?"

I looked at the bottles on the little ledge built into the tiled wall. "Yes," I said, giving in.

"Water warmin' up?"

It was. I ducked my head under the spray and felt it thrum against my scalp. "Yes."

"All right. Got any clean towels? The one out here's growing fungus or something."

"In the little closet."

The closet door squeaked open.

"I'll put this old one in the hamper, then I'll wait for you in the living room."

He was stripping the bed when I came out of the bathroom wrapped in a clean towel.

"These sheets are revolting," he said, bundling them into his arms.

"Oh, shut up." I clutched the towel tightly around me and leaned against the wall.

"I'll start a wash and then meet you at my house. If you're not there in twenty minutes, I'm comin' back for you."

I closed my eyes, waiting for him to leave. I heard him walk out the front door and clomp down the stairs to the laundry closet on the beach level. Resigned, I pulled the curtains closed against the darkening sea and began to dress.

I supposed having Marcus check up on me was Jamie's way of making his brother work for a living. Marcus had come over to the house one day, shortly before Jamie left with Maggie, and the two of them got into another of their heated battles.

"You need a job!" Jamie'd shouted at him. Marcus was the only person I'd ever heard him raise his voice to. I was in bed, and I pulled the pillow over my head but could still hear him. "All you do is surf, party, sleep, screw and drink!"

"I *don't* need a job," Marcus countered. "Neither do you. We're rich. Did you forget?"

"We weren't raised to be slugs," Jamie said.

"Let's face it, bro," Marcus said. "You were raised one way and I was raised another."

"You live off the income from family properties," Jamie said. "Don't you think you could manage a few hours a week on repairs and maintenance?"

"I suppose you'd expect me to be clean and sober while I worked?"

"Damn straight," Jamie said.

"Not interested," Marcus had answered.

Climbing the steps to the front door of Talos nearly did me in. I had no wind and my muscles felt flaccid and shaky. I opened the door without knocking and saw him standing at the stove, spatula in hand.

"Much better!" he said, appraising me. He wore the cute grin that had so captivated me when he was sixteen. "And you're almost smiling," he added.

Was I? I'd thought the muscles in my face had forgotten how.

The sharp smell of shrimp filled his kitchen. He pulled out a stool at the breakfast bar. "You better sit down before you keel over. What do you want to drink?" He was already well into a bottle of beer, and some empties littered the counter.

"Juice?" I lowered myself to the stool and put my elbows on the breakfast bar as Marcus opened his refrigerator.

"No juice. Beer?"

"Ugh. Have any wine?"

"No, but I do have these." He pulled out a wine cooler and set it on the counter. "I keep them around for the ladies."

I wrinkled my nose. "Just water," I said.

He opened the bottle. "Try it. You'll like it."

I took a sip. I could barely taste it. Although my sense of smell seemed overly developed, my sense of taste was shot, but the drink was cool and wet and I figured it would do.

Marcus set a plate of grits topped with shrimp and cheese in front of me. I liked shrimp and grits—at least, the old me did. The before-Maggie me. But I had no appetite at all anymore. My stomach was concave. When I woke up each morning, I could see the little mountains of my hipbones below the covers.

"It looks good, Marcus. I'm just not really hungry."

"Girl, you're wasting away." He circled my wrist with his hand. "Just eat as much as you can."

I'd been through all this with Jamie. With Sara. And I'd remained stubborn and unyielding with them. There was something about Marcus cooking for me, though. The second-best brother. I didn't want to hurt his feelings, so I slipped my fork into the grits and ate a bite. They might as well have been little bits of Styrofoam, but I managed to eat half of what was in my bowl. It was more than I'd eaten in months.

"Stay here for a while and we'll just veg," he said once we'd eaten. "I've got a couple of movies. Gotta get lonely over there by yourself."

I thought of telling him how much I liked the solitude, but it seemed cold and horrible to admit I liked being separated from my child and husband.

As soon as I stood up, I realized I had a bit of a buzz, and it was not at all unpleasant. I carried another wine cooler with me to the living room. Jamie and I rarely drank, and since Marcus moved out, there'd been no alcohol in the house at all.

Marcus knelt down in front of the VCR, two tapes in his hands. "Do you want to see *When Harry Met Sally* or *Born on the Fourth of July?*"

"I don't know anything about either of them," I said. "Put on whichever is lighter."

He inserted *When Harry Met Sally* into the VCR and sat on the opposite end of the sofa from me. We kicked off our shoes and put our feet up on his heavy wooden coffee table. I'd forgotten to put socks on and my feet were cold, so he loaned me a pair of his. They were too big and, as I wiggled my feet, the toes flopped back and forth.

I slid down on the sofa and lost myself in the movie. It made me giggle. When was the last time I'd giggled? Right after Meg Ryan faked an orgasm in the restaurant, Marcus said he was hungry again, so we stopped the movie while he made popcorn in the microwave.

"So what d'you think about the message in this movie, Laurel?" Marcus set the bowl of popcorn on the coffee table and handed me another wine cooler.

"There's a message?" I giggled again.

"Can men and women be friends without letting...you know...sex get in the way?"

"Of course!" I said. "You and I are friends."

"But you're my sister-in-law, so that's different."

"Well, I still think it's possible." I took a handful of popcorn. More Styrofoam, but it went down easy with the wine cooler. The image of Meg Ryan faking an orgasm in the restaurant slipped into my mind. "Speaking of orgasms," I said impulsively, "I had my first ever on the back of Jamie's bike."

Marcus's eyes widened. "That really happens? I thought it was a myth."

"Oh, it happens all right. There's something about fourth gear."

He laughed. "You're drunk."

"Am not." But I was and I knew it and I was grateful for it.

"Are, too." He grinned. "I like you drunk, though. Been a while since I've seen you look this happy."

I leaned forward for another handful of popcorn, but missed the bowl by inches. It swam in front of my eyes. I tried again, but moving my head made the room spin. Before *I'm going to be sick* was even a conscious thought, I threw up on Marcus's coffee table.

"Shit!" He sprang to his feet.

"Oh my God." Hands on either side of my head, I looked in disbelief at the pool of grits and masticated shrimp and wine cooler on his coffee table. "I'm so sorry."

Marcus darted for the kitchen. "My fault," he said. "I let you drink too much."

I was going to throw up again. I stood up, but fell against the side of the couch. Marcus came into my field of vision, a roll of paper towels in one hand, catching me by the arm with the other.

"To the bathroom," he said, half dragging me toward the hall.

I just made it to the toilet. He held my hair back as I got sick. When I was finally able to sit on the floor, my back against the shower door, he cleaned my face with a cool wash-cloth.

"I'm sorry," I murmured. "I made a mess in your living room."

"I'll clean it up. Stay right here."

I tried to say I'd help him, but the words wouldn't come out.

I must have fallen asleep—or passed out—because I woke up in a strange bed in a strange room. The door was closed, but I saw a line of light beneath it.

I sat up, my head pounding. "Marcus?"

In a moment the door opened and I winced against the light.

He walked into the room. "How d'ya feel?" he asked, sitting down on the bed.

"Did you have to carry me in here? Is this your bed?"

"Guest room. You know, the bedroom in the front of the house? And I only had to half carry you in here."

"What time is it?"

"Two in the morning."

"Why are you still up?"

He laughed. "I was afraid you were going to die on me. I told Jamie I'd get you to eat. He didn't say anything about getting you to drink, though." He patted my leg through the covers. "Can't hold your liquor, girl."

"I liked how I felt up until the time I threw up."

"Yeah, it was fun till then."

"What a mess. I'm really sorry." I giggled again, the sound surprising me, and Marcus smiled.

"C'mere, you," he said, gently lifting me into a hug. "You gotta promise me something, Laurel," he said.

"Mmm?"

"You'll try to work things out with Jamie. Because I want you to always be in my family. You're the only one who ever treated me like I was worth something."

"That's not true," I said into his shoulder. "Jamie treats you well."

"He kicked me out."

"You were a little shit."

Marcus was quiet for so long that I nearly fell asleep with my head on his shoulder.

"You're right," he finally said with a sigh. "We know our roles and we play them well. Jamie's the saint and I'm the sinner."

That night was the start of a new chapter in my life. Marcus and I ate dinner together at The Sea Tender or Talos most evenings, then watched TV or a movie, and I learned how many wine coolers I could drink so that I felt good without getting sick. Marcus usually cooked, but I shopped for any ingredients he needed, which felt like a huge step forward to me, since I hadn't grocery shopped in months. The outings to the store in Sneads Ferry wore me out and I usually napped when I came home, but I was no longer sleeping in my clothes or going for days without a shower. I looked forward to my evenings with him, although I worried at first that he felt the need to babysit me. I gradually realized he was choosing my company over that of his friends. We were proving *When Harry Met Sally* wrong, I thought. Men and women *could* be good friends and nothing more.

I started worrying about him. I felt scared when I'd see him out surfing alone, knowing he was probably wasted. I didn't want to lose him, not only because he was my brother-in-law and my friend, but also, frankly, because he was my drinking buddy.

The alcohol loosened my tongue, and I talked to Marcus in a way that I couldn't talk to Jamie or the therapist I'd seen or Sara. He was the only person I told about my fear of hurting Maggie.

"D'you miss her?" he asked me one night. We were curled up on opposite ends of the sofa at Talos.

I hugged my knees with my arms. "I miss..." There was no easy answer to his question. "I miss the woman I planned to be with her," I said. "The mother I expected to be. I thought I'd be such a great mother. Instead I'm the worst. I'm horrible."

"Don't say that."

"I'm actually *relieved* not to have her with me anymore." I plunked my forehead down on my arms. "I know that sounds terrible."

"You're too tired to take care of her," he said.

"That's not why I'm relieved." I looked him in the eye. "It's because I was afraid I was going to hurt her."

He laughed, but then realized I was serious. "You?" he asked. "You won't even go fishing because you think it's fish abuse."

"I know it sounds crazy, but I'd get frustrated with her and...I'd picture myself hurting her." I didn't want to tell him of the ways I'd imagined myself doing it. Those unwanted images that flew into my mind when I least expected them and made me feel both crazy and dangerous. I didn't want him to have to see them, too. "Just believe me," I said. "She's safer not being with me."

***

Once a week, Jamie would bring Maggie back to The Sea Tender. She was a beautiful child, with Jamie's large brown eyes and dark hair that already fell in silky waves over her delicate shoulders. I didn't see myself in her face at all. Maybe that's why she seemed more like a friend's child than my own. I wanted to feel love for her. When I'd see her get out of the car with Jamie, my heart would swell with a kind of longing, but it was as if the closer she came to me, the less I felt. I pretended, though.

"Hi, Maggie!" I'd say, in a voice that rang false to my own ears. "Would you like to play with your blocks? Or we could put together one of your puzzles?"

She'd cling to Jamie's leg, yet keep me in her field of vision. It would take all my energy and false cheer, but I could usually engage her in an activity if Jamie played along with us.

One day, Jamie gave me his usual hug when he arrived, then drew back with a quizzical look.

"Have you been drinking?" he asked.

My breath had given me away. "Just a wine cooler with lunch," I said.

"Be careful." He rested his big hand on Maggie's head. "You know alcohol's a depressant."

"Oh, I know." I brushed the comment aside. "You don't need to worry."

He smiled at me then. "You do seem a lot better these days," he said.

Alcohol might have been a depressant for most people, but it was having the opposite effect on me, I thought. It took away the ache inside me and let me feel a little bit like myself again.

The next time Jamie came over, I brushed my teeth and gargled with mouthwash. It sent a shiver up my spine to see my own deception. To realize I was drinking enough that I needed to hide it.

I was careful around Sara, too, in case Jamie told her to be on the lookout for my drinking. She'd occasionally bring lunch over, and I had the feeling she and Jamie had worked out some sort of schedule for their checking-up-on-Laurel visits.

One balmy November day, Sara suggested we go for a walk on the beach after lunch. "It's gorgeous out, Laurel," she said. "Do you feel up to it?"

My first thought was to plead exhaustion, but when I looked out the window, the sand sparkled and the sky and sea were the same rich shade of blue and I suddenly wanted to be walking in the sunshine.

"Sure," I said. "How chilly is it out?"

She was momentarily speechless at my response. "It's barefoot weather, believe it or not." She kicked off her tennis shoes and started tugging off her socks, leaning against the kitchen counter for support.

I took off my slippers and together we walked out on the back deck and down the steps to the beach. I felt a surge of happiness. How much was due to the splendor of the day or to the wine cooler I'd had before lunch, I couldn't say. I curled my toes deep into the cool sand as we started walking south on the beach.

"Bare feet in November!" Sara said. "I'm *never* going back to Michigan."

"Good," I said. "I'd hate for you to leave."

"Well, I'm not going anywhere, but things *are* about to change." She glanced at me, smiling. "I wanted to tell you before it became obvious." She rested her hand on her stomach.

"You're *pregnant?*"

She nodded. "Four months. Due in May."

"Congratulations!" I tried to get some oomph in my voice, but found myself suddenly consumed by envy. Sara would be a terrific mother—a mother filled with joy at the birth of her baby. "Is Steve excited?"

Sara laughed. "As excited as Steve gets. You know him. Always cool, calm and collected. That's why the military loves him, and he loves it."

Actually, I didn't know Steve very well. He was quiet and reserved and serious, and I sometimes had the feeling Sara liked it better when he was away on temporary duty, but maybe I was only projecting my own recent need to be apart from Jamie onto her.

I had a sudden thought. With a baby on the way, would Sara and Steve still want Jamie and Maggie living with them? I'd only been to their house once, and it was small. I was trying to formulate the question when Sara spoke again.

"You know that Jamie doesn't really want to be living with us, don't you? That he'd rather be here with you? He still loves you. He only left because you wanted him to."

"I know."

"Do you still love him?"

I blew out my breath and tipped my head back to search the sky for an answer. "I don't even love myself right now, Sara," I said finally, although an image of Marcus flickered in my mind. The warm gratitude I felt toward him was the closest feeling I had to love these days.

"I'm not sure it's the right thing for him not to live here. To separate you from your daughter."

I could read the writing on the wall and hated the way my heart sank. "Does he have to get out right away?" I asked. "You must need his room for the nursery."

"Actually, no," she said. "Maggie's in the third bedroom right now, but the baby will be in our room at least for a while, so it's not a problem. For the first week that we have the baby home, my mother will be coming from Michigan, so we'll need the room then, but other than that, Jamie and Maggie are welcome to stay as long as they want. Frankly, the rent helps. Plus, with Steve gone so much, Jamie comes in handy when the sink clogs up and the front door falls off its hinges and the toilet turns into Old Faithful."

I laughed, primarily with relief that my husband and child would not be coming home except for one week in May. "That all actually happened?" I asked.

"Last week," she said. "It was bizarre. Plus I'd miss Mags. She's such a delight."

I sidestepped a clump of seaweed. It jolted me, hearing her call Maggie "Mags," the way Jamie did. And it saddened me that Maggie was a delight around Sara and an uncomfortable little girl around me. How bonded had my daughter become to her? I didn't deserve any of the jealousy I felt.

"What happened, Laurel?" Sara asked. "I mean, you changed so much after Maggie was born, and here I am pregnant and I wonder if it could possibly happen to me."

I was glad of my sunglasses so she didn't see the way my eyes filled with tears.

"You'll be fine," I said. "I'm a freak of nature."

"Oh, no, Laurel. I think the baby blues got you and didn't let go."

"Well," I said, "I'm getting better." And I knew I would feel much, *much* better once I was back in The Sea Tender, a wine cooler in my hand.

Chapter Twenty-Four

Laurel

I BARELY SLEPT AT ALL THE NIGHT AFTER MARCUS told me that Andy was under suspicion for the arson. The words that kept running through my mind were *How absurd!* I wrote little speeches of indignation in my mind and nearly called Marcus in the wee hours of the morning because I needed to say the words out loud. *He is not capable of planning a crime, and he's certainly not capable of covering one up.*

I thought of the time he stole a candy bar while we stood in line at the grocery store when he was about five years old. I discovered it when I went to check his seat belt. I did what all good parents are supposed to do: I marched him back into the store and made him apologize to the manager, and I told him in no uncertain terms he was *never* to steal candy again. It was against the law.

A week later, though, I discovered he was carrying a toy water pistol when we got in the car after a trip to the pharmacy. He didn't even try to hide it.

"Where did you get that?" I asked him.

"In the store."

"I told you just last week it's against the law to steal!" I shouted.

"You said not to steal candy!" he shouted back at me.

Of course, he was no longer five years old. As frustrating as that experience had been, there was a cuteness about the story when I told it to friends. As he got older, his misunderstandings of the way the world worked were no longer quite so cute, as I'd discovered in the airport the week before. And people were not as quick to understand and forgive as the manager of the grocery store.

As soon as Maggie and Andy left for school, I went upstairs to Andy's room and stood in the doorway, trying to look at it through the eyes of a detective. On the surface, it looked quite neat. I'd drilled "everything in its place" into his head from the time he was little; otherwise his room would have been utter chaos. Even his bed was made. That was number one on his *Get Ready in the Morning* chart. It smelled a little stuffy, though. I opened the window that faced the sound and let in a tepid breeze.

I'd gotten him to pin some of the greeting cards and letters he'd received after the fire to his corkboard wall instead of strewing them around the room. There were about thirty on the board, and a large wicker basket on his dresser held the rest.

I went to his computer first. I had long ago installed parental monitoring software on both his and Maggie's computer, with their knowledge. I took the software off Maggie's a couple of years ago, at her reasonable request, deciding she was mature enough not to have her mother snooping through her life. She had a right to her privacy and was hardly the type to be taken in by a stranger in a chat room. It would probably be a long time before I could set Andy's computer free, though. I didn't like looking through his e-mail or instant messages, because they were always a reminder of his immaturity and lack of friends. His e-mails were usually about swim team practice and meets, or from Marcus or Emily. I didn't read the e-mails from Marcus and only a couple from Emily, whose spelling was so atrocious I wondered how Andy made sense of them. He had instant messages, the majority of which were from Maggie about little things—*Have an awesome day tomorrow!* I knew her motivation behind sending them, because I shared it. She wanted him to receive some IMs, the way his classmates did. I steeled myself for a few nasty ones from kids, because I knew they would be there. Andy would occasionally IM some random kid from school, someone he considered one of his many "friends." The nicer kids would IM him back with a non-committal response. But every once in a while, Andy would pick the wrong target. I read through them quickly with my new detective eyes.

Andy had received an IM from someone with the screen name *Purrpetual:* Thank U 4 saving my life! he or she had written.

Andy's response: Ur welcome. If I wasn't there U might of burned up.

I cringed. I'd forgotten to tell him to be modest in his e-mails and IMs. What would the police make of his self-aggrandizing?

There was an IM from BTrippett sent the day after the last swim meet: Andy, you rock!

Andy's reply, an appropriate: Thank U!!!!!

He'd sent an e-mail to someone named *MuzikRuuls:* Do U want to skate Satrday?

MuzicRuuls replied: Not w U, loser.

That was enough. I didn't want to read any more.

I went through his desk drawers one by one, but found nothing out of the ordinary. I opened his top dresser drawer, bracing myself for the disorder I knew was inside. I allowed him one drawer he could keep however he liked. He tended toward disorder, and keeping things neat and folded was so hard for him. Letting him have one drawer where he could simply throw things was my way of giving him some release.

I could barely pull the drawer open, it was so full. It smelled rank. I found dirty socks, a balled-up T-shirt that smelled like salt and fish, probably from the last time he and Marcus fished off the pier. I tossed the dirty clothes onto the floor. I found his old Nintendo and a slew of probably dead batteries. A couple of old matchbox cars I hadn't seen since he was little. Acne cream, although he'd only had one or two pimples so far. A few empty and half-empty packages of gum and lots of crumpled tissues. In the very bottom of the drawer, I found a foil-wrapped condom and told myself not to overreact. It was a rite of passage for a teenaged boy to own a condom, wasn't it? I thought of removing it from the drawer, but left it there. It would make Andy seem like a normal kid for once.

There was a note dated the year before from one of his teachers, apparently brought home for my signature but which I'd never seen, stating that Andy was repeatedly tardy to class. And finally, a new, unopened CD of the Beatles. I didn't know he bought CDs, much less the Beatles, and I worried he might have stolen it. I felt the way I had when the lighter had been discovered in the airport. I didn't know all there was to know about my son. A familiar niggling fear crept into my chest. How would I guide him through the next decade as he entered adulthood? Could he ever hold a job? Live on his own? I doubted it. Right now, though, I had more pressing things to worry about.

I opened the next drawer where his T-shirts were folded, not particularly well, but they were stacked three across in piles. I was about to close the drawer when I noticed something white jutting from beneath the middle stack. I reached for it and my hand closed around a fistful of balled-up paper. Receipts. I pulled them out, flattened them on his bed. I was relieved to see one for the CD. One for gum and a Snickers bar. One for the pocketknife he'd "always had," that he'd traded for the lighter. One for cigarettes dated four months earlier. I lifted the stacks of shirts and found a crushed pack of Marlboros, three missing from it. I sniffed them. A little stale smelling, as if they'd been in his drawer for some time. My baby. Trying so hard to fit in.

I looked through his underwear drawer. Not very orderly, but nothing suspicious.

I opened the folding louvered doors of his closet and spotted the green-striped shirt and tan pants he'd worn the night of the fire. I'd washed them twice trying to salvage them, successfully, I'd thought, but when I pressed my nose to them, I could still smell the hint of smoke. Bending low, I picked out the sneakers he'd had on that night. They were dark brown with tan detailing, and we'd bought them the day before the fire. I held them to my nose. The odor was faint. Maybe the smell of the leather? I held them away from my face, took in a breath of fresh air, then sniffed again. Not leather. Definitely something with a chemical edge to it. The lighter in his sock! He'd worn these same shoes to New York. Some of the lighter fluid must have seeped onto his shoes. I'd have to explain to the police about the lighter in his sock in case they, too, caught a whiff of something they didn't think should be there.

Everything will be okay, I told myself. There was nothing here for the police to sink their teeth into.

And I was so, so certain I could explain away anything they might find.

Chapter Twenty-Five

Marcus

I LOADED MY KAYAK INTO THE BACK OF MY PICKUP after my later-than-usual trip through the sound and climbed into the cab. My shoulders ached in that good way they did after paddling for an hour. Checked my cell for messages. There was one.

"It's Sara, Marcus." Man, she sounded strung out. "Keith is able to speak now and I need to talk to you. It's important. I'm back in Surf City and I'll be at Jabeen's today."

Jabeen's was my next stop anyway. I was off duty and planned to nurse a coffee while I read the paper. I guessed Sara wanted to tell me what I already knew: Keith had seen Andy outside the night of the lock-in. Or maybe she was pissed I'd been to the hospital and hadn't tried to see her while I was there. Or maybe she was just annoyed I'd seen Keith and hadn't told her.

I was wrong on all counts.

She looked up as I walked into Jabeen's, giving me a nod as she made some fancy, steamy, overpriced drink for a woman at the counter. I hadn't seen Sara since before the fire. Only two and a half weeks had passed, but they'd been a crappy two and a half weeks and every minute of them showed on her face. Sara was one of those women with a year-round tan. Today, her face was actually pale. Pasty. Ever since I'd known her, she wore her blond hair short with bangs. Now it was swept to the side and tucked behind her ears, like she'd had no time to fix it.

"Large, Marcus?" She handed the drink to the woman ahead of me.

"That'll do it," I said.

"For here?" She had dark circles beneath her eyes.

I nodded. I really felt for her.

She ran the coffee from the machine into a white mug, her back to me. Tan capris hung loose around her hips. Even too skinny and too pale, she was a good-looking woman. A few years ago, I'd toyed with the idea of starting something up with her. But although she was pretty and smart and damn nice, I wasn't attracted to her the way I should have been. I didn't want to start something I was sure I couldn't finish. Living in a little town where we'd have to see each other all the time, I was careful about things like that. Besides, she wasn't Laurel.

She handed me the mug.

"You wanted to talk?" I asked.

An unfamiliar middle-aged man and woman walked into the café and I glanced at them. Tourists.

"I'm alone here this morning," Sara said. "Dawn's at the dentist, so I don't have a lot of time—" she smiled at the tourists "—but I *have* to tell you something."

"I'm gonna be here a while." I nodded toward my favorite table by the window.

"Okay."

I sat by the window and opened my paper while she waited on the couple at the counter. Then she came over. Sat down across from me.

"Keith can speak now." She didn't look happy. "Did I say that in my message?"

"Yes. And I actually spoke with him myself yesterday. It's great he's doing better."

Her eyes flew open. "You did? At the burn center? What did he say?"

"He told me he saw Andy outside the church."

"Did he say anything else?" She was fishing for something.

"I wasn't there long," I said. "Sorry I didn't get to see you. They told me you went back to the hotel."

A couple of Realtors from the office down the block walked into the café.

"I'll be right with you," Sara said. Her hand shook as she brushed a wayward strand of hair off her forehead. She leaned toward me. "He found your old letter," she whispered.

"*What* old letter?" As soon as the words left my mouth, I knew. "You *kept* it?"

"Shh."

I lowered my voice. "Why the hell didn't you throw it away?"

"I filed it with my banking stuff when Keith was little. I never thought about it again. He went snooping through my files and found it."

What had I written, exactly? I couldn't remember the words, but the gist of what I'd said would be enough.

"What did he say?"

"He was furious. And very hurt. I told him he could never tell anyone about it, that it would hurt too many people."

"When did he find it?" I felt the impatient eyes of the Realtors on us. Or at least, on Sara.

"The day of the lock-in." She got to her feet. "I left a message for you, but then the fire happened and…I was just worried whether Keith would live or die, not whether he'd tell anyone about the letter." She tapped her hand on the table. "Later." She walked behind the counter.

I vaguely remembered getting a message from her the afternoon before the fire, making a mental note to call her after I got off duty.

Maybe Keith started the fire, Laurel'd said. The letter gave him a motive—if being angry at the world counted as a motive. But, again, why would he set a fire and then get trapped by it?

Couldn't answer that one. Suddenly, though, I got why Keith called Andy a little rich boy that night. Keith would go home to his double-wide after the lock-in. Andy'd go home to a two-story stunner on the water.

I'd always felt that was an injustice, myself.

Chapter Twenty-Six

Laurel
1991

TALOS HAD ONE THING THE SEA TENDER DID NOT: a hot tub. When winter finally hit with those winds that felt positively arctic at the northern end of the island, Marcus and I got in the habit of stripping down to our underwear and sitting in the hot tub in the evening—with our bottles of booze, of course. Leaning my head back on the edge of the tub, studying the crisp white stars against a background of black velvet, reminded me of those nights Jamie and I would bundle up on the beach in the winter and search for satellites. Only a couple of years had passed since then, yet it seemed as though those nights had taken place in someone else's life, not mine.

One night late in March, we must have stayed in the tub too

long, or the water had been too hot, or we'd had too much to drink. When I got into the house and quickly threw on my terry-cloth robe to stop the shivers, I suddenly felt woozy.

"Uh-oh." I closed my eyes as I leaned against the living room wall.

"You going to be sick?" Marcus asked as he threw a towel around his shoulders.

I opened my eyes. The room blurred but didn't spin. "I think I'm okay," I said.

"Want some coffee? Hot chocolate?"

"Ugh, no." I took one tentative step forward, then another. "I'm going to crash in your guest room."

"Party pooper," he said. Then hollered after me, "Call if you need me!"

In his guest room, which now felt like my home away from home, I slipped out of the robe, peeled off my wet underwear and crawled under the covers.

I don't know how long I slept. I only know that when I woke up, I was lying on my right side facing the wall and I slowly, very slowly, became aware that Marcus was lying behind me. I felt his arm around me, his finger lightly tracing the place where my breast met my rib cage, and the hard warmth of his erection pressed against my left buttock. I lay for minutes that way, neither asleep nor awake, sober nor drunk. Then I rolled over, and somewhere between facing the wall and facing him, I passed the point of no return.

Chapter Twenty-Seven

Andy

MISS BETTS LEANED BACK AGAINST HER DESK like she does sometimes and asked, "What is some of the evidence of global warming?"

I raised my hand first out of everybody. She called on Brynn instead of me, even though I hadn't raised my hand in probably ten minutes. I was only supposed to raise my hand every third time I knew the answer. I was good at things like "the evidence of global warming" because it was facts. I could memorize facts. That part of my brain was excellent. I wasn't so good when we were supposed to debate things, like should we use the electric chair. Things like that. That part of my brain was weak. The electric chair killed people and it was wrong to kill people, so that was simple. But when we did the debate part, we weren't supposed to think in black and white, as Miss Betts said. That was harder. Mom was the one who told me I should only raise my hand every third time I knew the answer. She said I drove the teachers crazy raising it all the time. So that's what I tried to do, but sometimes I didn't get called on anyway.

Brynn gave the same answer I was going to give: melting glaciers. Then a lady from the office came into the room. I saw her look right at me as she walked toward Miss Betts. She whispered to her. Then Miss Betts looked right at me, too.

"Andy," she said, "gather your things and go with Mrs. Potter, please."

"Why?" I asked.

"Mrs. Potter will explain why to you."

I stuffed my books and notebook in my backpack, kind of mad because I didn't want to miss the rest of my class. Mrs. Potter was very, very old. She smiled when I walked toward her. She put her arm around me and we left the room.

When I got in the hallway, I saw a policeman standing there looking at me. He wasn't smiling. Everything I did that day ran through my mind really fast. Did I do something wrong? I couldn't think of anything.

In the hall, Mrs. Potter said, "Andy, this is Sergeant Wood. He'd like to talk with you for a few minutes."

He was big. I didn't want Mrs. Potter to leave me alone with him, but I could tell she was going to. My heart beat hard as I walked with him to the office. He had a gun! I saw it on his waist, like inches away from me. I'd never seen a real gun that close up. Mrs. Potter said, "Use the counselor's office," so we went in there. The policeman closed the door. I had trouble breathing all of a sudden. My inhaler was in my backpack on the floor. I didn't need it yet, but I liked that it was there in case.

"You can sit," he said to me.

I sat down in a chair by the tall file thing. He sat down in a chair by the window. The room was little. I didn't like being that close to his gun. He had a big badge on his chest with the word *sergeant* on it and above the badge was a skinny flag, like an American flag, but without enough stripes.

"Andy, you have the right to remain silent," he said. Then he said a bunch of other things really fast, but all I kept thinking about was that I had the right to remain silent. He rubbed his chin when he was finished talking. "Did you understand what I just said to you, Andy?" His eyes were really blue, like Uncle Marcus's. "About your right to remain silent?"

"Yes, sir."

"It means you don't have to talk to me right now. I'm going to ask you some questions, but it's your right not to answer them."

I nodded. It sounded stupid for him to ask me questions if I could be silent, but sometimes people don't make sense. I guessed this was just one of those times.

"You also have the right to have a parent present while I talk to you," he said. "Do you understand that?"

"Yes, sir," I said, even though I was very confused. Mom wasn't there, but he was talking to me anyway.

"I want to talk to you about the night of the fire," he said.

"Okay," I said.

"Did you go outside at all during the lock-in?" he asked.

I didn't know what to do. I could be silent. Even though he'd turned a little in the chair and I couldn't see his gun anymore,

I knew it was still there. Any minute he could pull it out and shoot me. I thought I better answer him, but I was going to have to lie. What if he had one of those lie detector machines with him? My windpipe tightened up, but I was afraid to reach for my backpack. He might think I was reaching for a gun, too.

"Did you go outside at all during the lock-in?" he asked again.

"No, sir," I said.

"You didn't go outside during the lock-in?"

I shook my head. Why was he asking me another time? I leaned over to try to see under his chair to see if he had the lie detector machine hidden there. I only saw his feet.

"We had a few reports that you were seen outside the church during the lock-in," he said.

My shirt felt wet at my armpits. I'd forgotten to use the deodorant that morning. Mom added it as a new thing in pencil on the edge of my *Get Ready in the Morning* chart. I always missed it. "I didn't go out," I repeated.

"You were involved in a fight with Keith Weston at the lock-in, is that correct?"

Maybe that's what this was about. He was trying to figure out who started the fight first. "He called me a name," I said.

"And you were very angry with him."

"Yes, sir."

"Angry enough to start a fire."

"What?" He really confused me now.

"Did you start the fire, Andy?"

"No, I'm the one who *rescued* people," I said. He had me mixed up with someone else.

"Well, why don't you tell me how you rescued people?" he asked.

That was easy. I'd told the story so many times it came out of my mouth as easy as facts about global warming. I told him about climbing through the boys' room window and crawling over the air-conditioner box and everything.

"Okay, Andy." He stood up. The handle of the gun was right next to my eyes! "You can go back to your classroom now. Thanks for your help."

"You're welcome."

I left him and went back to Miss Betts's room. The class was over and she had to help me figure out where I was supposed to go next. Once my day gets out of order, it's confusing. She told me I should go down the hall to my art class, and then she said, "How did your talk with the policeman go?"

"Good." I tried to sound happy. Then I walked to art class. On my way, I thought about the policeman's questions and my answers, and I decided it would have been smarter to remain silent. Even if he did have a gun.

Chapter Twenty-Eight

Laurel

BONNIE BETTS POKED HER HEAD INTO MY office where I was taking a fourth-grader's temperature. "When you have a minute," she said, then ducked back into the hallway.

I took the thermometer from the girl's mouth. "Normal, sweetheart," I said. "I think it's allergies."

She twisted her mouth into a grimace. "My nose don't clear no matter how much I blow it," she said.

"That can be pretty frustrating," I said as I dropped the plastic sheath from the thermometer into the trash can. "Ask your mom to get some saltwater spray at the store. It'll help."

She stood up like she had a sack of potatoes on her shoulders and left my office.

I called Bonnie in. The elementary school where I worked

shared a campus with the middle school, as well as the high school where Bonnie taught, but it was unusual to see her in my building in the middle of the day.

"How are you, Bonnie?" I asked. "You want to have a seat?" I motioned toward the small chair the fourth-grader had vacated.

Bonnie stood in the doorway. "No, I'm fine, thanks, but I thought you'd want to know that Mrs. Potter took Andy out of my class to talk with a police officer last period. He seemed just fine when he came back, but I thought you should know."

"They talked to him without telling me?" I wasn't sure if that was even legal.

Bonnie shrugged. "I didn't think to question it." She looked at her watch. "I'd better get back, but wanted to let you know."

I thanked her, then sat at my desk, wondering if I should pull Andy out of his next class to find out what had happened. I'd really mess up his day then, but I'm sure he was already befuddled from talking to the police. Before I could decide, Flip Cates called on my cell phone.

"I just heard that one of your guys talked to Andy," I said. I'd known Flip for years and knew he'd be straight with me.

"That was Sergeant Wood," he said. I didn't recognize the name. "We needed to ask him some more questions about the fire."

"Shouldn't I have been there?"

"It's mandatory for a parent to be present when questioning a minor under fourteen," Flip said. "Sergeant Wood told Andy he had a right to have a parent present, but he didn't seem to have a problem with it."

"He was probably confused, Flip!" I stood up and shut my office door. "Someone should have contacted me."

"I think he did fine, Laurel," Flip said. "And I'm sorry to lay this on you right now, but we'd like to search Andy's room. We'll need you to sign a consent-to-search form, and we'd like to do it this afternoon. Can you take some time off work?"

"You want to search his *room?*" I thought I'd better sound shocked. Most likely Marcus had been out of line when he tipped me off.

"Yes. It won't take long."

I could say I wouldn't sign. That consent-to-search form wasn't the same as a warrant. But what would they find in Andy's room that I hadn't already found? The shoes, I thought. I should have simply thrown the shoes away. *Stupid.* Why didn't I toss them? I'd just have to tell them about the lighter fluid.

"I can be there in about forty-five minutes," I said. I'd let them search the room and clear his name, putting an end to the rumors. Then they could get on with the business of looking for the real criminal.

"Great," Flip said. "We'll meet you at your house at noon."

Even though I arrived home at eleven forty-five, a police car was already parked at the end of the street by the water, and I waved at the two figures inside as I pulled into my driveway. I wondered if they were intentionally early because they thought I might try to go through Andy's room before their arrival. Surely that would be a typical parent's response.

I met them on the front porch. Flip smiled and shook my hand. "Laurel, this is Sergeant Wood," he said.

"Ma'am." Sergeant Wood nodded to me but didn't offer his

hand. He was prematurely gray with bright blue eyes, and he would have been handsome if he'd allowed anything approaching a smile to cross his lips. I didn't like picturing Andy being questioned by him.

Flip handed me a clipboard and pen. "Here's the consent-to-search form," he said.

I looked at the form as if I were actually reading it, but the words ran together in front of my eyes. "You just need to look at Andy's room, right?" I asked as I signed. "You don't need to see the whole house?"

"Correct," Flip answered. I thought I saw an apology in his eyes.

"It's no problem." I led them inside. "I know you have to follow up every lead and I want Andy's name to be cleared."

They followed me upstairs to Andy's room. The sergeant carried a large canvas bag and I wondered if he planned to take items away with him. How would I explain *that* to Andy?

In the doorway to the bedroom, both men stopped and put on latex gloves.

"Can I stay while you look?" I asked.

"Yes, ma'am," Flip said, as if forgetting how long we'd known each other.

I took a seat on the very corner of Andy's bed, folding my damp hands in my lap, trying to stay out of the way as they started opening drawers and reading the cards on the corkboard wall. "When you spoke to Andy today, Sergeant Wood, did he say anything that made you want to search his room?" I asked.

"No, ma'am," Flip answered for the sergeant. "We'd already planned to ask your consent."

"What did you talk to him about?"

"You keep parental monitoring software on this computer, ma'am?" Sergeant Wood asked as if I hadn't spoken.

"Yes, I do. He's not much of an Internet surfer. He likes games, mostly."

Sergeant Wood sat down in Andy's desk chair and popped a CD into the writable drive. I thought of the nasty IM from *MuzicRuuls* and wondered what other hurtful messages he would come across.

While Sergeant Wood clicked mouse buttons and studied the computer screen, Flip started pulling out desk drawers. I knew what he was seeing in them and relaxed a bit. He asked me to stand up, then ran his arm beneath the mattress and box spring and peered under the bed.

"What exactly are you looking for?" I asked as I sat down again.

"We're particularly looking for lighter fluid. Matches. Arson instructions he might have looked up on the Internet. That sort of thing," Flip said. "I know this must be hard to watch."

"Well, Andy's not the kind of person who could or would set a fire, so I'm not concerned," I said. "You know that, too, Flip," I added, trying to remind him of our friendship.

He was into the messy drawer now, his back to me. I knew when he found the condom, because he asked me if Andy was sexually active.

"Not hardly," I said with a laugh.

I heard the front door slam shut.

"Mom?" Maggie called, and I suddenly remembered today was a half day for the seniors.

"I'm up here," I said.

"Why's a police car here?" she called from the stairs. She nearly flew into the room. "What's going on?"

"Hi, Maggie," Flip said.

"Are you—" she looked from me to Flip to the sergeant "—are you searching Andy's *room?*"

"Yes, they are," I answered.

"*Why?*" Maggie looked at me. "Shouldn't you...can they just do this?"

I nodded. "It's only Andy's room," I reassured her in case she was afraid of her own privacy being invaded. "Not the whole house."

"But it's ridiculous!" she said.

"I know, sweetie." I patted the bed next to me. "Sit down."

"Is this because of what Keith said?" She directed the question to me and I shrugged.

"Probably."

Sergeant Wood stood up from the computer, popped out the disk and dropped it in a small plastic bag he took from the canvas carryall. Then he pulled out a stack of paper bags. "We'd like to take the clothes Andy had on the night of the fire," he said.

"Sure, but I've washed them." I stood up, pulling open the louvered closet doors. "A couple of times, actually, to get rid of the smoke smell."

"We'd still like to have them," the sergeant said.

I reached into the closet for the green-striped shirt, but my hands, as if they had a mind of their own, moved to his solid sage-colored shirt instead.

"No, Mom," Maggie said, "he had on—"

I looked at her sharply enough to cut her off. She understood.

"Oh, I forgot," she said. "I thought he wore that other shirt,
but he had that on during the day, didn't he?"

I nodded, afraid she would say too much, embellish the lie
to the point of it being obvious. I handed the shirt to the
sergeant, who put it into one of the paper bags. Then I reached
for his pants. Thank God, he had several pairs of tan pants. My
hands passed over the ones he'd worn and handed some khaki
ones to Maggie, who gave them to Sergeant Wood.

Flip looked up from the basket of cards he was filing
through. "Don't forget shoes and socks," he said.

"I'm not sure which socks he wore," I said. I leaned over to
pick up the shoes, but Maggie beat me to it, pulling out a different pair of sneakers than the new ones he'd had on that
night. She avoided my eyes as she handed them to the sergeant,
who put each shoe in a separate paper bag. We were in it
together now, Maggie and I. I cringed at the realization that
I'd made her a party to tampering with evidence.

"We appreciate your cooperation," Sergeant Wood said, as
he added the last paper bag to his canvas carryall.

"Thanks, Laurel." Flip took one last look around the room.
"We'll let ourselves out," he said.

Maggie and I didn't look at each other as the men went
downstairs, even after we heard the front door close. We
listened to the sound of their car doors slamming shut and the
crunch of their tires on the gravelly end of the road where
they'd parked. I wondered if Maggie felt as stiff with guilt as
I did. I couldn't believe I'd dragged her into my lie.

I put my arm around her shoulders. "I'm sorry," I whispered.

"I would've done the same thing if I'd thought of it first," she said.

"But why?" I asked her. "Why did we do it? If we're one hundred percent sure of his innocence, why did we...why did we just tamper with evidence?"

She shook her head slowly. "To protect him. We don't know what they'd find on the clothes he wore that night," she said. "I mean, maybe he accidentally stepped in a puddle of gasoline or something and then they'd really go after him. This way, we know they won't find a thing."

My gaze drifted to the shoes he wore the night of the lock-in, and I thought I could still smell the scent of something caustic, something *flammable,* on them even from where I sat. I wouldn't tell Maggie. I didn't want to make her doubt him.

"I was afraid maybe his lighter leaked onto his shoes," I said.

I let go of her to reach for Andy's pillow, which lay on the side of the bed where Flip had tossed it after searching beneath the mattress. I hugged it to my chest. Andy's scent was on it, still more the scent of a little boy than a man. Even if he could have figured out how to get fuel to the church and how to set it on fire in a way that would make him appear heroic, he never would have done it.

I knew my son. I knew his heart. He would never hurt a soul.

Chapter Twenty-Nine

Laurel
1991

SARA'S BABY ARRIVED THREE WEEKS EARLY. She and Steve named him Keith, and he had a mild heart condition that might require surgery when he got a little older. I felt terrible for Sara. She deserved the perfect baby I'd had.

Sara and Keith spent two nights in the hospital in Jacksonville. The second night, Steve called to tell me that Jamie was in the emergency room. While visiting with them in Sara's room, Jamie had suddenly doubled over with chest pains.

I tried calling Marcus, but he was out, so I had to drive myself to Jacksonville. I'd had an accident the week before. I'd been parked in front of the grocery store, and when I backed out of the space, I somehow smashed into a light post. I got out of the car to check for damage and tripped over my own feet, cutting my cheek on the side mirror. A few people rushed to help me, but I scrambled back into my car, waving them away with a smile as though my cheek didn't hurt a bit and the parking lot wasn't spinning around me. I didn't want them close enough to know I was three sheets to the wind. When I got home, I discovered the long, deep crease in the fender of my car and hoped Jamie would never notice it.

As I drove to the hospital in Jacksonville, though, I wasn't drunk. Still, I'd had enough to drink that I knew I had no business being on the road. I drove slowly, my eyes wide open and fixed to the white line. There were few other cars on the road that late, but I worried about running into a ditch or smashing into a deer. I wasn't worried about Jamie, though. I was quite sure what was wrong with him.

Sure enough, the E.R. doctors could find no problem with Jamie's heart, but they kept him overnight for observation. I sat by his bedside, woodenly holding his hand. In his eyes, I saw that he, too, knew what was wrong, something he wouldn't try to explain to the doctors: Sara and Steve's pale little baby had triggered Jamie's empathy gene. His gift. His curse.

Jamie and Maggie moved back into The Sea Tender while Sara's mother stayed with the Westons for a week. The first night, Maggie had trouble going to sleep in the crib she hadn't slept in for nearly a year, and I listened to Jamie getting up with her from his bed in our guest room. I was relieved he hadn't expected to sleep with me.

I felt awkward with him in the house, especially the second evening when Marcus stopped by to greet his brother and niece. Marcus and I had made love only that once. In a sober, remorseful moment the following day, we'd made a pact never to let it happen again and we'd stuck to it in the month since that night. But we were close, emotionally bonded in a way I no longer was with Jamie, and I felt shaky and awkward when both brothers were around.

"Listen, bro," Marcus said as he played with Maggie on the floor. "I'd like to help out with the...you know, the property management. The maintenance you talked about a while back."

I caught Jamie's look of surprise. His smile. He probably thought Marcus was finally growing up or that his bout of chest pains had scared him. I knew the reason behind Marcus's offer though: good, old-fashioned guilt. In my sober moments, I had plenty of it myself. Whatever the reason, the sudden ease between the brothers helped settle my nerves.

The plan was for Jamie to stay home from work the first couple of days to help Maggie adapt to being back at The Sea Tender, but on the second day, he got a call from the fire department and had to leave. He'd just put Maggie down for her nap, so we were both hopeful he'd return before she woke up. With Jamie out of the house, my first thought was to get one of the wine coolers from the refrigerator, but I knew I wouldn't be able to stop at one. I wanted to be alert in case Maggie woke up. Instead, I took a nap to keep myself from drinking, leaving my door open so I'd hear her if she needed me.

I woke up to the sound of a distant chant coming from the nursery.

"Dad-dy. Dad-dy. Dad-dy."

I got up and walked into the nursery to see her standing in her crib, holding onto the railing, midchant.

"Dad—"

She saw me and her eyes widened.

"Hi, sweetie!" I worked at sounding cheerful.

Maggie let out a scream, flopping facefirst onto her mattress. "Dad-dy!" she wailed. "Dad-dy!"

"Daddy had to go to the fire station, but he'll be home soon." I rubbed her back, but she twitched away from me with another wail.

My hands shook as I reached into the crib and lifted her out. She writhed in my arms, pushing me away, and I set her down on the floor.

"Daddy!" She ran out of the room, diaper drooping, clearly on the hunt for Jamie. I watched her helplessly, following her from room to room to be sure she didn't hurt herself. I held the front door shut as she reached up to jiggle the knob.

"Come on, sweetie," I said, "I need to change your diaper."

"Nooooo!" She flopped onto the living room floor as she had on her mattress and let out one scream after another, punctuated occasionally by the word *daddy*. I stared down at her, uncertain what to do.

Finally, I sat next to her on the floor. I didn't touch her, but spoke quietly to her, telling her Daddy would be home soon. I doubt she even heard me. I tried singing "Itsy Bitsy Spider," but the screaming didn't cease. Was this the terrible twos? She was only twenty-three months old. I got up and moved to the toy box, where I took out the toys one by one, talking about each of them. "I *love* this puzzle," I said. "I wish Maggie would help me put it together."

She ignored me. I read from one of her books, while she continued screaming.

She hates me, I thought. *She truly hates me.*

I took a wine cooler from the refrigerator and drank the entire bottle in one long, sweet pull.

From the bookshelf in the living room, I pulled down the book on one-year-olds that I'd studied so long and hard during my pregnancy. *"Tantrums wear themselves out,"* it said. I turned on *One Life to Live* and watched it through my tears. My daughter hated me, and who could blame her? I was an atrocious mother.

The tantrum lasted forty-five minutes. I heard her voice dribble off into nothing as she finally fell asleep on the floor. I got up, lifted her into my arms and carried her back to the sofa. She smelled of poop and urine, but I didn't want to risk changing her and waking her up again. Having her sleep now would probably wreck Jamie's schedule for her, but she was so quiet and limp in my arms. I rocked her gently, her hair soft against my cheek.

"I love you," I whispered, although the feeling behind the words still escaped me. "I'm sorry," I said. That, I knew, was the truth.

She awakened and the cycle started again. I had another wine cooler; I had to. Maggie was still screaming for Jamie when he came home. I heard his car door slam and cringed, certain he could hear her screams from the driveway.

As soon as he opened the door, she ran to him and he scooped her up. "What's the matter, Mags?" He looked at me where I stood leaning against the side of the couch, knotting my hands together. "How long's this been going on?" he asked.

I hesitated, humiliated by the truth. "She was upset when she first woke up. Then she settled down for a while, but I didn't want to change her because..."

"She's soaked. You're soaked, Maggie-doodle." He walked past me into the nursery. I heard her protest a bit when he changed her; I never would have managed. I brushed my teeth and rinsed with mouthwash as he tended to her.

"Why didn't you change her?" he asked as he walked back into the living room, Maggie toddling at his side, sniffling, holding his index finger with her little hand.

"She was screaming for you," I said. "Jamie, she doesn't like me."

"Shh," he chided. "She understands more than you think. Of course she likes you. We just upset her routine, that's all."

Over the course of the week, things between Maggie and me improved a bit. I threw out the remaining wine coolers— except for three, which I stashed in the bedroom closet just in case. I lasted through two full days without one, proving to myself that I was *not* an alcoholic. I made an effort to play with Maggie. I'd read to her any time she'd let me, which grew more frequent. She never really warmed up to me, though, as if she could see behind my mask, and I might have been babysitting for a friend's child, for all the warmth I felt toward her in spite of my longing to fall in love with her. Yet, I pretended. I'd gotten very good at pretending.

Marcus's work on the Lockwood properties lasted exactly three days. The first day, he power washed decks. The second, he repaired a roof. Jamie was so pleased that the third day, he asked Marcus to replace a couple of windows in one of the Surf City cottages. Marcus removed the old windows and enlarged the openings for the new ones, but he made them too big and too crooked because he was, quite simply, too drunk.

He came to The Sea Tender that evening to admit his mistake.

Jamie handed Maggie to me and told me to take her into the bedroom. I did so gladly, not wanting to witness the fireworks. I sat on the bed with Maggie in my arms. The fireworks, though, pierced the thin bedroom door.

"Did you *measure?*" Jamie shouted.

"Of course I measured!"

"Daddy!" Maggie scrambled out of my arms toward the edge of the bed. I held on to the back of her shirt to stop her progress.

"Well, then how did this happen?"

"I don't know!" Marcus said. "It just did. It's not like it's the end of the world, Jamie."

"Daddy!"

I closed my eyes. *Please stop.* I couldn't take the yelling.

"Sloppy work, Marcus," Jamie shouted. "It's going to cost an arm and a leg to fix."

"We can get bigger windows."

"*We're* not doing anything! I'm not letting you near those windows again!"

"You've just been waiting for me to screw up!"

Maggie sprang free of my grasp.

"That's the *last* thing I wanted," Jamie said. "I was hoping you'd finally gotten your act together. It's about time. You're twenty-two years old! You're a damn *drunk,* Marcus. You need help. And you're fired."

I reached for Maggie, but she toppled headfirst off the bed.

I picked her up and saw that she was fine, but her face was quietly twisting into that I'm-getting-ready-to-let-out-a-bloodcurdling-scream expression.

"*No,* sweetie." I bounced her on my lap. "Shh."

Marcus was laughing. "Fired from *what?*" he shouted. "It's not like I'm getting paid. And I don't need the hassle, man. It's all yours."

The front door slammed, and Maggie let out the scream I'd known was coming.

I walked out of the bedroom and held her toward Jamie, who was staring red faced at the front door, hands on his hips.

"I need a nap," I said, handing Maggie over to him before he could protest. Back in the bedroom, I locked the door, took the third and last wine cooler from the bedroom closet, and drank it warm.

The following night—the night before Jamie and Maggie were to return to the Weston's—Jamie got another call from the fire station. Maggie was already asleep, thank goodness, and by the time Jamie returned, I was in bed. He knocked on the door.

"Can we talk for a minute?" he asked, opening the door a crack.

I wasn't yet asleep. "Uh-huh," I said. I sat up against the headboard, tucking the covers across my chest because I had nothing on.

Jamie's anger at Marcus had blown over sometime during the day—or at least he'd known better than to dump it on me. Now, he sat on the edge of the bed, the light from the hallway pooling on his cheeks, catching in his eyes. I'd so loved those big brown eyes! I wished I could feel love for them—for *him*—

again. And for my daughter, who deserved so much better than I was giving her.

"It's been good being here with you this week," he said.

I nodded, although I was anxious for them to leave. I wanted my easy sleeping-and-drinking life back. "At least Maggie doesn't scream when you leave her with me now," I said.

He didn't smile. "You made a big effort with her. I know you still aren't your old self, and I just want you to know that I appreciate how you tried to...to be a mom to her this week."

Tears welled up in my eyes.

He moved closer, taking my hand and holding it between those big teddy-bear paws of his. "What is it?" he asked. "Why the tears?"

"I just wish I could *feel* something for her." I swallowed. "For *you*. Like a normal mother and normal woman."

He leaned forward, surprising me with a kiss. "You will," he said, his hand on my cheek. Then he kissed me again. His lips against mine felt familiar, tugging at a place deep inside me— a place I wanted to get to again but couldn't seem to reach.

His fingers curled beneath the sheet where it lay across my chest. He started to lower it, and I let him, because I couldn't shut him out of whatever was left of my heart. He fumbled in the nightstand for a condom, tore it open and put it on.

I feigned desire for him, a gift I wanted to give him, but my body felt nothing as I opened it up to him. For the first time, I faked my orgasm.

When we were finished and he pulled out of me, he swore.

"Damn!" he said. "Well, that's a first."

"What's a first?" I asked, worried he was referring to my poor acting job.

"It broke," he said, and I realized he was talking about the condom. "It must have been old." He lay down next to me, his hand on my stomach. "Where are you in your cycle?" he asked.

I thought back to the last time I'd had my period, well over a month ago. *Well over a month ago.* I remembered feeling woozy for a few days the week before, a light-headedness I'd attributed to drinking too much. My heart gave a great, breath-stealing leap in my chest. I wanted to jump out of bed and run to the kitchen calendar, count off the days, hoping I was wrong. But I didn't budge, trying to stay calm.

"I'm not sure," I managed to say.

"That's the last thing you need now," he said. "Another pregnancy."

It may have been the last thing I needed, but I knew it was what I had.

Chapter Thirty

Marcus

COKE WITH PEANUTS WAS MY COMFORT FOOD, but it wasn't working for me that morning. I sat on the back deck of my tower, watching the waves make chop suey of the beach. The surf was high and rough, spraying my face and the Wilmington newspaper on my lap. I waved at a couple of beachcombers. Watched their yellow Lab fetch a ball from the water. Tried to pretend it was an ordinary day, which almost worked till I lifted the paper again.

Could Fire Hero Be Villain? the headline read.

The last couple of days, the rumors had started flying. The police had a press conference the night before to try to squelch some of them. It backfired. Too many questions asked. Too few answers given.

Even CNN had people there. That's what happened with exposure on the *Today* show. Suddenly a small-town fire was big news.

"Is it true several witnesses saw Andy Lockwood outside the church during the lock-in?" a reporter had asked.

How did this information get out? I'd wondered. Did it float through the air and settle in people's heads?

"As I said," the police chief repeated for the third or fourth time, "the investigation is ongoing and we're still conducting interviews and collecting evidence."

"Would you call him a person of interest?" someone asked.

"Everyone with a connection to the church that night is a person of interest," the chief said.

"We've heard reports of Andy Lockwood's temper," a reporter said. "Can you verify that he's lost his temper in public before?"

"That's not something I personally have ever witnessed," the chief said.

I remembered a time Laurel went out of town to give an FASD speech. The school called me, since I was Andy's second backup emergency contact. The first was Sara, of course, but they couldn't reach her. Andy'd been suspended for the day. He'd hit a girl who called him a jerk-off. There were other incidents Laurel had dealt with over the years, though not an infinite number. Andy could be unpredictable—calm and cuddly one minute, furious the next. I could see him beating up Keith at the lock-in. His temper was a flare, though. Impulsive. Never premeditated.

It didn't matter that nothing incriminating had been said about Andy at the press conference; the seed was planted by the questions themselves.

"Hey, Uncle Marcus."

Maggie walked across the sand near the corner of my house. I turned the paper upside down on the off chance she hadn't already seen it.

"Hey, Mags," I said.

"I knocked, but I figured you were back here when you didn't answer." She climbed the steps to the deck.

"Don't you ever go to school anymore?" I teased.

"I *had* to see you." She stood in front of me, her hair blowing in long wavy strands around her head. "You have to tell me what's going *on.*" She pulled an elastic band from her pants pocket and tied her hair back as she spoke. "That press conference last night was flippin' unbelievable, and I just don't get what's *happening!*" She grabbed the long ponytail and raked her fingers through it.

"Sit down, Mags."

She plunked down in one of the deck chairs. "I am so *totally* pissed off," she said.

"Can I get you a Coke?" I asked, although caffeine would probably be a mistake for her at the moment.

"No, you can tell me what's *really* going on in the investigation."

I watched the Lab get flipped by a wave. He shook himself off and ran in the water for more.

"Uncle Marcus! *Tell* me."

"You know I'm not on the team any longer," I said.

"They searched Andy's room yesterday."

I nodded. "Did they find anything?"

"A condom and some cigarettes." She shrugged. "They took the clothes he was wearing that night. Like they'd actually find something on them."

"A condom, huh?" Did Laurel ask Andy where he got it? Did

he tell her? She'd kill me, but he was fifteen and I didn't know
how much she'd talked to him about sex. *Someone* had to do it.

"It was so…*invasive*," she said. "Yuck." She sounded like a real
teenager. Most of the time, she seemed much older. I usually
had to remind myself she was only seventeen.

"Is your mom okay?"

"*No,* she's not okay. Everybody's suddenly saying Andy's an
arsonist. How could she be okay? It's insane." She looked at me.
Her face was crimson. "First of all, the guy at the press conference didn't even *call* it arson. Couldn't it have been some
kind of accident?"

"They won't officially call it arson until the investigation is
over, but a burn pattern like that doesn't happen by accident."

"Couldn't it have something to do with the electricity going
out in the youth building, though?"

"That still wouldn't explain the burn pattern."

"Tell me what evidence they have," she demanded. "Do they
have something on Andy I don't know about?"

"They know the type of fuel," I said. "A gasoline and diesel
mix."

She snorted. "Like Andy carried gasoline and diesel to the
lock-in. I drove him there. I think I would have noticed."

"I know, babe."

She looked toward the beach. "I feel like they're only
looking at Andy as a suspect now. Not even trying to figure
out what really happened."

"Andy just makes a colorful rumor, that's all. The truth will
come out eventually."

"Didn't a church burn down in Wilmington this year? Could
it be, like, a serial arsonist?"

"Pretty good, Mags." I was impressed. "I'm going to suggest the investigators hire you."

"Seriously?"

I laughed. "No, not seriously. If *I* can't be on the team, they sure won't take Andy's sister. But that was a good catch about the church in Wilmington. The big difference is, that church was empty."

"But they'll still consider the possibility, won't they?"

"Of course," I said. "Has your mom talked to a lawyer yet?"

"I don't think so."

"What's she waiting for?" I said. "She's in denial."

"I don't know. All I know is that Andy's so confused. He cried in bed last night. He kept saying, 'But I'm the *hero.*'" Her voice cracked. "I didn't want him to go to school today. Kids are going to be so mean to him."

"Maybe he should stay home for a day or two," I thought out loud.

"I'm starting to plan this fund-raiser at school for sometime in May," Maggie said. "A big makeover event with the beauty college coming in and a silent auction and everything. Now I don't even feel like doing it."

Couldn't keep that niece of mine down. Who cared if she was valedictorian or not? "Well, just remember it's for the victims," I said. "Don't punish them because people are spreading rumors about Andy."

She screwed up her face. "You're right," she said. She looked at her watch. Sighed. "I'd better go back to school."

"Listen, Mags," I said as she got to her feet. "The best thing you can do—and I can do—is be there for Andy. Be his support right now, all right? Don't let this get you down."

"Okay." She still looked glum as she leaned over to kiss my cheek.

I watched her walk down the steps. Once she'd disappeared around the corner of the house, I turned the newspaper over. Stared at the headline again. Could Fire Hero Be Villain?

I felt suspicion closing in on Andy, the way it had closed in on me years earlier. I knew how destructive it could be. How unstoppable. Like the waves ripping the sand away from my beach.

Chapter Thirty-One

Laurel

I WAS SUMMONED TO THE PRINCIPAL'S OFFICE like a wayward little kid. That's how I felt, sitting on one of the small, armless wooden chairs outside Ms. Terrell's office in my white nurse's jacket, waiting to be invited inside. From where I sat, I could see one end of the high school through the office windows. How was Andy faring over there today? Maybe I should have kept him home. I told him that if anyone called him names or said anything upsetting to him, to use it as an opportunity to practice self-control. He said he would do that and I knew he meant it at the time, but even I had little faith in his ability to tune out ugly words from his classmates.

Certainly, this visit to Ms. Terrell's office had something to do with Andy. I knew a few parents had called the high school principal, angry that he was still attending classes. They were worried that, like some other kids who didn't fit in, he might bring a gun to school and slaughter his classmates. I imagined his principal calling Ms. Terrell, asking her to persuade me to withdraw him for the rest of the year.

"Mrs. Lockwood?" Ms. Terrell had opened her office door and stood smiling at me.

I followed her inside. At my modest five feet, five inches, I towered over her.

This was Ms. Terrell's first year at my school, and I didn't know her well personally, although I did know quite a bit about her. She was fortyish with a doctorate degree in education, a petite African-American woman who'd grown up on the streets of Baltimore and who, despite her tiny size, the string of pearls she always wore, and the heels you could hear clicking through the halls, was tough as nails with the kids. They both feared and respected her. I found, sitting across the desk from her, that I had the same reaction.

"How are you holding up?" she asked.

"I'm managing." I smiled, trying not to look as wary as I felt.

"I wanted to touch base with you, given the situation with your son," she said, folding her hands neatly on her desk. "I thought you might want to take some time off while you're coping with this."

I hesitated, trying to read her face. There were frown lines on her forehead and what I read as concern in her eyes.

"Are...have parents complained that I'm here?" I asked.

"No," she said. "I *do* know that some parents over at the high school have complained that *Andy's* still attending school, but I've had no formal complaints about you at all. I simply—"

"You've had informal complaints?"

She sighed. "*Complaints* is too strong a word," she said. "Certainly there's no problem with your work here. The children adore you." She unfolded her hands and dropped them to her lap. "But people talk. You know how that goes."

"They have no right to speculate about my life or my son," I said sharply. Then I pressed my hands together in front of me as if in prayer. "I'm sorry," I said. "I'm not usually so defensive. I just...I know Andy's innocent and it's hard to...he's misunderstood enough as it is. This is the icing on the cake."

"I hear you," she said. She looked out the window toward the high school and I wondered what she was thinking. "I have a son, myself," she said finally.

I was surprised. "You do?" I didn't think she'd ever been married.

"I had him when I was fifteen years old. He's now twenty-five and in medical school at UNC."

"Oh my God," I said. She must have been a determined little dynamo right from the start to get where she was today. "How did you ever manage to..." I waved my hands through the air as if taking in her office and the diplomas on the wall. "You've accomplished so much."

"I had plans for my education even back then," she said, "and I would've had an abortion, if I hadn't been scared and waited too long, but of course I have no regrets." She smiled, looking at a framed picture on her desk. I couldn't see the picture, but I imagined it was a photograph of her son. "I was very lucky," she said. "My mother and grandmother helped raise him so I could keep up with school. When he got into his teens, the area we lived in...well, it was no good for an African-

American male. He wasn't a Goody Two-shoes, but he also wasn't a misogynist hip-hoppin' junkie, like a lot of the other boys his age. The cops didn't know that, though. They saw this black teenaged boy and lumped him together with the others. I was making enough money teaching by then that I could get him out of the city. As I said, I was lucky." She folded her hands on her desk once again and leaned toward me. "I'm telling you this to let you know that *I* know about being young and doing irresponsible things like getting pregnant at fifteen, or—" she nodded toward me "—like drinking while you're pregnant, and I know about ostracism and about motherhood. So, I'll understand if you need to take some time off while this is going on."

I stared at her for a moment, taking it all in. "Thank you," I said finally. "Maybe I could take a few days while I try to find a lawyer."

"You don't have one yet?" She seemed surprised.

I told her I'd called the attorney I used for my will and other documents, and he gave me the name of a woman in Hampstead who, as it turned out, had a nephew injured in the fire. She refused to take the case and didn't bother to offer me other names. I was ready to turn to the yellow pages.

Ms. Terrell wrote a name on the back of one of her cards. She tapped a few keys on her computer keyboard, then jotted a number beneath the name.

"I don't know this man well," she said, handing the card to me. "But I do know he's handled criminal cases. His name's Dennis Shartell and I met him through a friend of a friend. He's all the way in Wilmington, though, but he might at least be a starting point for you."

I stood up. "Thanks again," I said.

Walking back through the hallway, I clutched the card in my hand. I'd call this man, this Dennis Shartell. By the time I reached my office, my hopes were pinned on him. He'd be the one to stem the tide of suspicion that was rising against my son. I'd made mistakes in my life. Failing Andy a second time would not be one of them.

Chapter Thirty-Two

Laurel
1991–1992

WITH THE REALIZATION OF MY PREGNANCY came the sucking, sticky grip of a depression that made the black mood I'd experienced since Maggie's birth seem like little more than a rainy afternoon. A voice in my head repeated incessantly *You're a liar, an adulterer, a hideous mother.* I hated myself. I withdrew from everyone, including Marcus, never going to Talos, although he still came to The Sea Tender a few nights a week to drink and watch TV. He probably attributed the change in me to my desire to avoid the hot tub and a repeat of that night in his guest room.

I missed him. He was my best friend. My only real friend. I was afraid, though, that spending too much time with Marcus would lead me to tell him what I didn't want him to know.

I knew I couldn't have this baby, the child of my husband's brother, another child I would ruin with my lack of maternal instinct. A child I certainly didn't deserve and who didn't deserve to be born with me as his or her mother. But getting an abortion required picking up the phone, making an appointment, driving myself alone to the clinic in Wilmington as well as back home again, and every time I thought of all I needed to do to make the abortion happen, I crawled into bed and cried until I fell asleep.

I was lying in bed one afternoon when I felt the flutter of bird wings between my navel and my hipbone. Just a quick little ripple, but it scared me. Could I possibly be that far along? The sensation finally motivated me to get out of bed and call the women's clinic.

"When was your last period?" the woman asked me on the phone.

I glanced at the calendar on the wall of the kitchen. It was still turned to the page for May, although I knew we had to be well into June.

"I don't know," I admitted. "Probably two, or maybe three, months ago."

She gave me an appointment for the following day.

There were protestors, maybe twelve or thirteen of them, on the sidewalk in front of the clinic. They carried signs I avoided reading as I parked my car. *I have to do this,* I told myself.

I felt the hungry eyes of the protestors on me as they waited for me to get out of my car. I opened the door, shut it quietly behind me and started walking in the direction of the clinic door.

"Don't kill your baby!" they chanted as I passed them. "Don't kill your baby!"

One woman thrust her sign in front of my head so that I had to dart to the left to avoid running into it.

A young woman greeted me on the walkway to the clinic. "I'm your escort." She smiled, and I let her take my arm and guide me inside. I walked into a waiting room, where a receptionist sat behind a glassed-in desk. I wondered if the glass was bulletproof. Maybe today would be the day the clinic was bombed. The idea didn't distress me. I wouldn't mind, as long as I was the only person killed. Spare the greeter and the staff and the other patients, I thought. Just take me.

The receptionist gave me a clipboard covered with brochures to read and forms to fill out. I took a seat and set to work on them. Once I'd filled out the forms, I let my attention wander to the people sitting around me. Who was here for birth control? Who was here for an abortion? One teenager caught me looking at her and gave me a snarly, scary look that made me study my hands. I didn't lift my gaze again until a nurse brought me a paper cup and pointed to the water cooler in the corner of the waiting room.

"You need to drink water for the sonogram."

I stood up. "A sonogram?" I whispered to her. "I'm here for an abortion."

"We need to know how far along you are so you can have the correct procedure," she said.

I drank the water, cup after cup, until I was certain my bladder would burst. Finally, I was led into a dressing room where I changed into a thin yellow gown, gritting my teeth against the need to urinate. Once I was on the examining table, I became aware for the first time that my belly was round—a smooth, gently sloping hillock above the rest of my body. I felt the flutter of wings again.

"Hey, there." The technician, a woman with short, spiky dark hair, swept into the room carrying the clipboard and my forms. "How are you today?"

"Okay," I said.

She wasted no time, reaching for the tube of gel, smearing it across my stomach. The sonogram screen was turned toward her as she pressed the transducer on my belly.

"Hmm," she said. "About eighteen weeks. Do you want to see?"

"Eighteen *weeks?*" I asked in disbelief. Could it possibly have been that long since that night with Marcus? "What date is it now?"

Her gaze darted from the screen to me. "What do you mean?" she asked.

"Today. What date is today."

"Oh. July twenty-first. Would you like to see the sonogram?" she asked again.

I shook my head. No. I was still stuck on the fact that we were well into July when I thought we were still in June. I pressed my hand to my forehead, rubbing hard, as if I could stuff the cotton back into my brain. "I'm so confused," I said, unaware that I was speaking out loud.

"Well—" the technician turned off the ultrasound machine and wiped the gel from my stomach with tissues "—pregnancy *can* be pretty confusing sometimes. That's why we have counselors to help you think things through." She offered me a hand to help me sit up. "You can empty your bladder in the bathroom across the hall. Then get dressed and go to the first room on the left and the counselor will talk to you about the abortion. It's a two-day procedure at eighteen weeks. And you will absolutely have to have a support person with you to drive you home each day."

In the bathroom, I sobbed as I urinated. I felt completely alone. I knew a second-trimester abortion was a two-day procedure. I was a nurse; I knew what it entailed. In my alcohol-and-depression-fogged brain, I'd hoped I wasn't that far along, that an abortion would be easy. But it wasn't the complexity of the abortion or my inability to supply a "support person" that upset me. It was that I could remember Maggie's eighteen-week sonogram with perfect clarity. She'd sucked her thumb. Rolled a somersault. Waved at Jamie and me. The technician that day had told us she was probably a girl. She'd been so real. So perfect. A tender little bundle of potential, into which we'd poured our hopes and dreams and love.

In the counseling office, I sat across from a woman with short-cropped gray hair, thick white eyebrows and a deep leathery tan.

"Are you cold?" She looked at me with real worry and I realized my entire body was shaking.

"Just nervous," I said. I clenched my teeth to keep them from chattering.

She pulled her chair close to mine until our knees were almost touching.

"The technician doing your sonogram said you seemed surprised to learn how far along you were," she said.

I nodded. "I'm not going to have the abortion," I said, "so I guess I really don't need to talk to you."

"It's your decision," she said. "What made you change your mind?"

I knotted my hands together in my lap. "Because I remember my daughter's sonogram at that...at eighteen weeks, and I can't...it would feel wrong to me, with the baby being this developed."

"Ah," she said. "I understand. You must have very conflicted feelings about this pregnancy to have waited so long."

I nodded, thinking of the little market I'd passed on my way into Wilmington. I could stop there to get a wine cooler on my way home.

"Do you have some support at home?" She glanced at my ring finger. "Your husband? Did he want you to have the abortion?"

"He doesn't know I'm pregnant," I admitted.

"Is it his?" she asked gently.

None of your business, I thought, but I shook my head.

"What do you want to do?"

"I don't know," I whispered.

She looked at the clipboard on her lap, flipping through the forms. "You live on Topsail Island? I can refer you to a therapist in Hampstead," she said. "You have some hard decisions to make and I think you'll need some help."

I nodded again, although I knew I wouldn't go. I was still afraid of seeing a therapist, afraid I might end up in a psych ward if I opened up too much.

The counselor checked a Rolodex file, then wrote a name and number on a card and handed it to me.

"If you're sure you don't want an abortion, please see an obstetrician right away to get started with prenatal care," she said.

"I will."

"And one other thing." She leaned forward, studying me from beneath her white eyebrows. "The escort told me she thought you'd been drinking this morning."

I opened my mouth to protest, but didn't have the strength. I looked down at my hands where they clutched the card she'd given me.

"Alcohol is toxic for your baby," she said.

"I only drink wine coolers."

"They have as much alcoholic content as a beer."

I shook my head. "No, they don't," I said. "The label on the beer says you shouldn't drink it while you're pregnant, but the wine cooler label says nothing about it."

"It should. Right now the law doesn't require that they do, but trust me, they contain the same amount of alcohol as a beer."

I thought she was wrong, or maybe making it up to scare me. Probably, I thought, the brand of wine coolers I liked simply didn't have enough alcohol in them to merit the warning.

"Okay," I said to stop the lecture.

"Would you like me to find an AA meeting near your home?" she offered.

"I don't need an AA meeting." I felt my cheeks flush.

I was shaken by her words, though. Shaken enough to drive the hour home without stopping for a wine cooler, and once at The Sea Tender, I found the remainder of the prenatal vitamins I'd taken while pregnant with Maggie and popped one in my mouth. When I opened the refrigerator door to look for something to wash it down with, though, my choice was between the three-week-old carton of orange juice and the six-pack of wine coolers I'd purchased the day before, which was really like having no choice at all.

For another two weeks, I sat with my secret. I tried and failed to cut back on the wine coolers, but I forced myself to eat better and take the vitamins. I didn't see a doctor. I asked Jamie not to bring Maggie over, telling him I didn't feel well, which was certainly the truth.

Sara was so wrapped up with baby Keith that she rarely stopped by anymore, and that was a relief. Marcus still came over, and I wore loose beach dresses and was boring company, my dilemma the only thing occupying my mind. I knew I'd give birth to this baby, but I wondered if I should keep it. Maybe I could go away someplace where I could have the baby and place it for adoption with no one any the wiser.

One evening in my twenty-first week, Marcus was over and we drank too much and ate pizza as we watched *Seinfeld*. He carried our empty plates into the kitchen and I followed a moment later with our empty bottles.

"You look like you're pregnant in that dress," he teased me.

I was too taken by surprise to speak, and our eyes suddenly locked.

He reached over to touch my belly, then jerked his hand away. "Jesus!"

"It's Jamie's," I said quickly.

"Jamie's?" he asked, as though shocked I'd slept with Jamie during our separation.

"It was the week he and Maggie stayed here," I said. "Remember? When Sara had her baby."

"Does he know?"

I shook my head. "I haven't decided what to do."

"Looks like you've already decided to me. Why didn't you have an abortion?"

I rubbed my eyes, suddenly very tired. "Don't ask hard questions," I said as I walked back into the living room and sat down again on the sofa.

He followed me into the room. "What's hard about it?"

"I lost track of time and I waited too long," I said. "Now I have to decide if I should go away someplace, have the baby, and let someone adopt it."

He shook his head. "You need to tell Jamie."

I let out my breath, dropping my head against the back of the sofa in resignation. "I know." I'd known all along, deep in my heart, I would not go away, not because I felt any special bond to the baby I was carrying, but because I didn't have the energy to figure out where to go.

He sat down at the other end of the sofa. "How do you know it's Jamie's and not mine?" he asked.

"Because," I said, lifting my head to look at him again, "that's the one thing I *have* decided."

Jamie and Maggie moved back into The Sea Tender when I was nearly seven months' pregnant. Jamie was furious with himself for the broken condom, as though it was his fault. He should have checked the date, he said, and he shouldn't have made love to me when I was still so depressed. He wanted to take care of me, and he was upset that I hadn't felt able to tell him about the pregnancy from the start. I was nervous about being two weeks farther along than I said I was. I hoped the baby came two weeks late and would then seem like it was right on time.

Maggie was two and a half and talking a blue streak, but I couldn't understand most of what she said and Jamie needed to serve as her interpreter. I tried hard to understand her, struggling to make sense of the words.

"I'm sorry, honey," I'd say over and over. "Can you say that again, please?" And when she'd repeat her statement and I still didn't get it, she'd wail in frustration. Jamie, on the other hand, could listen to her nonsensical-sounding words and know their meaning almost every time. It was uncanny, as though the two of them shared a secret language I could not be part of.

He seemed to know better than to leave me alone with her, and he hired a nanny to babysit during his work hours at the real estate office and on Sunday mornings when he was in the chapel. He gave up the volunteer fire department altogether so he wouldn't be called away unexpectedly.

Although I was fully in favor of having the nanny take care of Maggie, I disliked being in the house when the middle-aged woman was there. I felt her judging me. I was certain my strained relationship with my child was obvious to her. Jamie had told her my doctor wanted me to rest during the last couple of months of my pregnancy, so that my withdrawal and constant napping wouldn't seem odd to her, but I felt in the way in my own home. So I spent most of my days at Talos. I napped on Marcus's sofa, watched TV, and drank the wine coolers that were forbidden to me at home. I needed them more than ever, with a craving that I knew had become more physical than emotional.

That's why I was drunk when I went into labor, three weeks early, a full five weeks before the fictional due date I'd told Jamie. And that's why I called Marcus to take me to the hospital, not wanting Jamie to see me until I was sober.

Andy was only ten hours old when the social worker came into my room at the hospital. Jamie was in the chair next to the bed, telling me he wanted to name the baby Andrew after his father, and I rolled the name around in my mouth even though I was thinking, *I don't care what we name him.* What I really wanted was to go back to sleep.

The social worker, whose name I instantly forgot, was about thirty, five years older than me. She wore an expression that I read as ten percent pity and ninety percent condescension as she sat in a chair near my bed and asked me questions I didn't bother to answer. I didn't care what she thought of me. I closed my eyes so I didn't have to see Jamie's frown as I ignored her.

"Your baby was premature, but even considering his gestational age of about thirty-seven weeks, he's smaller than he should be," she said. "He didn't grow well inside you."

My eyes still shut, I tried to figure out if anything she'd said could make Jamie doubt his paternity, but the words and the weeks clotted together in my brain and I couldn't sort them out.

"The staff called me in because of that, and because you were inebriated when you arrived."

"I still can't believe it," Jamie said. He'd already chewed me out for it and I hoped he wasn't going to start up again.

"You have what we call a dual diagnosis," the social worker said.

"What does that mean?" Jamie asked.

"First, you have a substance-abuse problem."

I opened my eyes, but only to roll them at her.

"Your blood alcohol level was .09 when you were brought in," the social worker said. "The man who brought you...your brother-in-law? He told the staff you'd been drinking through-out your pregnancy."

I was angry with Marcus. What right did he have to tell anyone anything about me?

"Well, I think she *was* drinking early on," Jamie said naively. "We were separated. But the last couple of months, I've been home and she hasn't had anything except I guess last night—" I saw the light dawn in his eyes. "Have you been drinking over at Marcus's during the day?" he asked.

"Just wine coolers," I said.

"Oh, Laurel."

I wasn't sure if it was disappointment or disgust I heard in his voice.

"The second part of the diagnosis is postpartum depres-sion," the social worker continued as if I'd said nothing. "I spoke with the nurse who talked with you, Mr. Lock-wood—" she nodded at Jamie "—and it seems like that's been a problem for your wife since the birth of your last child."

Jamie looked at me. "*Finally,* Laurel," he said. "Finally we know what's been wrong with you all this time."

I knew about postpartum depression, but whatever was wrong with me was so much worse than that. I'd imagined running a knife through my child's heart. Wasn't that more than depression?

The social worker gave us a tutorial about hormones and

DIANE CHAMBERLAIN

brain chemistry. She said, "I think you must have felt pretty isolated living on Topsail Island after your daughter was born."

In a flash, I relived the weeks after Maggie's birth when she cried constantly and I felt as though I had no one to turn to. I started to answer, but the words couldn't get past the knot in my throat.

"Your brother-in-law said that you barely drank at all before then," the social worker said. "I think you felt so bad after your daughter was born that you started to medicate yourself with alcohol to take away the pain."

I wanted a wine cooler right then, more than anything.

"The pediatricians in the neonatal intensive care unit believe your baby may have problems caused by your drinking."

I was suddenly alert. "What kind of problems?"

"His small size is probably related to your alcohol consumption," she said. "His Apgar scores were low. Fortunately, he doesn't have the facial deformities we often see in babies with fetal alcohol problems, but he did have some respiratory distress that was more than they'd expect in a preemie of his gestational age. There's often central nervous system involvement. Possibly intellectual or cognitive impairment. It's too soon to know how severely he might be affected or even if he *will* be affected that way at all."

I froze inside. What had I done? I felt the way I had the day I'd pulled into the street and cut off Jamie's motorcycle. I'd hurt another human being through my actions. I'd hurt my own baby.

"Jamie, I'm sorry," I said. "I'm so sorry."

He turned his face away from mine, and I knew that he would not be quick to forgive me this time. I didn't blame him.

"Is he..." I tried to picture the baby I'd seen only briefly in the delivery room. "Is he suffering?" I asked.

"It's hard to know how much neonates feel," she said. "What you need to know at this point, though, is that Andrew's now in the custody of Protective Services. When he's ready to leave the hospital, he'll go to a foster home until we can evaluate your home situation."

"*What?*" Jamie asked. "We can take perfectly good care of him." He didn't look at me. "At least *I* can."

"Protective Services will make that evaluation," she said. "You've had a nanny helping with your other child, is that right?"

Jamie nodded.

"She contacted Protective Services when Laurel went into labor. She was worried that your home isn't a safe environment for an infant."

"That woman hates me," I said. I couldn't even remember the nanny's name.

"So her report," the social worker continued, "on top of a substance-abuse problem and Andrew's fragile health means we have to do what's best for him, and that's to place him in foster care once he's released from the hospital and the home is evaluated."

"How do we get him back?" Jamie asked.

"The best chance of getting your baby back is for Laurel to go into a rehab program. There's one in Wilmington that's specifically designed for people like you with dual diagnoses. It's expensive, though, so—"

"The money doesn't matter," Jamie interrupted her.

I was frightened. "Jamie, please don't let them lock me up!"

"It's completely voluntary, Laurel," the social worker said. "But I highly recommend you go if you want a chance to regain custody of your baby."

"Please go into rehab." Sara leaned forward from the chair next to my hospital bed that evening. She'd come into my room and told Jamie to take a break. When she sat down next to me, that was the first thing she said. "Please do it for your family, if not for yourself."

"I wish y'all would just leave me alone," I said. Jamie'd been pleading with me about the rehab program for the last few hours and my nerves were brittle. Ready to snap.

Sara sat back in the chair, while I turned my head to look out the window at a darkening winter sky. She was quiet for so long, I thought she'd given up. I heard her shift in the chair and imagined she was getting ready to go, but she was only leaning forward again.

"I remember this woman," she said slowly. "I saw her a few years ago in a little chapel her husband built. Her husband got up and spoke to the people who were there, and this woman…well, she looked up at him like he'd hung the moon. I remember watching her with envy, thinking *I wish I could feel love like that.*"

I wanted to tell her to shut up, but my mouth wouldn't open. I stared through the window at a distant water tower as she continued.

"The man asked people where they'd felt God that week, and when no one answered, that woman got to her feet because she loved her husband so much she didn't want to see him fail. And she said how she felt God when she was under the stars the night before. She said she was overwhelmed by the beauty of the world."

I turned to her then. "You still remember that?"

"Oh, yes," Sara said. "I admired that woman. Admired her and envied her."

"Where——" my voice was tight, a whisper "——where did she go?"

"She drowned in a bottle of booze," Sara said bluntly. "Her husband wants her back. And her children need her back."

"Maggie doesn't care," I said. "She hates me."

"She's not even three years old!" Sara's voice rose. "She's not capable of hate, Laurie. She just doesn't *know* you. She doesn't trust you."

I shook my head. "All I want right now is a drink," I said.

Sara suddenly grabbed my wrist. I gasped in surprise, trying to wrench my arm free, but she held it fast. "You've become a selfish, self-absorbed bitch." She looked hard into my eyes and I couldn't seem to turn away from her gaze. "I understand that your hormones got screwed up," she said. "I understand you can't help the depression. But you can *fix* it, Laurel. You're the only one who can."

It was Sara's anger more than Jamie's pleading that propelled me into rehab. I didn't go to get my baby back——I was certain he'd be better off without me. But Sara had made me remember the happy, contented, honorable woman I used to be. If there was a chance I could reclaim that woman——the woman who'd drowned——I had to take it.

The rehab facility was in a peaceful, bucolic setting that belied the intensity of the work taking place inside its four buildings. In the beginning, I hated everything about it: the forced structure, the food, the exercise, the group sessions, my assigned individual therapist. I was surrounded by addicts and crazy people with whom I had nothing in common. They allowed no one to visit me, not even Jamie. They gave me the Prozac I'd resisted a couple of years earlier. I was there a full month before I began to feel a change come over me. I broke down during therapy, crying a river of tears that had been locked inside me, perhaps since the deaths of my parents so many years earlier. I remembered Jamie telling me, so long ago, *If you don't deal with loss, it could come back to bite you later.* Was that what had happened to me?

One memorable day, I laughed at a commercial on television and it was like hearing the voice of a stranger in my ears. I couldn't remember the last time I'd laughed.

And one morning, almost two months into the program, I woke up caring. I cared how Maggie and Jamie were doing. I cared about my newborn son whose face I'd barely noticed and wished now I could see and touch. I had a picture of him that Jamie had taken at the hospital and I kept it in my pocket during the day and on my night table at night. A palm-size, dark-haired baby, he lay in an incubator, his head turned away from the camera, hooked up to more wires and tubes than I could count. I knew he was now in a foster home, and I prayed he was with people who were holding him and loving him. It felt extraordinary to care about him and Maggie and Jamie. It felt extraordinary to care about *myself.*

By then, I knew the names of the addicts and crazy people and I knew they were not all that different from me. Some of them had lost their children for good. I wouldn't let that happen. I was going to fight to get well and then I would fight to get my baby back. And once I had him in my arms again, I would never, ever, let him go.

Chapter Thirty-Three

Maggie

BEN LEANED UP ON HIS ELBOW AND STRUCK A match to light the joint he held between his lips. In that quick flash of light, I saw the smooth, dark hair on his chest. I put my hand on his belly and rested my cheek against that hair. Sometimes I couldn't get close enough to him. Even when he was inside me, it wasn't really quite enough. What was wrong with me? He gave me so much and I still wanted more...though I wasn't sure what it was, exactly, that I wanted more of.

He held the joint to my lips and I pulled the smoke into my lungs, holding it there as long as I could before letting my breath out across his chest.

"I'm worried about Andy," he said suddenly.

"Me, too." I knew Mom was still upset we'd given the cops the wrong clothes, but I was glad. I wished I could tell Ben. I wanted to tell *someone* about that split-second decision Mom and I had made. That weird, sudden connection between us. That no-turning-back moment. I couldn't lay that on him, though. There were so many things I wanted to tell him but couldn't. "Everyone's turned against him all of a sudden."

"Well, you haven't. And I haven't. And I'm sure as hell your mom hasn't."

"True."

Ben took another hit on the joint. "Your mother's made Andy her life's work," he said when he finally exhaled. "I figured that out the first time I met her at the pool, when she gave me written instructions on the best way to deal with him." He laughed. My head bounced on his chest.

"That's my mom," I said.

"She doesn't mother *you* much, though, does she?"

"Well, I'm seventeen."

"But has she ever?" he asked. "Has she ever taken care of you the way she takes care of Andy?"

I felt a hurt inside me that I didn't want to feel. "I never needed taking care of the way Andy does," I said.

"Everybody needs to be taken care of."

"That's why I've got you," I said.

He didn't say anything, and the hurt expanded inside my chest. He held the joint to my lips again, but I shook my head. I felt a little sick from it now. I tried to think of a different subject we could talk about. His daughter. He loved talking about her. I could ask him when he'd see her again. I opened my mouth to speak, but the alert tones suddenly rang out from his fire department pager, which was buried somewhere in the pile of clothes on the floor.

Ben jumped to his feet, as I knew he would.

"Are you getting up?" He pulled his T-shirt over his head.

I stretched beneath the covers. "I'm going to stay here a while." The long window in front of the bed was full of stars. I could sit outside and try to make contact with Daddy's spirit. It had been so long since I'd been able to reach him, and all that talk about needing to be taken care of really got to me.

"I don't like you being here alone at night." He had no idea how often I came to The Sea Tender alone.

"I'll be okay," I said.

I listened to him walk through the living room and close the front door. I heard the *thump* as he jumped from the steps to the sand. I tried to hear his van start, but he must have parked too far away.

He'd handed me the joint before he left. I held it between my lips without inhaling as I pulled on my shorts and top. I blew out the candles, then walked outside to sit in my favorite spot on the edge of the deck. I dropped the rest of the joint to the sand below. *Wasteful,* Ben would say.

Closing my eyes, I took in a deep, salty breath as I tried to still my mind.

At least the fire had been good for Ben, I thought. He was happy in the department now. He wouldn't leave.

Stop thinking!

I took in another deep breath, and my mind was on the brink of clearing up when those damned posters from the memorial service popped into it again.

I groaned. "Daddy," I whispered in frustration. *"Please come."*

What if he was just as frustrated as I was? Maybe he was waiting on the other side for me to quiet my mind long enough for him to break through. Maybe I was failing him like I was failing everybody else.

I thought I heard a sound from inside the house. I turned to listen through the screened door, but all I could hear was the ocean.

A flash of light bobbed on the railing next to me. I jumped to my feet.

"Maggie?"

A woman's voice. I felt so busted and was glad I'd dropped the joint.

I tried to block the beam of the flashlight with my hand to see who was aiming it at me, but it was impossible. I was dizzy from standing up too quickly. I grabbed the deck railing. "Who are you?" I called.

"Oh my God, I don't believe this!"

Dawn. She pushed open the screened door. Her flashlight blinded me.

"What are you doing here?" I asked as I backed against the railing, shielding my eyes with my arm.

"I could ask you the same question."

What did she know? The light was trapping me. I had to get away from it. I pushed past her and into the house. She followed me inside.

"This is the cottage where I lived when I was little." My voice shook. "I visit it sometimes. I was just going to leave."

Dawn scanned the living room and kitchen with her flashlight. I could just make out that her hair was in a ponytail and she had frown lines like stripes across her forehead. She sat down on the arm of the sofa and put the flashlight on the floor, aiming it toward the corner of the room. She was too quiet. I wanted to get my pocketbook out of the bedroom so I could escape, but what if she followed me in there and saw the unmade bed? Did she have a clue what was going on? Why was she *here*?

I picked up my bottle of water from the breakfast bar and started talking to fill the silence.

"I'm sorry I didn't call you about the fund-raising yet," I said. "I was waiting till I worked out details, but we're going to have this massive makeover event at the high school, with—"

"Why was Ben here?" she asked.

Shit. Shit. Shit. "Ben?" I asked. "What makes you think he was here?"

"Don't play dumb," she said. "D'you think I just happened to show up here tonight? I followed him. I wanted to know where he disappeared to so many nights without explanation. When I saw him leave this cottage, I decided to see what was so...so *alluring* to him about it. Now I get it."

I opened the water bottle and took a sip to give me time to think. "We meet here sometimes to talk about the swim team," I tried.

"You can do better than that," she said.

"Dawn, it's really not like—"

"Don't give me that crap." She sounded harsh, not like the Dawn I thought I knew. "How long's this been going on?"

I sighed. Gave in. I felt my shoulders sag. "A while," I said.

"I can't believe he's cheating on me with a *teenager*. A *kid*. It's sick."

"He's *not* cheating on you!"

"What do you call it?"

"You're just friends."

"Oh, cut me a break," she said. "Did he tell you that?"

I was afraid of getting Ben in more trouble by saying the wrong thing, but I was so nervous I couldn't think straight. "I know when he first moved in, he...the two of you...you slept together, and I know you hoped you'd be more than just friends, but—"

"That goddamned son of a bitch." She rubbed her neck. "I thought he was different, but turns out he's like all the rest. He wants the thrill of doing something forbidden, behind closed doors. With a tight little body." She motioned toward me, toward my body.

"Ben's so not like that."

"Don't tell me what Ben's 'so not' like!" she snapped. "I *live* with him, sugar. I know him better than you ever will."

I twisted the cap of the bottle back and forth, afraid of her anger and what she might do. Who she might tell.

"Does your mama know about this?" She was a mind reader. "She can get him for statutory rape."

"The age of consent is sixteen."

She let out a nasty laugh. "You've figured this all out, I see," she said. "Even if it's not illegal, it's *immoral* for a twenty-eight-year-old man to sleep with a seventeen-year-old girl."

"Age is just a number." I wrinkled my nose as the cliché popped out of my idiotic mouth.

"And it's immoral to sleep with two women at once and lie to them about it."

"It's not at once. You are so *yesterday* to him!" I felt like a bitch, but she deserved it. "You think he's your boyfriend, but he's not."

She stared at me, then started laughing again. "Lord have mercy," she said, "I'm going to give that bastard one hell of a talking-to." She tilted her head to the side. "Was he your first?"

"None of your business."

"I just bet he was. Men love that, don't they? Popping the cherry."

"Don't talk that way about him!" I said. "Don't lump him together with all the losers you've been—"

"Does your mama know you're smoking weed?"

"*What?*"

"Don't play innocent with me, Maggie. It reeks in here."

Oh God. Now she had two things on me. My hand twisted the bottle cap back and forth. Back and forth.

Suddenly, she stood up. When she spoke again, her voice was totally different. She growled like a tiger. "Lay off my man, girl," she said. She picked up the flashlight and walked to the door. "If you don't, I'll have to tell your mama what you're up to, and she's got enough to worry about right now. You sure don't want to add to that now, do you, sugar?"

I threw the bottle hard—*really* hard—before I knew what I was doing. It caught her on the side of her neck and she screeched, dropping the flashlight.

"*Bitch!*" she said.

"I'm sorry!" I pressed my hands to my face. "I didn't mean to do that, Dawn! Honest!"

She picked up the flashlight and I thought she was going to come after me with it, but she opened the door and ran onto the front deck. I listened to the creak of the stairs and heard her jump to the sand.

I slammed the door shut and turned the lock. Then I

pulled my phone from my pocket and hit the speed dial for Ben's cell. No answer.

As fast as I could, I typed a text message into the keypad.

D knows.

Chapter Thirty-Four

Laurel

"HAVE A SEAT, PLEASE." DENNIS SHARTELL led me into his office and gestured toward one of the leather chairs in front of a massive mahogany desk.

"I appreciate you seeing me so quickly," I said as I sat down. I'd only received his name from Ms. Terrell the day before, but the attorney's receptionist said he'd be able to squeeze me in.

"I can imagine what you're going through," he said as he sat down on the other side of the desk. "I've heard the rumors."

"You've heard them here? In Wilmington?"

"The fire was big news," he said, "and although the officials aren't calling it arson, everyone knows it's arson—or in legal terminology, the 'burning of a church.' People love a good twist to a story. What better twist than the hero turns out to be the villain?"

"He's not, though."

He nodded, the overhead light glinting off his glasses. He was a slender man, but soft looking, as though he didn't have to work hard at keeping the weight off. His face was long beneath thinning dark hair, and he wore a smile that was equal parts kind and self-confident. I liked him. I was practically in *love* with him. He would help me make sense of this ridiculous mess.

"Tell me what you know," he said, clicking his ballpoint pen above a yellow legal pad. "What evidence do they have so far?"

"As far as I know, they just have the word of a few people that Andy was outside during the lock-in. I don't believe it, though. Even if it's true, so what? But my son is a very concrete thinker. If the rules say, 'this is a lock-in and you stay inside,' he'd stay inside."

"What do you mean, he's a concrete thinker?"

I explained FASD to him. Maybe it would have been better to find an attorney already familiar with the disorder. But Dennis took notes and appeared to be listening carefully.

"All right," he said when I had finished talking. "Who are the witnesses who claim they saw Andy outside during the lock-in?"

"One is a boy named Keith Weston." I told him about Andy's fight with Keith during the lock-in and about their long-ago history as childhood friends. "Another was a woman who was just passing by the church that night. Of course, she couldn't identify Andy by name, but she described seeing a boy who may have resembled him. Then his friend Emily—who's also a special needs child—said he disappeared during the lock-in."

He looked at me as if waiting for more. "That's it?" he asked finally.

"That's all I know of. They searched his room."

"They had a warrant?"

"No. I signed a consent-to-search form."

"Did they remove anything?"

"They took the clothes he had on the night of the lock-in. And I think some information from his computer."

Dennis tapped the pen against his jaw. "Andy seemed to be the only person who knew a safe way out of the building, is that correct?"

"Yes. But that's not a crime."

"Hardly." He chuckled. "From what I've read, your son is viewed as an outsider. Not very popular. Do you agree with that description of him?"

I nodded. "Yes," I said. "He doesn't fit in very well, but that doesn't mean he'd set a fire to make himself look like a big man on campus."

"Well." Dennis rested his pen on the legal pad and sat back in his chair. "Unless there's more to this picture than meets the eye, it would seem that all they have now is circumstantial evidence. Nothing they can use to pin a felony on your son, that's for sure. How did he get to the lock-in?"

"My daughter—his sister, Maggie—drove him."

"And I assume Maggie knows he wasn't carrying a couple of gallons of flammable liquid, right?"

I smiled. I was beginning to relax about this whole thing. It was, as I'd thought all along, absurd. "Right," I said.

"As long as his clothes don't come back from the lab with traces of accelerant on them, I'd say he's home free."

"That won't happen," I said. I knew that for a fact.

* * *

I was so relieved after speaking to Dennis that I sang along with the radio in my car. I opened the windows, letting my hair blow around my head in the warm spring air as I sang oldies-but-goodies at the top of my lungs all the way to the swing bridge.

I turned right after crossing the bridge and headed for Jabeen's. Maybe Sara was still in Surf City and would have some time to catch up. Once again, I felt out of touch with her. I'd called twice in the past few days, but she hadn't called back.

Dawn was cleaning the counter when I walked into the empty café. She looked up and gave me a halfhearted wave.

"Hi, Dawn," I said. "Is Sara in today?"

"She's back at the hospital." She barely glanced at me as she sprayed a spot on the counter, but I could see that her eyes were bloodshot and I was immediately worried.

"Is Keith okay?" I asked.

"He's actually doing better." She put down the cloth and spray bottle and picked up a paper cup, holding it under the spigot of one of the coffeemakers. "But those burn treatments don't sound like fun."

"I know," I said. "I had a couple of burn patients when I was in nurse's training." Scrubbing scorched skin raw had been, without a doubt, one of the most disturbing parts of my training. "Poor Keith. It's got to be so hard for Sara to watch him go through that."

Dawn snapped a lid on the cup of coffee I hadn't ordered and handed it to me.

"Thanks," I said, taking a sip.

"She makes out like she's doing all right with it," Dawn said, "but you know she must be wrung out." Dawn looked wrung out herself. There were puffy bags under her eyes.

"How about you?" I didn't want to pry, but something was clearly wrong. "Are you all right?" I asked.

She nodded. "Just tired." She sat down on the stool behind the cash register, her feet propped up on the rung, and rubbed her palms on her lean, denim-covered thighs. "You wouldn't believe how the money's been rolling in since the *Today* show," she said with a little more pep in her voice. "Thanks for your help with that."

"You're the one doing all the work." I took another sip of the coffee. "Is Ben's head healed?"

She ran her fingers through her pretty red hair, taking her time, as if she had to think about her answer. "Doesn't Maggie keep you informed?" she asked.

It took me a moment to realize that my children would see Ben at swim practices. "Oh, of course," I said, "I guess if he were having any problems, Maggie or Andy would have let me know." Actually, I wasn't sure either of them would think to tell me. "He *is* all right, isn't he?"

"He's fine," she said quickly. Then she chuckled, and I imagined she was thinking of a private moment between them, because when she spoke again, it wasn't about anything funny. "Listen, sugar." She leaned forward, resting her elbows on her knees. "I know there's all this talk about Andy, and it must be driving you 'round the bend."

"It is," I acknowledged.

"Well, I just want to say that, even if Andy *did* have something to do with the fire, I'm sure he'll be able to get off because he couldn't possibly understand the seriousness of what he was doing."

I stared at her, momentarily speechless. I knew she was trying to comfort me, but it certainly wasn't working.

"Andy didn't do anything wrong," I said.

"I'm just saying, even if he did."

I let out a long sigh. "All right." I gave up. People were going to believe what they wanted to and there wasn't much I could do about it. "Thanks for the coffee. And if you talk to Sara before I do, please tell her I was asking about her and Keith."

As I drove home, I wondered if Sara hadn't returned my calls because she, too, believed Andy was responsible for the fire. Ludicrous. Sara knew Andy nearly as well as I did. I'd try calling her again as soon as I got home.

There was a police car in front of the house when I pulled in my driveway, and the sight of it wiped Sara from my mind. I hurried into the house and found Maggie standing in the entryway with Sergeant Wood.

"They think we gave them the wrong clothes," she said quickly.

I looked from her to the sergeant.

"Sorry to disturb you again, ma'am," he said. "But we have some pictures from the lock-in that kids took with their cell phone cameras. The clothing and shoes you gave us are not what Andy has on in those pictures."

"You're kidding." I didn't look at Maggie. I never should have dragged her into this.

"I'd like to take another look in his room for the right articles of clothing."

I hesitated, maybe a moment too long. "Sure," I said. "Go ahead."

We followed Sergeant Wood upstairs, Maggie gnawing her lip. I wished she didn't look so guilty.

In Andy's room, I watched the sergeant pull the correct pair of sneakers from his closet. "These look more like it," he said. He withdrew a photograph from his shirt pocket and studied it, then handed it to me.

My hand was damp with sweat as I took the photograph from him. The picture was of two boys I didn't know, posing like bodybuilders, flexing their arms to show off their small adolescent biceps. Andy and Emily stood off to one side of the boys, vacant looks on their faces, clearly incidental to the main subjects of the photograph.

"I was sure he was wearing those others," I said, afraid the sergeant would lift the shoes to his nose and smell what I had smelled on them, but he simply dropped them into two separate bags. I looked at the picture again. "And I could have sworn he'd had on that sage-colored shirt."

"Me, too," Maggie added. "He had it on earlier that day, so I guess we got mixed up."

I wanted her to be quiet, afraid she'd give us away—if we were not already given away.

"Uh-huh," Sergeant Wood said. I didn't think he believed a word we were saying, but apparently he wasn't going to call us on it. At least not yet.

He finished his collection of clothing and we followed him downstairs again.

"Good day, ma'am. Miss." He nodded to us, then let himself out.

As soon as the door shut behind him, Maggie grabbed my arm.

"Why didn't you throw them away?" she asked. "The shoes and his clothes?"

"I didn't think of it," I said. "I never thought of pictures. But I should have given them the right clothes from the start. That was really stupid of me. I'm sorry, Maggie."

We fell quiet, neither of us moving away from the front door.

"What should it matter?" I asked. "He's innocent, so the clothes won't have anything flammable on them, right?"

"Oh God, I hope not."

"Maggie, you can't possibly think—"

"What if his cigarette lighter leaked, like you said?"

"Then we'll explain about the lighter," I said calmly. "I met with the lawyer this morning, and he said everything's circumstantial evidence so far. So as long as the clothes come back clean, Andy's in the clear."

She looked at me with worry in her eyes.

"Nothing will be on them, Maggie." I hugged her to me and she melted in my arms, unusual for my independent daughter. "We have nothing at all to worry about."

Chapter Thirty-Five

Maggie

I DIDN'T HEAR ANYTHING FROM BEN THE DAY after Dawn busted me, even though I left six messages for him. Between the cop coming back for Andy's clothes and me waiting for Mom to say, *I had a call from Dawn Reynolds today, Maggie,* I was ready to slit my wrists. And I had the tiniest—just the teeny tiniest—bit of doubt about Ben. That was the worst part of all.

He finally called on my cell that night. "I'll call you right back!" I said. Then I went out to our pier; I couldn't take the chance Mom would overhear me.

I speed-dialed him as soon as I was far enough from the house to talk. "I've been freaking out!" I said when he picked up. "What did Dawn say?"

"Everything's cool," Ben said. "At least for now. She was rabid when I got home last night, though."

"What did you tell her?"

"I calmed her down. That took a while." He laughed a little. "I told her...you know...how she thought we...her and me...have something that we don't."

I relaxed. I used to feel sorry for Dawn, but after last night when she was such a bitch, that was over. "Was she really upset?"

"Yeah. Sure. I think she got it, though."

"Do you think she'll tell?" I'd reached the end of the pier and sat down on one of the posts. "I thought for sure she'd call my mother today."

"Well, that could still be a problem, Maggie. She thinks it's wrong for us to see each other. That I'm robbing the cradle."

"That's *our* business!" I heard my voice carry over the dark water and wondered if the pier was such a good idea after all.

"Well, I just don't want her to make it *her* business, if you get what I'm saying."

"What do you mean?"

"I think you and I need to lay low for a while. Just till Dawn settles down."

"What do you mean, lay low?"

"Not see each other. Definitely not at The Sea Tender. We can talk and e-mail, but I don't think we should get together."

How could he even say the words? "Ben!" I said. "I *have* to see you! I'll go crazy if I can't see you!"

"I know," he said. "Me, too. But we can't risk pissing Dawn off. You're going to be eighteen soon and out of high school. Then it won't matter so much. So let's just——"

"Couldn't we... We have swim practice Saturday. Wouldn't it seem normal to get together afterward like we used to? You know, to talk about the team? Dawn couldn't make a federal case about that."

He waited a second, then said, "Dawn's coming to practice Saturday."

"What?" I stood up. *"Why?"*

"She said she misses watching the kids, but I'm sure it's to keep an eye on us. So we have to act cool, Maggie, all right?"

"Why didn't you tell her she can't come?"

"Because I'm trying to *protect* us." I thought he sounded a little fed up with me. "Not only could she tell your mother, but Marcus or the rec center staff or the parents of the kids we work with. Let me deal with her, okay? I know her better than you do. We just need to keep our noses clean for a while. Till you graduate."

"That's over a month away!"

"It'll fly by, angel."

"How can you sound so *calm?"*

"I'm not. It's just that I've had twenty-four hours to think of the best thing to do. It's fresh news to you."

I lowered myself to the pier and lay down on my back. It was too cloudy to see the stars. My eyes were full of tears, anyway. The thing was, I knew he was right. I sucked at being patient, but I could wait another month to have a lifetime with him.

"Maggie? You still there?"

"I think..." A plan was taking shape in my mind. "I think I won't live on campus next year," I said. "I'll commute. Maybe I could find a roommate here on the island and not have to live at home."

"What are you talking about? You've always planned to live on campus."

"I don't want to be that far from you."

"It's only forty-five minutes."

"That's too far." I wiped tears off my cheeks with my fingers.

"I think you should live on campus. It'd be a good experience for you."

"Don't you want me to be closer?"

"Of course. But I'll visit you there all the time, if you're not too embarrassed to be seen with an ol' man."

I smiled. "No way." I loved the idea of finally being able to show him off in public.

"Don't decide now, Maggie," he said. "I think it'd be good for you, though. You know. Get that whole college experience."

If it was *him* going away to college with me staying on Topsail, I wouldn't want him to live on campus. How could he just let me go that easily? I thought how it felt to rest my head on his chest. How content I felt when he wrapped his arms around me.

"Ben?"

"I'm here."

"Can we…maybe in a week…can we find someplace to be together. Just for a while? The beach at night or someplace? No one will know. Please?"

He was quiet and I tightened every muscle in my body, waiting for his answer.

"All right," he said. "I'd better get off now."

"I love you."

"Love you, too."

I clicked off my phone, and lay there on the pier until I fell asleep, hanging on to his "love you, too" by my fingertips.

Chapter Thirty-Six

Laurel

I HUNG UP THE PHONE, THEN RACED ACROSS campus from the elementary school to the high school. I was breathless and perspiring by the time I arrived in the main office.

"In there." The secretary nodded toward the room used for meetings. The door was slightly ajar and I pushed it open without knocking. Flip Cates sat at the long table, and although Flip was not a large man, he dwarfed Andy sitting across from him. Andy leaped up from his chair and ran into my arms, sobbing.

"It's okay, sweetie." I rocked him back and forth like I did when he was little. "Don't be scared. It's going to be all right." Was it? Could Andy feel how my own body trembled beneath his arms?

Flip had left a message on my cell that they had a petition requesting Andy be taken into custody. Now I looked at him over Andy's head. *"Why?"* I asked.

"His pants and shoes had traces of accelerant on them," he said. "I'm sorry, Laurel."

The lighter. "Maybe he spilled lighter fluid when he—"

Flip shook his head. "It's gasoline and diesel."

Was that what I'd smelled on his shoes? It couldn't have been. "That can't *be,* Flip!" Andy had settled into my arms as if he planned to stay there forever. "It's got to be a mistake. A conspiracy or something." I grasped at straws as my heart lost its rhythm behind my breastbone. "This is completely impossible!"

"I know you're upset, Laur—"

"Flip! You *know* this child." I hugged Andy even closer to my body. Tears slid down my cheeks that I didn't want him to see. "You've known him nearly all his life! Please! At least tell me you think this is some kind of crazy mistake!"

I supposed there was some sympathy in Flip's eyes, but I was blind to it at that moment.

"I'm sorry," he said, "but I need to take him to the juvenile detention center in Castle Hayne. You can follow in your car or ride with him in mine."

"With *him,*" I said. "I'm not letting him out of my sight."

I called Marcus's cell from the back of Flip's cruiser.

"Already on my way," Marcus said. "I just heard."

"I don't know what's going on, Marcus." I tried to keep my voice even for Andy's sake. I'd scared him with my hysterics at the high school. Now he shivered next to me, his body close to mine. I hadn't seen him this frightened since he was a little boy.

"Call his lawyer," Marcus said. "I'll see you there."

"Is he going to shoot us?" Andy whispered to me when I shut my phone.

"Who?" I asked. "*Flip?* No, of course not. No one's going to shoot us."

At the detention center, the thirty-something, balding intake officer had me fill out a form while he talked to Flip in legalese. Then he fingerprinted Andy, because of "the serious nature of the crime."

Marcus arrived just as another uniformed officer handed Andy a navy-blue jumpsuit and said to follow him. I suddenly understood that they meant to keep him there.

"He can't *stay* here!" I said to the intake officer as Marcus came to stand at my side. "I'll put up bail. Just tell me how much and—"

"There is no bond in juvenile cases, ma'am," the man said.

Marcus reached across the man's desk to shake his hand, and I was glad he was in uniform. "I'm Marcus Lockwood," he said. "The boy's uncle."

"You the fire marshal in Surf City?"

Marcus nodded.

"What do you mean, no bond?" I asked.

"He'll have a secure custody hearing within five days and the judge will decide if he waits here until his trial or if he can be released to home. Given the serious nature of the crime, though, I imagine he'll be staying here."

"Five days!" I said. "I won't let him stay here a single night!"

I grabbed Marcus's arm, knowing I was digging my nails into his flesh but unable to stop myself.

"Andy has special needs," Marcus said. "He won't do well in detention."

"Mrs. Lockwood here's explained about his special needs," the officer said.

"I didn't realize you expected him to actually *stay* here when I told you, though!" I said.

"What did you think the word 'detention' means, ma'am?" he asked.

"She didn't know it meant overnight," Marcus said with more calm than I felt. "He's never stayed away from home overnight."

"I'll recommend a hearing be scheduled as quick as possible," the officer said.

"Today," I said. "Please. It needs to be today."

"Ma'am, it's already three o'clock. This is not considered an emergency case. However, one thing you may not have thought of is that when this gets out, the community is going to be mighty angry. It may be best your boy remain here for his own safety, and the judge will take that into account."

"There's no way it would be best for him to stay here!"

"She's right," Marcus said to the officer. "Aim for tomorrow."

Andy returned to the room in a navy jumpsuit that was too big on him and blue flip-flops. The skin around his eyes was puffy and red, but he no longer looked terrified. More like defeated. I drew choppy breaths through my mouth, trying to keep from crying. That would only scare him more.

Marcus hugged him, and I wanted to pull him into my

arms again, but knew I'd fall apart if I did. Andy didn't say a word. It wasn't like him to be so quiet and I worried about what the other officer might have said—or worse, *done*—to him.

"Andy," I managed to say, "please don't worry, sweetie. We're going to get this all straightened out."

"Y'all can sit down again," the intake officer said, although he remained standing himself. "I need to make a copy of the petition. We'll be sending it along to your attorney, ma'am."

We sat down on the hard wooden chairs as he left the room.

"The man said I have to stay here." Andy looked at Marcus.

"For a couple days," Marcus said. "It'll be all right. Your mom has an attorney...a lawyer. He'll come talk to you."

"His name's Mr. Shartell, Andy." My voice sounded remarkably calm given how hysterically I was screaming inside. "He's on *your side,* sweetie, so you don't have to be afraid to tell him the truth when he comes, all right?"

"I don't want to stay here." He hadn't heard a word I'd said. I was sure of it. I wondered if Marcus caught the tremor in his chin.

"I know," I said. "I know you don't. And we'll get you out as soon as we can." Over Andy's head, I mouthed the words to Marcus, *I can't leave him here!*

Marcus reached across the back of Andy's chair to squeeze my shoulder.

Andy looked at Marcus again. "I don't understand, Uncle Marcus," he said. "I didn't do anything wrong."

Marcus moved his hand from my shoulder to Andy's, a small smile of encouragement on his lips. "I know, son," he said.

I stared at Marcus. I'd never heard him call Andy "son" before. Never. That was the way I'd always wanted it. But now, I wanted to hear him say that word again and again and again.

Chapter Thirty-Seven

Marcus
1992

JAMIE DIDN'T LET ME SEE LAUREL TILL SHE'D been in rehab three months. Not that I didn't *try* to visit her before that. Got turned away by the sentry at the front desk. "Only her husband and people he authorizes can visit her," I was told. Apparently, I wasn't one of those people. Jamie said I'd "enabled" her drinking. Give me a break. Laurel was no alcoholic and I didn't believe there was a damn thing wrong with her baby. Jamie and the hospital and Protective Services had made a fuss about nothing.

"You can see her," Jamie finally told me one afternoon at The Sea Tender. "She's strong enough now."

"She's got to be 'strong' to see me?" I was pissed.

"Yeah, exactly. She does."

"Go fuck yourself," I said.

Jamie closed his eyes the way he did when he was angry and trying to control it, like he was silently counting to ten. I hated when he did that. Hated his self-control.

"You know." He opened his eyes again. "I have a two-year-old daughter in the next room. Maybe she's napping, but maybe not, and I don't appreciate you using that language in her presence."

"You self-righteous—"

"Do you want to see her or not?" he interrupted me. "Because I can still tell them not to let you in."

"Yes, I want to see her!"

"Then shut up. And when you go there, go sober."

I hardly recognized her as she walked toward me in the rehab lobby. She filled out her jeans again—I hadn't realized how much weight she'd lost the past couple of years—and she wore a red V-neck sweater, a blast of color beneath her dark hair. She smiled at me as she came closer. I hugged her hard, not wanting to let go, because she'd see the tears in my eyes. I'd forgotten what the real Laurel looked like. Forgotten the smile. The light in her eyes.

I finally released her. "You look unbelievable," I said.

She knew it. Knew she gave off a glow. "It's good to see you, Marcus," she said. "Come on. Let's go to the lounge where we can talk." Taking my arm, she guided me through a maze of hallways until we reached a small room filled with armchairs. We were the only people there. We sat in a couple of chairs by the windows.

Kicking off her shoes, she lifted her feet onto the chair and hugged her knees.

"How are you?" she asked.

"I'm okay," I answered. "But I want to know about *you*. What's it been like to be locked up in here?"

She smiled again. A secret smile. It reminded me of Jamie when he talked about his "relationship with God," like it was something only he could understand and someone as low on the food chain as myself could never get it. I wasn't so crazy about the secret in her smile.

"It was bad at first," she said. "And I hated this place. But they've helped me so much."

"They convince you you had a drinking problem?" I asked.

That frickin' smile again. "I'm an alcoholic." She sounded like a parrot, repeating what she'd been told.

I leaned forward. "You drank little pink girly things."

"I had withdrawal symptoms getting off those little pink girly things," she said. "That's how bad it was. I'm an alcoholic, Marcus. And so are you."

I rapped the side of her head with my knuckles. "Hello? Is my favorite sister-in-law still in there?"

She rested her chin on her knees, her eyes pinning me to the back of my chair. "I hurt my baby," she said. "I was depressed after I had Maggie. That part I couldn't help, except that I should have taken antidepressants when my doctor told me to. I'm sorry I've been a crappy mother to her, but I have to forgive myself for that and move on. I won't be a crappy mother to my little boy when I get him back. My Andy."

I'd lost her. It wasn't like I wanted her to be a bad mother to her kids, but I still wanted her to be my friend. She'd been my *best* friend. More than that. The night in my guest room—a night I knew she regretted but I couldn't—would always be in my memory. That Laurel was gone now. I'd never get her back.

"What have they done to you?" I asked.

"What do you mean?"

"They've turned you into a Stepford wife or something."

"I'm sober, Marcus," she said. "And I'm happy and starting to feel good about myself again."

I looked out the window. Acres and acres of rolling pasture, bordered by dense forest. I supposed the setting would seem peaceful to most people, but I was suffocating, looking at it. I needed the ocean. Didn't she?

"When are you coming home?" I asked.

"I'm nowhere near ready to leave here," she said. "I feel safe here. Safe from alcohol." She pinned me again with her eyes. "Safe from you."

I wanted to say *Bullshit*, but stopped myself. Because I suddenly got it. I may have loved her. I may have been the closest thing she had to a friend for a couple of years. But I hadn't been good for her.

She pulled a picture from her shirt pocket and handed it to me. The baby. I'd seen him after he was born, hooked up to monitors in the intensive-care unit. He'd looked barely alive, his puny little chest struggling to rise and fall above ribs like bird bones. I hadn't been able to look at him for long. I felt sorry for her that this flimsy piece of paper was all she had of her baby.

"He was completely vulnerable," she said. "Completely dependent on me to take care of him." She pressed her fingers to her mouth as her eyes filled. "I don't care how hard this is, being here. I'd climb Mount Everest for him. I'll gladly give up alcohol to have him back. To be a true mother to him."

I stared at the baby, and something snapped inside me. I saw bruises where this tube or that entered his body. Saw veins under his skin. He was so defenseless. Fragile. Damaged. If they said it was alcohol that hurt him, then maybe it was. And I'd done my part to make his mother a drunk. For the second time in an hour, my eyes burned.

"Marcus," Laurel said. "Please get sober. If you don't, then I don't want you coming over to The Sea Tender once I'm home. Understand?"

"No," I said. "I don't understand."

"If you don't get sober, I'll have to avoid you." Her voice broke. What she was saying cost her something.

"You'd cut me out of your life? Out of Maggie and——" I lifted the picture in my hand "——this little guy's lives?"

She nodded. "Get sober, Marcus," she pleaded. "I love you, and you're a good man, deep inside. I know you are."

No, I wasn't. There'd been something off about me, right from the start. I always managed to push away the people I cared about. The people who cared about me.

I tried to give the picture back to her, but she cupped her hands around my hand, forcing my fingers to tighten around the photograph.

"Keep it," she said. "It's *yours*."

I stared at her, the moment so charged it stole my voice. *What's mine?* I wanted to ask. *The picture? Or the baby?*

But the moment passed. She looked away from me, quickly. So quickly, that she told me all I needed to know.

* * *

I drank half a bottle of whiskey that night, staring at the baby's picture. The booze didn't taste as good as it usually did. After a while, in a moment of monumental strength, I poured every damn ounce of alcohol I had in the house down the kitchen drain. I called AA's twenty-four-hour number. There was a meeting in Wilmington the next morning at seven.

I couldn't sleep that night, afraid I'd miss my alarm. I left the house at five-thirty and drove through a pink dawn to Wilmington. Found the church building where the meeting would be held. Forced myself to walk into the room and was bowled over to see Flip Cates inside the doorway. He was a rookie cop in Surf City, a year or two older than me, and he'd made that same hour drive I'd just made to get there. He gave me a surprised smile. An arm around my shoulders as he led me into the room.

"Glad to see you, Marcus," he said.

"This your first meeting, too?" I asked.

He laughed. "More like my hundred and first," he said, and I thought, *If he could do it, maybe I can, too.*

I hit meetings every night, piling the miles on my pickup. Flip got me a construction job with a boss who'd let me take off for a meeting on days when I knew I was sinking. I doubt I would have made it through without Flip, because eighty percent of me wasn't sold on sobriety. Eighty percent of me craved a beer. But that other twenty percent was stubborn as hell. It hung on to the image of a baby chained to tubes and wires. Of a woman who'd said the words "I love you" to me, even if she'd only said them as a sister-in-law to a brother-in-law. That part of me was stronger than I'd ever known.

I kept my sobriety to myself. I didn't want to hear Jamie say he was proud of me, when I'd wanted him to be proud of me all along. I didn't want to feel him watching me, waiting for me to screw up. And I didn't want to feel the burning guilt that seared me every time I remembered that I'd slept with my brother's wife.

I got jumpy as Laurel's release day neared. I wanted to see her, sure, but living near her again? A mistake—for both of us. I didn't want to be her brother-in-law. I wanted more than that. Not being able to have it, yet living next door to her, would be torture. The last thing I needed with only two months of sobriety under my belt was torture.

I had an AA buddy from Asheville. I decided to move there—a good six-hour drive from Topsail—the week before Laurel came home. Jamie was shocked, but pleased.

"Good for you, Marcus!" he said. "It'll be good for you to really get out on your own. Maybe get yourself straight."

Fuck you, bro.

After Laurel's return, my mother wrote to tell me it was like having the "old Laurel" back. I remembered the old Laurel. Very cool woman. I was glad for her.

Several months later, Mama told me that one-year-old Andy had been returned to Jamie and Laurel. I wanted to visit. Wanted to see Laurel and the boy I was sure was my son. I didn't go. I stayed in Asheville, joining the fire department— first as a volunteer, later as paid staff—and making a life for myself four hundred miles from my family. I was never going back, because seeing Laurel again would be like taking a sip of booze: I would only want more.

Chapter Thirty-Eight

Andy

I HAD MY OWN ROOM LIKE AT HOME, BUT IT was a bad room. I didn't have any windows except in the big metal door, and the bathroom was right next to my bed. When I went to the bathroom, I worried someone would look in the window in the door. I got nervous when I had to go and by the end of the first day, my stomach hurt.

I was a lot littler than the other boys. Everybody wore dark blue jump things and flip-flops. The man who gave me mine said it was the littlest size they had. At dinner, it was like the cafeteria at school with long tables and everyone being there except there were no girls. I said hello and smiled at everyone. It was hard because I was scared. And nobody smiled back. I asked everybody, when can I go home? Some of the boys said maybe never.

I couldn't sleep good last night. I was scared someone would come in the metal door and hurt me. I watched the door all night. Maybe I slept a little though, because I had a dream I was fishing on the pier with Uncle Marcus.

A bad thing happened at breakfast this morning. I said hi to a boy and smiled at him. He started laughing and said to the other boys, "We got us a little pansy," and the boys laughed too and started saying things. One of them nearly pushed my tray off the table and said, "We don't allow no faggots at our table." I knew what that word meant and I ran around the table and started punching him. Then they all started punching *me*. I don't know all what happened then except I ended up in the nurse's office. The nurse, who was a man but he said he really honestly was a nurse, put burning stuff on my cuts. It hurt and I was scared and wanted Mom. I said, when can I go home? The nurse said a bunch of words I didn't understand about a "pearance." I asked him to explain and he said, "You dumb as a bag o' hammers or you jes' playin' like it?" I sat on my hands to keep from hitting him. He said to me to "buck up." I didn't know what that meant except I thought it was swearing.

They said I could have meals in my room then, and even though my room wasn't nice, I was glad. That way, the boys wouldn't get to see me cry.

Chapter Thirty-Nine

Laurel

I WAS WORRIED ABOUT DENNIS SHARTELL. I couldn't believe I'd had such confidence in him in the beginning. He thought Andy was guilty. He didn't say as much, but I could tell. Before the secure custody hearing, he told me he thought Andy would be safer if he stayed in detention until his trial because, as the intake officer had predicted, people were angry.

"Absolutely not!" I said. "Get him out of there."

He shrugged as if to say *It's your funeral*.

The judge, a very young-looking woman who reminded me of Sara, was compassionate, and I knew we'd lucked out in getting her. She seemed to take the innocent-until-proven-guilty statute to heart. In the end, she reluctantly allowed Andy to leave detention.

"Mrs. Lockwood," she said, "I would suggest Andrew not go to school during this period. If he were to stay in detention, we could guarantee his safety. In the community, we cannot."

I nodded, already thinking about tutors and home schooling and other ways he could keep up. It seemed unjust, but I had to face reality. Somehow, the accelerant had gotten on his clothes. I believed that now. Marcus had managed to talk me out of conspiracy theories and lab errors. But he and I were both in agreement that Andy lacked the capacity to plan and carry out arson. I was afraid, though, that Andy's attorney was not so sure.

"Andrew," the judge addressed him. "Will you and Mr. Shartell please stand."

Andy and Dennis got to their feet.

"Andrew, you're being charged with the burning of a church, three counts of first-degree murder, and forty-two counts of attempted murder. Do you understand these charges?"

Although I already knew the charges being brought against Andy, hearing them spoken from the mouth of the judge gave them an unbearable credibility. I thought I might faint, and I was sitting down. I could only imagine what Andy was feeling.

Dennis whispered something to him.

"Yes, ma'am," Andy said, though I wondered if he knew what he was agreeing to.

"Your probable cause hearing will be scheduled within fifteen days," she said. "At that time, it will be decided if you'll be bound over to the superior court for trial."

"Bound over?" I whispered to Marcus.

He didn't look at me. He stared straight ahead but licked his dry lips, and a muscle twitched in his jaw.

"Adult court," he whispered. "They'll decide if they should try him as an adult."

Then, for the first time in my life, I actually did faint.

I had a long talk with Dennis on the phone later that afternoon. He explained that, "given the serious nature of the charges," a phrase I was quickly coming to hate, it was likely Andy *would* be bound over to the adult system at the probable cause hearing. He might—or might not—have a bond. I told Dennis if he did have one, I would pay it; I didn't care how much it was.

"*If* he has one, it could be in the millions," Dennis said. "But you need to prepare yourself, Laurel. Given the serious nature of the crime, they may see him as a danger to others and not let him post bail." He blathered on. "Murder committed in the perpetration of arson is considered murder in the first degree. If he's charged as an adult, he can enter a plea of guilty to the burning and maybe get the murder charges dropped."

"But what if he's *not* guilty of the burning?" I asked.

Dennis hesitated so long I wondered if we'd lost our connection. "We'll have time to talk about all that."

"Did you hear what I said, though, Dennis? I want you to *fight* this! You need to fight him being bound over." If they tried him as an adult and found him guilty, he was doomed. "What's the chance he can stay in the juvenile system?"

"I'd say there's still a small chance of that," he said. "They don't like to bind over juveniles. If no more evidence is found and no more witnesses come forward with incriminating testimony, we've got a shot at it."

* * *

Maggie, Marcus and I did our best to celebrate getting him home that evening. We ignored the camera crews outside the house, and I turned the ringers off on all the phones except my cell. We had a pizza delivered and Marcus picked up an ice-cream cake. We ate in the family room—although only Andy seemed to have an appetite. I'd felt dizzy ever since my fainting episode, and Maggie'd gone absolutely white when I explained to her about the upcoming probable cause hearing.

"They could try him in *adult court?*" she asked, wide-eyed. We were in my bedroom and she waved her arms around in outrage. "He's only fifteen!" she shouted. "This whole thing has ballooned into something insane! Is his lawyer totally brain dead? I don't know how gasoline got on Andy's pants, but he *could not have done it!*"

"It won't happen," I said quickly, taken aback by her outburst. "I'm sure his lawyer can make a good case to keep him in the juvenile system, so please don't worry about it."

I regretted giving her so much information. Maggie was suddenly more fragile than I'd ever guessed she could be. I'd caught her crying a couple of times the last few days. When I'd ask her what was wrong, I'd get the usual "nothing" in reply, but I knew she was frantic about Andy, as we all were. I decided right then to keep the gory details between myself and Marcus. She didn't need to know.

Sitting in the family room, nibbling on the edges of our pizza slices, we talked about everything other than Andy's experiences in detention or what had happened in court that morning or what lay ahead of us. For the moment, I felt safe.

Marcus's cell phone rang as I started cutting the cake I knew only one of us would be able to eat. He walked outside to answer it.

"This is like my birthday," Andy said as I handed him the first slice.

"Right, Panda." Maggie's eyes were red again, and I wondered when she'd found a private moment to cry. She was trying so hard to be upbeat for her brother, and it touched me. "So now we don't have to celebrate on your real birthday," she teased him.

"Yes, you still do," Andy said.

Marcus appeared in the doorway and motioned me to join him in the kitchen. I handed the cake knife to Maggie.

"What is it?" I asked once we were out of earshot of the kids.

"They found a couple of plastic gasoline containers in the landfill this morning," he said, "Might be the ones used to lay the fire, because they each contain a bit of a gasoline and diesel mixture."

I drew in a breath. "Are there fingerprints on them?" I hoped the real arsonist had been sloppy enough to leave his prints behind.

"They've sent them for testing." He nearly smiled. "Pretty miraculous they found them. If there are some good prints on them, Andy could be out of the woods."

Chapter Forty

Laurel
1996–1997

JAMIE HUNG UP THE PHONE, HIS SMILE bordering on incredulous. "He's coming," he said with relief. "He's driving down tomorrow."

I put my arms around him. "Good," I said, as though my feelings about Marcus's arrival weren't mixed. Miss Emma had died the day before after a long battle with cancer, and it was right that he come, yet I hadn't seen him or even spoken to him in the four years since he moved to Asheville. We knew little about his life there except that he had become a firefighter and was supposedly sober. He e-mailed Jamie occasionally and sent birthday cards and Christmas gifts to the kids, but other than that, he'd cut himself off from his family and I'd been frankly glad of it. Jamie'd been afraid Marcus wouldn't come for the service. He thought his brother had stayed away all these years because of his animosity toward his mother and possibly toward Jamie himself. He never guessed it could have anything to do with me.

Marcus arrived at The Sea Tender the next afternoon. The last four years had put muscle on his slender frame, chiseled his face with maturity and brightened the blue of his eyes. I knew instantly that the change in him was more than superficial. It was a confident man who drew Jamie into an embrace. The brothers held on to each other for a full minute before letting go, eyes glistening.

"I've missed you, bro," Marcus said. Then his gaze fell on me. Smiling, he reached for me and I hugged him, both of us pulling away after only a few seconds. How different he smelled! Shampoo and soap. Not a trace of booze or tobacco. "I've missed y'all," he said.

"We've missed you, too," I said with stiff formality. I couldn't look him squarely in the eyes without feeling a tug I hadn't expected—and certainly hadn't wanted—to feel.

Marcus leaned over until he was eye to eye with seven-year-old Maggie. "Do you remember me, Mags?" he asked.

"Uh-uh." She shook her head.

Marcus laughed. "That's good." He straightened again. "I wasn't the best uncle when you were little. And where's Andy?" He looked at me. "I've never even *met* him."

I was afraid to have Marcus meet Andy. To me, the resemblance was as strong as a positive DNA test.

"He's napping," I said, wrapping my arm around Jamie's waist to ground myself in him. In our marriage. I'd fought hard for the peace of the past four years. I didn't want it disrupted now.

My six months in rehab had profoundly changed me. I'd cried my lifetime allotment of tears during those months, tears of guilt and remorse, along with fierce tears of determination. When I got home, I embarked on the adventure of getting to know my three-year-old daughter, the child I'd been so unable to mother. Maggie clung to her daddy at first, cutting her eyes shyly at me. I was a stranger to her. I looked different and I'm sure I smelled different from the woman she'd known as Mommy. I imagined she connected the scent of alcohol to me the way some children connected their mothers with the scent of perfume.

The first night I was home, Jamie and I'd sat with her between us on her bed as we read to her. She leaned against Jamie, and I found my voice breaking when it was my turn to read. I felt her curious gaze on me instead of on the pictures in the book. Jamie rested his chin on the top of her head as I read. Sometimes love is nearly palpable, and the love between my husband and my daughter was like that—a presence I could feel in the room. I was not a part of it, and although my relationship with Maggie grew over the years, I knew I would never have the closeness to her that Jamie had earned.

Although I adored my little girl, my love for her so new and rich, I was preparing for the return of my son. I learned all I could about children with fetal alcohol syndrome. There was precious little information available, but I searched it out. I became an evangelist for healthy, alcohol-free pregnancies the way reformed smokers became intolerant of cigarette smoke.

Sara coached me in what to expect from a year-old boy. She

and Steve had recently divorced and she was raising Keith alone. I felt sorry that she was losing her husband just as I was getting mine back. We drew her into our fold, and I delighted in discovering that I had enough energy and love inside me to extend to her and Keith as well as to my own family.

Now that Marcus was back for Miss Emma's funeral, I couldn't deny that I was attracted to him. But although that attraction made me feel awkward around him, I wasn't afraid of my feelings. I'd grown up. In my four years of sobriety, I'd learned how strong I could be. I had a husband spun from pure gold—how many men would stick by the sick, self-destructive, cold woman I'd been in the years after Maggie's birth? I had two amazing children I was devoted to. And every time I saw Sara, now living in one of the many old mobile homes in Surf City, I was reminded of how precious my marriage was and how far I would go to hold it together.

Jamie couldn't stop smiling in those first few days after Marcus's arrival. He lit up around his brother, and the kinship between the two of them was fun to watch. Certainly he was sad over his mother's death, but his joy in rediscovering his now sober, respectful and thriving brother tempered his sorrow over the loss of Miss Emma.

Both children fell in love with Marcus. He played with them on the beach, tossing a beach ball, letting them bury him up to his chin in sand, roughhousing with Andy in a way that made me nervous but that put a smile on Jamie's face. Jamie wasn't the roughhousing sort, but I could see that he admired his brother's playful rapport with the children.

"He needs to have some kids," Jamie said to me one night in bed. "He's great with them."

"He needs a wife first," I said.

"Yeah," Jamie said. "Sounds like he hasn't had much luck in that department. He told me he's had a few relationships, but nothing serious."

"He's only twenty-eight," I said. "He's got plenty of time."

Jamie sighed. "I only wish Mom had gotten to see him this way."

"I know." I thought of Miss Emma, how her love for her sons had hinged on their achievements, with Marcus never able to measure up to Jamie in her eyes. I kept the thought to myself; it wasn't the time to criticize Miss Emma.

"I'm going to try to persuade him to move back here," Jamie said.

I stiffened at the thought of watching Andy grow into Marcus's image right before our eyes. I wasn't one hundred percent certain that Marcus knew Andy was his, but how could he not? How could anyone look at the two of them and doubt their relationship?

"Do you think he would?" I asked. "Would it be okay for him? I mean, this is where he got so screwed up drinking."

"I don't know. Topsail might make him remember some bad times, but it's obvious how much he's changed. I can hardly remember what he used to be like. It won't hurt to ask him, anyway. Wouldn't it be great for the kids to have an uncle here?"

"Yes," I said. It would be. And it would be great for Jamie to have his brother back.

Jamie talked to Marcus the next night over dinner. We were on the deck eating grilled catfish, macaroni salad and hush puppies, and the sun was beginning to set on the other side of

The Sea Tender. In a couple of weeks, the mosquitoes would make it impossible to eat outside, but that night was one of those magical June evenings. It was warm but not hot, and the sea was calm—a pale opaque blue—swaying like gelatin. I thought, how can he possibly resist?

Marcus took a long swallow of iced tea, as if mulling over the question. "I don't know," he said, setting the glass down on the picnic table. "I do miss it. Being back here…it's part of me, you know?" He looked at his brother. "I love the mountains, but it's not the same as living on the water, and it'd be great to see y'all all the time." He smiled at Maggie and Andy, who was pulling apart catfish with his fingers. "It's very tempting."

"So what's holding you back?" Jamie asked. "There's an opening coming up at the Hampstead fire station."

"Move here! Move here!" Maggie jumped up and down on the bench and I put a hand on her shoulder.

"You're rockin' the boat, sweetie." I smiled at her enthusiasm.

"I'll think about it, Mags," Marcus promised.

Jamie got the kids ready for bed later that evening, while I cleaned the kitchen. Marcus came in and began to wipe the counters with a sponge. He'd been with us five days, but this was the first time I'd been alone with him.

"How would you feel about me moving back here?" he asked quietly as he wiped the breakfast bar.

I kept my eyes on the soapsuds in the sink. "Jamie really wants you here," I said. "And the kids are crazy about you."

"But how do *you* feel, Laurel? Would you be okay with it?" He lowered his voice. "Comfortable with it?"

"I'd like you to be part of the family again," I said as though I'd never felt anything other than friendship for him.

"It's important to me you're all right with it," he said.

I didn't want him to say another word. I was afraid he'd say something about Andy. I looked at him then as though I had no idea why he was so concerned. As though I didn't share those concerns. "It will be fine," I said.

"I'm not proud of—"

I put my fingers to his lips, then dropped my hand as quickly as I'd raised it. "Let the past stay in the past," I whispered. "Please, Marcus."

He stared at me a moment, long enough for me to turn away.

"Okay," he said. "You don't need to worry."

Marcus became a fixture in our lives and on the island. He moved into the most unlikely of the properties he and Jamie had inherited from their father: one of the Operation Bumblebee towers. He added on to the three-story tower, remodeling it with amazing speed, painting the exterior a sea-foam-green with white trim.

He was respected at the fire department, and he and Jamie loved working shoulder to shoulder. I respected him as well. I knew how difficult it had been for me to get sober in a struc-tured rehab environment. The fact that he'd gotten straight with only the help of AA earned my admiration.

As for me, I felt as though I had my cake and was eating it, too. I loved my husband, but I also loved being around Marcus once it was clear he'd keep his promise not to bring up the past. I loved his spirit and sense of fun, and any attraction I felt for him I filed neatly under *i* for *in-law*.

With Andy in preschool, I took a part-time job in a derma-tologist's office. The rest of my energy went into fetal alcohol projects—developing a Web site, writing a newsletter and speaking occasionally at a medical or education conference. Maggie and Andy loved it when I went out of town on a speaking engagement because Marcus would stay at the house, and he and Jamie would take them to the movies and play games with them and feed them pizza and other junk food that was forbidden when I was around.

About a year after Marcus moved back to Topsail Island, he picked me up at the Wilmington airport when I returned from an out-of-town conference.

"Where's Jamie?" I asked, surprised to see him waiting for me in the terminal.

"He and the kids wanted to sleep in, so I volunteered to come get you." He took my rolling carry-on and pulled it behind him as we walked toward the exit.

"Did y'all have a good weekend?" I asked.

"Great." We were walking across the parking lot toward his pickup. "Only I deserted everybody yesterday to buy a new boat."

"A new boat?" I laughed as I got into the passenger seat. I rolled down the window to let in some of the sticky June air. I'd flown in from New York. It had to be fifteen degrees hotter in Wilmington. "What was wrong with your old one?"

"It was old, that's what."

We pulled out of the parking lot, and he told me about the movie they'd watched the night before and how many times they let Andy win at CandyLand.

"Maggie's such a little honey-bunch," he said, looking over his shoulder to change lanes. "She'd let Andy win every time if she could."

"I know," I said. "I worry about her that way."

"Well, I don't think you have to *worry* about her."

"I think she has Jamie's...you know...his *empathy* thing."

"Oh." He understood. "I hope not."

I was thinking about his statement—that he hoped Maggie didn't have Jamie's overdeveloped capacity for empathy—when I realized he'd fallen silent.

"Thinking about your boat?" I asked him. "Have you named her yet?"

He licked his lips, flexing his hands on the steering wheel. "I have to ask you something," he said as if he hadn't heard my question.

Oh, no. Was this why he'd wanted to pick me up at the airport? I'd finally relaxed about the subject of Andy's parentage; Marcus never seemed to concern himself with it. Finally, though, the question was coming, and I braced myself.

I watched his Adam's apple bob in his tanned throat. "I thought it would be okay when I moved here," he said.

"Thought what would be okay?" I asked cautiously.

"I thought I had my feelings for you under control."

That was not what I'd expected. "What are you talking—"

"Stop." He glanced at me. "Don't say anything. Just let me talk for a minute, okay?"

"No," I said. "I—"

"Every time I see you, my feelings get stronger," he said. "It doesn't have anything to do with the past, all right? It has to do with the here and now. Not with the people we used to be. We were both sick then. Now we're healthy and...I admire you, Laurel. The way you deal with Andy. The way you've taken on the whole FASD cause, and—"

"Marcus, please don't," I said. "I mean, thank you. For the compliment. I admire you, too. We both turned our lives around. Let's not do anything that could screw that up again."

"I'm in love with you."

"Please don't say that." I looked out the side window, not wanting to see whatever had been laid bare in his face.

"I've been fighting it all year," he said, "and I'm tired of fighting it. I need to know if there's a chance. That's all I'm asking. You tell me there isn't and I'll shut up and never mention it again. But I need to know if you'd ever consider—" He shook his head. "I'm not talking about an affair. I wouldn't do that again. I'm talking about you and me, out in the open. With you divorced from Jamie." Although my gaze was riveted to the side of the road, I felt him looking at me. "I love my brother," he said, "and I hate the thought of hurting him, but I don't know how to keep my feelings for you hidden any longer. Every woman I go out with...I keep wishing she was you."

"Marcus, please stop!" I said, turning to face him. "I won't ever divorce Jamie. He stood by me through so much. He—"

"Are you saying you have feelings for me?" he interrupted. "That if it weren't for Jamie, you'd—"

"I love you like a brother-in-law," I said.

"I don't think I believe you."

"Why not?"

"I catch the way you look at me sometimes."

Had I been that transparent?

"I love Jamie, Marcus," I said evenly. "He and I have a family together. Please support that. Don't..." I let out my breath in frustration. "This year's been so much fun with you here. Please don't mess it up."

He was quiet for a moment. "You're right," he said then. "Absolutely right. I'm sorry, Laurel. I had to ask."

"Now you know."

"Now I know."

An awkward silence fell between us. Finally I spoke.

"You need to find yourself a woman who's free and who'll love the dickens out of you," I said, wondering how it would feel to see him touching, loving another woman.

"You're right," he said grimly. "I'll do that."

The next day was Monday and both Marcus and Jamie had time off from work. The sun had just broken over the horizon, sending a pink glow into our bedroom, when the phone rang. Jamie answered it from his side of the bed. I listened to his groggy end of the conversation.

"Yeah," he said after a few minutes. "I'd like that." He set the phone back on the night table.

"Was that the fire station?" I asked. No one else would call that early.

"No. It was Marcus." He sat up and swung his legs over the side of the bed. "I'm gonna meet him at the pier and check out his new boat."

"*Now?*" I asked. "It's your only day to sleep in."

"Yeah, but look outside." He motioned toward the sunrise and I could understand his desire to be on the water. He leaned over to kiss me. "You go back to sleep. I won't wake the kids."

A few hours later, Marcus called me from the police station in Surf City. He was sobbing, and I could barely understand him. There'd been an accident on the boat, he said. A whale had lifted it into the air, tossing him and Jamie out. Marcus had searched the water, trying to find his brother, but had to finally give up.

I hung up the phone, trembling and nauseated. The kids were right there, and I did my best not to show the terror I felt. I called Sara to come stay with them, although she was nearly as upset as I was. She blew into the house with six-year-old Keith and hugged me, crying, while the three children anxiously tried to figure out what was wrong.

I sped to the police station and when I looked into Marcus's eyes, the eyes of the man who only the day before had asked me if I'd leave my husband for him, I realized exactly how well I knew him—well enough to know that the story he was telling was a lie.

Chapter Forty-One

Laurel

THE PROBABLE CAUSE HEARING WAS SCHEDULED for Wednesday, two short days away and too soon for my comfort. I knew that the hearing could literally mean the end of Andy's freedom forever, "given the seriousness of the charges." Dennis sounded more and more certain that Andy would be bound over to adult court, and less and less certain that he would get any sort of reasonable bail. That meant he would stay in prison until his trial, which could be months, if not years, away. His sentence could be life without parole.

"He can't get the death penalty, though," Dennis said, "so don't worry about that."

What an asshole! I only needed to worry about my FASD

son getting life in prison. I should have gotten a new lawyer when I first started having doubts about Dennis.

I thought he should make a case at the probable cause hearing that Andy shouldn't be bound over to the adult system because of his FASD, and I tried again to educate the lawyer about the disorder, but it was like trying to educate Andy himself. It was as though Dennis's brain shut down when I talked about it now.

"It's a very weak argument," he said. "It used to hold water as a defense, but now every Tom, Dick and Harry claims their mothers drank before they were born. Andy's IQ is in the normal range, he's not insane, and he knows right from wrong, and that's what the judge will be looking at."

"Whose side are you *on?*" I was losing it with this man. Every time I spoke with him, I felt panic bubble up in my chest. "You're not hearing me! First of all, I'm not talking about his *defense.* I'm talking about why he shouldn't be tried as an adult. He may be a teenager and he may have a IQ in the normal range—the *low* normal range—but he *thinks* like a child. I'm an expert in FASD. I speak to groups about—"

"You're his mother," Dennis interrupted me. "Your expertise doesn't count."

One night a few years earlier, I woke up and saw Jamie sitting on the edge of my bed. I was probably dreaming—it had happened a few times before—but it felt so real. He sat there in jeans and a blue T-shirt, his empathy tattoo as big as life. I wasn't afraid. I was happy to see him. He spoke to me, although his lips didn't move. He said, *You're a fighter, Laurie. You're the champ.*

I had thought about that dream—or whatever it was—

often since that night. Every time I faced a challenge, I thought of his words. Words he'd never said to me when he was alive, but that I could imagine him saying. I'd had more than my share of challenges, that was for sure. Now, though, I was facing the biggest challenge of my life, and I was going to fight with all my power to keep Andy out of jail.

So if *my* expertise didn't count, I would find someone whose expertise did. I was fired up. I'd find someone with experience testifying in court cases for people with FASD. I went online and, through my network of FASD parents around the country, found the name of a neurologist in Raleigh. I called his office and set up an appointment to meet with him the next day. He suggested that at this point, I come alone but bring Andy's medical and psychological records with me. If the case actually went to trial, then he would do a thorough evaluation of Andy. For now, he would give me ammunition to share with Dennis that might prevent Andy from being bound over to the adult system. I cried with relief when I got off the phone. He was optimistic, and his optimism gave me hope.

I made arrangements for Andy to spend the next day with the mother of one of his swim team members. Ben had convinced me that Andy should stay on the team, and I appreciated his willingness to deal with whatever repercussions arose from that decision. Andy didn't understand why he wasn't going to school; taking him away from the swim team he loved would leave him more confused than he already was.

I tucked him into bed that night and told him about the plans for the next day.

"I have to go out of town tomorrow," I said, "so you'll—"

"To make a fetal alcohol speech?"

"No." I smiled. "Not this time. I'm just going to Raleigh for the day. So you'll stay at Tyler's house with his mom, and—"

"Will Tyler be there?"

"He'll be at school, so you'll take your books with you and—"

"Can I take my iPod?"

"Yes, but I want you to do some reading and that math we talked about, okay? I marked it in your book. And I'll tell Tyler's mother so she'll be watching to be sure you do it."

"Can I have lunch?"

"Tyler's mom will make you lunch. Then after school, she'll take you and Tyler to swim team practice and Maggie will pick you up afterward."

"Tyler's not a good swimmer."

"No?"

"Even though Ben explains things good."

"*Well,*" I said. "Ben explains things well."

"Ben said if I work hard, I can be a top swimmer."

"I think you already *are* a top swimmer."

"No, Mom. Not just a top Pirate swimmer. A top swimmer of all time. A champion."

I ran my hand over his curly hair. "What a wonderful aspiration," I said.

Andy yawned. "What's a 'aspration'?" He rubbed the back of his hand over his eyes. My sleepy boy.

"A goal. You know, how we have your goal chart?"

"Uh-huh." He shut his eyes.

"I love you," I said.

"Mmm." He was already breathing steadily, a tiny smile on his lips.

I watched him for a few minutes, biting back tears. Then I leaned over, whispered in his ear, "You're a fighter, sweetie," I said. "You're already a champ."

Chapter Forty-Two

Marcus

THE BOAT IS TOO SMALL FOR SUCH A ROUGH day on the ocean. I realize that as soon as we pass through the inlet into open water. A monster yellow boat the size and shape of a school bus passes us. We rise high on its wake, then plunge down in the gully, water pouring over us. For a moment, I'm afraid, but when Jamie starts to laugh, peeling his wet T-shirt over his head, I relax and laugh with him. I open the throttle, and the nose of my boat rises as we speed across the water.

"Look!" Jamie's eyes are wide and he's pointing to the east. I turn my head to see a pod of jet-black whales, all in a row, all spouting at the same time. Like a drawing in a children's book.

"God's swimming with us!" Jamie says.

* * *

I woke up from the dream gasping for breath, like I always did, even though I'd managed to wake up before the bad part. My heart hammered in my chest. For nearly ten years, that dream had dogged me. I got out of bed to shake it off. Was I going to have that damn dream for the rest of my life? I doubted my heart could take it.

In the bathroom, I splashed water on my face. If I went right back to bed, the dream would turn into the nightmare. No way I was letting that happen.

I got on the computer and started playing Freecell, but my mind was muddy. I stared at the cards until they blended together. Closed my eyes.

I could have changed the outcome that day. I could have suggested we take the boat into the sound instead of the ocean. Go in the afternoon instead of the morning. I could have bought the boat the week before or the week after. It wasn't the first time I'd made myself crazy thinking about the what-ifs.

The day before the accident, I'd picked up Laurel at the airport and asked her the question that had been in my mind for months: was there a chance for us? She'd given me her answer and I was determined to live with it. I had to. I dropped her off at The Sea Tender, but Jamie came out before I pulled away.

"Hey." He got in on the passenger side. His hair was wet from a shower or a swim. "Do you have time to hang out later today?" he asked. "Just with me, I mean."

Weird request, but that didn't register. All I could think about was that I didn't want to spend time with him right then. Not after the conversation I'd just had with Laurel.

"How about tomorrow?" I asked. "You have the day off, right?"

"Okay," he said. "I'll call you in the morning."

"You can help me christen the new boat," I suggested.

"Whatever." He looked toward The Sea Tender, then got out of the pickup.

When I called at sunrise the next day, I expected him to balk at the early hour. He liked sleeping in on his days off. But he sounded like he couldn't wait to go out on the new boat. That should have tipped me off right there.

We met at the boat docks and I could tell something was up. Forced smile. Kept his hands in his shorts pockets as he admired the boat. He asked me questions about her, but I knew he wasn't listening to my answers. Just the early hour, I told myself. He wasn't awake yet.

I jumped into the boat with a thermos of coffee and a couple of foam cups, and he followed. "I wanted something small enough to maneuver well, but large enough to fit all of us," I said. In my imagination, I'd pictured Laurel and the kids with me in the boat while Jamie worked. I was one hell of a brother.

I sank into the cushy seat at the helm. "Coffee?" I held the thermos out to him as he sat down in the front passenger seat. He shook his head, still smiling that not-quite-real smile.

"You okay?" I asked him.

He shrugged. "A little preoccupied," he admitted. "So!" He motioned to the boat. "Show me what she's got."

"You game for the ocean?" I asked as we pulled away from the pier. I'd already cruised the sound and the Intracoastal Waterway. I wanted to see how she handled in the open water.

"Sure." He adjusted his sunglasses. "Got a name for her yet?"

I'd thought about naming her *Laurel*. Seriously. I was such a fool.

"Maybe *Maggie*," I said.

"Cool," said Jamie. "She'd love having a boat named after her."

In a few minutes, we were cruising through the inlet. I felt a thrill, as I always did, when I saw the open sea in front of us. So wide, I swore I could see the curvature of the earth. How I'd survived four years in the mountains, I didn't know.

As we sailed into the ocean from the inlet, a massive ship appeared out of nowhere. Materialized from thin air. Steamed past us with a killer blast from its horn. I tightened my hands on the wheel as we headed straight into its wake.

"Holy shit!" I said, as we climbed the first swell.

"Hang on!" Jamie shouted. Like he needed to tell me.

We crested the wave, dropping like a stone on the other side of it, and the next wave was on us before we recovered. It tore off my sunglasses, blinding me with a wall of water and nearly swamping the boat. I hung on to the wheel. Jamie let out a *whoop* like he was riding a bucking bull.

Two more waves, and then finally, the worst was over. I turned to see Jamie laugh as he peeled off his sopping wet T-shirt. He took off his sunglasses, looking around, I guessed, for something to dry them with. "I couldn't see a damn thing," he said.

"No shit," I said, able to laugh now myself. "And I lost my frickin' sunglasses."

He propped his own sunglasses on top of his head. Wrung his T-shirt out over the side of the boat. "Well, your boat handled well," he said.

"Thought I might lose her there for a minute."

We sailed into the sea, and I opened the throttle wide. After a while, Jamie cleaned his sunglasses with his damp T-shirt. Slipped them back on his face. Then he pointed south.

"Is that a *whale?*" He had to shout for me to hear him over the roar of the engine.

"Where?" The surface of the water was calm.

"He's gone under."

"Can't be a whale!" I shouted. "Not the season."

"You're right," he said. "Sure looked like one, though."

We soared across the water. "Is this baby smooth or what?" I shouted.

"She's great!"

She was *dynamite*. We were flying.

"There he is again!" Jamie pointed. "We're practically on top of him."

I saw him this time. Couldn't miss him. He breached just south of us, a thirty- or forty-thousand-ton mountain shooting straight up from the sea, then slipping back into the water.

"Holy…" I slowed the boat, and we scanned the water to find him again. "I don't believe it. It's *June!*" You'd see humpbacks in December or January as they headed south, and in the spring as they returned north. But late June?

I heard the *pop* of the whale's blow spout and turned to see a fountain of water spray into the air not twenty yards away. Then the massive tail rose in the air like a great bird, wings spread above the water. The tail thwacked the surface as he dove under again. I throttled back the engine until we were simply drifting.

"Is he alone, do you think?" Jamie nearly whispered.

"I have no idea," I said. "Should've brought my camera. No one's going to believe this."

The whale suddenly breached a second time, rocketing toward the sky in front of us.

"Is that the same one?" Jamie asked.

"I don't know, but damn! That's one big Mama Jama!" And too damn close for comfort. I'd seen whales up close before. Close enough to scratch their backs with a net from a fishing charter. This was different. This guy dwarfed us. Dwarfed my boat. I could imagine Jonah setting up house in his belly.

"How can anyone see this and not feel God's presence?" Jamie asked.

I didn't answer. I'd found my own higher power through AA, but Jamie's God and mine were not the same.

The whale slipped underwater again. We waited a few more minutes, swiveling our heads left and right for the next sign of him. He was gone.

I reached for the throttle.

"Wait," Jamie said. "Let's sit here a while longer."

"I think he's gone."

"Yeah, I know," he said. "I want to talk to you, though."

I let go of the throttle. Shit. Had Laurel told him about our conversation?

"I'll take some of that coffee now," he said.

I handed him the thermos and a cup. Watched him pour. His hand had a tremor, but so did mine after our close encounter with Moby Dick.

He took a sip of the coffee, then blew out his breath. "Damn, bro," he said, "this is hard to say."

I wiped my sweaty palms on my shorts. "What's going on?"

"I've made a hard decision." His sunglasses masked his eyes, but I knew he was looking right at me. "It's selfish. Really selfish. And I'm gonna need your help, bro."

I relaxed. No way this was about Laurel and me. "Anything, Jamie," I said.

He looked toward where we'd last seen the whale. "I'm going to ask Laurel for a divorce," he said.

The muscles around my heart squeezed so tight that I rubbed my hand across my chest. "What are you talking about?"

"I know it's a shocker," Jamie said. "You probably think I'm crazy. Like I have the best marriage going and why would I screw it up?"

"Exactly," I said. "You're...I don't know anyone more into his family than you."

He reached beneath his sunglasses with his thumb and forefinger. Maybe rubbing tears away. I couldn't tell. "I love her, but it's like loving a friend," he said. "It's been that way for a long time. When she was in rehab, I started feeling different about her. It's not fair, I know. What happened wasn't her fault, and I kept hoping the old feelings would come back, but—" He shook his head.

"How can you not love her?" He was crazy. How could he want to leave her? And wasn't that what I'd wanted only twenty-four hours ago? No. It wasn't. I'd wanted Laurel to ask *him* for a divorce. I wanted *her* to be the one calling the shots. Not the one getting hurt.

"I'm not sure how to tell her," Jamie said. "I don't want to hurt her more than I have to."

"Is that a question?" I asked. "Because if it is, the answer is, there's no way you won't be killing her." I wanted to tell him how she'd turned me down out of her devotion to him. I wanted to rub his face in it.

"I know," Jamie said. "And I'm sorry to lay this on you. I wanted you to hear it from me first, though, because they're going to need you. You care so much about her and the kids. They'll need to lean on you for a while."

A couple of gulls flew overhead. I watched one of them dart to the surface of the water, then glide into the air again with a small fish in its mouth like it took no effort at all.

"This is unbelievable," I said. "I mean, so you tell her and then what? You move away? Go to California to start a new life or what?"

"You're pissed," he said.

"Just...I don't get it."

"Yeah, I don't blame you." He blew out his breath again. His jugular pounded beneath the damp skin of his throat. "Look," he said, "here's the truth, all right? I'm in love with someone else."

I wished I could see his eyes behind the dark lenses. "You've been cheating on Laurel?"

"That's an ugly word."

I laughed. "You got a better one?"

"It's not like that."

"Well, why don't you tell me what it's like then." I folded my arms across my chest, suddenly the nobler of the two sons of bitches in my boat.

"I shouldn't have told you."

I didn't want him to stop talking. I needed to know everything. "You can't blame me for being pissed," I said. "You're not Jamie anymore. You're somebody else."

"It's Sara," he said.

His words hung in the air for a few seconds before they sank in. "Oh, nice," I said. "You pick your wife's best friend."

"It wasn't...that isn't how it happened." He lifted his damp T-shirt from the bottom of the boat and wiped his forehead with it. "I lived with Sara and Steve back when Maggie was little, remember? I fell for her then. We clicked. Laurel was such a mess and Sara was... Her marriage wasn't so great and Steve was gone a lot. We needed each other."

"That was a long time ago," I said. "This has been going on all these years?"

"No. At least not physically. Once Laurel got pregnant with Andy and I moved back into The Sea Tender, it was over with Sara as far as I was concerned. But it's one thing to say something's over and another to feel it." He rubbed his chin. "Sara's been great." A smile curled his lips. I wanted to smack it off his face. "She always told me it's up to me what happens. During the last few months, I realized I've been living a lie, pretending I love Laurel, telling her I love her when I don't. Living a lie isn't fair to anyone."

"You son of a bitch. You're just going to walk out on your kids?"

"I'd never do that," Jamie said quickly. "That's why we'll stay here. Either on the island or maybe inland. We're thinking of Hampstead. That way I can still be a part of Andy and Maggie's lives but Laurel won't be tripping over me at the grocery store. I'll always provide for them," he added. "For Laurel, too."

I really wanted to hit him. When we were kids, I'd try to beat him up and he always won. He had the brawn and the years on me. Now, though, I had the anger. I could take him down if I tried.

"Marcus." He spoke in the quiet, calm voice that echoed in his chapel on Sunday mornings. "Look at me."

I did, my lips pressed together so tightly they hurt.

"I have another child to provide for," he said. "To be there for."

"What are you talk…" I pictured Keith. Six years old now. Handsome kid. Big brown eyes. Dark wavy hair. Slowly, I shook my head.

"Keith," Jamie said, as if I hadn't figured it out. "I've been giving Sara money for him since he was born. She deserves more from me than just a few hundred bucks every month."

"I feel like I don't know you," I said, staring at the stranger in my boat. "You encouraged Sara to help Laurel. You practically forced them to be friends. Your wife and your…mistress. How many times have you had your wife and your mistress in your house at the same time?"

"Shut up, Marcus."

He was getting angry with me and I was loving it. *Damn*. I hated his self-control. His calmness.

"And your bastard kid," I said. "Do you expect him and Maggie and Andy to be playmates? All one big happy family, except without Laurel?"

"Look in the fucking mirror, Marcus." Jamie crushed the empty cup in his hand and tossed it over the side of the boat. "You screwed my wife."

I must have shaken my head, because he leaned toward me.

"Don't try to deny it! You think I was born yesterday? You screwed her and you got her pregnant and hooked on booze. Andy is the way he is because of you."

I dove for him. Punched him hard on the side of his jaw. His head whipped to one side, but he recovered quickly, grabbing my arm and wrestling me to the bottom of the boat. I fought him with strength I didn't know I had. I bent my legs, put my bare feet on his chest, and sent him flying across the boat. He grunted as he crashed into the back of one of the seats.

I was dizzy in the bottom of the boat. The sky twirled above me. Scrambling to my knees, I felt like I was rising into the air. Jamie started toward me, but then he felt it, too. The shifting of the boat.

"What the—" He tried to steady himself, his legs wide apart, arms out at his sides.

I looked around for a boat that might have created a freak wave. Then I saw it—the huge tail over the gunwale. Before I could grab hold of one of the seats, I flew into the air.

Jamie shouted as we were tossed from the boat. He flew upside down, and I heard a *thud* as his head hit the bow. Then I was deep under water, unsure which way was up, unsure if the dark shadow above me was my boat or the whale.

I found the surface of the water. Gulped air. My eyes stung from the salt. The boat was already yards away from me, and my anger at Jamie turned into a fight to survive. I swam to the boat, grabbing onto the short ladder at the stern as I scanned the water for my brother.

"Jamie!" I shouted, listening hard for his voice. A few seagulls cawed from the air overhead, but that was the only sound. I climbed into the boat for a better view of the water. *"Jamie!"* I shouted again and again. The sound of that *thud* replayed in my head. I dove into the water once more, opening my eyes in the murk as I searched for him. I swam underwater until my muscles gave out, and still I stayed in the water, crying hard, gagging on each watery intake of breath.

Climbing into the boat again, I scanned the water once more from that height. He couldn't be gone. He *couldn't* be. I expected him to rise out of the water any minute. Laughing. Getting me back for being asshole enough to try to fight him. I couldn't leave. Leaving would mean giving up on him.

"Jamie!" I called, until finally, I was only whispering the word. I wanted my brother.

Even as I sailed back through the inlet, crying openly, I thought he might greet me at the pier. He'd say I deserved his cruel hoax and chew me out for being such a hypocrite.

But of course, he wasn't there, and my real nightmare began when I told the police what happened: a whale lifted the boat and tossed us out. In *June,* when the humpbacks should be somewhere north of New England. Ludicrous. Sometimes I wondered if I'd imagined the great thwacking tail. I told no one about our fight, no one about our conversation, but I had scratches on my shoulder. Bruises on my neck. Was it any wonder I failed the polygraph I'd stupidly agreed to take?

People who'd known our family for many years remembered the old rivalry between Jamie and myself. Did we fight on the boat, they wanted to know? They remembered my drinking. Had I been drinking out there? In the end, they had no evidence against me and had to let me go. The firefighters, whose love and admiration for me was nearly as strong as it had been for Jamie, stuck by me, but Laurel didn't believe a word I said. And she was the only one who mattered.

Chapter Forty-Three

Maggie

"YOU'RE REALLY BRAVE TO VISIT KEITH," AMBER said. She was slumped in the passenger seat of my car with her bare feet flat against the dashboard. I'd warned her that if we crashed and the air bag burst open she'd end up with two broken legs and her knees would smash her nose, but she told me I worried too much. I *did* worry too much. I couldn't help it. The fire showed me how quickly things could go wrong. You think you have control over your life, and then *bam!* Major wake-up call.

"What's so brave about it?" I asked.

"I've heard burn units are beyond gross." Amber had always been a wimp. When we took the elementary schoolkids' handmade cards to New Hanover Hospital, she stayed in the lobby while I went to the patients' rooms. Most of them were there for smoke inhalation and minor burns, so it wasn't that bad. It seemed like my duty, taking the cards to those kids. I was one hundred percent healthy. It was the least I could do. I even got out of school legitimately today, since my counselor said a visit to Keith counted as "community service," just like planning the makeover event. I'd been working my butt off on that thing, but no way was I talking to Dawn about it again. I'd send her a big fat check when the event was over. I was never talking to Dawn again about anything.

"I feel bad that I haven't gone before now," I said to Amber. "I've been carrying the cards for him around for a week."

Amber had interviews in the business department at UNC in Chapel Hill, where she'd be going in the fall. I'd said I'd drive her there, and her parents would pick her up later in the week. I wanted to see Keith, and not just to give him the cards. Keith was the one person who swore he saw Andy walking around outside just before the fire. No way did that make sense. I wanted to know exactly what Keith was telling the police so I could figure out how to poke his story full of holes. Mom had found the world's lamest lawyer, so it was up to me to get Andy out of this mess. While I was in Chapel Hill, Mom would go to Raleigh to talk to a neurologist who specialized in FASD. The probable cause hearing was tomorrow, and although Mom said everything would turn out fine, I could tell she was nervous about the whole thing.

"Travis's parents had a meltdown when they found out I'd be going to Carolina," Amber said with a laugh. Travis's parents thought he and Amber were getting too serious too soon.

"Not much they can do about it," I said. "Travis is a big boy."

"Exactly."

I didn't care about the ongoing saga of Amber and Travis, but there I was, stuck for two-and-a-half hours listening to every stupid detail about their relationship from the girl who used to be my best friend, while I couldn't tell her a single thing about Ben. She'd never understand. She'd probably write about it on her Facebook page. Amber had no idea what it was like to have *real* problems.

God, I was so *jealous* that Amber got to be with Travis, out in the open, hanging all over each other. It was so unfair. I missed Ben! We talked on the phone, but I wanted to *be* with him. We planned to meet Friday night on the beach at the very north end of the Island, where what was left of Daddy's old chapel stood. I hoped it didn't rain, but even if it did, I was going. Every time I thought about being with him again, my heart sped up.

Amber hugged herself through her UNC sweatshirt. "I'm glad I'll be inland tonight," she said as we got on the Beltline.

"Why?"

"Where've you been?" She brushed a speck of something off her pink toenail. "There's like a major nor'easter coming. Supposed to blow hard on the coast. I mean, I guess I'll see some of it at UNC, but not like you'll get on the island."

Was that why it seemed so dark? I took off my sunglasses and saw that the clouds looked like clumps of ashes. Maybe the storm could screw up the hearing tomorrow. A really good storm might make them close the courthouse for the day. Maybe the hearing would have to be postponed and we could find a better lawyer or something.

I dropped Amber off on the UNC campus, and then spent forty-five minutes trying to find the hospital and parking lot for the burn center. I forgot the blue gift bag of cards on the backseat of my car and was almost to the elevator when I remembered. It was already starting to rain a little when I went to my car for them. I didn't want to have to drive in a nor'easter, thank you. I'd have to rush.

I found the burn center. There was a big desk with a bunch of nurses, and I asked them for directions to Keith's room.

One of the nurses—overweight, blond and about Mom's age—looked up from a computer keyboard. "It's not visiting hours, sugar," she said.

I cringed at the word *sugar*. I didn't need any reminders of Dawn.

"I looked the hospital up on the Internet and it said visiting hours were from six to ten," I insisted.

"The burn center has its own hours," she said, but she stood up. "Who're you here to see? Keith Weston, did you say?"

I nodded. "I drove all the way from Topsail Island."

"Bless your heart," she said. "Oh, you go ahead. His mama's not here today and he can probably use the company." She pointed down the hallway. "Second door on the right."

I stood in Keith's doorway, suddenly scared to walk inside. I could see him in the bed closest to the door, watching a TV suspended from the ceiling. I thought he had two long, thick tubes of white fabric lying at his sides until I realized they were his arms and hands, completely covered with bandages. This is what the fire did, I thought. This is only a *tiny part* of what the fire did. My knees went soft and I leaned against the door frame. Amber was wrong. I wasn't brave. I wanted to run back down the hallway and out of the hospital.

But I had to do this. I made my mushy knees walk into the room.

"Hey, Keith," I said. I'd known Keith his whole life. We had a picture of me when I was three holding him on my lap. For years, I thought it was Andy in that picture, until Mom told me Andy didn't live with us until he was a year old. I was eleven when she told me about drinking too much while she was pregnant with him and that's what made him the way he was. I was so angry with her that I tried to hit her when she told me. She caught my hand, and in typical Mom fashion told me she understood my anger, that she felt angry at *herself* for what she'd done, but she'd tried to forgive herself and she hoped I could, too. I still wasn't sure I had.

Keith turned to look at me and I saw the bandages covering one whole side of his face. I felt like crying. He seemed sort of spaced out, staring at me like he didn't know who I was.

"It's Maggie." I moved right up against his bed.

"I know who you are," he said. "What are you doing here? Slumming?"

Slumming? What was he talking about? I held up the blue gift bag. "The kids at Douglas Elementary made a bunch of cards and pictures for you," I said.

Obviously, he couldn't reach for the bag. I looked at his arms and noticed skinny metal rods sticking out from the bandages around his left hand. I thought I might get sick. There was a chair next to his bed and I sat down.

"Would you like me to read the cards to you?" I asked.

"Does this ease your conscience or something?" he asked. "The rich girl visiting the poor boy in the hospital?"

His attitude shook me up. What was his problem? I knew

he'd called Andy a rich kid or something at the lock-in and now he was doing the same thing to me.

"What are you talking about?" I asked. "Why are you suddenly calling Andy and me rich?"

"Because you *are,* aren't you? Especially compared to me and my mom. Rich and lucky."

I figured he meant that Andy had escaped from the fire with minor injuries, while he was lying there covered with bandages. "I know we're lucky," I said. I glanced at the TV and saw a weather map on the screen before looking at him again. "Keith, tell me what you told the investigators about seeing Andy outside before the fire."

He either coughed or laughed, I wasn't sure which. It took a minute for him to catch his breath. "So that's it," he said finally. "You're not here to visit poor Keith. To bring poor Keith some crap made by second-graders. You're here to convince him that your precious, lame-o baby brother is innocent."

"Not true," I said. "I just wanted to know what you think you saw."

"I've got a news flash for you, Maggie," he said. "He's not just *your* brother."

"What do you mean?"

"He's *my* brother, too."

Maybe the pain drugs were messing with his head. "Did you really see him outside the church, Keith?"

"Did you hear me?" He looked like he was trying to sit up but couldn't manage it. I didn't know if I should help him or not. "Andy's my brother," he said. "And *you're* my sister."

I stood up. "I'll ask one of the nurses to come check on you," I said.

"Why? You think I'm talking crazy? Full of shit?"

"I don't know what you're talk—"

"Your father fucked my mother," he said.

"What?"

"You heard me. He fucked my mother and nine months later I was born. That makes me your half brother. The side of the family that lives in a trailer and eats ramen noodles while you and Andy-the-hero eat steak."

"I don't believe you," I said.

"Go ask your uncle," he said. "He knows all about it."

I took a step backward, my knees mush again. "You're full of it," I said. "My father would never do something like that."

He croaked out that half laugh, half cough sound again. "Looks like you didn't know him very well, big sister."

"I knew him better than anyone!" I pictured myself as a little girl sitting next to Daddy on the deck, running my fingers over the tattoo on his arm. "You're just trying to piss me off."

"You don't look pissed," Keith said. "You look like someone just kicked you in the gut. What's the matter? Don't you want another brother?"

I stared at him and suddenly felt like I was looking in a mirror. The dark wavy hair. The enormous brown eye. Lashes thick and black. The room felt as long as a tunnel, its dark walls closing in on me. I took another step backward and my hand grasped the doorjamb.

"Go ask your uncle," Keith said again. "He can fill you in on all the juicy, sicko details."

I turned and flew out of the room, nearly tripping over my rubbery legs in my rush to escape, but his voice followed me all the way to the elevator:

"Bring me some of your money next time, sis!" he shouted, and I pushed the elevator button with my elbow, my hands pressed tightly over my ears.

Chapter Forty-Four

Maggie

I DIALED MY CELL WHILE DRIVING SEVENTY-FIVE miles an hour through the rain.

"That you, Mags?" Uncle Marcus answered.

"I need to talk to you." I heard radio static in the background. "Are you at the station?"

"I am. You at school?"

"I'm driving back from Chapel Hill." I had to slow down because the car in front of me was practically crawling. "I talked to Keith."

Total silence.

"Oh my *God!*" I wailed. "Don't tell me it's true!"

"Listen, Maggie. Calm down. How close are you? When can I see you?"

"I'm like still two hours away! You need to tell me now."

"Uh-uh. Not over the phone. It's nearly two. Call me when you get closer and I'll try to get away, okay?"

"Is Keith my half brother?"

"Maggie. I'm *not* talking about this now. Turn on your radio or a CD or whatever and put this out of your mind. Is it raining where you are?"

My wipers slapped back and forth. "Yes," I said.

"Concentrate on your driving, babe, all right? I love you. Call when you get closer."

I tossed my phone onto the passenger seat. Then I screamed out loud. Just screamed until I was hoarse.

The turtle in front of me was actually slowing down even more. I had to pass it or I knew I'd snap. I checked my mirror. No cars behind me. As soon as I started to steer to the left, though, someone laid on his horn and I jerked back into my lane and saw a black Saab in my mirror. Where'd *he* come from? I pressed my brakes to slow down to the turtle's speed. Adrenaline raced down my arms to the tips of my fingers. I had to be more careful. I could have died right there, and if I died, who would help my brother?

I picked up my cell again and tried to call Ben to tell him about the whole Keith thing, but I got his voice mail. "This is Ben Trippett. If that's who you're trying to call, please leave a message." I didn't know what to say that wouldn't worry him, but I loved hearing his voice. I kept hitting redial over and over again to listen to it. I didn't want to repeat what Keith had told me anyway without knowing the truth, but I knew there was something to it for Uncle Marcus to go quiet like that.

I passed the turtle when I was sure it was safe. I turned on the radio like Uncle Marcus suggested. I couldn't get my regular station that far from Surf City, so I hit scan and listened to snippets of country music and Bible talk for the next hour, not even noticing that I was getting the stations only in ten-second bursts.

"Daddy," I whispered to the only perfect person I'd ever known. "Please don't let it be true."

Uncle Marcus said he'd meet me at Sears Landing. I got there first and sat in the far corner of the restaurant. I wanted to be as far from the door and the kitchen as possible because I knew I was going to cry. I watched the rain beating down on Topsail Sound outside the window. It came down at an angle to the water, the wind already kicking up. The sky was so heavy and low, the clouds almost touched the water.

Uncle Marcus showed up looking wet and old. My phone call had gotten to him. I didn't have the energy to stand up for a hug, so he bent over and kissed my cheek.

"How're you holding up?" he asked.

"Awesome," I said sarcastically.

"Yeah." He sat down kitty-corner from me. "I can imagine." He rested his forearms on the table. "So, tell me what Keith said."

"That he's my half brother. Andy's and mine. He said Daddy and Sara...you know." I could not—absolutely could not—think about it. "I thought maybe he was just trying to piss me off. He's so angry about getting burned. Not that I blame him."

Uncle Marcus played with the saltshaker on the table, moving it back and forth with his fingertips. I tried to be patient, but he was getting on my nerves. And then the waitress, a girl named Georgia Ann who graduated from my high school a few years earlier, showed up at our table.

"Hey, Marcus. Maggie," she said, opening her little notepad. "You must be fixin' to graduate, huh, Maggie?"

"Soon." I knew coming to a restaurant had been a bad idea, but it was too rainy to meet on the beach and Uncle Marcus didn't want to talk at the station.

"I'll have a beach dog and onion rings and iced tea." Uncle Marcus got right to the point with her, although I didn't see how his appetite could be all that great. "How about you, Maggie?" he asked.

"I'm not hungry," I said.

"Bring her a sweet tea," Uncle Marcus told Georgia Ann.

"Sure will," she said, and I was relieved when she walked away.

Uncle Marcus started working on the saltshaker again. "I've decided to tell you everything," he said, "because if I start…leaving parts out, I…" He leaned back in the chair and looked at the ceiling. "The thing is, your mother should hear all this first."

"She doesn't *know?*"

He shook his head. "And I was going to wait at least until after the hearing tomorrow, because she has enough on her mind. Is she in Raleigh?"

I nodded. "She might be on her way home by now."

"Where's Andy?"

"His team has a special practice today and he was getting a ride there. I'll pick him up later." I was getting antsy. "You can't leave me hanging until after you tell Mom," I said.

"Right. I know." He gave the saltshaker a few more back-and-forth taps. "Well, it's true," he said simply. "I'm the only one who knows everything that happened, Mags. I never wanted Keith to find out. I sure never wanted you to find out."

"How can Keith know, but nobody else?"

Georgia Ann brought our teas and tossed a couple of straws on the table. "Food'll be up in a jiffy," she said.

Uncle Marcus waited until she walked away again. "Well, he doesn't know everything." He unwrapped his straw and dropped it into his tea. I didn't touch mine. "You know how your Dad died, right?"

"The whale."

"Yes. And I know you've probably heard old-timers' suspicions that I had something to do with it."

I shook my head. No way.

"Well, some people thought that."

"Is that why Reverend Bill is so weird about you?"

"Partially, yeah. And he didn't like Jamie because Jamie's brand of religion didn't fit with his."

"I don't get why anyone would think you had something to do with Daddy dying, though."

He poked his straw up and down in the tea. "Well, first of all, it wasn't the right season for whales to be off the coast," he said. "Plus Jamie and I didn't always get along when we were young, so some people thought maybe I...that I killed him."

"That's totally ridiculous," I said.

"You're right. It is. We *did* have a fight on the boat, though, and that's the part nobody knows about. Not Keith. Not anyone, except you and me."

Georgia Ann showed up with his beach dog and onion rings. The smell of them turned my stomach.

"Y'all need anything else?" she asked.

"We're fine," Uncle Marcus said.

"You holler if you do now, hear?"

Uncle Marcus sipped his tea as she walked away. "While Jamie and I were on the boat," he said, "he told me he was in love with Sara and wanted to divorce your mom so he could marry her."

"No *way*," I said.

"I'm sorry, Mags. He did. And he told me he was Keith's father." He took a bite of an onion ring, the onion pulling from the batter. I tried to be patient while he chewed it.

"I never told anybody about that conversation, because I figured the secret would die with Jamie," he said once he'd swallowed. "He'd been giving Sara money for child support, and once he died, that stopped, of course. I wished that he'd never told me, but he did, and I couldn't sit back and watch Keith who was only what…six at the time? I couldn't watch him grow up with nothing when I knew he was Jamie's son, as well as my nephew. So, what I did was start a trust fund for him with forty thousand dollars of my own money."

"Get out!"

"I wrote a letter about it to Sara and gave it to her with a check. Wrote something like, 'This is Keith's college fund. I know Jamie loved you and wanted to provide for you and Keith.' I wanted to let her know that I knew. That I got that she was grieving, too, but wasn't allowed to show it. I felt sorry for her."

"What about for *Mom?*"

"I felt sorry for your mom, too," he said, "but the thing was, she didn't know the truth. As far as she was concerned, Jamie died her loving husband. Sara, on the other hand, had lost someone she had to pretend she was only friends with."

"How can you sound so sympathetic about her?" I nearly shouted. "She's Mom's best friend, and she was..." I couldn't even say it.

"I know it's hard to understand, Mags. I was angry at first, too. Angry enough to fight with your father. People make mistakes, though. And their feelings change over time."

I thought of Ben, trying to imagine my feelings for him changing. Impossible.

I took the wrapper off my straw so I'd have something to play with. I wadded the thin paper into a tiny ball and squeezed it between my fingertips. "So, I still don't get why Keith is talking about this all of a sudden," I said.

"Sara kept my letter," Uncle Marcus said. "She stuck it with the account information someplace where Keith stumbled onto it. He found it the morning of the lock-in, which explains why he was so mean to Andy that night."

"He said things about me being rich when I saw him at the hospital."

"Well, you *are* rich. You live on a tidy inheritance from Jamie, plus his life insurance kept you and Andy and your mom going for quite a few years. Sara and Keith had very little, and even though I was thoroughly pissed at your father for what he did, I couldn't let his son end up with nothing."

I looked out the window at the sound. The rain had stopped, at least for now. "I always thought Daddy was perfect," I said. "I don't understand how he could do something like that. Cheat on Mom and his family that way."

"You know, Mags, he was a great man in a lot of ways. A really good father. He had high standards for himself. I almost never heard him curse, not as an adult anyway. He stuck by your mom when she got pregnant with Andy even though she wasn't much fun to be around. Neither was I," he added quickly. "We were both drunks. I lived next door at the time and your mom and I drank together and were pretty bad for each other."

I nodded. I knew Uncle Marcus was a recovering alcoholic like my mother, but I'd never imagined him and my mother getting drunk together. It was totally impossible to picture either of them drinking at all. Together? No way. My mother was such a cold fish around him. Suddenly, though, things started to make sense.

"Did Mom think…was she one of the people who thought you might have killed Daddy?" I whispered.

He nodded. "I…" He hesitated. "I really liked your mom and she knew it. She thought that was motivation for me to…get rid of your father."

"Oh, Uncle Marcus, that's insane!"

"Damn straight." He took a bite of his hot dog, washing it down with a swallow of tea. "So I guess the moral of the story is, we're all fallible," he said. "We all screw up at least once in our lives."

Some of us were more fallible than others, I thought.

"Do you know about your Mom's depression?" Uncle Marcus asked.

"Just that she says she medicated herself with alcohol."

"Right," Marcus said. "After you were born, your mom fell into what's called a postpartum depression. Hormones out of whack, which sometimes happens to women after they have a baby. Anyway, we thought she was upset at being a mother or whatever. Your dad tried to help her, but she wouldn't see a counselor or anything, and she wanted...they decided to separate for a while."

"They separated? I didn't know any of this."

"He moved in with Sara and the man she was married to at the time, Steve. Steve was gone a lot in the service, and I guess your dad and Sara...comforted each other."

"Oh, ick." I cringed.

"Mags." He covered my hand with his on the table. "Please, babe. Be an adult about this."

I rolled my eyes. "I'm sorry," I said. "I'll try. Where was I while he was living with Sara?"

"You were with him. Your mother could hardly take care of herself. Sara helped him with you. Even though I was angry with him at first, I think they really needed each other."

"He was going to *leave* us, though," I said. "Leave Andy and me." I felt a tear roll down my cheek before I even knew I was crying.

"No, he planned to be there for *all* his children." He covered my hand again. "You were his baby girl, Maggie. The person he was closest to. He adored you. He was both father and mother to you for your first three years."

That explained so much. "I still feel so attached to him," I admitted. "I think about him a lot. I remember him so well from when I was little, but I hardly remember Mom at all. Like she wasn't there."

"She wasn't, really, but don't blame her either, okay? She became a very good mother to you and Andy once she got sober, so there's no use blaming her or Sara or your dad for any of this now. It's in the past and everyone's tried to move on."

"If Keith told *me*," I said, "he might tell *Mom*." She wouldn't be able to take it. I thought my father had been perfect, but Mom thought he walked on water. "You said she has no idea."

"I know, and I'm going to tell her, but not yet. Not with the hearing tomorrow. So keep this between us for now."

"What if Keith calls her?"

"I don't think he can manage a phone right now."

I remembered his bandaged arms, the metal rods sticking out of his fingers.

Uncle Marcus's pager suddenly went off, and he was on his feet in an instant, wrapping his food in a napkin. "Gotta run, babe," he said, dropping a ten dollar bill on the table. "You okay for now?"

I nodded, and watched him head for the door. Then I stood up to leave myself. I didn't want to have to talk to Georgia Ann again.

My phone jangled on my hip when I got outside. A text message from Ben.

Had fite w/ D. She's on rampage. Keep ur cool. ILU, B.

Chapter Forty-Five

Laurel

THE RAIN WAS COMING DOWN IN BUCKETS BY the time I left Raleigh and I knew I had a miserable drive ahead of me. It was after four, and I'd just hung up on Dennis. I couldn't remember another time when I hung up on someone, but I was furious. I was starting to hate him, and that's a bad way to feel about the man who holds your son's life in his hands. First, it took him two hours to return my phone call when he *knew* I was trying to find someone to help us tomorrow at the bind over hearing. Second, even after I told him about my nearly two hour long meeting with the neurologist in Raleigh, he still didn't think it was worth talking to the man himself.

"I told you, it's an overused defense, Mrs. Lockwood," he said. "It's lost its punch."

"Well, it hasn't been overused in Andy's case!" I shouted into my cell phone. "You're not using it at all?"

"Once the case reaches the trial level, then the neurologist's testimony could be helpful in negating intent."

"But he'll be in adult court by then!" That's when I hung up. I knew I was going to start crying or cussing or both. Shartell didn't seem to get it. Andy wouldn't survive in jail. He simply wouldn't.

I was still crying twenty minutes later when my cell phone rang. I hoped it was Shartell, having reconsidered, although I knew that was unlikely. I answered my phone.

"Hold on," I said quickly into the mouthpiece. I put the phone on my lap and drove through the spiking rain to the shoulder of I-40. I picked up the phone again as I came to a stop.

"Hello?" I hoped it wasn't obvious that I'd been crying.

"Laurel, this is Dawn." Her voice sounded strange. Tight. Scaring me. I was afraid Keith had taken a turn for the worse and she was making the calls for Sara. The rain thrummed on my roof and I turned the volume up on the phone.

"Is everything okay?" I asked.

"That depends on your definition of okay," she said. "Where are you? What's that noise?"

"It's rain. I'm driving back from Raleigh. What's going on?"

"I'm calling because I think you need to know what your daughter's up to."

"Maggie?" I asked, as though I had more than one daughter.

"She's having an affair with Ben. He's been cheating on me with her."

"*Maggie?*" I repeated.

"It's been going on since they started coaching together."

"Dawn, what makes you think—"

"Ben told me everything. He says he's trying to end it with her, but he's taking his sweet time about it."

"Maggie doesn't even date," I said.

Dawn laughed. "They're doing a lot more than dating, Laurel."

I was quiet, thinking of the time I watched Maggie comfort Ben in the emergency room. "He's...how old is he?"

"Twenty-eight. A mere eleven-year difference."

"Did he start it?" I felt a rare emotion—an overwhelming need to protect my daughter. All my protectiveness had gone toward Andy; I'd had none left over for her. Quickly replacing that need, though, was rage. How dare he!

"Does it matter who started it?" Dawn asked. "Lord have mercy, Laurel! My boyfriend's banging your teenaged daughter. Not only that, but she smokes dope with him."

"I don't believe that." Maggie knew—I'd made sure both my kids knew—that substance abuse was *out* in our family. I had zero tolerance for it.

"Then you're hiding your head in the sand."

"I've got to get off the phone, Dawn. Sorry." My hands shook as I clicked off that call and then speed-dialed Maggie's cell phone.

"Did you have any luck?" she asked when she picked up.

"That's not why I'm calling." I ran my free hand around my steering wheel. "I just had a call from Dawn."

Maggie's silence told me all I needed to know.

"Oh, Maggie." Disappointment welled up in my chest. "It's true?"

"Mom, let me explain. It probably didn't come out sounding too good from Dawn."

"No, it sure didn't. You've been lying to me all year. 'Oh, I don't want to date, Mom. I want to concentrate on studying, Mom.' How could you lie to my face like that?"

"Because if I told you the truth, you wouldn't let me see him."

"Damn straight I wouldn't! He's twenty-eight and living with his girlfriend."

"She's not his girlfriend. And why does his age matter?"

"Because there's a huge difference between seventeen and twenty-eight."

"You always say how mature I am, so I don't get what's so shocking and terrible. I love him. He's the best thing that ever happened to me."

"You're smarter than that," I said. "Don't you realize he's taking advantage of you? He's living with Dawn and has you on the side. Where's the future in that?"

"He and Dawn are just housemates."

"She seems to think they're more than housemates."

"Well, she's wrong!"

"Everyone knows they're a couple, for heaven's sake."

"He doesn't love her. She's just our cover."

"Maggie!" I was shocked. "How dare you! If that's true…how can you use someone like that?"

"They are *not* a couple!"

"Maggie—"

"I'm not going to let you ruin this for me!"

"Ruin *what*? Do you think he's going to leave Dawn for you?"

"How many times do I have to tell you, he's not *with* Dawn!"

"What kind of future do you expect to have with him?"

"A *long* one!" she yelled.

"I wouldn't count on it. If he's cheating on Dawn, he'll cheat on you, too."

"You're not *listening* to me! If Dawn thinks he's her boyfriend, she's living in a fantasy world."

"I'm afraid you're the one living in a fantasy world, Maggie. She said he wants to end it with you."

"She's so full of it! I'm hanging up."

"Don't you dare."

"We can talk about it later."

"No, now!" I said. "We can talk about it *now*, because I want you to call him up and tell him it's over."

She laughed. "All of a sudden you want to be involved in my life after ignoring me for seventeen years?"

"Maggie!" One of my heartstrings broke. *She's upset,* I told myself. *She's just trying to hurt you.* "Never mind," I said. "I'll call him myself."

"No!"

"He's probably had any number of lovers," I thought out loud. "Do you realize that? He could have a venereal disease, for all you know. You could get pregnant."

"Mother, give me some credit. I'm not stupid."

"Yes, that's *exactly* what you are!" The rain was so loud that I had to plug my free ear with my finger. "You're being incredibly stupid. How could you trust a man who'd have a secret affair with a girl half his age?"

"Because I'm not like *you!*" Maggie snapped. "I *trust* people. You don't trust anyone. You don't even trust Uncle Marcus.

You're going to end up alone forever and I don't want that to happen to me."

"I do so trust people," I said, grabbing her bait. "I trusted your father completely."

"Well, guess what, Mom. Turns out that was pretty stupid of *you*."

"Maggie! Why would you say that?"

"Because he was cheating on you, that's why."

"That's ridiculous," I said. "Don't try to turn this into something about me," I said.

"It *is* about you," she said. "You think Ben's so untrustworthy and you talk about Daddy like he was a saint. Well, guess what? He wasn't. He was in love with Sara."

"Sara?" Where in God's name was this coming from? "Sara helped him a lot when you were little. Is that what you're remembering?"

"Keith is Daddy's son!"

I nearly laughed, it was so ludicrous. "Maggie, where are you? You're scaring me." I'd never heard her sound so vicious and desperate before. "I'm going to ask Marcus to come stay with you."

"Mother! It's Uncle Marcus who told me everything. Daddy confessed it all to him when they were on that boat the day he drowned. He was going to leave you for Sara and Keith."

My mind spun as her words sank in. *Impossible.* "Even if this is the truth, why would Marcus tell you?"

"Because Keith knows and Keith told me."

"What?"

"Uncle Marcus never wanted you to know. You play ice queen with him because you think he had something to do with

Daddy's death, but all this time he's just been trying to keep you from finding out. He set up a college fund for Keith after Daddy died and Keith found the papers or something, so now he knows the truth. Uncle Marcus was going to wait until after the hearing to tell you."

My car closed in on me, the rain sheeting down my windows like a second layer of glass. I felt the blade of a knife slip into my heart, then twist.

Maggie was crying.

"I'm sorry, Mom," she said. "I didn't mean it to come out that way. I know this is a bad time, but you pushed me about Ben. Please, please, just accept that he and I are together. Dawn's jealous, that's all. It's not like he's cheating on her. He told her he just wanted to be friends a long time ago. She's angry that—"

"Maggie—" I wasn't really listening to her "—I'm on my way home. It's been a terrible day."

"Why? What did the neurologist say?"

"We can talk about it in a few hours when I get home. It's raining here and the wind's blowing and I want to miss the worst part of the storm if I can." I sounded remarkably calm to myself even though the knife was turning and twisting and cutting me deeper.

"Mom, just tell me you understand," she pleaded. "That you believe Ben and I are together for the right reasons. I love him."

"We'll talk when I get home," I said. "And don't forget to pick Andy up from swim practice."

"Have I ever once forgotten him?" Maggie snapped, and then the line went dead.

I flipped the phone closed, pressing my forehead to the

steering wheel. Jamie had always been mine, I thought. Solid and supportive and loving. We had a few good years after I got sober. All those *I love you*'s. Tender moments with the children. With each other. They were excellent years, weren't they? Had they been my imagination? Were those *I love you*'s meant for Sara, not me?

Sara?

Why *wouldn't* Jamie have fallen for Sara? She was pretty, sweet and his helpmate. Her husband had been frequently absent and emotionally distant even when he was around, while for years I'd been drunk, slovenly and very, very hard to love.

And Marcus. Had he really been keeping the truth from me all these years, while I froze him out? I wanted to call him, to separate what was true from my angry daughter's manipulation of things he'd told her. But I needed to get home and I couldn't possibly drive in the pouring rain and talk on the phone at the same time. Not today. Not about this.

I turned the key in the ignition and pulled back onto I-40.

Chapter Forty-Six

Maggie

ANDY RAN TOWARD ME THROUGH THE RAIN as I got out of my car in front of the rec center.

"I'm getting good at butterflying!" he shouted to me in greeting.

"Good, Andy," I said, opening my umbrella. "Wait in the car, okay? I need to talk to Ben. I'll just be a minute."

I ran into the building and downstairs to the pool. Ben was talking to the parents of one of his team members. He demonstrated a stroke, his arm arcing through the air. He was so amazing. *Oh, God, please don't let this be the end.* I sat down on the lowest bench of the bleachers to wait for him. He spotted me and excused himself from the parents.

"Dawn told my mother," I said when he was close enough to hear me.

"Damn." He sat next to me. "I'm sorry. I was afraid she would. Your mother had a fit, I bet."

"Yes, but there's so much else going on," I said. I'd tried to call Uncle Marcus to tell him I'd blown it with Mom, but he hadn't picked up. I thought of texting him, but he was totally lame at text messages. Besides, I was afraid to tell him what I'd done. I'd been so mean to my mother. Part of me felt guilty about it, but another part loved every second of hurting her. I'd had the empathy of a rattlesnake. "You won't believe it all." I looked up to see another mother walking toward us. "I have to talk to you. Can you call me later?"

He stood up, turning his back to the woman who waited a few feet away. "I'll try," he said.

"Ben…" I got to my feet. "My mother said that Dawn told her you want to break up with me."

He shook his head. "You know Dawn," he said. "She's just trying to make trouble for us. We'll talk later, okay?"

Outside, a gust of wind nearly blew me off my feet. I put up my umbrella, hanging on to it while the wind tried to tear it out of my hands. I was soaked by the time I got to the car.

"You look like you fell in the pool," Andy said.

"I feel like it, too." I shivered as I turned the key.

"Did you bring my iPod?"

"I forgot it. Sorry."

"The thing with the butterfly is you have to get the breathing right," he said, as I pulled into the street.

"Just like everything else in swimming." I knew I sounded snippy, but he didn't seem to notice.

"I want to be the champion."

"Andy, you don't need to be the best at everything all the time."

"Yes, I do."

"Why?"

"So I'll be happy."

I had to laugh. "Your life is pretty simple isn't it?" I asked.

"Yes."

Did he know about the hearing tomorrow? He sure didn't sound worried about it. "It's good that you try hard," I said, "but part of growing up is learning how to lose gracefully."

"What does that mean?"

"You know when Ben tells you to congratulate the winner on the other team?" I liked hearing myself say Ben's name.

"I hate that."

"That's losing gracefully."

"It's still better to win, though, right?"

"I guess so." I sighed. I couldn't focus on the conversation any longer. "I'm in charge of dinner tonight because Mom won't be home till later." Oh, I dreaded seeing her! "What do you feel like eating?"

"Pizza!"

"I think there's one in the freezer. I'll make it while you get changed."

I was sliding the pizza into the oven when the phone rang. I checked the caller ID. Uncle Marcus. He was going to kill me.

"Hey, Maggie," he said when I answered. "Is your mom home yet?"

"No, and I blew it," I said. "She called and I got mad at her about something and I told her." I bit my lip, waiting for his reaction.

"*Why,* Maggie?" He sounded more shocked than angry.

"She was giving me grief, and then she said how Daddy was the only trustworthy man she ever knew or something like that and it just came out. I know I shouldn't have. I couldn't help myself."

He was quiet, and I scrunched up my face, waiting for him to yell at me.

"Do you know how she made out with the neurologist?" he asked finally. "She left me a message, but I think her phone's off."

"I don't know. She said it was a terrible day."

"Damn."

"It'll be okay, though, won't it? Tomorrow, I mean?"

"Not if Andy's bound over to adult court, it won't be."

"But——" I was confused "——Mom said that probably wouldn't happen."

"She said that *today?*"

I tried to remember my phone conversation with her. "No. She told me the day Andy came home from jail. I was going off about it and she said not to worry. That it wouldn't happen."

Uncle Marcus was quiet again.

"Could it happen?" I asked.

"I think your mother was just trying to keep you from getting upset, Mags," he said. "If she said it was a terrible day, it sounds like she either didn't have any luck with the neurologist or else with the lawyer. And if that's the case, then there's a really good chance Andy will end up in adult court."

"So..." What did that mean exactly? "When would he have a trial? He could stay home while he's waiting for it, right?"

Andy came downstairs. I watched him walk into the family room and turn on the TV.

"No, Mags. Look, I know your mom doesn't want to worry you, but here's the deal. If he gets bound over, they'll lock him up right away and—"

"What do you *mean,* lock him up right away?" I whispered, turning my back to the family room.

"I mean, after the hearing tomorrow, they'd take him back to jail. And it's very doubtful he could get bail, so he'd have to stay in jail until his trial. And sometimes it can take a year or even longer for a case to go to trial. Then if he's found guilty, he could end up in prison for the rest of his life."

I couldn't speak. This couldn't be happening.

"So that's why your mom's been knocking herself out to find the right expert and why she's been so worried and why you really were...you were cruel to her today, Maggie. She didn't need that on top of everything else."

"I can't believe it," I said.

"What part of it?"

"Any of it." I looked into the family room. I could see the back of Andy's head where he sat on the sofa. He had no idea how his world might change tomorrow. *I'd* had no idea. "I'm so sorry," I said to Uncle Marcus. "I didn't realize...I knew it was serious, but I didn't get how bad it was."

"It's worse. That's what I was calling to talk to your mother about."

"How could it possibly be worse?"

"Here's how," he said. "Those empty containers from the landfill? One of them has Andy's prints on it."

Chapter Forty-Seven

Laurel

I HAD TO STOP ONCE MORE ON THE DRIVE home from Raleigh, this time because of the blinding rain. Mine wasn't the only car to pull over with its emergency blinkers flashing, but I bet none of the other drivers were in the sort of turmoil—the sort of emotional pain—I was in. I'd failed to get the necessary help for my son, and my daughter had been lying to me for the past year, turning into a girl I didn't know. I thought of all the times Ben Trippett had talked to me about Andy's swimming, all the while chortling to himself about the wool he was pulling over my eyes.

And then there was that knife beneath my breastbone, the most visceral pain of them all. My beloved Jamie had led a double life. My best friend had deceived me. I'd been blind to it. Why did I always *lose* people? My parents. My aunt and uncle. Jamie. And now even Jamie's memory would be lost to me. And Sara! How could she? Even Marcus had betrayed me in the guise of protecting me—an act of nobility I could barely fathom, given the wrath with which I'd blamed him for Jamie's death. Nothing was as it seemed. The only person in my life I felt sure about was Andy, and tomorrow, he could be ripped from my arms for being too naive, too defenseless against a world he didn't completely understand. I started to cry. To sob so hard that, even as the rain let up and the other cars took off, I stayed on the side of the road trying to get a grip on myself.

By the time I got home, the nor'easter was in full swing. The sky was eerily dark for so early in the evening, and the thunder made a ripping, growling sound that reminded me of when the church roof caved in during the fire. The slender trees in my yard bowed toward the sound. I caught them in my headlights, and that's when I realized that my headlights were the only lights near the house. The power must have gone out.

The garage door opener worked, though, and as I pulled inside, I noticed that Maggie's Jetta wasn't there. I let myself into the house, feeling even more unsettled. Something wasn't right.

"Maggie? Andy?"

The wind rattled the windowpanes, but even so, I could hear the refrigerator's loud hum. The power *was* on. I flipped the kitchen switch and the room filled with light. An uneaten pizza rested on a cookie sheet on the granite counter. Where were they?

I walked through the house, calling for them, afraid the

police might have taken Andy away again. Why, though? And where was Maggie?

I sat on the family room sofa and dialed her cell phone, but she didn't answer. She was probably afraid to talk to me after our conversation earlier. I tried Andy's phone but, as with Maggie's, I was dumped to his voice mail.

"Hi! This is Andy. Leave…leave me a message when the tone rings." It had taken us an hour to get that message properly recorded.

"Andy, this is Mom," I said. "Call me right away!" I tried Maggie's phone again, this time leaving a message. "Where are you and Andy? I'm home and very worried!"

Then I dialed Marcus's cell.

"Do you know where Maggie and Andy are?" I asked when he picked up.

"I spoke to Maggie about an hour or so ago," he said. "She was home with Andy. She said they were making pizza."

"Well, I just got home and the house is dark and empty and a whole pizza is on the counter. Her car's not here. She was mad at me. We had a fight on the phone." I ran my hand over the green fabric on the arm of the sofa, unsure how much to say about that conversation.

"Then you don't know about the containers?"

"What containers?"

"The ones found in the landfill." He hesitated. "At least one of them has Andy's fingerprints on it, Laurel."

"No!" I stood up. "Oh, Marcus, that's impossible! It's just impossible. I don't understand what's happening."

"I'm coming over."

"Could the police have picked him up?"

"I doubt it. I think they have other things to worry about with this storm, but I'll call them on my way to your house to make sure."

"Please do." I hung up. I tried to make a pot of coffee, but forgot to add the grounds and ended up with a carafe full of murky-looking water. Sobs shook my shoulders as I tried again. I remembered the grounds this time, but the power died as the first dark drops poured into the carafe.

Fumbling in the darkness, I found my hurricane lanterns and flashlights. I lit the lanterns, setting them on the tables and fireplace mantel in the family room.

If the police had Andy, could Marcus somehow get him out again? Or was this it, now that they had his prints on those containers? Would Andy be locked up tonight, then sent to jail after the hearing tomorrow, never to get out again?

It was nine o'clock when Marcus arrived. I heard the slamming of his pickup door and I raced to my front door, anxious to talk to him. He literally blew into the house, the wind lifting him off his feet.

"Damn!" he said, knocking into the small table in the foyer. "My pickup hydroplaned half the way here." He helped me close the door against the wind. "We need to go out there again," he said. "We need to get your patio furniture in the garage."

I was usually a clear thinker in a storm. Tonight, though, I could barely picture the furniture he was talking about.

"Do the police have him?" I asked.

"No. I'm worried about tomorrow, though, Laurel. I mean, I thought maybe we had a chance till these containers turned up."

"I don't understand!" I said for the hundredth time.

"Let's get things secured outside and then figure out what to do."

"I don't care about the patio furniture!" I said. "I don't care if the house falls down. I just want to know where my children are!"

"You stay here, then. I'll do it."

I knew he was right. A nor'easter last year had sent some-one's trash can through my front window. I followed him outside and together we managed to get the chairs and patio table into the garage. My trash can was already gone, blown away who knew where. I cried in the windy darkness, letting myself break down unheard. I just managed to pull myself together before we went into the house again.

"Let's think," he said, as I relit one of the lanterns that had gone out. "How could Andy's prints have possibly gotten on the container?"

"Someone set him up," I said. "That's the only possibility. Maybe Keith, since he was angry that…" I stopped, pressing my hands to my temples as all that Maggie had told me rushed back. "Marcus." My voice cracked as I leaned against the stone of the fireplace. "I know about Keith. Maggie told me. Is it true about Jamie and Sara?"

He lowered himself to the sofa. "I'm sorry Maggie told you the way she did," he said. "I wanted to wait until a better time."

I shook my head, sinking into the chair behind me. I had no time to wallow, I told myself. Right now, I just needed to focus on Andy. "We should go out and look for them," I said.

"We wouldn't be able to see two feet in front of my pickup."

Again, he was right. I rubbed my arms with my hands,

watching the hurricane lantern flicker on the mantel. "What do you think?" I asked. "Could Keith have set Andy up?"

"But then we come back to the question of why he'd get trapped by the fire if he set it himself."

"Ben!" I said suddenly, getting to my feet and grabbing the wireless phone from the coffee table. "Maggie and Andy might be with Ben!"

"With *Ben?* Why?"

"Well, here's the other piece of terrific news I got today," I said. "Dawn called to tell me that Ben and Maggie have been seeing each other for nearly a year."

"Seeing each other?" Marcus's eyes grew wide. "You mean...intimately?"

"That's exactly what I mean. That's why Maggie got mad at me. I talked to her about it and I was furious. She—"

"Ben?" Marcus was incredulous. "I saw him with Dawn the other day, all lovey-dovey. And he's pushing thirty, for God's sake."

"I know it. I'm going to strangle him."

"I'll beat you to it."

I sat down again, glad to have something to do. Some action to take. "Do you know his phone number?" I hit the talk button on my phone, but there was no dial tone. Of course. "The power," I said, holding the dead phone in the air.

Marcus pulled his cell phone from his belt. "Cells are iffy tonight," he said, frowning at the display. "I only have one bar."

I watched as he dialed. He listened, shaking his head. "Voice mail," he said to me. Into the phone, he said, "Ben, it's Marcus. Call me."

I leaned back against the chair, feeling defeated. "It's my

fault, Marcus," I said. "Maggie and Ben. I've been a terrible mother to her. An absent mother. I made her parent Andy with me without giving much thought to *her* needs. Jamie raised her until he died and then I let her be. I expected her to take care of herself."

"She seemed really good at it."

"How could I not have known she was seeing Ben? And for so *long?*"

"Man!" Marcus got to his feet, pacing toward the stairs and back again. "I'm going to flatten him!"

"Could they be over there?" I wondered. "At Ben's?"

"Since it's actually *Dawn's* house, not likely."

I massaged my forehead. A headache was starting, or maybe I'd had it for hours and hadn't noticed. "This thing about the containers," I said. "It makes no sense." I rubbed my temples harder. "But if Maggie had a secret life, maybe Andy did, too." There was no other way to explain it all. "I think about the mothers of those kids who shoot up schools. I'm sure they never suspected their child could do such a thing." I dropped my hands to the arms of the chair. "Marcus, I *knew* there was something on his shoes," I admitted. "I hoped it was fluid from his lighter. You know, how he put it in his sock when we were at the airport? With all the time and attention I gave Andy, did I still screw up with him? Is there a side to him he's managed to keep hidden from me?" Just then, I felt as though everyone in my life had deceived me.

"Don't *you* start doubting him, all right?" Marcus stopped pacing. "You're the one person who can't afford to ever doubt him."

"But how do you explain it?" I raised my hands in the air,

palms up. "He needed to feel powerful and looked up to. He loved being a hero. Maybe he—"

"How can you even think that?" he asked.

I looked across the room at the man I'd mistrusted for the last fifteen years. "Because," I said, "today I learned that I don't know a thing about the people that I love."

Chapter Forty-Eight

Maggie

THE UNIVERSE WOULD HAVE TO PICK THIS night for a storm.
I parked on a side street at the northern end of the Island. The
rain sounded like nails hitting the roof of my car. The houses
were dark: people must have gotten the word about the
weather and stayed away from the beach. That was totally fine
with me. The darker and emptier, the better.

"Where are we?" Andy asked when I made no move to get
out of the car.

"We're near The Sea Tender. *You* know. We've driven past
it a couple of times."

"The circle house where I lived when I was a baby?"

"When you were little, yes. That's the house. We're going
to stay there tonight. It'll be fun."

"Cool," Andy said. He peered into the dark rain. "Where is it?"

"Just a short walk away." It didn't seem as though it would stop raining anytime soon, so I grabbed the flashlight and a trash bag I'd filled with clothes for each of us, along with Andy's iPod. "We're going to have to get wet." I opened the door, hanging on to the handle to keep the wind from tearing it from my hands. The ocean roared in my ears as if I'd parked right on the beach. "Be careful getting out!" I shouted, too late. The wind grabbed Andy's door and he went sprawling onto the sandy side of the road. He got up, laughing. He was clueless. About tonight. About tomorrow.

I was practically blinded by the rain as I walked around the car to help him shut the door. The wind was like a living being, pushing the door toward us. It spooked me, like we weren't alone out there. Everything I was doing spooked me, but I had to do it. This wouldn't be the first crazy thing I'd done. I wished Mom had told me how bad things were! I would have done something sooner. Made a better plan. *Something.* Tomorrow, Andy was supposed to sit through a hearing he could never understand that could lead to him being locked up and the key thrown away. I would *not* let that happen. I hadn't thought things through past tomorrow, but if they couldn't find Andy for the hearing, they couldn't lock him up. That was all that mattered.

"Can you carry the food?" I shouted, handing him a brown paper bag I'd filled with bread and peanut butter and fruit. There was nearly a case of bottled water in the cottage. That would last us through tonight and tomorrow. "Hold the top closed so everything doesn't get soaked," I said as he took the bag from my hand. I swung the garbage bag over my shoulder and we started walking toward The Sea Tender.

"I can't see *anything!*" Andy said.

"We're almost there." I could hardly make out one house from another. I squeezed my eyes nearly closed to keep out the wind.

We walked right past the narrow boardwalk that led to the house and had to backtrack.

"Come on," I said, turning onto the boardwalk. "Stay close to me."

We reached the puny dune in front of the house. Even in the darkness, I could see the waves crashing into each other as they raced toward the beach. I shone the flashlight toward the sand below The Sea Tender. Something was different, and it took me a moment to realize that the silvery glow in the beam of my flashlight was not sand at all but swirling water. The ocean churned around the pilings of the cottage, tossing foam and spray up to the deck. I'd never seen the water so high on this beach. I didn't want to let Andy know how it freaked me out.

"The rain is biting me!" Andy shouted.

"It's the sand blowing." The sand stung my face and hands. "Come on," I said, jumping down the sharp angle of the dune.

"This bag's—" The wind cut off whatever Andy said, and I didn't ask him to repeat it. I was too busy reminding myself that the cottage had survived dozens of hurricanes and plenty of nor'easters. It would survive this one, too.

I found the cinder block and moved it into place beneath the front stairs. "I'll go up first, then I'll help you up," I shouted. It took me three tries to throw the heavy trash bag onto the little front deck. Then I climbed on the block and hoisted myself onto the steps.

"I can do that," Andy shouted. "I don't need help."

"Okay, hand me the bag of food."

He lifted it toward me, and I grabbed the top edge of the bag. It was soggy and before I could get a better grip, the wind ripped it from my hands, spilling everything onto the wet beach.

"I'll get it all, don't worry, Maggie!" He scrambled around on the sand, the wind tossing the loaf of bread in the air like it was made out of feathers.

"I'll be down in a sec, Panda!" I shouted. I unlocked the door and tossed the trash bag into the house. Then I jumped off the deck, and together we picked up as much of the food as we could find.

Once we were both up on the deck, Andy made me shine my flashlight on the sign.

"Condem-ned," he read.

"Condemned," I shouted. "When we were kids, Hurricane Fran demolished a lot of the island."

"I know that," Andy yelled back at me. "I learned it. And *condemned* means *keep out,* but we're not going to keep out."

"You've got it," I said. I pushed the door open again and ducked under the sign.

"Are we doing a bad thing?" Andy asked as he walked into the living room. His tennis shoes squeaked on the floor, and I knew he was twisting his feet to make them squeak louder.

I picked up a second flashlight from the kitchen counter. "Here's one for you." I handed it to him. "About this being a bad thing, some people will think so, but I don't."

"Will Mom?" Andy turned the flashlight on and off, shining it in my face.

"Stop that." I pushed it away. "You're blinding me."

"Sorry. Will Mom think this is bad?"

"There's a bunch of candles all around this room. Let's light them and then I'll answer your question." I handed him a box of matches.

"Can I use my lighter?" He reached into his pocket and I shone my flashlight on the green lighter in his hand.

"You still have that thing? I thought the security people at the airport took it away from you."

"This is a different one."

My baby brother had some rebel in him after all. "Why?" I asked. "Are you still smoking?" I thought I'd smelled smoke on him a few days ago, but since the night of the fire, the whole world smelled like smoke to me.

"Don't tell Mom," he said.

"I won't. But it's so bad for you, Panda Bear. I wish you wouldn't."

"I lied to Mom," he admitted.

"Yeah," I said. "I've done some of that myself."

"I told her I didn't suck smoke into my chest, but I do."

"Great for your asthma." I lit one of the candles on the counter.

"I like to make it come out of my nose."

I tried to picture him smoking. "Where do you smoke?" I asked. He was always supervised, really. We'd smell it if he smoked at home and he sure couldn't do it at school.

"I do it when I'm hanging in with my friends on the days I don't ride home with you."

"Hanging out," I corrected him. I pictured him waiting for the bus with other kids from school, kids he thought of as his friends but who probably bummed cigarettes off him and called him names behind his back.

"If a fire started in this house, I could jump out this window onto those boards out there." He shone his flashlight through one of the living room windows onto the back deck.

"Right," I said. "And there's a door in the kitchen we could use to get out on the deck, too."

"Deck, I mean. Not boards."

He sounded embarrassed by his mistake. "It's okay," I said. "I knew what you meant. And decks are made out of boards, so you were technically correct."

"We have a big deck at home."

"Yes, we do."

"When do we go home?"

I set out the food on the kitchen counter. "We'll stay here tonight, and then decide what to do tomorrow." I opened the bag of bread. "You want some bread and peanut butter?" I asked. I should have figured out a way to bring the pizza with us. What would Mom think when she saw the whole pizza on the counter?

"Okay."

In the candlelight, he watched me spread peanut butter on two slices of bread. I handed one to him.

We sat on the couch together facing the dark window, eating the bread and peanut butter and drinking from bottles of water. "The ocean's out there," I said. It was so dark and we were up so high that I couldn't see the white froth of the waves.

"I know that. I'm not an imbecile."

"Good word, Panda," I said.

We munched our bread in silence for a while. I kept imagining how Mom would feel when she walked into the house to discover Andy wasn't there. I'd dumped all the stuff about Daddy on her when her day had been crap to begin with. Then she had to drive home in the wind and rain worrying about tomorrow and then discover that her children had disappeared. There were two voices in my head, one telling me to let her know we were okay, the other telling me to keep quiet. My tattoo burned into my hip every time I thought of her worrying.

"I'm going to call Mom and let her know we're okay," I said when I'd finished eating. I got his iPod out of the trash bag and handed it to him. Then I checked my phone. No bars at all. Weird. I could usually get reception in the cottage. The storm, probably. I wondered if Ben had been trying to call me. I didn't want to think about Ben. That would totally mess me up right now.

Andy's phone was on the counter, but he had no reception either. I pictured Mom growing more frantic by the minute. Why why why had I told her about Daddy? I had such a mean side to me. I'd wanted to turn the tables on her. Get her off my back about Ben.

"Andy, I'm going out on the deck because I can't get a phone signal inside."

"Okay." He didn't look up from his iPod.

On the deck, I had to grab the railing to keep my balance in the wind. Even if I could get a signal—which I couldn't— I'd never be able to hear her. I'd have to call from my car.

In the kitchen again, I tore a hole for my head in the trash bag and put it on like a poncho.

"Be back in a few minutes, Andy," I said, glancing at the candles scattered around the room to make sure they were burning safely. Just what we needed was my brother in another fire.

I made it to the car, but still had no signal, so I started driving. There was water on the road and I drove very slowly, afraid of skidding into the sand. Getting stuck. What if something happened to me and Andy was left alone at The Sea Tender? *Oh God,* I told myself. *Stop thinking that way!*

I didn't see a single light in any of the houses and knew the power was out. I was all the way to the huge condominium building, Villa Capriani, before I got a signal. I had three messages from Mom. She sounded scared to death, her voice shaking, and I knew I was making the right decision to call her. I pulled into Villa Capriani's nearly deserted parking lot and dialed my mother's cell number.

"Maggie! Where *are* you?" She sounded so bad. I knew she'd been crying. I should have called earlier or at least left her a note.

"I'm just calling to let you know Andy and I are fine," I said. "We're perfectly safe."

"Where are you, Maggie? What are you doing?"

"I can't tell you. I just wanted you to know that we're fine."

"She won't say," Mom said to someone.

"Who's there?" I was afraid it was the police.

"Maggie?" It was Uncle Marcus on the phone now. "What's going on? Are you with Ben?"

"*No,*" I said. Oh God. So now Uncle Marcus knew about Ben

and me, too. "He doesn't know anything about this, so leave him out of it. I just wanted to let Mom know that Andy and I are fine."

"Why are you doing this?" he asked. "Come home. You're only going to make things worse, babe."

"How could they get any worse?" I asked. "Can you picture Andy in a jail cell without bail? Waiting a year for a trial, like you said? Getting picked on and maybe beaten up and maybe raped by the other prisoners? And not really getting it?" My voice broke as the images ran through my mind. "Not understanding what's going on?"

"I know, Mags," he said. "But try to calm down, all right? Maybe the judge will see reason tomorrow and not lock him up. Maybe he'll even let him stay in the juvenile system."

"Oh, sure," I said. "That's not what you said a couple of hours ago. Especially now that they have his fingerprints on that container."

"If he doesn't show, it'll be worse for him," Uncle Marcus said.

"I'm hanging up." I turned my phone's power off so I wouldn't have to hear it ring when they tried to call me back. I wondered if, by now, even Mom and Uncle Marcus believed Andy had done it. Was I the only one who knew he was innocent?

I was scared driving back to the cottage. I drove faster and faster, thinking again about the candles. I was so relieved when I saw that The Sea Tender was still standing. I parked the car on New River Inlet Road this time and ran as fast as I could back to the cottage. Inside, Andy had his earbuds in and barely seemed to notice when I burst into the living room.

I talked him into playing a game of Concentration with the sticky old deck of cards from one of the kitchen drawers. We spread them out between us on the sofa, and my hands shook when it was my turn to turn over a pair. Now that we were here, with my brother fed, my mother called and nothing more that needed to be done, I was starting to freak out. What was I doing? What had I done?

"I win!" Andy shouted, when we counted our pairs. For once, I envied his ability to see life so simply.

We played a few more hands. Then I blew out the candle on the windowsill and we watched the rain and salt water tap against the glass in front of us. The cottage vibrated, I guessed from the water swirling around the pilings. My nerves were going to snap any minute.

Andy had kicked off his shoes and now he put his feet on the windowsill. "I wish we could see the ocean," he said.

I leaned forward to see if the white water was visible.

"Do you mind getting wet again?"

"Are we going back to the car?"

"No," I said. "It's not raining that hard right now. Let's sit out on the deck and watch the ocean."

He followed me out the kitchen door onto the deck. It may not have been raining hard, but the wind made balloons out of our shirts and whooshed in our ears. I sat down where I always did, on the edge of the wet deck with my legs dangling over the side, my arms on the lower rung of the railing. The vibration was much stronger out here. The deck shook as if someone was running across it.

I patted the boards next to me and Andy sat down, too.

"Now we can see the ocean." I could tell from the frothy

white water that the waves were very high, crashing crazily into each other. The darkness scared me, though, because I couldn't get a good sense of how high up the beach the waves were coming. I felt the spray on my bare feet as the water swirled around the pilings.

"We could fish from here," Andy said. "If we run out of food, we can catch fish."

Right, I thought. Like *that's* in my plans.

"Yes, we could," I said.

I put my arm around Andy's shoulders. A different fifteen-year-old boy probably would have knocked my arm away, but Andy didn't seem to mind. What I really wanted to do was wrap both my arms around him. Hold him tight. I'd resented my mother for pouring one hundred percent of her love and attention into Andy, giving him the fifty percent that should have been mine. But I'd never resented Andy. It wasn't his fault she loved him more.

"Do you remember Daddy at all?" I asked him.

"I rode on his shoulders," Andy said. In his room, he had a framed picture of Daddy holding him on his shoulders when he was about two. I was sure his memory wasn't of Daddy, but of the picture.

"Sometimes," I said, "when I sit out here, I feel his spirit."

"Like a ghost?" Andy asked.

"No, not exactly. It's hard to explain. You remember Piddie?" Piddie had been his goldfish. We'd found him belly-up in his bowl a few months ago.

"Yes. He was pretty."

"Do you ever, sort of, feel him around? Like, you know perfectly well he's not there, but you feel like he is."

"No. He's dead."

"Well, okay. I'm trying to explain what I mean by Daddy's spirit, but I don't think you can understand it." I lowered my arm from his shoulders and leaned on the railing again. "I just feel like he's here with me sometimes."

"He's *dead!*" Andy sounded so upset that I laughed.

"I know, Panda Bear. Don't worry about it."

Between the wind and the light rain, it was chilly on the deck but I didn't want to go inside. I thought I should keep an eye on the ocean, although I was sure we were okay. If the deck started to actually sway, though, maybe we'd have to leave the house.

"My friends think I'm going to go to jail," Andy said suddenly.

"You won't go to jail."

"I'm scared I'll have to because I lied to the policemen. I lied to everyone."

I was confused. "What do you mean, Andy? When did you lie?"

"I said I didn't go outside while the lock-in was there, but I did."

"You *did?* Why?"

"To see if the bugs were dying. To see if the bug spray worked, but it was too dark."

I shut my eyes. I knew what he was talking about. I knew everything.

"I promise you, Andy," I said, "I will not let you go to jail."

"Cross your heart and hope to die?"

"Cross my heart and hope to die." I felt a chill up my spine, saying those words.

"How can you stop the police from putting me in jail?" he asked.

"I can stop them."

"But how?"

I put my arm around him again. "By telling them what really happened that night."

Chapter Forty-Nine

Laurel

IT WAS NOT DAMP IN MY HOUSE SO MUCH AS RAW, as though the weather had crept in through the windows. I huddled on the sofa beneath an afghan, while Marcus tended the fire he'd built.

"At least you know Maggie's got him someplace where he's safe." Marcus sat down on the sofa near my feet. "Do you think you should call Shartell?"

"I don't want to." I realized that whatever insanity had made Maggie spirit Andy away tonight, part of me shared it. As long as he was with her, he wouldn't be afraid and he wouldn't be in jail. "But I don't know what I'll do in the morning when we're supposed to show up for the hearing."

"I guess we'll deal with it then," Marcus said.

I lifted my head to look at him. "Thank you for saying *we*,"

I said. "You've always tried to be...a *we* when it came to Andy. I'm sorry I made that hard."

"I understood." He shifted on the sofa. "I don't know how much Maggie told you, but Jamie and I had a colossal fight on the boat. I was angry with him about the whole Sara thing, and when I got on his case about it, he turned on me, saying I didn't have much room to talk. He'd figured out that Andy was mine, and—"

"He *did?* I was never even sure that you knew." Relief washed over me now that it was out in the open. It should have been for years.

The light from the hurricane lantern caught his smile. "I was pretty sure about that right from the start. From when you told me you were pregnant. Jamie probably was, too. We just let it be the elephant in the room. But that elephant didn't fit on my boat with us."

I remembered the bruises on Marcus's body that had caused the police to suspect foul play. "Do you mean you had a *fist-fight?*" I couldn't picture the brothers physically fighting.

"Most definitely. That's why I was scratched up, but I only told the cops about the whale. I couldn't tell them the rest of it without getting into what led to the fight and all that."

"Was there really a whale, Marcus?"

He nodded. "We watched it for a while, and then it disappeared. While we were...having at it, the boat suddenly shot up in the air and we were tossed out. Jamie hit his head on the bow. All of that part is true."

"You should have told the truth," I chided. "If I'd known the truth, it would have made me more open to you. You had to know that."

"At what cost?" he asked. "I didn't want to hurt you or your memory of Jamie. I didn't think it would ever have to come out."

"Keith is really Jamie's son?" I whispered.

"Jamie told me he was. And once he said it, I could see Jamie in him. Do you see it?"

I thought about Keith's dark hair, the body that was already growing thick and brawny. I rubbed my breastbone. "My heart hurts," I said. "Ever since Maggie told me. It just hurts so much."

"I know." Marcus rested his hand on my foot through the afghan. "I'm sorry."

I drew in a long breath and blew it out. "Maggie said you set up a college fund for him."

"I did," he said. "That's how Keith found out. It just seemed so wrong that Jamie's other kids had so much when Keith had so little."

"Oh!" I suddenly remembered the day I tried to pay Sara's hotel bill. "You're paying for Sara's hotel room!"

He nodded.

I dropped my head back against the sofa. "I'm so humiliated," I said. "Sara...I thought she was my best friend."

"She *is* your best friend."

I shook my head. "How could she have done that to me, though?"

Marcus squeezed my foot through the afghan. "How could you and I have done it to Jamie?" he asked.

I don't know how I managed to fall asleep. Marcus shook my shoulder and I jerked awake, flinching at a pain in my neck from the cramped position I'd slept in on the sofa.

"Did they come home?" I sat up and looked toward the stairs.

"No." He shook his head. "It's a little after five and the weather's settled down. I'm going to try driving over to Ben and Dawn's. I can't just sit here any longer, and maybe Ben'll have a clue where they are."

I tossed the afghan onto the back of the sofa and stood up, my legs wobbly beneath me. "I'm going with you," I said.

I felt as though I was riding in a boat rather than a pickup as we turned onto New River Inlet Road from my street. Marcus's headlights illuminated the water on the road, but it was impossible to know how deep it was. Tall wings of it rose up on either side of the pickup, although Marcus drove slowly. The wind had let up and it was no longer raining, but aside from our headlights, the island was in complete, disconcerting darkness that my eyes couldn't pierce. The sky felt as though it was mere inches from the roof of the cab.

"I don't think I've ever seen a night this dark," Marcus said as he drove. He sat upright, close to the steering wheel, and I knew he felt as tense as I did.

Although there wasn't another vehicle on the road, it took us half an hour to drive the seven miles to Surf City. Marcus got out of the pickup a few times to shine his flashlight on the road ahead of us, making sure the water wasn't too deep or too swift to drive through. Finally, we turned onto the beach road near Dawn's cottage, and Marcus inched along as we tried to make out one dark building from another.

"I think that's it." I pointed to the barely visible cottage.

"Isn't that Dawn's car on the street in front?" Marcus asked.

I followed the beam of his headlights to the car and saw that it was parked in front of Ben's van.

"Why are they on the street?" I asked.

Marcus pulled into the driveway, his headlights answering my question: the parking area beneath the cottage was under at least a couple of feet of water.

"Oh boy." Marcus turned off the engine. "I bet this storm did a number on the beaches."

We got out of the pickup, each of us carrying a flashlight, and Marcus put his hand on my back as we walked toward the cottage. At the top of the front steps, he banged on the door with the side of his fist.

We waited thirty seconds, then Marcus tried the door.

"Locked." He banged again, relentlessly this time. "Ben!" he shouted.

I saw a flicker of light inside one of the windows, and a second later Ben opened the door, a flashlight in his hand.

"Is there a fire?" he asked. Then he noticed me. "What's wrong?"

"Let us in." Marcus pushed past him and I followed.

"Do you know where Maggie and Andy are?" I asked.

"Aren't they home?" Ben wore a pair of tan shorts, unbuttoned at the waist, and nothing more. I didn't want to think about Maggie touching him, touching that bare chest.

"No, they're not home," Marcus said. "Maggie took him away, hoping to keep him from the hearing tomorrow."

"Shit." Ben ran a hand through his hair. I suddenly hated him.

"How dare you take advantage of her!" I smacked his bare shoulder with my flashlight, creepily aware of his manliness. My assault barely made him flinch. "She's in high school!"

I felt Marcus's hand against my back again. "Time for that later," he said. "Did Maggie tell you anything about her plans?"

"Who's here, Benny?" Dawn came into the room, tying a short robe closed over her legs and carrying a lantern. She stopped short when she saw us.

"Maggie and Andy are missing," I said.

"Missing?" she asked. "What do you mean? Like kidnapped?"

"Maggie took Andy somewhere to keep him from the hearing in the morning," I said.

Dawn looked at Ben. "Do you know anything about this?" she asked.

Ben shook his head. "Nothing." He was avoiding my gaze.

"I bet I know where they are," Dawn said. She looked at Ben. "You do, too."

"Where?" Ben said, then shut his eyes. "Oh, no. The Sea Tender."

"*The Sea Tender?*" Marcus and I spoke in unison.

"But it's condemned," I said.

"That's where Ben was meeting Maggie," Dawn said with disgust.

That was too much reality for Marcus. "You son of a bitch!" He threw a punch at Ben's jaw, snapping his head back and knocking him halfway to the floor.

I grabbed his arm before he could lash out again. Now that I knew where my children were, I wanted to get to them. Hold them in my arms. "Let's go," I said.

"I cared about her!" Ben held his hand to his jaw as he regained his balance. "It's not like I didn't have any feel—"

"Shut up, Ben!" Dawn said.

Marcus flexed the fingers of the hand he'd struck Ben with.

"I'm not done with you, Trippett," he growled to Ben as he flung open the front door. "I'll catch up with you later."

"The Sea Tender," I said as we drove through the darkness. I wanted Marcus to drive faster, but knew he didn't dare. "How would Maggie even think of that?"

"That place is dangerous," Marcus said. "It was condemned for a reason. It should have been torn down long ago."

"I thought Maggie had a good head on her shoulders," I said, knotting my hands in my lap. "I thought she didn't need my guidance. My *mothering*. I don't know her, Marcus."

"Yes, you do." Marcus let go of the steering wheel to hunt for my hand in the darkness. He found it, squeezed it. "You know she'd do anything for Andy," he said. "Same as you."

Chapter Fifty

Andy

I OPENED MY EYES, BUT COULDN'T SEE anything. I blinked and blinked to be sure my eyes were really open. I thought I was going to barf. My brain was rolling around inside my head. The only other time I felt that way was on a boat. I could go in a boat on the sound, but not in the ocean. Last time I went on a boat in the ocean was with Emily and my brain rolled around inside my head the whole trip. I threw up three times and one almost time. Mom said I never had to go on a boat in the ocean again. Mom didn't like boats, anyway.

I knew I wasn't on a boat, though. I was in the house where I was a baby. I was on the couch. It was dark but I could see some things and it was kind of cold. And loud. Under me and over me I heard popping noises and screeching noises and creaking noises. I was afraid if I sat up, I'd throw up. But finally I did and there was no glass in the window. The sky was pink by the ocean. I couldn't see Maggie, but I heard her call my name.

All of a sudden I fell off the couch and my brain rolled and rolled and I couldn't remember where the bathroom was to run to throw up. Maggie said the bathroom didn't work anyway. I could hardly stand up. I had to hold on to a wood thing. And then I saw that I wasn't in the cottage anymore. I was on a kind of boat and big chunks of wood and things floated around me. Water went over my feet. The beach was far away. I forgot about throwing up. I started thinking about how to save our lives, because I knew we were in trouble and it wasn't like the fire where I could climb out a window.

"Maggie!" I hollered, and I ran across the floor trying to find her, as it bounced and broke apart beneath my feet.

Chapter Fifty-One

Laurel

THE PREDAWN LIGHT HAD CHANGED FROM coal to pale gray by the time we turned off Sea Gull Lane onto the continuation of New River Inlet Road. Marcus's pickup rolled forward slowly in a foot of water. Between the oceanfront cottages, I could see the wash of pink above the horizon. Then I spotted the first of the condemned cottages behind those lining the street and heard Marcus suck in his breath.

"What?" I asked.

He shook his head.

I rolled down my window and saw what had caused his reaction. I knew where the second condemned house should be, but a pile of rubble stood in its place. The sliver of sun resting on the horizon glinted off shards of glass and metal.

"Oh, no." My heart kicked into gear.

"Is that Maggie's car?" Marcus braked the pickup so quickly, I flew forward a couple of inches before my seat belt caught. Parked on the opposite side of the street was the only other vehicle in sight—Maggie's white Jetta.

"Maybe they're in the car!" I jumped out of the pickup into water up to my knees and sloshed across the street. I shone my flashlight through the car windows. Empty.

"Anything?" Marcus called through his open window.

"No." I waded back to his pickup. "But Dawn must be right. Why else would Maggie park here, a block from The Sea Tender?"

We inched forward, passing another of the old condemned cottages that had been reduced to a pile of rubble. Had The Sea Tender—had my *children*—stood a chance?

"Let me out!" I said, pulling open the door. "I can't stand it!"

"Laurel—"

I didn't hear the rest of his sentence as I lost my footing and fell into the water. I got quickly to my feet, not bothering to close the pickup's door as I waded toward the space between two of the front row of houses. I needed to get to the beach. *Please, God, let my babies be okay.*

I was barely aware of Marcus catching up to me as we slogged through the water between the houses.

"Where's the little dune?" I searched the gray light ahead of me, thoroughly disoriented. The water was only up to our ankles here but I couldn't see the little rise of sand that marked the boundary between the front row of houses and those on the beach.

"I think it's gone," Marcus said.

We ran forward now that the water wasn't holding us back, and what I saw turned my knees to jelly. "Oh God, Marcus!" I grabbed the back of his shirt to keep myself from keeling over.

"Ah, no," Marcus said with such quiet resignation that I wanted to shake him.

In front of us, the beach looked like a war zone. None of the condemned houses were still standing; they'd been reduced to mountains of debris covering acres of sand, although many of the pilings still poked from the rubble, like totem poles against the lightening sky. The Sea Tender had been the last house in the row and I needed to get to it. Although I felt weak and nauseated, I started running north.

"Be careful!" Marcus called from somewhere near me. "There's glass everywhere."

It was hard to tell one demolished house from another and when we reached the final pile of rubble, panic gripped me. "I'm turned around!" I said, searching the strange, unrecognizable beach for something familiar. The explosion of boards and glass and metal in front of me simply couldn't be The Sea Tender.

"Maggie!" Marcus called into the massive pile of debris as he circled it. "Andy!"

I stood frozen, my hands covering my face, afraid of seeing a lifeless arm or leg poking from the rubble. I peeked between my fingers to the deceptively calm ocean, littered with the remains of the cottages, and my eyes were suddenly drawn to the splashes of peach and purple above the horizon.

"Marcus, look!" I pointed toward the sunrise.

"Where?" He straightened up from the ruins. "What are you looking at?"

"There!" I kicked off my sodden shoes and started to run into the chilly water.

"Laurel, don't go out there!" He caught up to me, grabbing my arm. Then he saw what I'd seen. On a floating piece of debris, far in the distance, were two tiny silhouettes.

My children.

Chapter Fifty-Two

Maggie

AT FIRST I THOUGHT WE COULD SWIM, BUT AS WE psyched ourselves up to jump from the floating wreckage, I caught Andy around his waist.

"We're too far, Andy," I said. The current was pulling us away from the beach more quickly than I'd realized, sucking us toward a blinding orange sun. The beach, lit up like pink gold, looked very far away. "We won't make it."

We lost our balance for the fourth or fifth time, dropping to our knees. I stared again at the beach. What choice did we have but to swim?

I had to think. I wasn't sure what part of the house we were kneeling on. It had been a bigger surface at first, but it had morphed into a Huck Finn–type raft, with a chunk of built-in bookshelf jutting up from one side of it. The floor of the living room, maybe. It didn't matter. Whatever it was, it kept breaking apart, leaving us with a smaller and smaller barrier between life and death. It wouldn't float forever.

"We can swim," Andy said. "We can pretend it's laps."

"But it's not," I said. "It's much colder than the pool, and a pool doesn't have a riptide. See how we're being pulled out to sea? That's what would happen to us if we tried to swim."

I was so scared. What if instead of saving my baby brother, I was killing him?

Another piece of our creaky raft broke away and Andy yelped as I pulled him tight against me. I watched the part of the flooring with the bookcase float away from us, then buckle and slip underwater. I was watching our fate.

"Are we going to drown?" Andy asked.

The pink beach seemed farther away than only a few seconds earlier. I grabbed Andy's shoulders and looked him in the eyes.

"Listen to me," I said. "We'll have to try to swim, but we have to stay together as much as we can. Don't lose sight of me and I won't lose sight of you. And listen! We can't swim straight toward the beach! Okay? Swim *parallel* to the beach."

"What's 'parell'?" He looked scared. He was picking up my own fear.

I let out a sob, surprising both of us. I brushed tears away with the back of my hand. "It means we'll swim in this direction." I pointed north.

"How will we get to the beach then?" His voice was so tiny.

What have I done? "Panda." I hugged him quickly. "I promise. We swim in that direction for a little bit and then we'll be able to swim to the beach. But you have to stay calm. Don't panic."

"You're not calm." His lower lip trembled.

"You know how you're supposed to pace yourself during a race?" I asked.

He nodded, even though I'd never once seen him pace himself.

"You've *got* to pace yourself this time, Andy." My voice cracked. "Please, Panda. Don't swim all-out, okay? Slow and steady, in that direction—" I pointed again "—and we can do it."

Andy's gaze had drifted from my face, and I suddenly saw the whole of the sun reflected in his brown eyes.

"Look!" He pointed behind me.

I turned in time to see a wall of water headed for us, rising out of a sea that was totally calm. I clutched Andy's arm, letting out a scream as the wave bore down on us. It tore us from our flimsy deck and ripped my brother from my hands.

I tumbled underwater like a gymnast through the air. I held my breath, my eyes open, searching the frothy, swirling water for Andy as the wave turned me in corkscrews. I couldn't see him. Panicking, I batted at the water as if I could clear it away from my face like a curtain.

"Andy!" I shouted into the ocean, water filling my mouth, my lungs.

I rose in slow motion to the crest of the wave. It felt like someone was lifting me up, carrying me. My lungs hurt as they sucked in the amazing pink air, and when I plummeted into the water again, I gave in. Gave up. Gave myself over to the sea.

Chapter Fifty-Three

Laurel

"I CAN'T SEE THEM ANYMORE!" I SHOUTED TO Marcus. I couldn't see *him,* either, but I knew he was searching the yards of the front row of houses for a boat or raft.

"What?" He appeared suddenly, running toward the water with a surfboard.

I pointed toward where we'd last seen Maggie and Andy. "They've disappeared!"

He stopped running to look toward the horizon.

"I don't know what happened!" I said. "I blinked and they were gone."

He headed for the water again, dropping the surfboard on the surface and starting to paddle.

"Let me go, too!"

"Stay here and keep trying the phone!" he shouted.

We'd been trying to get a signal with both of our phones ever since we got there. I lifted my phone to punch in 9-1-1 again with my cold, shaking fingers, but something caught my eye on the beach a good distance north of where I stood. People? A small figure, pink lit in the shallow water, nearly to the inlet. It couldn't possibly be one of my children. There was no way either of them could have swum to shore that quickly under the best of circumstances.

But whoever it was had dark hair and was very slight.

"Marcus, come back!" I shouted as I started running. The wet sand was like concrete beneath my bare feet. I tried to make sense of the tiny image on the beach. What was he or she doing? Not standing, that much was clear, and I ran faster. The sandpipers and gulls dashed out of my way. I'd never run so fast in all my life.

"Be careful, Laurel!" Marcus shouted from behind me. I heard his own thudding footsteps on the sand. I knew he was warning me about the debris scattered along the beach in front of me, but I wasn't going to slow down for shards of glass or rusty nails. I knew he wouldn't either.

Andy was getting to his feet in the wet sand, gentle waves lapping at his legs.

"Andy!" I waved my arms. He was alive! "Andy!"

He tugged at something in the water and it wasn't until I was nearly on him that I realized it was Maggie.

"Oh my God!" I ran into the chilly knee-high water, splashing it behind me.

"Mommy!" Andy lost his footing and sat down again. When I reached him, Maggie's head was in his lap.

"Maggie!" I dropped to my knees next to my children.

Andy was wheezing, his breath whistling above the soft murmur of the waves and his chest expanding and contracting like an accordion.

"Baby!" I grabbed his neck and kissed his forehead, but quickly turned my attention to Maggie.

"Is she all right?" Marcus dropped to the water next to us as Maggie started coughing. Her eyes were closed, her skin an icy blue, but she was alive.

She gasped, choking on salt water, and I rolled her head from Andy's lap to mine, turning her onto her side.

"Maggie, sweetie, it's Mom. You're okay, baby."

She hacked and coughed, but I wasn't sure she was conscious. She was a deadweight on my lap and an incoming wave washed over her face.

"Let's get her out of the water," I said.

"Is she breathing okay?" Marcus asked as we carried her a few feet higher on the beach, turning her onto her stomach.

Andy knelt next to her face. "Maggie!" he shouted. "Are you okay, Maggie?"

I saw blood on Andy's legs. "Andy, you're bleeding! Where are you hurt?"

Andy looked down at his legs. The blood appeared to be pouring from his knee.

"It's Maggie!" Marcus rolled her onto her back, and I saw what I had missed when we'd been sitting in the water: a deep cut on her neck, gushing blood onto the sand. Marcus lifted his T-shirt over his head and pressed it to the wound.

Maggie coughed, and we started to roll her over again, but she seemed to get her breathing under control.

"Maggie, sweetie, can you hear me?"

She mouthed something I couldn't understand.

"What, honey?" I leaned closer.

"Did you swim all the way from out there?" Marcus asked Andy incredulously.

"We didn't have to swim," Andy said. "A big wave came and lifted us way up." He reached his arms toward the sky.

Maggie whispered something again, her mouth moving soundlessly.

I leaned my ear against her lips, "What, Maggie?" I asked.

She mouthed the words silently, then cleared her throat. "It was Daddy," she said.

Chapter Fifty-Four

Maggie

SOMEONE HELD MY HAND. I THOUGHT IT MIGHT be Daddy. My lungs burned when I breathed in. Everything hurt, especially my neck, and I wanted to reach up and touch the place that ached, but my arms were too heavy, and anyway, I didn't really care. My head seemed disconnected from the pain somehow. If heaven existed, did it feel like this? Floating above the pain, holding Daddy's hand? I thought it probably did.

"She's smiling," a man's voice said.

Uncle Marcus? I tried to open my eyes, but my eyelids were as heavy as my arms.

"Maggie?" *Mom.* It was Mom's hand holding mine.

I remembered the wave. I remembered losing Andy.

"Andy?" My eyelids flew open and I tried to sit up.

"Whoa." Uncle Marcus put his hands on my shoulders and lowered me down again.

"Not so fast, sweetie," Mom said.

I was in a strange white room. Mom was on my right, still holding my hand; Uncle Marcus was on my left, running his hand over my hair.

"I lost Andy," I said. My voice was raspy, not like my voice at all.

"Andy's fine," Mom said.

"I'm sorry!" I started to cry. "I lost him in the wave!"

"He's fine, Mags," Uncle Marcus said. "Don't cry. He'll come see you later."

My neck hurt. The pain cut through the floaty feeling in my head. I felt sick to my stomach and swallowed once. Twice. I was definitely not in heaven.

"You're in Cape Fear Hospital," Mom said. "You have a cut on your neck. It probably hurts a lot."

I nodded, my eyes shut. Andy was safe? Would they lie to me about something like that?

"Does it hurt to breathe?" Mom asked.

"Yes," I whispered.

"You're going to be fine," she said. "You and Andy were incredibly lucky."

"Is Ben here?" I opened my eyes again, squinting from the bright light in the room. I didn't care who knew about Ben now. I wanted him with me.

"No, Mags," Uncle Marcus said. "Just your mom and me."

"You said something about Daddy saving you," Mom said. "Helping you. What did you mean, sweetie?"

I closed my eyes again. I remembered the sense of calm I'd

felt as the wave lifted me high in the air, but I was awake enough to know how crazy that would sound to Mom. How crazy it sounded even to *me*. I'd keep it to myself. "I don't know what you're talking about," I said.

Mom hesitated, and I thought she wasn't going to give up. "Okay," she said finally.

I suddenly remembered the whole reason I was there. "The hearing!" I said, trying to sit up again. "Is it—"

"Postponed." Mom held me down. "Don't think about that now."

I remembered Andy in The Sea Tender, telling me he'd gone outside to check for bugs during the lock-in.

"I need to talk to someone," I said.

"What you need is rest." Uncle Marcus rubbed my shoulder.

"No. *No.* I need to talk to Andy's lawyer. No! To the *police*. Right now."

"You have a lot of pain medication in you," Mom said. "It's not the time."

"Yes, it's time!" I insisted. "*Yesterday* was the time. Last *week* was the time. Last *month* was the time."

"Mags, what are you talking about?" Uncle Marcus asked.

I couldn't tell them. They might stop me from doing what I needed to do. What I should have done weeks ago.

"I'm awake," I said. "I'm not out of it, and I need to talk to the police now." I looked from my mother's face to Uncle Marcus's and saw their confusion. *"Now,"* I said again. "You've got to let me. Before I chicken out. I need to tell them what really happened."

"What do you mean, 'what really happened'?" Mom asked. She looked a thousand years old. "Did Andy tell you something?"

She was scared. Was she afraid I'd reveal something that would send Andy to prison for certain? I wondered if the same fear would be there if she knew that *I* was the one who was going to be locked up for good.

"You really should have a lawyer here," Uncle Marcus said for at least the tenth time, when Flip Cates finished reading me the Miranda Warning. I knew he'd asked Flip to come instead of that weird Sergeant Wood and I was glad. But no way was I waiting for a lawyer. I'd already waited an hour for Flip.

I shook my head—a mistake. The doctor had told me not to move my head or I might open the cut on my neck again. I touched the bandage lightly with my fingers. The cut burned and my whole body ached, but I refused to take any more pain medication until after I talked to Flip. I didn't want anyone to say that I wasn't in my right mind when I spoke to the police.

Mom stood up from her chair to check my bandage. "It's not bleeding," she said. "I wish you'd reconsider, Maggie. Maybe Mr. Shartell could just talk to you on the phone before you say anything."

"I can wait, Maggie," Flip said. He was sitting where Uncle Marcus had been earlier, and he'd put a tape recorder on the rolling table. Uncle Marcus stood at the end of my bed.

"I don't *want* to talk to him," I said again. Mom and Uncle Marcus had been badgering me about a lawyer ever since I said I wanted to talk to the police. "He'll spin things around until I don't understand what I'm saying myself. I want to tell what really happened the night of the fire."

My mother twisted her old wedding ring on her finger. "You can't cover for Andy, sweetie," she said.

I was surprised. "I'm not," I said. "He didn't know it, but he's been covering for *me* all this time." I looked at Flip. "Can we get started now?"

"Sure, Maggie," Flip said. "Do you want me to question you or would you rather just talk?"

"I'll just talk," I said.

"Okay, then." He did something with the tape recorder, moved it a little closer to me on the table. "Go ahead," he said.

I took a deep breath and began.

Chapter Fifty-Five

Maggie

WHEN YOU REALLY LOVE SOMEONE, WHEN their joy feels like your joy and their hurt like your hurt, it's both a wonderful and a terrible thing. That's how it was with Ben and me. I was like a living, breathing clump of empathy around him. I thought he was so amazing, inside and out. Always patient with the kids on the swim team. Always encouraging my baby brother. Believing in Andy the way I did. I loved Ben for that, and for his tenderness with me, and for the way he adored his daughter. For the way he kept trying to do well in the fire department when it was so hard and scary for him.

"When I was a little kid," he told me one night when we were in bed at The Sea Tender, "my father would punish me by locking me in a cupboard under our stairs. I felt like I was suffocating. I'd panic. I'd pound on the cupboard door, but no one would come."

I rubbed his arm as he spoke. I couldn't imagine a parent being that cruel.

"I didn't have any more problems with claustrophobia, though, until the first time I had to put on SCBA gear during my fire training," he said. "It was like I was five years old again and trapped in the cupboard. That's the way it is every time I put on the face piece. I can't seem to get past it. I've mastered everything else. Your uncle says to give it time, but I think it's getting worse instead of better."

I was amazed he'd tell me something so personal. He trusted me with a secret. It made me feel like I could trust him back. With *anything*.

A couple of weeks later, I was in Jabeen's with Amber and some other girls, back when I could still stand hanging around with them. We sat in a booth, and the next booth over had some of the volunteers from the fire department. Two men and a woman.

I looked up from my latte to see Ben walk in the door. He nodded to me and I nodded back. We were good at acting cool around each other, like we were the coaches of the swim team and nothing more.

"Hey," Ben said to the volunteers as he walked up to the counter where Sara was working.

"Hey," the volunteers said back to him.

He ordered a coffee to go. Amber was blathering on about Travis, but it was like a white noise in my ears because I was so focused on Ben, while trying not to *act* like I was focused on him.

As soon as Ben left Jabeen's, the volunteers burst out laughing. It took me a second to realize they were laughing at *Ben*. One of the guys cackled like a chicken.

"Chickenshit," he said.

"What a pussy," the other guy said.

My cheeks grew hot, and my heart broke. Just cracked apart inside my chest.

"I told Marcus, no way I'm going in with that FNG again," the woman said. "He ditched on me in that warehouse last week. Hyperventilatin' like a fool."

FNG. *Fucking new guy.* I knew more firehouse slang than was good for me.

"And Travis said if he ever, *ever* saw Marty touch me again, he'd castrate him," Amber was saying.

"If he can't hang," one of the guy volunteers said, "he needs to just keep his butt on the truck."

"Damn straight," said the other guy. "I'm not lettin' him screw with me in a fire."

"Shh!" The woman lowered her voice. "His girlfriend works here."

"Dawn? She ain't here now."

His girlfriend's sitting right behind you, you dork, I thought.

Ben had told me the other volunteers teased him because of his problem with the SCBA gear, but this was more than teasing. This was just plain vicious.

I'd never tell Ben what they said. Some girls might have thought less of their boyfriend, hearing stuff like that. It just made me want to help him more. To be a comfort to him.

He'd told me he was working hard on the claustrophobia problem. He had some workout equipment at home, and when he'd exercise, he'd sometimes put on the SCBA gear so he'd get more comfortable with it. He went to Washington, D.C., to take a special class in using SCBA. He did exercises to slow down his breathing: five seconds breathing in, five seconds breathing out. I wished those volunteers who were making fun of him could see how dedicated he was.

"I'm so ready," Ben told me one night when we were lying out on the beach. It was one of those strange warm nights that could pop up for no reason in winter. We'd made love on the beach, and now we were cuddling together, wrapped in a quilt. "I told Marcus I can do it now," he said. "Not sure he believes me, though. I just need a chance to prove myself."

A few weeks went by without a fire where he'd need the SCBA gear. Then a couple more. I knew the other volunteers were being cold to him. Freezing him out. Ben was torn up about it, and I started hating some of them.

One day in March, he called me upset because someone had stolen his pager while he was in the shower. Whoever it was left a note in its place, saying something like, *we're taking your pager out of self-defense.*

"I'm thinking of leaving," Ben said to me on the phone.

"What do you mean?" I was afraid I knew. I was in my car coming up to the only stoplight in Surf City, and I turned left, sailing right through the red. Didn't even realize it until a few seconds after I turned.

"I could go back to Charlotte," he said. "Be closer to my daughter. Join the fire department there where I could start fresh. I love the beach, but this abuse is getting to me."

"Please don't go!" I was having my own sort of panic attack.

I stepped on the brake and pulled to the side of the road so I could concentrate on talking. I'd die if he left.

"I know," he said. "I'd hate leaving you. You're the best thing about being here."

"Then don't leave!" I wondered if I could still get into UNC-Charlotte for the fall. It was too far away, though. Too far from Andy.

"I won't make a decision for a week or two," he said, sighing. He sounded really tired. "I'll have to see how this mess plays out. I just wanted to let you know what I'm thinking."

So, I came up with a way to make the "mess play out." Drury Memorial was going to be demolished and rebuilt in a couple of years, so what would be the big deal if it burned down? In the back of my mind, I knew it was a crime. No one would be hurt, though. If anything, I'd be helping ol' Reverend Bill get his new church faster. And I'd be giving Ben a chance to shine.

Ben had told me about a church that burned down in Wilmington, and I remembered he said the arsonist used a mixture of gasoline and diesel and hadn't been caught yet. I figured if I used the same mix, the investigators would think it was the same arsonist.

I wasn't sure how much fuel I'd need or how to get it without attracting attention. I got a couple of those big plastic gas containers at Lowes. Then, a few nights before I planned to burn the church, I drove to two different gas stations outside of Wilmington where no one would recognize me. I got the gas at one station and the diesel at the other. No one said a word to me. I kept the containers in my trunk.

I waited for the right time. That Saturday night, I knew Ben was going to Daddy Mac's for dinner with a couple of guys, so he'd be right near the station. When the call went out, he could get there fast and be on the first truck. I was all set. I had to time it right, though. I had to wait until it was dark enough that no one would see me pouring the fuel, but not so late that Ben had gone home already. I thought I could pull it off. I felt pretty calm about the whole thing.

Then Mom asked me to give Andy a ride to the lock-in that night.

"I'm going over to Amber's to study," I said as I loaded the dishwasher. I *did* plan to go to Amber's as soon as I'd set the fire. That way, I'd have an alibi if I ever needed one.

"Well, you can drop Andy off on your way," Mom said. "I need to work on a speech."

"It's not exactly on my way," I said. To be honest, I'd totally forgotten about the lock-in, even though I was the one to talk Mom into letting Andy go to it. Did I really want to burn down a church less than a block from the youth building where a bunch of kids would be hanging out? I wasn't worried about the youth building catching on fire. It was far enough away. I just didn't want to freak out the kids—especially not Andy. But I already had everything planned so perfectly. And who knew how fast Ben was going to make his decision about moving back to Charlotte?

"I'll take him," I said.

That sudden change in my plans, though, made my nerves start to act up.

Around seven-fifteen, I called Ben on his cell.

"Hey." I tried to sound normal. I could hear restaurant noise in the background. Talking. Glasses clinking.

"Hey," he said. "What's up?"

"You still at Daddy Mac's?"

"Uh-huh. Where are you?"

"Home. I'm going over to Amber's to study. You gonna be able to talk later?"

"I expect so. I'll call you?"

I was trying to figure out how to casually ask him how much longer he'd be at Daddy Mac's. I couldn't think of a way other than just blurting it out.

"What time are you leaving there?" I asked.

"Oh, we'll probably be another forty minutes. Maybe an hour. Why?"

"Just making conversation." That didn't give me much time to work. "I'll let you get back to dinner. Later?"

"Later."

I got off the phone with my mind ready to explode. This wasn't going to work. The lock-in didn't start till eight. Ben would probably be gone by the time I set the church on fire. I'd just have to drop Andy off early at the lock-in. That was the only way.

When Andy and I pulled up in front of the youth building, it was so early that none of the other kids were there yet.

"You can't drop me off without other kids being here!" Andy shouted when I told him to get out.

"I can see an adult inside," I said, giving him a nudge. Through the youth building window, I saw Mr. Eggles with his back to us. I recognized him by his ponytail. "Go ahead. You'll be fine."

"I'm not going until kids are here and that's that." Andy folded his arms across his chest and wouldn't budge.

I didn't have time to argue with him. I'd just have to pour

DIANE CHAMBERLAIN

the gasoline mixture with Andy in the car. I made up my story as I drove down the block.

"I have to do something at the church," I said. "So you can wait in the car and then I'll take you back to the lock-in." I was really jumpy now. How was I going to make this work? I couldn't *light* the fire with Andy in the car, so I'd pour the gasoline, drive him back to the lock-in, then go back and toss a match on the fuel. I just hoped Ben stayed as long as he said at Daddy Mac's. If he wasn't on the first truck, the fire could be out by the time he got there.

I pulled up around the corner from the church and turned off my car.

"You stay here," I said. "I have to pour some insecticide around the church. They have a bad bug problem and they asked me to—"

"What kind of bugs?"

"I don't know, Andy." I reached for the door handle. "Just stay here."

"Is it ants? Or bees? Or those crepe paper wasps like we had by the deck?"

"Paper," I said.

"What?"

"Just paper wasps. Not crepe paper wasps."

"Is it cockroaches?"

"It's all kinds of bugs!" I said.

"I'll help you." He started to get out of the car.

"No!" Perspiration was dripping down my back beneath my T-shirt and jacket. "Just stay here. And listen." I grabbed his shoulder and turned him to face me. "This is a secret. The person who asked me to pour the insecticide told me never to tell anyone about it because the people who go to the church would freak out if they knew there were bugs."

"But bugs are *interesting*," Andy said. He opened the car door and hopped out before I could stop him. "I want to help."

It would be quicker to let him help than to argue with him about it. I opened my trunk and got out the two containers. My hands shook so hard I could hear the gasoline sloshing around. I'd brought latex gloves with me to keep my finger-prints off the containers, but only one pair. I gave Andy some tissues to use to hold the second container with.

"Be very careful not to touch the container without the tissues," I whispered, even though there was no one anywhere around. "The insecticide could hurt you if you get it on yourself."

"Right," he said. "Even though I'm not a bug."

"Right."

We started walking toward the church. I had on flip-flops because I planned to just throw them away after in case I left footprints. I didn't think about Andy's shoes. I just wasn't thinking, period. "You pour on this side, right where the ground and the building come together, okay? Make sure to get every single inch. I'll pour on the other side."

"Every single inch," he repeated.

"And remember, don't touch the bottle. And be careful not to splash any on you."

Now my entire body was shaking. I started pouring. It was dark, but I could tell I was pouring on top of crisp pine straw. It would catch right away when I lit it. The smell was so strong. I turned my head away to inhale, then held my breath as long as I could while I poured. Then I turned away for fresh air again and worked my way down the side of the church like that. I hoped Andy wasn't passing out on his side.

The air-conditioning unit was right up against the building, so close that I couldn't pour the fuel behind it. No problem. With all that pine straw, a few feet without gasoline wouldn't matter.

Andy walked around to my side of the church just as I finished up. "I ran out," he said.

"Me, too."

We walked back to the car. Thank God that part was over! I put the containers in a big trash bag I'd brought with me. Stuck my flip-flops in there, too, then put the bag back in my trunk. I'd brought sandals to change into and I slipped them on before getting into the car.

Andy was already back in the passenger seat.

"Okay!" I tried to sound cheerful. "You ready for your very first lock-in?"

"If the other kids are there," he said.

"I think they will be by now." At least the early birds. "Remember what I told you about the insecticide," I said as I pulled away from the curb.

"What?"

"What did I say about telling anyone?"

"It's a secret. Because the people would freak out."

"Excellent!" I said.

There were other kids in the youth building now. Andy spotted Emily Carmichael, which made him forget he'd felt shy a few minutes earlier. He ran out of the car without even saying goodbye.

I drove down the block to the church again, but just sat in

my car with the box of matches on my lap. *It's okay to do this,* I told myself. *They're going to demolish it soon anyway.* I thought of the old houses the fire department sometimes burned down to train the firefighters. How was this any different?

I decided I'd better drive over to Daddy Mac's, though, to make sure Ben's van was still in the parking lot. I was stalling, but I convinced myself I had to make sure as I drove to the restaurant.

Ben's white van was parked right smack in front of the entrance. I felt disappointed. I didn't realize until that second that I'd wanted the van to be gone to save me from my crazy plan. But it was still there, and I could see it all playing out in my imagination. The fire starting. Someone calling the department. Ben reaching for his pager. Ben racing down the street to the fire station, climbing on the truck. He'd be so excited. A little scared, but ready to show the other guys that he was one of them now. That he could be trusted.

It was like a movie in my mind as I drove toward the church. I decided to park over by Jabeen's, which closed at six. That way, I could walk to the church, set the fire, and run down the block in the dark with nobody noticing me.

I got out of my car and tossed the bag with the containers and flip-flops into the Dumpster behind Jabeen's. Then I realized if anyone found the containers, they'd also have my flip-flops, so I reached into the Dumpster, got the bag and just tossed the containers back in. My flip-flops I threw in the trash can out front along with the wadded-up bag.

I started walking to the church, but I suddenly saw a ton of kids around the youth building, which was completely dark. What was going on? I stuck the box of matches in my jacket pocket and headed toward the youth building. The kids were starting to walk in my direction and I was totally flustered. I found Andy and pulled him aside.

"What's going on?" I asked.

"The lights went out," he said. "We're going to the church instead."

I couldn't believe my relief! I felt it from the top of my head to my toes. I didn't have to do it! Now I *couldn't* do it, even if I wanted to. It was like some crazy girl had planned the whole thing and expected me to pull it off for her. I was free!

I ran back to my car and started driving toward Amber's, but I suddenly felt sick to my stomach. I pulled into the driveway of a deserted house, opened my car door, and threw up in the sand.

Then I knew where I wanted to go. It was Daddy I needed, not Amber.

I headed for The Sea Tender.

Chapter Fifty-Six

Laurel

I COULD BARELY BREATHE FOR THE TEARS. AS Maggie spoke, I wanted to leave so she wouldn't see me fall apart. At the same time, I wanted to gather her in my arms and tell her everything would be all right. I chose to stay because the thought that ran through my mind as she told her story was, *Where was this girl's mother?*

How had I missed all the signs? How could I not have known that she was sneaking out of the house in the middle of the night? That she rarely was where she told me she would be? That she was not only in harm's way, but capable of *doing* harm? Where had I *been*?

I knew the answer, of course: I was with Andy. Letting

Maggie fend for herself, as I had since her birth. I wiped my cheeks with my hand.

"Are you saying you felt like two different people?" Marcus asked Maggie, when she seemed to be finished speaking. "The crazy girl and you?"

"You mean like a split personality?" Maggie crossed her arms, tucking her hands beneath them as if they were cold. "No," she said. "It was all me."

Flip, Marcus and I exchanged looks. I knew what we were all thinking, and Flip finally put it into words. "But you ultimately *did* light the fire, Maggie, correct?" he asked.

"No!" Maggie started to shake her head, then seemed to remember the wound on her neck. "That's what I'm trying to explain," she said, touching the bandage. "When I realized the kids were going to be there, I just forgot about it. I would never set fire to a building with people in it!"

Flip didn't believe her. His expression didn't change, but the flat look in his eyes betrayed him.

I reached for Maggie's hand, prying it from beneath her arm. Her hand *was* cold and I held it between both of mine to warm it. I remembered how Maggie had held my hand as we rode together to the hospital after the fire. How she didn't want to let go of me. And I remembered her shock—her *genuine* shock—when I called to tell her the church was on fire.

"So, after you spoke with Andy, you drove directly to The Sea Tender?" Flip asked.

"Yes. And I called Mom to tell her the lock-in was moved to the church."

Flip looked at me.

"She did," I said. "But you were at Amber's then, weren't you?"

"You thought I was, but I wasn't."

"Do you recall hearing anything in the background when Maggie called?" Flip asked me.

"No." I'd been working on a speech for a meeting with a teachers' organization and remembered little of the call other than that the lock-in had been moved. That had worried me—that the change might be confusing for Andy.

"What did you do at The Sea Tender?" Marcus asked Maggie.

"I..." Maggie looked toward the end of the bed, where the covers bulged a little over a bandaged toe—her only other real injury. With her free hand, she brushed a nonexistent lock of hair from her forehead. I had the feeling she was stalling. "I sat on the deck for a while," she said. "I was...I felt like I'd dodged a bullet or something."

"Did anyone see you there?"

"It was...you know. Still March. No one was in the houses."

Flip shifted in his chair, folding his arms across his chest. "So how *did* the fire start?" he asked.

"I don't know." Tears filled her eyes. "Honest, I don't. All I know is that I didn't start it. And neither did Andy."

"Let's take a break," Marcus said, and I was relieved. Maggie had been stoic and brave throughout the past hour. Now, though, she was beginning to crumble. I wasn't doing too well, myself.

Flip clicked off the tape recorder and stood up. "Good idea," he said. "I could use a cup of coffee."

"I'll join you." Marcus got to his feet as well. "You all right, Maggie?" he asked.

She gave a little nod, not looking at him. Not looking at any of us.

"Coming with us, Laurel?" Marcus asked. I supposed he and Flip wanted me to join them so we could discuss all we'd heard, but I wasn't leaving.

I shook my head, still holding Maggie's hand. "I'll stay here," I said.

Once the men left the room, Maggie began crying for real.

"I'm sorry, Mom!" she said, gripping my hand. "I'm so sorry for everything."

"Shh," I said. "I know."

"I'm so relieved, though!" she said. "I'm so...I should have told the truth as soon as people started thinking Andy did it."

Yes, she should have. But she didn't. "You've told us now," I said. "That's the important thing."

"There's more," she said. "I mean, not so big. It's big, but not like that. Like the fire. And it'll only matter to you. It's about The Sea Tender."

"I know you've been meeting Ben there."

She shook her head. "Not just that," she said. "I've been going there ever since I got my driver's license. My permit, actually. Alone, I mean. Not with...a boy or anything."

"Why?" I asked. I remembered Dawn telling me she smoked marijuana. Did she go there to do drugs?

"You're going to think I'm crazy. Or crazier than you already think I am."

"I don't think you're crazy."

"I felt close to Daddy there. Sometimes I'd sit on the deck at night and I'd close my eyes and suddenly feel like he was there. His spirit or something."

I felt a chill. I could almost feel Jamie in the room with us.

"Do you think I'm deranged?"

"If you are, insanity must run in the family, because I've dreamed he's...visited me at night sometimes, too."

Her pretty brown eyes opened wide. "Honest? Do you really think it's him?"

"I have no idea, Maggie. I just think he left a mark on both of us—in different ways, of course—and we must both have a need to stay attached to him."

She suddenly stopped crying, looking right at me. "I'm sorry about how I laid that whole Daddy and Sara thing on you. That was so mean."

"It hurt, finding that out," I acknowledged. That pain already seemed weeks old instead of hours, usurped by a more immediate heartache. "It helps me understand how you must be feeling about Ben right now, though."

She turned her head toward the window. In her eyes, I saw the rectangular reflection of sunlight.

"If he cared about me, he'd be here with me," she said. "At the hospital. Wouldn't he?"

I thought that even if Ben *did* care about her, he was wise to stay away from Marcus and me right now.

"I think he would be," I said.

"Do you think Ben was really...you know, *with* Dawn the same time he was with me?"

"Yes, sweetie, I do." I remembered Dawn at her house the night before, wrapping her satiny little robe over those long legs as she swept into the living room. *Who's here, Benny?*

"I trusted him totally. I loved him so much. I still do."

"I know it hurts."

She turned back to me. "Aren't you totally *furious* with Sara?"

I sighed. I *was* furious. That was something I'd have to deal with on my own, though. "It was so long ago, Maggie," I said. "And there are things I did that I regret from long ago, too."

"Drinking."

"That's for sure. Other things, as well. I guess most people do things when they're young that they come to regret. Sara and I have been friends for so long. I hope we can find a way to put it behind us." I thought of Keith's injuries. How could Sara ever forgive my daughter? In her place, I wasn't sure I could.

"Mom, I just hurt so much!" she said. "I want to erase everything. The fire. Ben. Everything!"

"I'd love it if you could wipe all of that from your memory," I said. "But you know what your father said to me one time?"

"What?"

"You know that my parents died when I was little, and then my aunt and uncle cut me out of their lives, right?"

"Yeah."

"I tried, especially with my parents, not to think about them. To just keep going on with my life. Moving forward. Never looking back. And when I told your daddy that, he said that if you don't think about your losses, they'd come back to bite you."

"Bite you?" Maggie smiled. "That's his exact words?"

"Yes, because I've never forgotten them, even if I haven't always followed his advice. He meant that sometimes you just have to go through the pain."

"So did you try to think about them?" she asked. "Your parents?"

"Not until I was in rehab. I cried buckets about them then.

But the thing I learned was that you don't just get over one loss and then you're home free. Life keeps tossing them at you, and you have to learn how to handle them. How to keep going. Ben won't be your last heartbreak, honey. But there'll be wonderful experiences to make up for the hard times."

My own eyes teared up at the thought of the hard times ahead of her. She read my mind.

"Will Andy still have a hearing?"

"I don't know how that works, but he won't be going to jail."

"But I will be, won't I." It was a statement, not a question.

"I'm going to find an excellent lawyer for you. And I'll be by your side the whole time, Maggie. I will." I'd been so strong for her brother for fifteen years. I wanted to be strong for her, now. Finally. "I'm sorry for not being a better mother for you. You were so independent and Andy so dependent, that I sometimes forgot you needed me as much as he did."

"I didn't, though," she said. "But I think I really do need you now." She licked her lips and looked squarely into my eyes. "I know it looks like I set the fire, Mom," she said. "I could tell Flip totally didn't believe me."

"No, I don't think he does. But I believe you."

"You do?"

I smiled. "Absolutely, sweetheart."

There was so much I didn't know about my daughter. At this point, I barely felt certain she wouldn't burn a church with children inside. But one thing I did know with absolute certainty: she would never burn a church with *Andy* in it.

Chapter Fifty-Seven

Marcus

ONE MORE TIME, I WAS IN A HOSPITAL room, this one hotter than blazes. I'd driven to Chapel Hill to tell Sara about Maggie's confession; it was the kind of thing I didn't want to say on the phone. I wasn't sure about telling her with Keith there, but decided he had a right to know. Maybe a bigger right than any of us. I just didn't want to be there when his rage hit. He'd been pissed off enough when he thought it was Andy who started the fire. When he found out it was Maggie, who had no mental handicap to use as an excuse...well, I wanted to be any place else.

But there I was, standing at the end of the bed while Sara adjusted the bulky bandage on the left side of Keith's face.

"Maggie was having a relationship with Ben Trippett," I began.

"*No,*" Sara argued, as though I had no idea what I was talking about. "Ben was with Dawn."

"It looks like he was involved with both of them," I said.

"Oh, no." She sat down in the chair next to Keith's bed. "Poor Dawn."

"Maggie didn't realize he was still seeing Dawn, though." I came to my niece's defense. I had the feeling I'd be doing a lot of that in the coming days. "He told her they'd broken up."

Sara frowned. "That's horrible," she said. "And I thought Ben was so nice."

"Why are we talking about Maggie's pathetic love life?" Keith muttered. His right eye was squinched shut and he looked like he was in pain. Lines on his forehead. A deep crease in the peeling red skin between his eyebrows.

I went on to tell them how Ben was getting ragged on by the other firefighters for his claustrophobia. How Maggie had wanted to help him and how she'd been afraid he'd leave town if she didn't. I said it all without emotion because my whole body felt like it'd gotten a massive shot of Novocain. I was numb all over. I couldn't even get my lungs working right. It was hard to pull air in and out. I *still* couldn't wrap my mind around Maggie doing it.

Neither could Sara, apparently. She wasn't getting it.

"What does this have to do with the fire?" she asked.

I shifted from one numb foot to the other. Folded my arms across my chest. "Ben thought he finally had the claustrophobia thing under control," I said, "but he needed a fire to prove himself. So—"

"You're not saying *Maggie* set the fire?" Sara asked.

I nodded. "She confessed to it. But she didn't mean for the

kids to be there," I added quickly. "Remember, the lock-in wasn't—"

"I just don't believe it!" Sara interrupted me. "Maggie wouldn't do something like that. Could she be protecting Ben? Maybe he set it and she's taking the fall?"

"Maggie wanted to help him," I repeated. "She was so...hooked on him. So nuts about him. She wasn't thinking straight."

Sara's face went white. She clasped a hand over her mouth like she was holding in a scream.

"She poured fuel around the church," I said. "Andy helped her because...it's a long story, but he didn't know what he was doing. That's how his prints got on the gas container."

"Oh my God," Sara nearly whispered. "I just can't picture it. Little Miss Perfect. How could she hurt so many people?"

I couldn't picture it either, and yet everything about Maggie's story fit into place like the pieces of a jigsaw puzzle. All except her denial that she didn't light the fire. It was like she looked up the law on the Internet and learned the charges against her wouldn't be as bad if she didn't actually burn the building down. I talked to her till I was blue in the face, trying to get her to own up to it, but she wouldn't. I believed her because she was Maggie. And I didn't believe her, because that part of her story just plain didn't hold together.

"I don't think she meant to hurt anyone," I said.

"How can you *say* that? She burned down the church!" Sara had found her voice and, with it, her anger. The pallor in her face was gone now. Her cheeks were splotched with red, and I knew that, in a split second, she'd gone from loving Maggie to despising her. "She *killed* people!" she shouted.

"She swears she didn't ignite the fuel," I said. "She said once she saw the lock-in was moved to the church, she gave up the whole plan."

"Oh, right," Sara snapped. "Spontaneous combustion."

"I know," I said. "I don't know what to make of it either."

Keith had gone quiet in the last minute or so, and when I glanced at him, I saw tears running down his unbandaged cheek.

"Oh, baby!" Sara leaned forward, mopping his face with a tissue. "Oh, honey."

"I thought it was all *my* fault." Keith was just about sobbing. "I thought *I* did it."

"What do you mean?" Sara asked. "How on earth could it have been your fault?"

It took a few seconds for him to catch his breath. "I was on the back porch of the church, getting ready to have a smoke," he said. "I lit my cigarette, and when I threw the match on the ground, flames shot up. *Massive* flames. They blocked the back steps, so I ran back inside and then I was stuck in the fire, like everybody else. I thought it was my fault."

"Oh, Keith." Sara tried to hug his quivering shoulders. With the gigantic stiff bandages on his arms and hands, it must have felt like holding a block of wood. She pressed her face against his and I watched their tears mix together. "My poor baby," she said. "All this time you were thinking you did it? It wasn't your fault, honey. Not at all."

I stood there watching, letting Keith's words sink in. Sometimes relief feels like a trickle from a faucet. Other times, it's a tidal wave. *This* was a tidal wave. My eyes burned. I could suddenly feel my arms. My legs. My lungs moved air in and out. My heartbeat was rock steady.

Maggie'd been telling the truth! There wasn't much to celebrate about the whole damn mess, but just then, I felt like
shouting for joy.

I called Flip from my pickup and told him to get someone
up to Chapel Hill to take Keith's statement. Then I stepped on
the gas. I wanted to get back to Cape Fear. To the hospital and
Laurel and Maggie. I wanted to see Andy. To see where we
went from here.

People asked me why I'd never settled down. Never started
a family. "Not my thing," I'd say. Or "Just haven't met the right
woman." I'd dated a fair amount. Lots of one-night stands. A
few three-month-long relationships. Some six months. A
couple lasted a year. But there was one good reason why I'd
never settled down. Never started a family. I already had one.

Epilogue

Six months later
Andy

I SIT ON THE BENCH AT THE POOL WAITING for my turn. I don't like swimming as much as I used to. I don't win as much now that my startling reflex is gone, but Mom says I have to swim until Christmas. Then I can quit. Our new coach, KiKi, is a girl. Ben went to live with his wife in Charlotte. I cried at first because I missed him, but now I don't remember what he looked like. Mom said I got so upset because he left right after Maggie did. It was like losing two people at once, she said.

I like a new girl on my swim team, so I watch her swim the butterfly that she does better than anyone. Uncle Marcus says I have to be extra careful about personal space now that I'm getting older. He's not careful about it at all, though. Right now he's sitting on the bleachers with his arm around Mom. Sometimes they kiss. The first time I saw them kiss I said, "Yuck! What are you *doing?*" Mom said I better get used to it, that there would be a lot more kissing from now on. But she meant her and Uncle Marcus. Not me. I'm not supposed to kiss anybody that's not family.

I get to see Maggie every month. I like seeing her but not at the prison because the people are scary. Like the lady with the spider tattoos on her neck. Maggie shouldn't be with them. She's the best person and I won't ever get why she has to be there. At least, I don't get why me and my friend Keith aren't there with her. Me and Maggie put the bug spray which was really car gas around the church. Keith threw a match and made it burn. If me and Maggie and Keith all had something to do with the fire, I don't know why only Maggie is in jail, but that is what happened.

At night sometimes I think about how I can sneak her out. I told her about that the last time I went there and she laughed. "Oh, Panda, you're a goofball!" She got real serious then and told me she belongs where she is. "I'll get a second chance at life, but the three people who died in the fire only got one," is what she said.

I have a big calendar on my corkboard wall, and every day I cross off is one day closer to having her home.

Then she can start her second chance.

Laurel

They took my daughter from me the week before her eighteenth birthday. They convicted her of attempted arson and obstruction of justice, and her lawyer was able to get involuntary manslaughter charges dropped. She was incredibly brave.

She'd done something terrible. Insane. I thought she needed counseling instead of incarceration, but it was not my opinion that mattered. I worry what she'll be like at the end of twelve months in prison. How will she be different? The only thing I'm sure of is that I will be a very different sort of mother. I plan to smother her with love. She'll be nineteen, but she'll still be my beautiful little girl. And once I have her back in my arms, I'll never, ever, let her go.

Read all about it...

MORE ABOUT THIS BOOK

MORE ABOUT THE AUTHOR

DON'T MISS!

Read all about it...

QUESTIONS FOR YOUR READING GROUP

1. Empathy is a theme that runs throughout the book. Jamie's mother talked about him having the "gift" of extreme empathy, being able to feel what others were feeling. Do you believe that some people have this gift and, if so, do you believe that Jamie had it? Maggie? Why or why not?

2. Discuss Maggie's feeling that she could connect to her father's spirit. Do you think she believed he was coming to her from "the other side"? How did her connection to him influence her actions? How did it influence her relationships with Laurel, Ben and Marcus?

3. Even though Andy was clearly the favoured child, Maggie seemed to love him unconditionally and without resentment. Why do you think this was?

4. Maggie was an honours student with college plans and a bright future. What in her upbringing and personality allowed her to achieve so much? What in her upbringing and personality contributed to her falling so far?

5. Speculate as to why Jamie and Marcus were treated differently by their parents and the impact that treatment had on them and their relationship.

6. Were you able to remain sympathetic to Laurel during her postpartum depression and alcoholism? What other emotions did you feel towards her?

3

Read all about it...

7. Do you think Laurel ever doubted Andy's innocence? What do you think played into her assumptions and emotions?

8. Could you relate to Laurel's desire to tamper with evidence to protect Andy? What would you have done in her place? Did you have doubts about his innocence yourself? Why or why not?

9. After learning that Keith had called Andy a "little rich boy," Laurel worried that Sara might resent her wealth. Do you think Sara was resentful of Laurel? Discuss the dynamics in their friendship and how they changed – or didn't change – over the years.

10. Which characters garnered the most sympathy from you? How did your feelings about Andy, Maggie, Laurel and Marcus change throughout the story? In your opinion, should Andy be told about his relationship to Keith? What are your feelings about family secrets?

4

Read all about it...

INSPIRATION FOR WRITING
Before the Storm

Several years ago, I was invited to participate in the Authors Movable Feast sponsored by Quarter Moon Books in Topsail Island, North Carolina. I've always had a soft spot in my heart for the Carolina beaches, but this was my first trip to Topsail and I fell instantly in love with it. Right away, I started to imagine a story set somewhere on that long (twenty-six miles), very narrow strip of land.

Around the same time, I was thinking about a story that would involve a teenager who becomes a hero by saving others in a fire, only to later be suspected of starting the fire him- or herself. Gradually, my story and my setting began to come together. For me, that's when the magic really begins.

"...plotting is often a circular process!..."

At the story's heart is fifteen-year-old Andy Lockwood, who was born with foetal alcohol syndrome. Although Andy has an IQ in the low normal range, he's a concrete thinker...and a lovable character. I never set out to make him a special-needs teen, but as I started writing Andy's first chapter, his voice sounded very simple to me. I knew I had to come up with a reason for how young and naive he sounded. I had some experience with kids with foetal alcohol syndrome in my previous career as a clinical social worker and Andy reminded me of them. Of course, after I settled on his developmental issue, I then had to think about his mother and why she drank while pregnant with him. Plotting is often a circular process! I like it when my characters surprise me the way that Andy and his mother did, because I know they'll probably surprise my readers as well.

"...I think I'm good at writing about emotions..."

I made several trips to Topsail to research my story. I'm lucky to have friends who have homes on the Island and who have been more than willing to let me use those homes as my base while doing research. I've found the people who live on or near Topsail, from the real estate agent I stumbled across on my first trip to the fire marshal of Surf City, to be equally generous in helping me.

I needed the house from Andy's childhood to be nearly ready to fall into the sea. Unfortunately for some residents of Topsail Island, this is not hard to imagine. Most houses at the beach have names, and I christened the house The Sea Tender, which has a double meaning in the story. *The Sea Tender* was the original title of *Before the Storm*, but my publisher didn't like it. That's often a problem with book titles: the author may be looking at the meaning of the title, while the publisher is looking at the market. I went back to the drawing board on the title. It was actually one of my blog readers who came up with *Before the Storm*, for which I'm most grateful!

Before the Storm has a subtle spiritual thread running through it due to Andy's sister, Maggie, and her connection with their late father, Jamie. Jamie started his own little chapel on the Island, which he called the Free Seekers Chapel. I planted the chapel at the very northern tip of the Island, which is surrounded by water (the ocean, the inlet and the Intracoastal Waterway) on three sides.

I think I'm good at writing about emotions and relationships, but when it comes to subjects I know nothing about (fighting fires, for instance), I need help. I received that help from Surf City Fire Marshal Ken Bogan. Surf City is

Read all about it...

one of the three small towns on Topsail Island. Ken and his wife Angie were amazing! Over several visits, they answered pages and pages of questions from me.

The final challenge – and one of the biggest – in writing *Before the Storm* was telling the story from four different first-person points of view. It's important when writing multiple points of view to make each voice entirely distinct from the others. A reader should be able to open at any page and know within a few sentences which character she's reading about. It was a huge task, but I enjoyed getting to know those four characters and their distinct voices very much. I hope you did too.

Read all about it...

"...I began writing and couldn't stop..."

WHY I WRITE...

I always wanted to be a writer and wrote many small, terrible books as a pre-teen. But I also had a strong desire to be a social worker, having read a book as a teenager about the different ways social workers could help people. By the time I was ready for college, becoming a successful writer seemed like a pipe dream, so I received both my bachelor's and master's degrees in social work. Then a funny thing happened. I was at a doctor's appointment and the receptionist told me the doctor was running very late. There were no magazines in the office, but I had a pen and a pad...and I had an idea that had been rolling around in my head for more than a decade. I began writing and couldn't stop. At first, I thought of my writing as a hobby, but after about four years I had a completed novel. A year later, I had my first contract. I continued working as both a social worker and a writer for several more years until I decided to write full time. I love writing. It's hard to imagine a better career and I have plenty more stories to tell.

AUTHOR BIOGRAPHY

Once a medical social worker, Diane Chamberlain is the award-winning author of twelve novels that explore the complexities of human relationships — between men and women, brothers and sisters, parents and children. Diane lives in northern Virginia.

8

Read all about it...

"... I love creating characters and breathing life into them..."

Q&A ON WRITING

What do you love the most about being a writer?

It's so rewarding to be able to touch thousands of people with my stories. I love hearing that a reader lost a night of sleep because she couldn't put down one of my books! That's the best compliment I can receive.

Where do you go for inspiration?

When I begin to think about writing a new book, I see story possibilities everywhere. My mind and imagination are suddenly open to all the universe has to offer. I devour newspapers and magazines, watch movies, go to art museums, talk to people and even listen in on conversations in restaurants (not intentionally – I just can't help myself when I'm in story-gathering mode!). The story that ultimately arises from all of this is a composite of so many different ideas that I can rarely recall the initial inspiration.

What one piece of advice would you give to a writer wanting to start a career?

First, study the craft of writing. I have read many manuscripts in which the idea is brilliant, but the writing is so poor that I know it stands no chance of ever being published, which is heartbreaking. Read as much as you can so that you understand how stories are told. What draws you in? What keeps you interested? Take a class and share your writing with others to get feedback. Finally, get out and live your life so you have experiences to write about. Writers often tend to be introverts who like to closet themselves away, but we really do need the stimulation of being part of the world in order to understand people and the situations they get themselves into.

You have a master's degree in social work and worked as a youth counsellor and in the field of medical social work, as well as having a private psychotherapy practice. How does this background inform and influence your work?

My background helps me understand how people "tick." It also gives me a deep appreciation of the struggle people face as they try to cope with tragedy. I loved being a social worker and love being a writer. I feel lucky to have had two careers that let me touch people in a positive way.

"...If I'm surprised by what happens, I'm quite sure my readers will be as well..."

How did you feel when your first book was signed?

It's impossible to explain the joy I felt that day! It had been a long time coming and the realisation that my story would finally reach readers was simply amazing and very rewarding. I called my family and my writer friends. It was exciting... However, the book wasn't actually published for a very long two and a half years!

Where do your characters come from and do they ever surprise you as you write?

They surprise me all the time! I love creating characters and breathing life into them. I want them to be both believable and memorable to my readers and I spend much of my writing time getting to know them. When I was a clinical social worker, I took a seminar on hypnotherapy. During that training, I not only thought about how useful the techniques I was learning would be for my psychotherapy clients, but how they could help me understand my characters as well. In the beginning, I approached using this new tool in a very formal way. I'd sit in a comfortable chair with a pad and

"...I love working in coffee shops..."

pen, put myself in a light trance and imagine I was the character. Then I'd start writing about "my" life, in the first person, from the character's point of view. I didn't censor myself, but simply let the words flow. As my subconscious took over, I learned things about my character I never would have come up with consciously. It's an astonishing experience and often full of surprises. If *I'm* surprised by what happens, I'm quite sure my readers will be as well. Our subconscious minds are amazing things if we just tap into them. Now that the technique is second nature to me, I often use it when I'm feeling perplexed by, or simply out of touch with, a character. I close my eyes and ask her to tell me what's going on with her or perhaps how she's feeling about another character in the story. Sometimes the answers I receive are pure gold.

Which book do you wish you had written?

E.B. White's *Charlotte's Web*, and not only because I would now be very wealthy! I have always loved that children's book and it was an early inspiration in my longing to write. It's a beautifully crafted book and a lovingly told story.

Do you have a favourite character that you've created and what is it you like about that character?

I have many favourites, but CeeCee from *The Lost Daughter* is definitely one of them. I like that she's a blend of vulnerability and strength. I think many readers can relate to those qualities in her. I also like that, despite the fact that she's done something very *wrong*, she's still a person with high moral standards. It's that conflict that forces her to make a devastating choice at the end of the book and it's that conflict that truly humanises her.

A WRITER'S LIFE

Read all about it...

Paper and pen or straight on to the computer?

Both. I often start with paper and pen and then hit a certain point when ideas are coming too quickly for me to keep up. That's when I move to the computer.

PC or laptop?

Both. I am more comfortable working on my PC because I love my big monitor and ergonomic keyboard. But I also love working in coffee shops, so my laptop is a must.

Music or silence?

Music, but without lyrics. I listen to particular soundtracks when I write. I like soundtracks with high drama, such as *Braveheart*, *Blood Diamond* and *Dances with Wolves*. They make me feel very emotional and that is reflected in what I'm writing.

"...I'll have a crazed, frantic look in my eyes..."

Morning or night?

I'm a night owl, definitely.

Coffee or tea?

Coffee. Half caffeine, half decaf, with a little milk.

Your guilty reading pleasure?

Hmm...I don't think I have one. I really must work on that.

The first book you loved?

Charlotte's Web by E.B. White.

Read all about it...

A DAY IN THE LIFE

This depends on where I am in the writing process. If it's early on, you might find me lolling around the house with a faraway look in my eyes as the story begins to take shape in my imagination. If I'm outlining, you'll find me hunched over my dining-room table, surrounded by note cards, each one containing a scene from the book as I move them around to form a cohesive story. If I'm in the middle of the book, I'll often start my day at a local coffee shop, going over what I wrote the day before. Then I'll come home and get to work at the computer. If it's the last few months before deadline, you'll find me at the computer bright and early, then all day long, then late into the night. And I'll have a crazed, frantic look in my eyes!

Read all about it...

TOP TEN BOOKS

Poisonwood Bible by Barbara Kingsolver, which was not only a great read, but an eye-opener for me into the twentieth-century history of the Congo.

Gift from the Sea by Anne Morrow Lindbergh, because of its connection to the sea and beach and because of its exploration of a very real marriage.

White Horses by Alice Hoffman, because it was the first book of hers that I read and it inspired my early writing. When I reread my first novel, *Private Relations*, I can recognise the passages that were written during my "Alice Hoffman phase."

Prince of Tides by Pat Conroy, because it's beautifully told and a fantastic, gripping story about a wildly dysfunctional family – my favourite kind.

The Time Traveller's Wife by Audrey Niffenegger, because it's so inventive and so very touching.

The Colour Purple by Alice Walker, because I started sobbing on page one.

The Miracle of Mindfulness by Thich Nhat Hanh, because it keeps me centred.

I Know this Much is True by Wally Lamb, because it's an amazing story, wonderfully told. I reread it when I want to write from a male character's point of view. It helps me understand how a man thinks and feels.

Beloved by Toni Morrison. I didn't love it until I had to reread it for a book club. Then it suddenly came together for me and I've reread it several times since.

Eat, Pray, Love by Elizabeth Gilbert, because it's about three of my favourite things: food, spirituality and relationships.

14

Read all about it...

The story continues in

SECRETS SHE LEFT BEHIND
by Diane Chamberlain

Read on for an exclusive look at Chapter One

Coming in August from MIRA Books

SECRETS SHE LEFT BEHIND

Maggie

THEY MOVED ME FROM MY CELL HOURS LATER THAN I'D expected because of some paperwork issue Mom had to straighten out. I was afraid they weren't going to let me go. There'd been some mistake, I thought. A prison official would show up at my cell door and say, *Oh, we thought you were in prison for twelve months, but we read the order wrong. It's really twelve years.* It's amazing the things you can imagine when you're alone in a cell.

I sat on my skinny bed with my hands folded in my lap and my heart pounding, waiting. An hour. Two hours. I couldn't budge. Couldn't open the book I was reading. Just sat there waiting for them to come tell me how twelve months was a mistake and I couldn't get out today. I deserved the twelve years. Everyone knew that, including me.

But finally, Letitia, my favorite guard, came to get me. I let out my breath like I'd been holding it in for those two hours and started to cry. Outside the bars of my cell, Letitia's face was nothing more than a dark, wavy blur.

She shook her head at me, and I knew she was wearing that half sneer it took me a few months to recognize as a kind of affection.

"You crying?" she asked. "Girl, you cried the day you come in here and now you crying the day you leave. Make up your mind."

I tried laughing but it came out more like a whimper.

"Let's go," she said, unlocking the door, sliding the bars to the left, and I thought, *that's the last time I'll ever have to hear that door scrape open*. I walked next to Letitia as we started down the broad central hall between the rows of cells, side by side like equals. Two free women. *Free*. I needed a tissue, but didn't have one. I wiped my nose with the back of my hand.

"You'll be back!" one of the women called to me from her cell. Others hooted and hollered. Cussed and shouted. "Yo, bitch! Gonna burn some more kiddies, huh?" *BB* they called me. Baby Burner, even though the people who died in the fire were two teenagers and an adult. I didn't fit in. It wasn't just that I was white. There were plenty of white women in the prison. It wasn't that I was young. Sixteen was the age at which you were tried as an adult in North Carolina, so there were plenty younger than me. It was, as Letitia told me the first week I got there, that "they can smell the money on you, girl." I didn't see how. I didn't look any different from them, but I guessed everybody knew my story. How I'd laid a fire around a church to let my firefighter boyfriend shine in the department. How I didn't set the fire when I realized kids would be in the church, but how Keith Weston lit a cigarette, tossing the match on the fuel I'd poured without realizing it was there. How people died and burned and had their lives totally screwed up. They all knew the details, and even though some of them had murdered people, maybe sticking a knife in their best friend's heart, or they sold drugs to junior-high kids or robbed a store or whatever, they stuck together and I was the outcast.

At the beginning of the year I'd thought about Martha Stewart a lot, how even though she was a rich white woman, she made all these friends in prison and they loved her. Adored her, even. How she came out on top. I told myself maybe that's how it could be with me.

As Letitia and I went down the wide corridor between the cells, I remembered the first time I'd made that long walk. The hooting and name-calling. I didn't think of the women as people then. They seemed like wild dogs and I was afraid one of them would break loose and run after me. Now I knew better. They couldn't get out. I learned it wasn't when they were in their cells that they could hurt me, but out in the yard. I was beaten up twice, and for someone like me who'd never even been hit, it was terrible. Both times, it was a girl named Lizard. She was six feet tall with thin, straggly, almost colorless hair. She was skinny and her body seemed out of proportion to the long arms and legs she could wrap around you like strands of wire. She let me have it, for no reason I could think of except that she hated me, like so many of the others hated me. I wasn't good at getting beaten up. I didn't fight back well. I cowered, covering my face with my hands, while she pounded my ribs and tore handfuls of my dark hair out by the roots. I had one thought running through my mind: *I deserve this.* You see people getting beaten up in the movies and TV all the time. There'll be cuts and some blood, but you don't get to feel the fear while it's happening. The not-knowing-how-bad-it'll-get kind of fear. Or the pain that goes on for days. Letitia saved me both times. Then I was "Letitia's pretty baby." LPB. They had initials for everything. A lot of the initials I never did figure out because I wasn't part of the in crowd. I wasn't the only outsider, though. Not the only one getting picked on. I wasn't the weakest by far. They'd find the ones who were least able to defend themselves and move in for the kill. All I could think was, thank God Andy wasn't the one to land in prison. He would never have survived.

I got over the whole Martha Stewart fantasy real fast. After the first couple of days, I didn't even try to make friends. I kept to myself, reading, thinking about how I was supposed to be in college at UNC Wilmington this year. Maybe a business major, which seemed totally ridiculous to me now. Business? What did that matter, really? Who could I help with a degree in business? What good could I do for anybody but myself and maybe some blood-sucking company? I tried to keep a journal, but I threw it away after a couple of months because I couldn't stand rereading what I'd written in the first few days about Ben and how I still loved him even though he betrayed me. How I did something so stupid out of love for him. How I killed people. *I took lives.* I wrote those words over and over on four or five pages of the journal like some third-grade punishment. I'd touch the latest cut on my lip from Lizard or the bruises that crisscrossed my legs and think *these are nothing.*

Letitia led me into a room that was the closest thing to freedom I'd seen in a year. It was the room where I'd checked into the prison, but it didn't look the same to me now that I was facing the windows instead of the door that led to the cells. There was a long counter, a few people working at desks behind it. There were orange plastic chairs along one wall. The windows looked out on a sky so blue I barely noticed the rows of barbed wire at the top of a tall chain-link fence. There was something else out there, too: a crowd on the other side of the fence. News vans. People with microphones. People carrying signs I couldn't read from inside the room. People yelling words I couldn't hear, punching the signs in the air. I knew that the crowd was there for me, and they weren't there to welcome me home.

"Yo, girl," Letitia said when she saw them. "Sure you don' wanna stay here wit' the devil you know?"

Letitia was a mind reader. I was shaking so hard my teeth chattered. There was a kind of protection I had in my cell that I wouldn't have once I walked through the prison gate.

"You sign over here, Lockwood." A man behind the counter handed me a sheet of paper. I didn't bother reading it. Just scribbled my name. My hand jerked all over the place.

I spotted my mother and Uncle Marcus on the sidewalk leading up to the building. Delia Martinez, my tiny but tough lawyer, was with them, along with two guards, helping them push through the crowd. I reached for the doorknob.

"It's locked, girl," Letitia said. "They goin' buzz 'em through. Just hold on."

I heard the buzzer. One of the guards opened the door, and Mom and Uncle Marcus burst into the room, Delia behind them.

"Mama!" I said, though I'd never called her "mama" before in my life. We crashed into each other's arms, and then I started crying for real. I held on to her, sobbing, my eyes squinched shut, and I couldn't let go. I didn't care who was watching or if anyone thought I was holding on to her for too long. I didn't care if I seemed nine instead of nineteen. I didn't care if Mom had had enough—though I could tell she didn't care about anything either. It felt awesome, knowing that. Knowing she'd hold me as long as I needed to be held.

Uncle Marcus hugged me when Mom and I finally let go of each other. He smelled so good! If anyone had asked me how Uncle Marcus smelled, I would have said I didn't have a clue. But now that I could breathe in his aftershave or shampoo or whatever it was, I knew I'd been smelling that scent all my life. His hand squeezed my neck through my hair and he whispered in my ear, "I'm so glad you're coming home, babe," which started me crying all over again.

"When we go out there, Maggie," Delia said when I finally let go of Uncle Marcus, "you don't say a word. Okay? Eyes straight ahead.

No matter what you hear. What anybody says. No matter what questions they throw at you. Not a word. Got it?"

"Got it." I looked over my shoulder at Letitia, and she gave me her weird sneer.

"Don't ever wanna see you in here again, hear?" she said.

I nodded.

"Okay," Delia said. "Let's go."

The guards led us out, and the moment my feet hit the sidewalk, the people went crazy. I could see some of the signs now: Life for Lockwood. Murderer Maggie.

"Eyes straight ahead," Delia repeated, her hand on my elbow.

Mom's car was parked right outside the gate so I wouldn't have to walk very far through the crowd. Still, when we got close to the car, the camera crews threw microphones toward us on long poles. They shouted so many questions I couldn't separate one from another, not that I planned to answer any of them. I nearly dived into the car, Mom right behind me. Delia got in front, and Uncle Marcus jumped in the driver's seat.

People pressed against the car as Uncle Marcus slowly drove through the crowd. The car swayed and shook, and I pictured the mob of people lifting up one side of it and rolling it over, crushing us. I put my head down on my knees and protected it with my arms—the crash position for flying. I felt Mom lean over me, covering me like a blanket.

"All clear," Uncle Marcus called as we turned onto the road.

I lifted my head and the angry shouts of the crowd faded away. Would they follow us to our dead-end street in North Topsail? Surround our house? Who would protect me then?

I could hear Delia and Uncle Marcus talking quietly, but not what they were saying. After about a mile, we pulled to the side of the road behind a black Audi.

Delia turned around and reached for my hand. "I'm getting out here," she said. "Call if you need me. You stay tough."

"Okay," I whispered, thinking that I wasn't the tough one in the car. Delia was, and I owed my puny twelve-month sentence to her. She'd gotten a bunch of charges against me dismissed or reduced. I had mandatory counseling ahead of me, where I guess I was supposed to figure out why I did what I did so I never did it again. The fire had been a one-time deal. No question there. I didn't feel like talking to anyone about the whole frickin' mess. I wasn't sure *what* I needed, but I knew it had to be some kind of total overhaul, not a few sessions with a shrink. Then I had three hundred hours of community service. No college for me for a while. Restitution to the families, but Mom was managing that by taking money out of my inheritance from Daddy. How did you pay families for their dead kids?

You'd think after a year in prison, we'd have a lot to talk about, but it was quiet in the car. Sometimes there's so much to say that you don't know where to begin.

Her family's cottage was a place
of innocence for twelve-year-old
Julie Bauer – until her sister
was murdered.

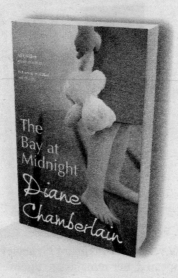

It's been many years since that August night. Now
someone from her past is asking questions about
what really happened. About the person who went to
prison for Izzy's murder – and the person who didn't.

Now Julie must revisit her past and untangle the
complex emotions that led to one unspeakable
act of violence on the bay at midnight.

www.mirabooks.co.uk